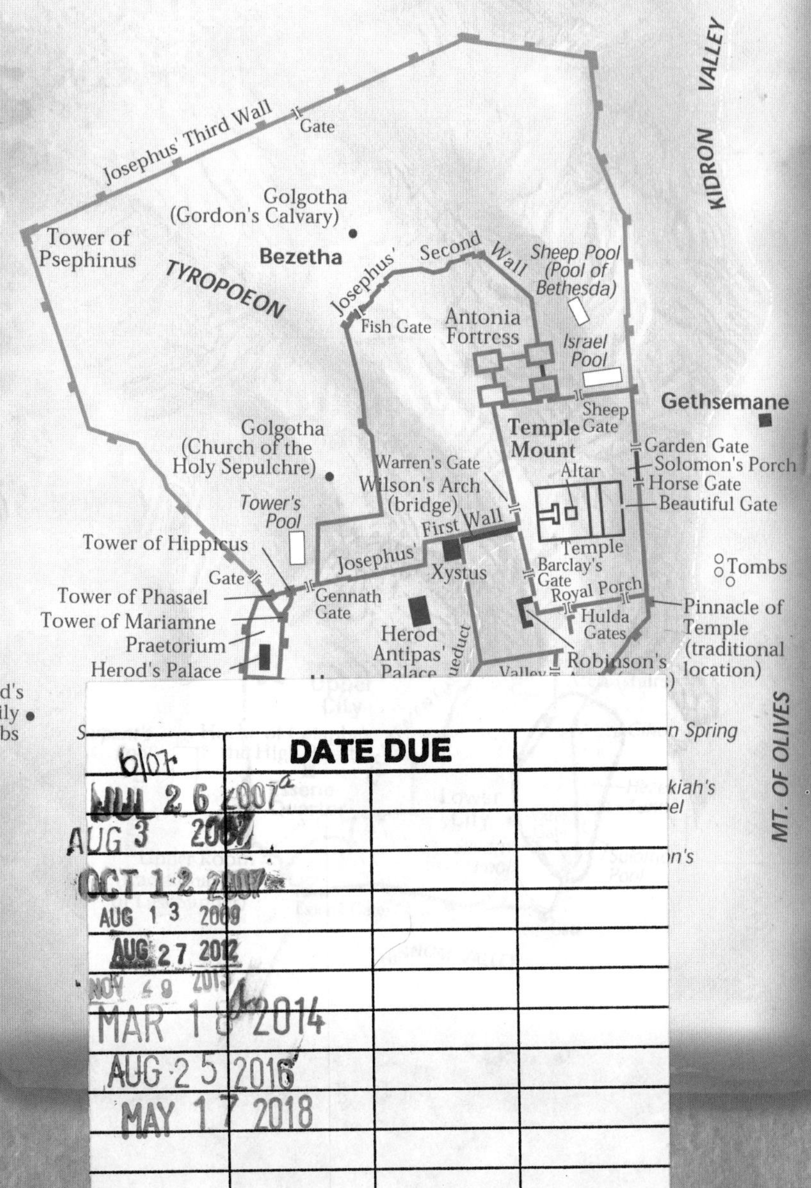
JERUSALEM
FIRST CENTURY A.D.
Josephus' Third Wall
Gate
KIDRON VALLEY
Golgotha
(Gordon's Calvary)
Tower of
Psephinus
Bezetha
TYROPOEON
Josephus' Second Wall
Sheep Pool
(Pool of
Bethesda)
Fish Gate
Antonia
Fortress
Israel
Pool
Gethsemane
Sheep
Gate
Temple
Mount
Garden Gate
Solomon's Porch
Horse Gate
Beautiful Gate
Golgotha
(Church of the
Holy Sepulchre)
Warren's Gate
Wilson's Arch
(bridge)
Altar
Tower's
Pool
First Wall
Temple
Tower of Hippicus
Josephus'
Xystus
Tombs
Gate
Barclay's
Gate
Royal Porch
Tower of Phasael
Gennath
Gate
Hulda
Gates
Pinnacle of
Temple
(traditional
location)
Tower of Mariamne
Herod
Antipas'
Palace
Praetorium
Robinson's
Herod's Palace
Herod's
Family
Tombs
MT. OF OLIVES

FIFTh seaL

BOOK FIVE

A.D. CHRONICLES®

Fifth Seal

Tyndale House Publishers, Inc.
Carol Stream, Illinois

BODIE & BROCK
THOENE

Visit Tyndale's exciting Web site at www.tyndale.com

Fifth Seal

A.D. Chronicles series designed by Rule 29, www.rule29.com

Interior designed by Dean H. Renninger

Edited by Ramona Cramer Tucker

Library of Congress Cataloging-in-Publication Data

Thoene, Bodie, date.
Fifth seal / Bodie & Brock Thoene.
p. cm. — (A.D. chronicles ; bk. 5)
ISBN-13: 978-0-8423-7518-4 (alk. paper)
ISBN-10: 0-8423-7518-X (alk. paper)
ISBN-13: 978-0-8423-7519-1 (pbk. : alk. paper)
ISBN-10: 0-8423-7519-8 (pbk. : alk. paper)
1. Jesus Christ—Fiction. 2. Bible. N.T.—History of Biblical events—Fiction. I. Thoene, Brock, date. II. Title. III. Series : Thoene, Bodie, date. A.D. chronicles ; bk. 5.
PS3570.H46F54 2006
813'.54—dc22 2006013900

Printed in the United States of America

12 11 10 09 08 07 06
7 6 5 4 3 2 1

This book is for Mama,
Bettie Rachel Turner,
who has joyfully entered
into the presence of the Lord.

Those of you who have read our books from the beginning may recall that she was responsible for my turning from a career in the secular film industry to writing for Yeshua. When I was still a writer for John Wayne's Batjac Productions, she said to me, "Bo-Bo! What are you doing in Hollywood? You need to be writing books to tell the world about Jesus!"

She prayed daily for Brock and me and for our writer sons, Jake and Luke, through the research and writing of every book. She celebrated with us at the completion of every story. She was the first person I called when the last sentence was written.

When a book was published, although she could have had as many free copies as she wanted, she was the first customer in the local Christian bookstore to buy a few dozen to pass out to everyone she knew!

At her memorial service her pastor remarked, "Now that she's gone, Bodie and Brock's local book sales will certainly drop off!" This drew a great laugh because everyone who knew her had received a Thoene book in Berean bookstore gift wrapping.

And who can forget how she gave a Bible to everyone the Lord brought into her path? She personally gave away several thousand Bibles in her lifetime.

If you are enjoying the A.D. Chronicles, you have Mama to thank. She was instrumental in turning our writing focus from twentieth-century historical novels to Yeshua and the time He lived here on earth. If you enjoy the audiobooks Luke produces, you also have her to thank, ever since it became difficult for her to read and she first requested audiobooks.

Even as I consider her last years, I remember the clear message she gave to me every time we were together. I can hear her singing, "Jesus, Jesus, Jesus . . . there's just something about that name."

Because she sang this song even when the words of other old familiar hymns dimmed, we believe she was speaking to us under the direction of the Holy Spirit. From her instruction we began delving more deeply into the power and glory and beauty of the Word and seeking to understand the folks who met the Son of God face-to-face. The study has changed our lives in ways we cannot begin to express.

How Mama loved and served the Lord! We—her forty-seven children, grandchildren, and great-grandchildren—miss her every day. We honor her and love her still. We are confident we will all be safely home with her one day.

Mama was the Christmas spirit all year-round for us. I know how much she would have loved the story of Mary and Yosef and the birth of Yeshua in *Fifth Seal.* She had a heart like Mary's . . . accepting God's will . . . wanting to serve Him. She now knows all the details of the truths we write about in the A.D. Chronicles.

Her prayers for our ministry continue as she is now among the great cloud of witnesses spoken of in Hebrews 11 and 12.

One day, if the Lord allows me time, I will write a book about her remarkable life. There is no one in my life who made such a difference or reached out to so many through her faithful prayers and straight talk.

So, this book is for Mama, who believed the promises first among us all. Watching from heaven, she knows how much our hearts long to share God's love with you so you will also see Yeshua face-to-face, experience His mercy, and live eternally with Him.

One day, when we are all with the Lord in His kingdom, I promise I will introduce you to her in person.

Bodie Thoene

Many have undertaken to draw up an account of the things that have been fulfilled among us, just as they were handed down to us by those who from the first were eyewitnesses and servants of the Word. Therefore, since I myself have carefully investigated everything from the beginning, it seemed good also to me to write an orderly account for you, most excellent Lover of God, so that you may know the certainty of the things you have been taught.

LUKE 1:1-4

Prologue

It was the first Sabbath after the wedding of Zahav, daughter of Rabbi Eliyahu, and Alexander bar Dan, the flute maker. Tomorrow, Yeshua said, they would return to the territory of Herod Antipas in spite of the danger. Peniel sat among the seventy talmidim of Yeshua of Nazareth and listened to the Master teach.

Peniel scribbled notes on a few things beginning with the Beginning.

In the Beginning, God . . .

. . . was too big for man to comprehend.

Like the Sea of Galilee at sunset that had dazzled Peniel's newly sighted eyes with beauty, God could not be scooped up in a bottle, carried home, and placed on a window ledge with the declaration that He occupied the bottle.

During autumn nights in the hill country, Peniel took in the vast expanse of the universe and was so overcome with the wheeling multitude of stars that he trembled and prayed for daylight. Too many stars! Too much light! Ever changing! Never changing! Never still!

Peniel was a simple fellow. He preferred it when the sky was only blue and only one sun shone above him.

Light. The simpler the better, to Peniel's way of thinking. For a fellow who had been born blind and who now could see, day sky versus night sky was the fact that somehow explained how little men really knew about the enormity of God.

In the Beginning, God could not be embraced.

In the Beginning, God could not be seen even by angels.

In the Beginning, God's presence was a terrifying, roiling furnace of creation born out of chaos.

From the Beginning, Yahweh was wrapped in the Cloud of Unknowing, and He alone in the person of Yeshua Messiah, Angel of the Lord's Face, Son and Heir, could enter and emerge from Yahweh's presence to speak to the legions of angel armies.

Lucifer wanted to enter the cloud and take Yahweh's throne. Thus began the great conflict.

In the Beginning, Yahweh created man and woman with a loving relationship in mind.

Peniel had learned from Yeshua that mankind's first father and mother had not loved God in return. They had turned away. After that, they had feared Him. The kind of fear that made them run and stumble away from Him instead of running toward Him for mercy.

From that time on, what mankind could not touch they proclaimed did not exist. What they could not comprehend they mocked.

Like color and light to a man blind from birth, they could not imagine God's power and righteousness and love for them. Instead, they ran to the lakeshore, filled their little bottles with water, and declared that god was in their bottle and that this was all the god they needed. The bottle was big enough to contain their truth, which was very small indeed.

The last autumn Yeshua lived among mankind He led His disciples south from the snowy peaks of Mount Hermon, where He had shone like molten silver in the company of Elijah and Mosheh. On that summit the voice of the Almighty God had declared, **This is my beloved Son. . . . Listen to him**!

As He left Caesarea Philippi to return to the shores of Galilee, the *am ha aretz* were listening and perhaps, at last, believing that Yeshua was the Messiah, the Redeemer of Israel.

Men who had never walked before ran after Him.

Sons who had never spoken a word sang praises to His name.

Women who had lived lonely lives, barren of hope, danced at their own weddings while others carried babies in their arms.

Beautiful daughters, once marred by leprosy, were healed and whole and reunited with families who had grieved as though their girls were dead.

It was true what the prophets had said about Messiah: Yeshua healed them of all their diseases.

So it had come to pass. *"Those who have long lived in darkness have seen a great light."* [1]

Yeshua was that Light.

The twelve disciples thought they understood what it meant. Certainly the seventy talmidim who studied Torah in Yeshua's academy thought they had grasped it. The host of four hundred men, women, and children who traveled south with the great Teacher believed His homecoming meant that soon Jerusalem would be rid of the Herodian dynasty and the tyranny of Rome.

At last the kingdom of David would rise, and Yeshua Messiah would ascend like a star to reign forever on David's shining throne. It was Judgment Day. Death to all enemies. The impending redemption of Israel!

This is what most . . . well, all but a few . . . believed lay ahead as they moved south toward Galilee.

Peniel, the man born blind who now could see the world clearly, had celebrated his eighteenth birthday in Caesarea Philippi. He slung his birthday present, a leather satchel containing pen and ink and parchment, over his shoulder. He marched on the right flank of the procession beside old Onias and his daughter, Rabbi Eliyahu bar Mosheh and his family, and Onias' robust brother Zadok, once Chief Shepherd of the Temple flocks.

Zadok's three adopted boys—Avel, Emet, and Ha-or Tov—scampered along, laughing and tossing stones into the creek beside the highway. Zadok, who bore scars upon his face as badges of honor, called the trio to his side. He commanded them to stay near him as the company approached the customs checkpoint at the northern border of the Galil.

Roman soldiers held posts beside the guards of Herod Antipas.

Their heads turned to consider Yeshua. Hate-filled, scornful eyes locked on the Master. Soon enough word would reach the court of Herod Antipas and the ears of the Roman governor, Pilate, that Yeshua was returning.

Peniel clearly saw Yeshua's mother beside her son. When the two neared the crossing, Mary linked her arm with that of her son, as if she needed His strength to support her in that last step from safety to danger. Yeshua put His arm around her waist, consoling, supporting, urging her onward.

"All right. Yes." Mary's voice was barely perceptible. She leaned her cheek on Yeshua's arm. "I know. We've come so far. So far. It seems like only a few moments since the morning and now twilight . . . so close. Where has our day gone? Forgive me, Son, if for this moment I want to look back. Forgive me if, in this moment, I wish it could be different."

Yeshua smiled down at her. Mother and son were so much alike, Peniel noted. Sun-streaked dark brown hair . . . only Mary's was streaked with gray. Wide-set brown eyes, flecked with gold. Yeshua's smile was sad, as if Mary alone, in all the multitude, was suffering, and He could not help her, heal her, vanquish her agony. Did some gaping wound await her?

Peniel shivered. Black-winged vultures wheeled patiently above. Were they anticipating what was ahead? Peniel made a mental note to remember this moment. To record it in his writings.

Yeshua returns from the territory of Phillip to the peril of Herod Antipas. . . .

Here you are, Lord. I see you as plainly as I ever saw anything. I see you clearly with the eyes you gave me. Yet suddenly I am afraid. All-seeing Lord, do you see how afraid I am?

In that instant Yeshua turned toward Peniel. Yeshua nodded slightly, confirming that He knew Peniel's unspoken fears and understood them too. Then Yeshua turned His attention back to His mother.

As they passed the stone pillars into the territory of Herod Antipas, a terrifying premonition seemed to fall over everyone and, with it, silence. Dust rose from the shuffling of helpless feet that moved forward toward either final judgment or redemption. The people grew solemn and introspective.

That night they camped beside the upper Jordan. Bonfires blazed in concentric rings out from the central fire of Yeshua's inner circle. Supper was finished. The unexplained weight of foreboding was like dark water pulling them down into despair.

Peniel stretched out his hands to the warmth of the flames. "What is it?"

"In the morning some will turn back," Rabbi Eliyahu answered.

Zadok, his boys snuggled beneath his wide arms, agreed. "Aye. That they will. Turn back. Aye."

Yeshua, seated on a stone beside the largest fire, began to recite the Torah portion and the Haftarah of the day. Through the Scriptures He would teach them what was to come. "It is written by the prophet Isaias why Messiah must come as a redeemer: '*He was despised and rejected by men. A man of sorrows, and familiar with suffering. Like one from whom men hide their faces He was despised, and we esteemed Him not. Surely He took up our infirmities and carried our sorrows, yet we considered Him stricken by God, smitten by Him, and afflicted. But He was pierced for our transgressions, He was crushed for our iniquities. The punishment that brought us peace was upon Him, and by His wounds we are healed.*'"[2]

In his mind, Peniel rehearsed the rest of the passage he had learned by heart as he had sat in darkness, begging at the gate of the Temple: *We all like sheep have gone astray. Each of us has turned to his own way. And the Lord has laid upon Him the iniquity of us all.*[3]

Yeshua paused, then continued the reading. "*He was oppressed and afflicted, yet He did not open His mouth. He was led like a lamb to slaughter. And as a sheep before shearers is silent so He did not open His mouth.*"[4] Attention was riveted upon Yeshua as He gave the interpretation of the reading. Each word that followed resounded in Peniel's heart like a hammer blow against a spike. "The Son of Man is going to be betrayed . . . into the hands of men."[5]

Peniel saw Mary bite her lip and shudder, as though the images of some almost forgotten nightmare played out before her. She sighed. Her breath caught. A tear escaped, spilling down her cheek.

She believes him!

Two of Yeshua's talmidim, Peter and John, exchanged looks of disbelief. Levi Mattityahu stuck out his lower lip in protest but restrained his comments.

Peniel heard a low rumble within Zadok's chest as if the old shepherd had taken a blow to his stomach. Covering his face, Peniel longed for darkness again so he would not see their expressions. Yeshua's single sentence explained the prophecy and amplified the heaviness of the day.

Peniel prayed that he was only dreaming. That Yeshua was not saying what Peniel's ears heard. *Betrayed? Who would do such a thing?*

Yeshua drew a deep breath. "I will be betrayed . . . yes. Men will kill me. But on the third day I will be raised to life. It is written in Torah and by the prophets, and it will be fulfilled."[6]

The earth seemed to quake at Yeshua's warning. Even the air trembled around Him. Had Peniel ever known such anguish? Grief swelled up until he thought his heart would burst. Truth fell on the talmidim like flaming meteors from the sky. Hope and anticipation cracked and crumbled. There was no chance Yeshua was not telling the truth. The joy of life and healing and the expectation of a better future had turned suddenly to the horrible fact of death! And they all—*all*—mourned as though Yeshua's death was a present reality.

Zadok's shoulders shook with great sobs. "The lamb . . . the manger . . . aye! I see it! I understand! Firstborn male from the flock of Migdal Eder! Aye!"

Children wept and burrowed against parents who could not hold back their own grief.

Mary's voice broke as she looked up at Yeshua and asked quietly, "That night. Oh, Yeshua! In the stable . . . the lamb . . . covered by the fleece of another. Near us! You turned your little face toward him! Even then! It . . . meant something."

Thus ended the lesson.

Hours passed. The camp lapsed into a silent gloom.

Zadok, his shaggy head bowed, spoke in a hoarse voice to those who were still awake around the campfire. "Aye. Do y' remember, Eliyahu? Do y' remember what those days were like? How we all were lookin' at the signs in the stars? The hopes we cherished for Israel? for our wives? our sons? Remember the hope?"

Eliyahu prodded the embers with a stick. "And the fears. I remember."

Zadok gazed into the face of Onias. "Ah, Onias, my brother . . . and here you are with us tonight. You've come hopin' to see a better end of the story. You, who knew all along what was ahead. You knew he was comin'."

Onias cleared his throat. "What a time it was, eh? What a terrible time when Herod the Butcher King sat on the throne."

Zadok eyed the setting moon. "The moon. Thirty years and more gone. We're old men. Aye. But the moon . . . it looks the same, eh? It shone like this that night in Jaffa, eh, Onias? Thirty years and more, yet I see it as if only an hour has passed. . . ."

PART I

In the time of Herod king of Judea . . .

LUKE 1:5

CHAPTER 1

At over six feet in height, wrapped in a dark cloak from ankles to prominent, bushy eyebrows, Zadok was an imposing figure atop the dune. He scanned the horizon in all directions, anxiously searching for the signal lantern.

Zadok feared that the moaning wind, the waves, and the sand underfoot would combine to muffle the sounds of guards approaching from Jaffa. The port city lay less than a mile to the south. Lights marking the summit of Andromeda Hill, which crowned the town, were visible.

The night was finally pitch-black. Moonset had occurred not long before. Darkness helped hide Zadok and his charges from Jaffa's Herodian guards and Roman customs agents, but the wind was a problem. Tossing surf made a boat's entry to the rock-bound inner harbor dangerous, if not impossible. Zadok fretted and paced. Would the smugglers never arrive? Had Zadok wasted a gold piece making this plan? Or worse, had the smugglers sold him out to the authorities?

A low moan made Zadok descend to the hollow to his crippled, fugitive brother Onias and Onias' daughter, Menorah. The shepherd dropped to his knees beside the ragged bundle of cloak and torn flesh that was Onias.

"Won't be much longer," Zadok rumbled reassuringly. "That Cypriot smuggler may fear the guards and the sea . . . but he'll come for more gold. Aye, he'll come."

Eyes glinting feverishly, Onias wrapped his bony forearms around Zadok's muscular right arm. He tried to haul himself upright, but his weakened state and the pain in his pierced hands defeated him. He sank back into the wicker stretcher on which Zadok had toted him from Beth-lehem during two days and nights.

"Promise me . . . Zadok." Onias was racked with a fit of coughing, but he shook off the offer of a drink from a waterskin. "Promise me . . . don't let Menorah be taken! If guards come . . . save her and raise her . . . as your own. Save her, Zadok!"

"Papa, I won't leave you!" five-year-old Menorah protested sharply. "You can't make me leave him, Uncle Zadok!"

"Hush, child." Zadok the Shepherd placed a large calloused hand on Menorah's shoulder to calm her as he would a frightened lamb. "I've told y' before: The two of you are goin' t' Cousin Japeth in Alexandria. Once there, your love and care'll nurse your father back t' health."

Zadok wondered what part of those encouraging words Menorah actually believed. Even if she and her father escaped capture, Onias might die during the voyage to Egypt. Onias had been crucified on the wall of his own home by order of King Herod for complicity in an imaginary plot. It was a miracle Onias had survived this long.

"If he stirs, offer him water again," Zadok instructed, returning to his perch on the dune.

No sound from the landward side. To the north, nothing in sight. Due west, nothing. Southwest?

Zadok froze, peering into the blackness with the intensity he used to seek the skulking form of a marauding jackal among his sheep. A pinpoint of light appeared. It danced nearer.

But was it on the prow of a boat or a lantern in the hand of a soldier? It was near . . . too near the shore for Zadok to be certain. Farther out in the bay a line of white breakers crashed against the rocks, but inside that boundary all was blackness.

Was it a routine patrol of the beach? Had Herod's butchers been alerted to the presence of the man they considered an escaped criminal?

Should Zadok grab the cripple and the girl and run? How long could their presence near Jaffa go unremarked? How long could Onias live if he had to hide in barns and caves by day, sleep rough by night, and go without proper food?

What if they missed their one chance of escape?

As the light drew nearer, it bobbed even more wildly—up and down and side to side. At last a skiff was revealed, riding the swells. Crewed by six men and captained by the Cypriot smuggler, the skiff slid onto the shingle, just below Zadok's position.

Moments only were required to load Onias and Menorah. Zadok pressed a money pouch—all that remained of his inheritance—into the captain's hand. "There'll be that much again for y' when they're safely with Japeth the Carpenter in the Jewish Quarter of Alexandria. Mark me! Take good care of them . . . or you'll have me t' deal with."

The captain, half a head shorter and forty pounds lighter than Zadok, started to laugh. Then he must have seen the intensity of the shepherd's eyes in the lamplight or heard the threat in his voice. The captain's amusement was cut short. "Pray to your god, Jew, that your brother is spared of dying from his wounds. Beyond that you may rely on me. I'll see them safe to Egypt."

There were quick hugs and parting blessings. Then, all too soon, Zadok stood on the sand alone. He continued staring after the swaying beacon as it wove between the rocks toward the trading scow anchored offshore. The light grew smaller and smaller until it disappeared in the distance, swallowed by the night and the sea.

Dawn ripened to red on the rim of the horizon beyond Beth-lehem. Red sky at morning meant trouble, yet the baby crowned and, with one great groan of effort, was pushed from Sharona's womb. As the child breathed in Zadok's wife Rachel's capable hands, she knew everything would be all right.

First light exploded over the distant mountains in the east. A newborn's wail of protest erupted within the birthing cottage behind the house of Zadok in the village of Beth-lehem.

Seven women who had come to watch and wait through the night for the birth of their cousin's child awoke suddenly. "The baby!"

The father, a shepherd named Lem who had four sons already, acted as if this were his first child. He ran his fingers through his red hair and embraced Rabbi Eliyahu, who pounded him on the back.

"It's a strong one, eh? Listen to that! A strong one!" Lem remarked, wiping his eyes with the back of his hand.

"Blessed are you, O Adonai!" Rabbi Eliyahu responded. "That's the sound of a son." Eliyahu laughed. "Congratulations, Lem."

"Rabbi Eliyahu, can I go in now? Havila and Rachel kept me out this time. I've been frightened before, but never like this. Do you think I can go in? see Sharona?" Lem asked the rabbi.

Rabbi Eliyahu, whose wife, Havila, was Zadok's sister and assistant midwife, discouraged him. "Wait! Wait. Rachel will say when it's time. My Havila will come out to you."

As the watchers stirred, Rachel, midwife of the territory of Ephratha, passed the newborn to Havila, who washed him, rubbed his skin with salt and oil, then wrapped him in swaddling cloths. Rachel finished bathing the mother. "You did well, Sharona. It gets easier every time, eh?"

Sharona, reaching for the infant, shook her head in disagreement. "Let me hold him. Oh! Look! Rachel! He looks just like Lem."

"They all look like Lem," Havila quipped. "Ask that husband of yours for a daughter next time, will you?"

Sharona sighed and kissed her son. "It doesn't matter. A boy. A girl. Ten toes. Ten fingers. Perfect. Perfect."

Rachel rose stiffly to her feet. The truth was, this had been a difficult delivery. The baby had come into the world turned upside down. He had not dropped into the birth canal without Rachel's coaxing. When he had finally emerged, the cord was wrapped around his neck. If Sharona had been so unlucky as to live anywhere else, she would not have survived, and the baby certainly would have been stillborn.

Rachel made her way to the open door of the house. Arms extended, she clasped the lintels and drank in the morning.

There, beneath the arbor, were Lem and Eliyahu. And beneath the tree, the women of the town. All looked to her expectantly.

"All is well!" Rachel announced.

"Boy or girl, Rachel?" called Sharona's sister.

"What else? It's Lem's child."

The women twittered with laughter. Five sons! Surely a blessing, but every woman should also have at least one daughter.

"Such a voice, eh?"

"The bellow of a prophet!"

Lem called, "Rachel!" And then again, "Rachel! Is . . . everything all right?"

Havila's weary face appeared. "Bless me! Bless all of us! It's a bright red angry boy child with bright red hair and hands this big!"

Rachel exhaled loudly with relief. And did anyone mention the shoulders? So broad! Too broad for a posterior baby. Eighteen hours of labor!

Lem walked toward the cottage. "May I?"

Rachel nodded and wiped her eyes. She put a hand out to him. "Lem, it was a difficult delivery," she whispered. "The lamb was turned wrong way up. You know how it is."

Lem frowned. Yes, he knew. Lambing season in the lambing caves always brought one or two that were turned that way. "But she'll be all right?"

"Yes, but if this had been her firstborn, Lem . . ."

There was no need to say more.

He nodded. "Thank you, Rachel. Thank you. You've got a gift. Zadok says it. It's true. You've got a gift." He shouldered past her and knelt beside Sharona's bed.

Rachel did not move from the doorway. The fresh air felt good. She scanned the road in hopes Zadok would appear. Where was he? Had he managed to get his brother Onias onto the boat? Had he been caught by the Herodian patrols who scoured the beaches these days in search of people attempting to flee Herod's maniacal purges?

Havila joined her. "It was a hard one, eh?"

"Not one I would like to see repeated," Rachel replied.

"She'll recover. And the baby . . . he's a lover if ever there was one." Havila placed her hand on Rachel's shoulder. "Any sign of Zadok?"

"No." Rachel's voice was hoarse with exhaustion. "But he'll come soon. I know he will. I sensed the danger last night. I prayed. I know . . . somehow . . . he's safe. I am sure of it."

There was also a prophetess, Hannah, the daughter of Peniel, of the tribe of Asher. She was very old; she had lived with her husband seven years after her marriage, and then was a widow until she was eighty-four. She never left the Temple but worshipped night and day, fasting and praying.

LUKE 2:36-37

CHAPTER 2

The prophetess was, by virtue of her age, untouchable. Herod could have killed her for the things she said about him and his reign. In fact, he longed to kill her. But he did not dare lay a hand on her.

The old woman's life story was an artifact of Jerusalem before Herod and before Rome. She was a living tower dwelling within the Temple grounds. Her face, venerable as weathered stone, had witnessed too much turmoil to be affected by Herod's threats.

Had Herod tried to dismantle her, his kingdom would have been toppled by riot and revolt.

She was called Hannah, which meant "favored." But in hearing her history, one could only wonder why she had been given such a name. She was the daughter of Peniel the Great and descended from the tribe of Asher, whose women were reputedly the most beautiful in ancient Israel. And so she was, once, very beautiful. Hannah had married a Pharisee, whose name was now forgotten by everyone but Hannah. Hannah loved her husband and loved the Lord. Her gentle spirit and infectious laugh made her a favorite with Queen Alexandra, the last righteous ruler descended from the brief line of Maccabee kings.

When the queen died, the nation reforged by the Maccabee dynasty dissolved into civil war, and Hannah's husband of seven years died defending the Temple grounds from Herod's allies, the Roman armies of General Pompey.

For many weeks, Hannah had hid under the Temple Mount. When she emerged, her countenance was forever altered. A light seemed to shine from within her. She would not leave the Temple grounds by night or by day, but lived in a converted spice-storage room.

Every word Hannah uttered came true. No one had the courage to ask her to leave.

Now Hannah was eighty-four years old. Her birthday was the month signs and portents first appeared in the skies above Jerusalem. Eighty-four was a significant age, because the life expectancy mentioned in Holy Scripture was only seventy. Hannah had survived fourteen years beyond that! On her eighty-third birthday she had her second bat mitzvah and declared she was living into her second life span. She had further declared that she and Old Simeon, son of the renowned sage Hillel, would live to see the coming of Israel's true King.

This prophecy had sent Herod into paroxysms of rage. The people prayed that Herod would break a blood vessel and die from anger. Instead he had arrested two of his sons for treason and crucified a number of local rabbinic scholars who agreed with Hannah that this year might well be the year Messiah appeared.

Herod's father-in-law, Boethus, a corrupt fellow whom Herod had appointed high priest, warned Hannah that she should hold her tongue.

She who had witnessed revolution, civil war, and the Roman general Pompey's desecration of the Holy of Holies had no fear of what Herod the Butcher King could do to her. Hannah was a tower. A cornerstone. A tree that cast shade on the humble. If she were felled, her fall would crush a king.

Hannah was correct in her fearlessness. Herod was helpless against a foe so beloved. His chief steward, Talmai, warned him, "You can't slit the throat of an old woman and expect to be loved."

Letting her live, however, was not a point in Herod's favor. The truth was, Herod could do nothing to earn the affection of the *am ha aretz*. Rebuilding the Temple after his Roman friends had destroyed the walls had not bought him gratitude. Raising taxes and placing his relatives in positions of authority had added fuel to the fire of rebellion.

Banquets for the Romans and the construction of a gymnasium and Hippodrome in Jerusalem had renewed the objections that Herod was not a Jew, that he never had been a Jew, and that no matter what he called himself, he was not king of the Jews.

Herod's response had been to burn the genealogy records in the Temple.

It had been Hannah, sleeping in the cinnamon cupboard, who raised the cry of "Fire!" But to no avail. The public records of generations and centuries of Jewish heritage were forever destroyed.

The people despised Herod as much as they adored Hannah. Young women looked for her when they brought babies in for redemption. Widows brought her flowers. Housewives brought her cakes of raisins when they paid their two-penny sacrifices or dropped a coin into the trumpet-shaped container for widows and orphans.

"Pray for my daughter, will you, Hannah? She needs a good husband."

"Please, Hannah, what do you say? Put in a good word for my grandson. . . ."

Today a wealthy female visitor, veiled in silks and followed by a retinue of slaves, walked across the Court of Women in search of Hannah.

The prophetess was found dozing in a chair on the steps of the Temple treasury, where the rabbis of various Torah academies gathered to teach their young talmidim.

The wealthy woman was of the Herodian court—that much was clear. Who else in the city had so much money and so many slaves?

There was a murmur among the common folk as the woman knelt and prostrated herself before Hannah. Her shoulders shook with grief.

The old woman reached down and lifted her chin. "Poor child. Poor child."

The woman whispered, "Hannah, you are the prophetess of the Almighty. Tell me, please, do you know what the fate of the two princes will be? Has the Lord spoken to you about Ari and Alexander, the sons of the Maccabee princess Mariamne? Will they also be killed like their mother?"

Hannah closed her eyes for a long time. Her lips moved. Then she looked about her, rose from her seat, and hobbled past the rich woman to where a female child, a black slave of around twelve, held the train of her mistress. The girl, ebony skin beautiful in the sun, smiled into the face of Hannah.

"Come with me, child." The old woman gently took her by the shoulders and led her to the shade beneath Solomon's Portico.

The girl glanced nervously back at her mistress, who remained kneeling by Hannah's chair.

"It's all right. Your mistress won't hurt you. She does not know I am speaking to you. The Lord has covered her eyes so she can't see us together. No one in the house of your master will hurt you ever again. The Lord has shown me the evil that has come upon you. The heart of the Lord is grieved by your anguish."

"Please. Please, kind old grandmother. I miss my mother. Will she find me? I miss her so very much."

"I know." Hannah kissed her head. "Your mother is waiting for you. Listen to me, child. There will come a night when the storms descend. With the thunder will come your pain. In that same hour you must leave Yerushalayim. Do not be afraid of what men can do to you. They will never again lay a hand on you. You must go quickly to the well of Beth-lehem. Call out for Rachel, wife of Zadok. She will hear your voice and answer." Hannah embraced the girl and escorted her back to her place.

Hannah returned to her chair. The slave girl looked up fearfully, but, true to Hannah's word, the rich supplicant had not noticed what had passed between Hannah and the girl.

The rich woman whispered, "Please, honored prophetess. Spokeswoman of the Most High. Tell me . . . please . . . if you see the fate of my hus . . . I mean, Herod's sons. Can you see?"

Hannah blanched and began to weep as certain images played out before her eyes in startling detail. "It is written: '*Rachel . . . weeping for her children . . . and she will not be comforted.*'[7] Thus says the Lord. Herod will have his revenge. The sons will not live to the third year."

Beirut had been a city for more than fifteen centuries before Herod took his sons there to stand trial. Its full Roman name was Colonia Julia Augusta Felix Berytus, to honor Caesar's daughter. Phoenician by heritage, Greek by preference, Syrian by provincial government, and Roman by conquest, Beirut was happy to absorb all its visitors.

The most recent settlers were retired Roman soldiers, veterans of the Third Gallic and Fifth Macedonian legions. Pensioned with free land—dotted with date palms and cedars and bordered by the brilliant blue cloak of the Great Sea of Middle Earth that curled around the shoulder of Beirut's harbor—the veterans eagerly accepted their role as an outpost of the Roman Empire against the Parthians to the east.

Over many years Herod's reputation in this port city had become very favorable indeed. He had built colonnades, market squares, even a magnificent temple. Herod correctly surmised that such benefits bestowed on Roman veterans would be reported back to Rome, to the ears of Caesar.

But all the agreeable images—sights, sounds, smells—conjured up by Beirut did not soothe Herod's tormented spirit. The darkness of mind with which he contemplated the treachery of his sons made him unswerving in his purpose . . . and murderously angry when irritated. Here, in this non-Jewish state, no one would mourn the loss of the last of the Hasmonean bloodline.

The outcome of the trial of Alex and Ari was never really in doubt. Presiding over the affair was Saturninus, Roman governor of Syria. Over a hundred Syrian nobles, all of whom had benefited from Herod's largesse, attended the court.

The two princes were not even present.

Herod's chief steward, Talmai, had been suggested as prosecutor. But he had demurred, afraid of Herod's wrath if anything went wrong. Instead Talmai encouraged Herod to speak for himself. Let the court see how aggrieved a father was at such dastardly treatment by two well-beloved and pampered sons, Talmai advised.

So, in a voice choked alternately with grief and rage, Herod pronounced the charges against them: treason, conspiracy, attempted murder, usurpation. Any one charge was sufficient to warrant a death sentence. The king also read aloud from a letter said to have been written by Alex to the commander of Herod's garrison at Alexandrium:

"When with God's help we have achieved all that we set out to do, we will come to you. Only take it upon yourself to receive us into the fortress, as you promised."

Murmurs of shock and condemnation rippled through the spectators.

Herod asserted, "What else can this mean but a treasonous conspiracy following an assassination attempt?"

"What does the commander of the guard say?" Saturninus inquired.

"He confessed all before he died."

"Execute them!" insisted a voice from the crowd, right on cue.

"Death to traitors!"

Governor Saturninus, who knew Herod well but also knew Caesar's desire to save the princes, asked, "And your sons . . . have they confessed?"

"No," Herod grudgingly admitted. "Prince Alex says the letter is a forgery." Then, bursting with fury, he added, "But he has confessed they were attempting to leave my realm and go to Cappadocia . . . without my permission."

"Guilty!" another onlooker bellowed.

"*Guilty . . . guilty . . . guilty*," was the chant.

That the proceedings should take place in Beirut with Saturninus as judge was all Caesar required. Justice would seem to have been done.

Herod himself would pronounce the sentence.

"*Death!*" goaded the crowd.

Privately, in Herod's ear, Saturninus suggested, "Caesar approves of clemency. Lock them up forever, or send them into exile. Caesar will never let them succeed you—of that you may be certain. And since there is no kingdom for them to seek, there is no longer any reason to try to depose you. Mercy, Herod. Caesar . . . recommends it."

"I will . . . consider further."

When Yosef woke up, he did what the angel of the Lord had commanded him.

MATTHEW 1:24

3 CHAPTER

The hot summer day was softened by a cool evening breeze sweeping through the canyons from the Great Sea to Nazareth. The air was redolent with the scent of grapes newly harvested from ancient vines clinging to terraced hillsides.

Carefree music from the wine-harvest celebration drifted across the valley as Mary and her family said farewell to Zachariah, Aunt Elisheba, and their baby son, Yochanan.

Old Zachariah gazed toward the market square where all the citizens of Nazareth gathered. "This is the best time for us to slip away. You go on to the party. They'll never notice we've gone."

Mary and her sisters Naomi and Salome huddled around their mother, Anna, and Aunt Elisheba.

"You'll send word to us, Sister?" Anna asked tearfully.

Elisheba wiped her cheeks with the back of her hand and nodded. "When it's safe. Safe for us and for you. You're my sister. This will be the first place Herod's soldiers will look when they turn their attention from imaginary plots to true portents of Messiah's coming. Zachariah's dream was very clear. Leave the Galil and Herod's territory *now*! Leave quietly."

Thus far the brutal purge in Jerusalem had resulted in the arrest and trial of Herod's sons and the murder of over two hundred others. This had prompted Aunt Elisheba and Uncle Zachariah to rent out their vineyard in Beth Karem to tenant farmers. East of the Jordan the couple could live in obscurity and raise their child in safety. The angel who had appeared to old Zachariah in the Temple had spoken treason against the Herodian dynasty. The miraculous birth of Zachariah's baby boy nine months later was a very real threat to the aging monarch.[8]

Yosef the Carpenter stood apart from the family, not willing to intrude on what would certainly be their last moments together for a very long time.

Jerusalem still reeled from Herod's attacks on imaginary enemies. Might Herod wake up some morning and remember an aged priest, an angel, and a baby boy? Like Pharaoh of old, was it possible that Herod could consider a newborn his rival and seek to destroy him?

Zachariah and Elisheba could not take the chance.

Aunt Elisheba placed baby Yochanan in Mary's arms for the last time. "Mary, the birth of our son is proof that the angel's promise to you is true. Don't be afraid. Nothing is impossible with God."[9]

Zachariah put his arms around Mary and Yochanan. "The Lord has placed four sons as royal seals from his signet ring upon the covenant he made with Avraham. By Avraham's faith and through Avraham's seed all the nations of the world will be blessed. The first seal is the miracle of Avraham and Sarai's son Yitz'chak, who was father of Jacob and grandfather of the twelve tribes.

"The second seal, Mosheh, at whose birth the stars shone like they shine now. He survived the massacre of the Hebrew firstborn babies and grew to lead Israel out from the bondage of Egypt.

"The third seal is the miraculous birth of the prophet Samu'el, who anointed David as king over Israel. Through Samu'el, Hannah's son, the Lord announced the promise that David's son will sit on the throne of Israel forever. Now, in our day, here is the miracle of the birth of Yochanan. The angel promised me that Yochanan will grow up to be the prophet of the Most High and forerunner of our Messiah.[10]

"Four miraculous baby sons, each born and swaddled as is the custom and laid in his happy mother's arms. Listen to the Word of the Lord! Oh, how the Lord delights in wordplay when he speaks to us of mighty things! The word for a 'swaddled' baby is *chathal.* The word for the 'seal' of a covenant is *chatham.* The word for 'bridegroom' is *chathan.*

"The miracle of each of the four swaddled babes is God's seal on his covenant of love and the coming of the heavenly Bridegroom to redeem his bride, Israel.

"The miracle of Yochanan's birth is the fourth seal, set by the Lord's own signet ring, upon the scroll of mankind's final redemption."

There were last embraces and tears; then Zachariah, Elisheba, and the baby were gone. When would they ever see one another again? Yosef wondered, as the women wept and the men clapped one another on the back.

As Zachariah and Elisheba headed away from Nazareth, Mary and her family hurried to the center of Nazareth, where they would pretend that nothing was out of the ordinary.

Just after sunset three bright stars appeared low in the western sky.

Flocks of children welcomed the encroaching darkness as they shouted challenges in a game of hide-and-seek. Men gathered about Mary's father, Heli of Nazareth, in twos, fours, sixes, and eights to discuss livestock, crops, and politics. Their women likewise compared solutions for all the problems of the world.

Yosef, the newly wedded husband of Mary, was a quiet man, uncomfortable in crowds. A carpenter by trade, he had been shy and reserved even before the extraordinary events that led to his marriage.

Because he lacked the blushing exuberance that usually shone on the face of a new groom, there was some gossip that perhaps he was not altogether happy with his bride.

"They're talking." Mary slipped her hand into his. "You know how it is."

"Let them talk." Yosef squeezed her hand gently. "They're so busy talking, talking, talking . . . why should I talk?" He kissed the top of her head.

From the light in Mary's eyes, Yosef could tell that his simple gesture had reassured her. "I'm happy with my wife. As a matter of fact, I'm so happy with just your company that I wish we were staying home alone to sit on the roof and count the stars together."

"Stay close by me tonight, Yosef. In case . . ."

Though this request surprised him mildly, he did not ask her, *"In case of what?"*

"Yes. Of course." He raised her hand to his lips. "And if you need to leave . . ."

The responsibility of providing for Mary and the baby she carried was a heavy one. Yosef shouldered the burden with the prayer that he would never let The Lord of All the Angel Armies down.

That meant never letting Mary down.

Tonight, when the women separated from the men and natural conversation groups formed, Yosef lost track of Mary. A vague sense of uneasiness settled on him. Where had she gone?

Masculine conversations revolved around cattle. Crops. Politics.

Where is Mary?

Politics had become a dangerous subject even here in the Galil. Yet the topic of treason was irresistible to the group clustered around the rabbi.

"They say Caesar insisted the trial be in Beirut. To be fair. Just so the lads would have some chance."

"Some chance? The court'll judge the princes according to Herod's whim all the same. . . . They'll live or die according to how the king feels about his sons when he wakes up in the morning. What do you say, Rebbe Mazzar?"

The old rabbi, his back bent from years of study, stroked his gray beard as he pondered the question. "The Lord watches over the way of the righteous. True? Of course true."

Nods of assent all around.

"Well spoken, Rebbe."

"Whether Herod believes in miracles or not, he fears the miracle we all hope for."

"And what's your opinion, Yosef?"

"Aye, Yosef. You worked in Yerushalayim. On the Temple construction. Heard the gossip about the high priest, Boethus, Herod's father-in-law, eh? Dangerous times we live in. When the king appointed by Rome then appoints the high priest, eh? So! Where do you think we here in the Galil stand? In relation to the politics of Yerushalayim and Rome and such?"

"I think . . ." Yosef frowned, contemplating the question. He raised a finger to make a point. "I think . . . that Nazareth is quite far from Yerushalayim. And the territory east of Jordan is farther still. And Egypt even more so. And Rome is very far away from us indeed."

Like the rabbi's remark, Yosef's comment elicited favorable responses.

The rabbi was impressed. "True, Yosef!"

"Of course true!"

"Well spoken, Yosef."

"Wise words indeed."

"Why should we in the Galil worry?"

"Yerushalayim is very far from Nazareth."

Yosef was pleased that his recitation of a simple fact of geography was confused with wisdom. He excused himself and went in search of Mary.

He spotted her beside her mother. A neighbor's baby lay faceup on Mary's lap. The infant grasped her forefingers in his fists. Mary kissed his tiny feet as he paddled spindly legs. She cooed to him as though there were no one else at the festival.

The scene seemed so ordinary.

Mary's born to be a mother, Yosef thought as he watched her. *Good with babies. Really good. Look at her smile. Yes, Adonai, you have chosen well the woman to raise your Son.*

None outside Mary's immediate family knew the true circumstances of Yosef's marriage to Mary. Even to his closest friends Yosef had not dared speak of the angelic messenger who had appeared in his dreams telling him that the one he was engaged to wed was the virgin of the prophecy of Isaiah: *Therefore the Lord Himself will give you a sign: The virgin will be with child and will give birth to a son.*[11]

Yosef was certain Mary was blessed by Adonai and chosen from all the women of Israel to carry in her womb the Messiah, the only begotten Son of the Most High. Yet she did not seem to be pregnant when he looked at her.

To help her, the angelic messenger had appointed Yosef to be protector, friend, and brother to Mary.

As a carpenter, Yosef was a man of great physical strength. His prowess would be used to defend her life and the life of the child if required. He carried a short sword concealed beneath his tunic these days and was willing to fight and die shielding her if called upon to do so.

Yosef's standing as a righteous man would also shield her reputation and deflect emotional assaults when they came. His calm, quiet spirit would stand between her and the dark, unseen force that must surely be seeking to destroy her respectability even now.

Yosef cherished Mary beyond what he'd imagined, but they lived as husband and wife only in the eyes of the world.

Fear of betraying the holy secret and the weight of his responsibility made Yosef even more contemplative than usual tonight. He keenly felt added irritation as wine flowed and jokes about newlyweds swarmed and multiplied around him.

Arms crossed, Yosef stood apart. He watched over Mary from a distance.

A familiar voice boomed behind him.

"Yosef! What's this? What! Bridegroom! Can't take your eyes off your bride, eh?" Perez, the scruffy, pop-eyed uncle of Mary, linked arms with Yosef. "Come on, man! Come on! Women have to gossip without us listenin' in. Come on! You'll only be away from her a short time." Perez led him into a group of eight rough-hewn stockmen.

The fellows chimed greetings around the circle:

"Ah! Yosef! The bridegroom! Out from the bedchamber at last! How long has it been since we've seen you?"

"Yosef! How do you like married life, eh? Eh?"

"A pretty girl, your wife!"

"Pretty can be headstrong!"

"Aye! Marry an ugly girl, says I. Then you've got her gratitude all her days."

"And when the light is out, they're all the same."

"But then there's homely children to deal with."

"Too late for Yosef, eh? He's married a beauty."

"A homely child is a humble child, says I."

"Remember, Yosef! Use a stick on her if she disobeys!"

"Beat them early and often! That'll keep a woman from rebellion."

Yosef felt color climb to his cheeks. If they only knew who she was! Chosen of all women! His to care for and protect and love! If they could even imagine! Angry, he tucked his chin in and did not respond.

"Ah, now look! You've embarrassed him!" Perez elbowed Yosef. "Don't let the louts get under your skin, man! All the wisdom they have about the female gender they picked up from their cows."

"So it seems," Yosef fumed. Wrongly perceived as an attempt at humor, Yosef's comment was met with uproarious laughter and hearty backslapping.

To Yosef's relief, the topic soon turned to the scourge of summer bag among milk cows, and he was forgotten. Try as he might, intelligent conversation about cause and treatment of putrefied udders escaped Yosef. From there they leapt upon all that could go wrong in the castration of colts. Constipated heifers and calves with diarrhea rounded out the dialogue.

So passed the pleasant summer evening in the Galil. Yosef was relieved when Mary's sister Salome tapped him on the shoulder. The girl whispered too loudly, "Yosef, Mary's feeling sick. Sent me to fetch you. Wants to go home to bed, please."

This information was met with knowing nods and winks and many *ah-ha*s among the stockmen. As Yosef turned to go, he heard new speculation make the rounds.

"Sick is she?"

"Aye. She's sick after supper? Y' know what that means."

"Could she be . . . so soon . . . ?"

"Young Yosef wasted no time, eh?"

"Nay! It's only in the morning when they're sick. And later in the term. They've only just wed."

Perez exclaimed, "Not so! When my woman was expecting the first one, she was sick cookin' supper and sick as I ate it and sick when I came to bed of an evenin'."

Perez certainly left himself wide-open, Yosef thought.

The verbal blow came swiftly from Perez's elder brother. "And so would any woman be sick—watchin' you eat and sleepin' in your bed!"

Thus ended the evening.

Mary was indeed ill when Salome led Yosef to her at the end of the lane. Pale and shaky, she clung to Yosef's arm for support on the way home and had to sit twice to rest until the world stopped spinning.

"I need air," she gasped.

Air? She needed air? They were out beneath the stars, Yosef thought. Plenty of air all around. Still, she was sick. "Of course. It's so hot tonight."

"The smell of fish, Yosef! The smell!"

"What should I do?"

"Don't worry, Yosef." She gulped and wiped her mouth with the back of her hand. "Mama says it's part of it. But I'll never bear the smell of fish again!"

"I'm not worried. The fellows tonight, they were talking about cattle and . . . things. Women . . . pregnancy. And babies."

Yosef was, in fact, worried but he pretended he was not. After all, there was the case of Perez's wife to consider. Pregnant women commonly threw up at odd times.

But there was something about the word *pregnant*! The reality of what it meant to have Mary nauseated by the smell of fish crashed down on him.

This was the first hint, the first tangible sign, that every detail Yosef had been told by the angel about Mary and the child was indeed a fact!

And yet, it seemed so ordinary!

Could it be that Mary, chosen by the Almighty to carry the Messiah of Israel in her womb, would experience pregnancy with the same discomfort as every woman since Eve? Was such a thing possible?

Yosef raised his gaze to the stars rising in the east. From childhood he had heard from the rabbis that Messiah would descend from heaven to earth to establish His Kingdom with a host of angel armies and a flaming sword of judgment against the nations.[12] He thought of the babies of whom Zachariah had spoken: Yitz'chak, Mosheh, Samu'el, and finally little Yochanan.

Yitz'chak, the promise of God's provision for redemption through the chosen *family* of Abraham.

Mosheh, the visible expression of God's redemption of mankind through His chosen *nation*, Israel.

Samu'el, the prophet to anoint David as chosen king of Israel from whom the eternal *kingdom* of a redeemed world would one day be established.

Little Yochanan, the chosen forerunner to prepare the way of King Messiah who would unite *Family*, *Nation*, and *Kingdom* beneath One Righteous Banner and One Name.

The first three men had been mighty in the history of Israel. But the record of their eternal significance had begun with accounts of their births. God, family, nation, kingdom . . . could it be that the Almighty and Eternal God planned all along to begin His greatest miracle with something as small and insignificant as the birth of a baby?

Instead of a flash of lightning and the sound of trumpets, here is Mary, Lord. My sweet Mary. Pregnant. Sick from smelling fish.

So ordinary!

This was not at all what Yosef or anyone else in Israel had expected.

Ecbatana, Kingdom of Parthia
31st year of King Phraates IV
Supplement to Journal of Court Astronomer Melchior
Summer, Year of Creation 3753

There was neither New Moon nor Full Moon tonight. Nothing in my position as court astronomer required my presence atop the palace observatory, yet I came directly after the synagogue's Sabbath service ended. The weather was too hot for sleeping. Mercury (The Messenger star in Hebrew) set immediately after the sun. Its passage was followed by Venus (Splendor) in the constellation known to the Jews and others as The Virgin.

It was from this same balcony some five months earlier that I, a Gentile believer in Yahweh, watched Mars (The Adam) closely approach Porrima (The Star of Atonement), near the heart of The Virgin. My mentor, the Jewish elder Old Balthasar, became excited to the point of agitation at the sight, linking it to a prophecy in Isaiah about a virgin giving birth to a son and calling his name God-with-us.

Tonight Mars was in the constellation of Libra (The Scales)—the heavenly image of justice—and it, too, drifted after the sun.

I walked to the opposite parapet and stared eastward. At precisely that moment, as if responding to a tug from descending Mars, the planets Saturn (known to the Jews as The Lord of the Sabbath) and Jupiter (The Righteous) and the moon (the symbol of the Holy Spirit) popped over the horizon. These three rising celestial bodies kept close company in the constellation of Nun (The Two Fish).

According to Old Balthasar, the sign of The Two Fish has always represented the nation of Israel.

The close conjunction of Jupiter and Saturn has occupied much of my attention for the past many months. The two wandering stars reached their closest approach to each other some two and a half months earlier. Since that date, Saturn and Jupiter have remained inside the boundary of The Two Fish but have drifted slightly apart until only two weeks ago. Since then the two bright lights are again closing the gap that separates them.

As Old Balthasar noted, the signs mean that something extraordinary is going to happen in Israel to the Jewish people. Something important for their nation . . . about their King . . . their promised Messiah.

In truth, I still do not fully understand the significance. But each clear evening since two Sabbaths ago, my observations record a decreasing distance between the two planets as they again approach each other.

I turned north, away from the sight, then stopped and pivoted back again.

The moon had visibly closed the gap separating it from Saturn.

Was it possible? Could this be one of those rare occasions when the moon passed in front of one of the other six major heavenly lights?

Hours passed, but I was no longer sleepy.

Three hours after midnight, when the trio of Holy Spirit, Sabbath, and Righteousness shone due south in the sky, the edge of the moon kissed Saturn.

Over the next hour, as I watched, transfixed, the moon's disk covered Saturn until the wandering star was completely hidden.

Though I waited and considered until the last hour before dawn, The Lord of the Sabbath did not reemerge. The pale blue tide of returning daylight sluiced darkness from the sky.

Exhausted, I watched the moon set, then went home. I forced myself to remain awake to record these impressions before I went to bed. I must remember to seek out Balthasar and report what I have seen.

Magi from the east came to Jerusalem and asked, "Where is the one who has been born king of the Jews? We saw his star in the east."

MATTHEW 2:1-2

CHAPTER 4

Yosef bar Jacob lay on his back, staring up. It was still night. The black Galilean sky was star-studded. The air was pleasant on the rooftop of his Nazareth home.

Blessed are you, O Adonai, who made so many stars. Your heavens are the roof over my head tonight. Help me, Lord. Help me look at Mary like a brother looks at his sister. I'm safe now on the roof. But Lord, you know I love her.

It was easier for his prayers to take effect with Mary sleeping in the house below. Yosef eyed the area and considered how easy it would be to construct a small chamber on the roof for himself. This arrangement would work even when the weather turned cold. She could sleep downstairs in the house, and he would live above her.

He dozed off, dreaming of construction plans.

A footfall scraped on a stair tread, rousing him.

"Yosef?" Mary called. "You awake?"

He sat up. "Yes. Awake. Is anything the matter?"

"Can't sleep . . . the heat. I'm . . . sick. The house is too hot. Cooler up here. Do you mind?"

Yosef felt a stab of guilt. "Here. Take this place. I'll go down. I should have thought of it. Such a hot night."

She put a hand firmly on his shoulder. "Stay awhile. Let's talk." Then, "Cool. Nice. I feel the air. Better."

There was an awkward silence for a time as Yosef moved to make room for Mary to sit beside him. He arranged his blanket, folded double, as padding for her.

What would they talk about? He blurted the last thing he had thought before he had fallen asleep. "I'm going to build myself a little room up here. Like the Shunnemite's husband did for Elisha."

"Hmm. A room. I would sleep out under the stars forever if I could."

"The rain, you know. In two months. I'll need a roof."

"So many stars, Yosef." She clasped her knees. "Like the jewels in Solomon's mines. The stories, you know? I'd like to see diamonds and such close up. What do they look like, do you suppose?"

Her question was so sincere, his sense of awkwardness melted away. He answered, "I saw Herod in his jeweled crown once when I was working in the Temple. I was carving clusters of grapes on the beams. Standing high on the scaffolding. He came with his bodyguards to have a look at the grapes. His crown was nothing compared to a night sky in Nazareth."

"No, I suppose not. Nothing like the sky above the Galil."

"And I had the feeling that under his jewels was something rotten." It was easy to talk to her. Not at all what he had expected.

"He is an old man, they say. Looks older than he is. A madman."

"His own sons arrested. If he will not spare his own sons . . ." Yosef left the thought unspoken.

"How could he?" Mary rested her chin on her knees.

"He's truly mad." A meteor streaked, dazzling white, across the sky from east to west, but was gone in an instant.

"I suppose he'd kill me if he knew. Would he, Yosef?"

Yosef nodded, his eyes downcast. "And try to kill the baby too. So he must never know, Mary."

"That's why we mustn't speak of it to anyone."

Yosef wondered aloud, "Could a mortal man like Herod kill the Son of God, you think?"

She contemplated his question. "I suppose he could. Like Pharaoh tried to kill Mosheh." She covered her stomach in a protective gesture.

"I feel the baby move and I know . . . he's still just a baby. Vulnerable. Sharing my heart as every baby shares its mother's heart. We're meant to protect him, you and I. Together. Both of us strong, I think. We must've been chosen because we're both strong."

Jupiter, the wandering star called The Righteous, stood just a little east of south. Beside its left shoulder was the paler dot of Saturn, The Lord of the Sabbath. Both planets boldly proclaimed the names of Messiah for those who could read the language of the heavens.

"I've been trying to figure it out. Why you and I were chosen, I mean."

"I try not to think about it much." Mary seemed so content. "It is what it is. Too big for me to understand it all. So I don't try."

"Me? I'm thinking all the time," Yosef admitted. "Herod would hurt you both if he knew about the angel. About my dreams."

The two considered the danger to the infant Messiah. Cygnus, the constellation of The Swan, flew into the west. The outline of a cross stood out vividly against the sky.

Mary exhaled slowly. "It's good Uncle Zachariah and Aunt Elisheba took baby Yochanan out of the territory."

"He'll be safe east of the Jordan."

"The angel said we must name this baby Yeshua: 'God is Salvation.'[13] I wonder what he'll look like when he's born. King David had red hair, they say. Who will the baby look like?"

"I hope he has your eyes, Mary. Brown with flecks of gold."

"Blue, I think. Like the sky. Like heaven. Like the blue thread in the fringe of a prayer shawl."

There was so much Yosef had intended to tell her after they were married. For months he had considered all the things he would say to her on their wedding night. In the end he had said nothing, for fear of saying too much. Tonight she seemed more like a friend—someone who could forgive him for loving her so much.

"I want to say . . . I mean . . . when I first saw you . . . you were a child. But I noticed your eyes. I was with my mother in the market square. It was about this time of year. You were with your mother and little sisters selling cheeses."

"I thought we met at synagogue."

He smiled. "It was just after we moved to Nazareth. You had a plate of samples, and you were giving them out. I was very hungry. And then

I noticed your eyes. Such wide, dark brown eyes with gold dust sprinkled in. Pretty, yes."

"I probably thought you were very handsome."

"Really?"

"I don't remember. But I suppose I would have thought so. If I was noticing such things about boys that day. Was the cheese good?"

He nodded. "Very good."

"Did your mother buy some?"

"Yes. We took it home and sliced it and had it with wine vinegar and tomatoes. With dates and nuts."

Mary smiled, and her eyes twinkled. "Some cheese is better, depending on the cow . . . and the feed too. In a year with lots of rain and lush grass the milk and cheese are better. Like vintage wine, I suppose. Only milk."

"I told my mother I would marry you. That if it was acceptable, my father should hire the matchmaker and maybe we could make a match."

"That was precocious of you. Choosing your own bride."

"I liked you. You were pretty. I liked your eyes."

"And my cheese samples."

When she laughed, Yosef knew they would be friends. Friends sharing a great adventure.

"Yes. That too. It was good. My brother waited too long and never expressed any preference for a girl. So at last my father betrothed him to a homely girl in Bethsaida with a large dowry. Nice, but homely."

Mary added, "I was only eleven when the match was made. When Papa and Mama told me the match had been made, I tried very hard to picture you. But I couldn't. I asked someone in synagogue. She pointed down through the lattice. And there you were. I saw the back of your head from the gallery. Black curls. So the first time I really looked at you was in synagogue."

"Ah. That's why you thought we had met in synagogue."

"Papa said you would make a good husband. A carpenter."

"My father taught me carpentry from age six, when I could hold a hammer and nail. There was a stump outside his shop. He taught me to hammer nails into the stump until I could drive a nail with one blow." Yosef pantomimed the action, gently smacking a fist against the other palm.

"And here you are."

"Yes. Here we are. I would have liked Papa and Mama to have seen me married. I mean . . ."

"I know what you mean."

"At least they both knew who you were. The betrothal contract signed."

"Yes. It's good."

"And I've done all right for myself. This house. The shop."

"You'll teach our son what you know."

Yosef sighed. "I wouldn't presume."

"But you must. You must teach him everything."

"You think a prince, the Anointed One written about in Torah, would want to learn carpentry?"

Mary raised an eyebrow. "Wasn't David a shepherd in Beth-lehem before he became king?"

"I just never thought of it. That I could teach him anything."

She smiled and patted Yosef's hand. "He'll be a boy like other boys. With a father. You. The Lord chose you. And a mother. Me. He'll learn from his father. From me too, I guess. And we'll protect him while he's growing up."

"Who could imagine such a thing? How will it work, do you suppose? Do you think he'll pretend he's like any other child?"

"Maybe he will be. What do you think he'll look like? The angel didn't give details. Oh! There! He just moved. Here—give me your hand." She grasped Yosef's fingers and placed his hand on her stomach. The baby moved.

Yosef laughed. Tears brimmed. So this was a real person. Immanu'el. God-with-us. God come to live among man.

The Lord of All the Angel Armies tapped from within Mary's womb again.

"Feel that?" Mary exclaimed.

"Yes. Yes."

"He's saying 'Shalom, Yosef. Glad to meet you.' He's saying, 'I will be happy to be a carpenter like you until I can become king and build a kingdom.'"

Yosef looked up. The Pleiades stood out clearly in the east—a cluster of jewels in the silent sky.

"Shalom!" he said to the baby.

And inside his heart Yosef murmured, *Blessed are you, O Eternal, who made the stars. Blessed are you because you love us so much you are coming to live with us. Like an ordinary man. I promise, Son of David, I will take care of you! Protect you! Oh, Lord. Messiah. Maker of stars! I'll do my best to be a good father to you while you're here. Like my father was to me. Someday when you're old enough I'll teach you how to choose only the best wood to build with. I'll show you how to hold a hammer. How to drive a nail so deep it will never come loose.*

Such a celebration! The courtyard of the Nazareth home of Nathan the Spice Merchant and his wife, Em, was packed with members of the congregation celebrating the bar mitzvah of the couple's eldest son.

A lamb turning on the spit above the fire pit outside the kitchen filled the air with the delicious aromas of garlic and pepper. The second of Nathan's sons tended the fire. A gaggle of smaller boys fought a great battle with wooden swords atop the stone wall.

Yosef and Mary, along with Mary's two sisters, her mother, Anna, and father, Heli, arrived together.

Heli called to the children, "So, boys, who's winning? Eh?"

"We're the Maccabees, Reb Heli!" The clack of blades grew more fierce.

Heli encouraged, "Drive them out! Drive them out!"

Mary leaned close to Yosef. "Papa should have had sons," she whispered. "Oh, the toy swords he would have made!"

Anna linked arms with Mary. "Grandchildren. There is hope yet for your papa to make swords."

The scent of cooking meat made Yosef's stomach rumble. "Smells good."

Mary blanched. "Like burning shoes."

"Soon enough lamb will be lamb again," Anna consoled.

"There's Nathan. Proud . . . proud. And his boy Mordi, a fine handsome young fellow. A good son, eh?" Heli hailed his friend.

Mary had prepared an enormous tray of sliced apples, honeyed walnuts, and four kinds of cheese to contribute to the supper that would follow the celebration. But Mary wanted nothing cooked. No meat. Her stomach would not abide meat.

"Yosef, kind husband, will you take this to the banquet table? Hide it somewhere so I can find it later." Mary winked—a friendly, wifely gesture.

"Save me a place." Holding the tray above his head and working his way through the crowd, Yosef entered the courtyard. A long table beneath the portico was heaped with food covered with long strips of cloth.

A clique of five women, heads together, continued their conversation, evidently without noticing his approach.

"Well, of course she is! Morning sickness. Sick at the smell of food . . . what else?"

"And putting her poor father and mother through the whole megillah of a wedding!"

"The expense of it! For what?"

"Poor Heli!"

"The shame!"

"The expense! Why put on a wedding when there's already been a honeymoon, eh?"

"Poor Anna!"

"What sort of example is she to her little sisters, I ask you?"

"Never mind Anna! Anna's blind to it! Mary's her daughter; what do you expect? Poor Yosef! What if it isn't his?"

Yosef paused midstep, smile frozen on his lips. He cleared his throat, warning them of his approach.

The women, eyes wide in horror, glanced up in unison. *Guilty! Caught midslander!* Resentment of Yosef's intrusion filled their faces.

"Yosef!"

"Sneaking up on our private conversation!"

He ducked his head, pretending he had not heard anything. "Mary sent me with this. Cheese. She made it herself. Walnuts. Em likes honeyed walnuts. Apples for luck, you know. But it looks like there's plenty here to chew on without it. Did I interrupt?"

Eyes narrowed to angry slits. *How dare he blunder in!*

"Never mind, Yosef!"

"It's nothing."

"Women's secrets men should not hear."

"Come. The toasts are about to begin."

In a unified huff the women moved off.

Tray still in his hands, Yosef stared at the mounds of food offered by the neighbors. His mouth tasted like rusty nails. His stomach churned as he considered the vitriolic curse of women who knew nothing but judged everything.

Blessed are you, O Adonai, who knows the hearts of all mankind. Turn these curses into blessings for your servant Mary, I pray.

He placed Mary's platter on the table and returned to the house. He took his place beside Mary as the proud father and son stood together at the front of the room.

It was clear by the guilty expressions of neighbors that the incident beside the table was not isolated. The private lives of Mary and Yosef had been sliced, laid out, and served up long before the party began.

Yet Mary and Anna kissed the cheeks of the most vicious one of the women and asked about her health and her children and grandchildren.

"Here comes the rabbi." The woman sniffed and raised an eyebrow. "So, Mary, perhaps there'll be a *Bris* to celebrate soon in your home? Eh? How soon?" A pause and a conspiratorial whisper. "Does Yosef know?"

There was nothing subtle about the questioning.

Anna stepped between the woman and Mary. "A son to carry on the name of Yosef! May the day come! We pray for such a day! A little lion cub for the tribe of Judah. Someday a bar mitzvah for the son of Yosef and Mary, eh? May the Eternal One, blessed be he forever, answer our prayers!"

Though Anna and Mary knew very well what was being inferred, to Yosef's amazement, Mary appeared immune to the remarks. If she heard the gossip, her perpetually sunny disposition seemed unaffected by it.

How was it possible, Yosef wondered, that beneath a hail of Satan's flaming arrows, she was not wounded?

It is your will, Eternal my God, to save blessed Mary this day and every day from the arrogant enemy who seeks to destroy her and the child who grows now within her. Blessed are you, O Eternal!

Was Mary's unruffled demeanor in part because she spent so much time with her mother and her sisters, talking, laughing, praying about every concern?

As evenly yoked as a matched team of fine horses, mother and daughter laughed alike, had the same intonation of voice and identical mannerisms. Side by side on their way to market, Mary and Anna would advance with a cheerful march, arms swinging in unison. Their purposeful stride indicated they had cheeses to sell and bread to buy and no time for nonsense.

Physically, Mary was the younger version of her mother. Pretty. Yes. But not like the silk found in palaces. She was more like a fine homespun fabric.

She wore her thick dark hair plaited in a single braid hanging down to her waist. Dark brown, honest eyes held the gaze of others and conveyed an unspoken message of both sweet humor and kindness.

Yosef could see Anna had once been a beauty too, before the sun and the harsh weather of the Galil had etched themselves into her skin. Anna's eyes were still youthful.

Both women had featherweight figures, projecting a first impression of frailty. But either could easily heft a seventy-pound basket of grain over the fence. In defense of her family Anna would have taken on a Roman legion without a second thought.

Her physical strength was matched by her strength of character. When a legion of whisperers closed in on Mary, as well as Yosef, Anna's sound advice, fierce faith, and constant prayers of intercession kept the hounds of hell at bay.

Along with Yosef, Anna was Mary's greatest defender, her most ardent supporter. Yosef knew that Anna had been the first to hear of the appearance of the angel to Mary. She had been the first to believe with unwavering faith the heavenly message given to her daughter: *You will conceive in your womb and bear a son and you will name Him Yeshua. He will be great and will be called Son of the Most High; and the Lord will give Him the throne of His father David . . . and His Kingdom will have no end.*[14]

Only yesterday Anna had instructed, "*Head high at the bar mitzvah. And keep your mind clear. . . . Smile at them if they fall silent as you pass. Remember, when they're talking about you, they're giving somebody else a rest. Pray for them, children. They violate the commandment not to murder with words as sharp as daggers. With speculation and lies passed on to others they bear false witness against the Lord's Anointed. Against the Son of David! An unkind word is a sword aimed at your heart, Mary. Meant to pierce you through with discouragement. The Lord, who is judge of all, will break the blade of the slanderer one day. Pray for those who speak badly of you. Pity them.*"

This was especially good advice in Nazareth, where the weaving of tales was a form of entertainment exceeding sewing, cooking, singing, or dancing.

Perhaps, Yosef reasoned, it was this powerful bond between mother and daughter that gave Mary the deep emotional keel by which she sailed on fearlessly through high seas.

Each day the women of Mary's close family circle were together as they kneaded bread or tilled the garden or churned butter. It came to Yosef in a sudden revelation that the Eternal One had carefully selected this family—these women—from among all in the tribe of Judah to help raise the Lord's Anointed. They were a clan not easily rattled.

What he saw today at the bar mitzvah was further confirmation of that fact.

How easy it was for Yosef to understand "Why Mary?" as he observed Anna. Was it not written "the apple does not fall far from the tree"?

Anna of the steady heart! Anna of the easy laugh! Anna of the Lord's keen insight! Anna, believer in miracles. Anna of praise and prayer. Anna selected as grandmother to the promised King of Israel! Mary needs you now and will need you when the time comes!

But Yosef still had no real conclusion to his own recurring doubt: *Who am I, Lord, that you have chosen me? I am only Yosef, son of Jacob.*

Believing in the importance of the question, he waited patiently for the answer.

CHAPTER 5

Four Herodian scribes arrived at the caravansary of Nazareth just after noon. In the courtyard of the inn they ate and drank and speculated openly about the fate of Herod's sons. Each Nazarean within earshot pretended not to listen. Within the hour gossip from the court in Beirut had crossed the threshold of every home.

In spite of Caesar's support, things were not looking good for princes Alexander and Ari. Anyone who had something pleasant to say about the sons of the Butcher King had better keep silent or risk loss of a tongue or worse.

A collective shudder passed through the marketplace of Nazareth as the Temple scribes strolled from stall to stall, asking questions in regard to the whereabouts of Zachariah and Elisheba of Beth Karem. High Priest Boethus was anxious to speak to the old man who claimed he had seen an angel in the Temple, they said. It was reported in their hometown of Beth Karem that Zachariah had brought his wife and newborn to Nazareth to visit relatives.

The scribes, pens drawn like swords, questioned Heli, who was related by marriage. "The high priest wishes to interview the fellow who spoke with an angel. Lord Boethus would like to honor him. Perhaps the priest Zachariah has some word from the Lord to help direct Lord Herod in the matter of his treasonous sons? Lord Boethus is most eager to speak with Zachariah on the matter. Where are Zachariah and his wife now? Where have they taken their baby?"

Heli informed them he was unsure exactly where Zachariah and Elisheba had gone. "They visited awhile in Nazareth, then went away. Out of the country. They mentioned several places they might like to move. Perhaps Egypt. Alexandria is a great city where a scholar like Zachariah might want to settle. If not Alexandria, then perhaps Antioch. Or Cyprus. They're gone; that's all I know."

But where they had gone, Heli simply could not say.

The scribes pressed Heli's replies into the soft wax of their tablets. "You will send word to the Temple, eh? You will inform Lord Boethus when you receive word of where Zachariah and Elisheba have taken their child? Lord Boethus will count it a personal favor."

Heli promised that if Zachariah was in contact with relatives in Nazareth, the high priest of Israel would indeed be informed.

Thus ended this probe by Temple officials into the strange rumors of angelic visits to the Temple.

It was not to be the last.

The single room with one tiny window in which the Herodian princes were imprisoned was the best accommodation the village of Platana had to offer. That description implied nothing sumptuous. Platana was a dusty, windswept settlement inland from Beirut and away from the sea. It smelled strongly of the camels milling in the courtyard, but little else.

Ari complained about their treatment a great deal. Alex reminded him they were not in chains nor even in a dungeon—both of which were possibilities.

Ari subsided.

The day for the trial had come and gone. No one from the court came to bring them word of their fate. That fact by itself was not conclusive. Carrying news—good or bad—to suspected traitors was tantamount to suicide.

Neither brother could sleep.

Finally, about midnight, with Jupiter and Saturn continuing their yearlong dance in the southwest and the constellation Aries—"the sacrificial lamb," Ari muttered—due south, there was a knock at their chamber door.

Ari panicked. "They've come, Alex! Will it be poison or the noose, do you think? I never wanted to be king! This is all your fault!"

"Shut up!" his brother hissed. "We aren't even bound. I'll die fighting before anyone pours poison down my throat! Besides, they wouldn't knock first!"

Ari gulped, then nodded.

Posting themselves on either side of the narrow entry, Alex and Ari readied themselves to fight for their lives if Alex was wrong.

"What is it?" Alex demanded.

"It's me, young masters. Tero. May I come in?"

Tero was one of the oldest of Herod's retainers. The man, a soldier by profession, had accompanied Herod on every military campaign. Tero had once saved his sovereign's life during the Parthian War some thirty-three years earlier.

Tero was one of the few people living who could speak his mind to King Herod . . . and continue living.

"You . . . you come with news?" Alex asked.

"Yes. It's very bad, young masters. You both stand condemned."

Ari sank down in a heap on the dirt floor, staring at nothing. A moan escaping his lips brought a look of reproach from his brother.

"Is that all?" Alex replied, raising his chin.

"Bless you, no, Lord Alex. Not a'tall. The king, your father, is pondering what to do with you both. Now, some says you should die. . . ."

Ari moaned again.

"But Emperor Caesar's man suggested otherwise."

"Caesar did?" Ari said, brightening.

"Oh, he'll not order it. Your father is king, after all. But the emperor has left it up to your father to decide."

Ari slumped back. "We're doomed, then."

"Not yet! Your father looks so glum! He doesn't want you dead . . . not really. And listen, young sirs. My boy . . . young Tero . . . you know him?"

Alex grasped Tero by both forearms. "Get on with it, man!"

"My son says the army doesn't want Antipater for king. Says he's a commoner, a sneak, and a coward."

Antipater, half brother to Ari and Alex, was, along with Steward Talmai, the chief architect of the princes' present dilemma.

"I'll go to your father, see? I'll speak to him. Remind him of the good times before all this was stirred up. Perhaps he'll pack you both off to Rome, but he'll never have you killed. Why, before he killed your mother, he loved her as much as his own life . . . almost, anyway. It'll come out all right. You'll see. The court's to leave Beirut soon. Rest easy tonight, and tomorrow or the next day I'll have my talk. Leave it to me."

The evening sun still shone on the white marble and honey-colored sandstone of Caesarea Maritima. Begun as a showpiece to demonstrate Herod's architectural prowess, Caesarea's aqueducts and arches, its temples and market squares had been fifteen years in the making.

Warm light still illuminated the blue-tiled pools in the garden spaces, but it could not penetrate the heavy woven drapes drawn tightly across the windows of Herod's bedchamber. The interior rooms of Herod's royal palace were steeped in gloom. The king, suffering a migraine, had taken a sleeping potion hours before and been unconscious ever since.

The sentries tiptoed on their rounds. Orders and responses were whispered.

As if suddenly conscious of an uninvited presence, Herod awoke with a start. A figure standing in the corner of his room stirred, then advanced toward him.

The apparition startled the monarch. He tried to scream but choked. A fit of coughing stopped him from calling out for the guards.

"Your pardon, Majesty," muttered a voice hoarse with age. "It's Tero. You remember me—your old comrade-in-arms. Tero."

When the king's heart stopped its wild palpitations and he regained enough breath to speak, he demanded, "Tero? What are you doing here?"

"Sorry to disturb you. I waited till I thought you was awake."

"How did you . . . ?"

"Well, it's like this, Majesty. I know you want to do right by your boys Alex and Ari. You've been lied to about them, see? Well, I've come to put your mind at ease."

Herod might have demanded an explanation for this outrageous affront, but another paroxysm of rasping gasps allowed Tero to continue.

"The army won't have it, see? Putting Antipater in charge, that is. Now, I don't know what all's behind the trouble with Alex and Ari, but the soldiers trust them. Nobody much trusts Antipater. So, you see, I told them I'd speak up for them. Straight talk, eh? One old soldier to another, eh?"

"You . . . met with them?"

"Oh yes. And my son . . . you call to mind my son . . . young Tero, he is. In your palace guard. Hermes is off duty, so my son's the one let me into your room so we could have this chat. You can ask him too, if you've a mind to. The army thinks Antipater . . . well, his mother is a commoner, eh? Not a princess like the Lady Mariamne. Now, mind you, everyone says it's not your fault . . . just your wit's clouded by your illness is all. Why, when you were younger, you'd've seen through him right enough. Antipater's always been one to carry tales when it served his purpose. But now you know the truth, eh?"

"I do indeed! Guards! Seize this man! And bring me Hermes!"

At spearpoint Tero was gagged before he could utter one more startled syllable.

Ecbatana, Kingdom of Parthia
Supplement to Journal of Court Astronomer Melchior
Summer, Year of Creation 3753

Despite Ecbatana's elevation of over a mile above sea level, the midday heat is oppressive. It is the season of the seistan, the "wind of 120 days," when much of the central plateau of Parthia is dust-blasted and sun-parched. The coolest air in Old Balthasar's home is nearest the ground, so he and I sat on the flagstone-covered floor next to a study table barely six inches in height.

Old Balthasar reviewed with me the signs in the sky. He explained that the constellation of The Scales was known in Hebrew as Mozanaim, and that every nation of men called the cross-shaped constellation by some form of that name: The Balances.

I asked him, "Since Mars (The Adam) has moved from The Virgin to The Balances, does that mean that One is coming from heaven to set things right on earth?"

Old Balthasar said, "Truly! Does not Isaias record of the Sovereign Lord: 'Who has held the dust of the earth in a basket, or weighed the mountains on the scales, or the hills in a balance? . . . Surely the nations are like a drop in the bucket; they are regarded as dust on the scales.'"[15]

Then he warned me to be careful. He told me believers in Yahweh as the One True God are not like those who see portents in every shooting star or tie a man's fortunes to the hour of his birth.

He urged me to remember what is written in this psalm of King David: "The heavens declare the glory of Yahweh; the skies proclaim the work of His hands. Day after day they pour forth speech; night after night they display knowledge. There is no speech or language where their voice is not heard."[16]

Then Old Balthasar added, "So this is the message every time Mars

(The Adam, Star of the Son of Man) arrives in the sign of The Balances: Yahweh is keeping accounts. Someday King Messiah will come. Someday he will judge. Someday he will put things right."

I had been keeping back what I considered the most intriguing observation, but I could contain it no longer. I reminded him of the significance he found in the conjunction of Saturn (The Lord of the Sabbath) with Jupiter (The Righteous) in the sign designating Israel.

Then I burst out with my news: Not only were those two stars drawing nearer together again, but I saw The Lord of the Sabbath hidden by the moon, emblem of the Ruach HaKodesh (the Holy Spirit).

Old Balthasar nodded vigorously, sharing my excitement. He stopped, as if debating whether to share more with me, then evidently decided to include me in his conclusions.

Reminding me about the life and words of Dani'el the prophet, he said, "It was here—right here in Ecbatana—that King Darius located the scroll of King Cyrus, ordering that the Jerusalem Temple to the Most High God must be rebuilt.[17] This is the same King Darius of whom Dani'el writes. Later Dani'el also prophesied of the coming of the Anointed One . . . King Messiah."[18]

My heart pounded in my chest. "And . . . when?"

Old Balthasar lowered his voice, as if fearful of being overheard. Speaking with great precision, he said, "I have done the calculations. I am convinced what we have seen in the skies, including what you observed with The Holy Spirit and The Lord of the Sabbath, means the time is near. Very near."

6 CHAPTER

s the planets danced closer together, declaring signs and wonders to observers in distant lands, the children of Israel slept.

Yosef slept on his mat on his roof in Nazareth. A breeze stirred, carrying the aroma of Temple spices and the soft ringing of bells.

He heard a voice whisper, *Yosef!*

He sat up and rubbed his eyes. The stars of Israel's constellation, The Two Fish, gleamed brighter than he had ever seen them before. Was he dreaming?

He rose and called, "Mary? Are you awake?"

She did not reply from inside the house.

Yosef stood a moment and listened before gazing at the two planets, shining like jewels. Tzadik and Shabbatai so close in the sky. Was this sign the heavenly proclamation of the secret Mary carried?

He reached as if to touch the stars and tried to pray. "Blessed are you, O Adonai. . . ." His mind was sluggish with exhaustion. "Adonai . . . who selected us from all people, to love and take pleasure in us."

Lying down again, he closed his eyes and tried to recite the blessing. But halfway through, he fell asleep again. . . .

A call penetrated the fog of heavy slumber.

Yosef!

Had some stranger found his way onto the roof? Was Mary in danger?

Yosef muttered, "Who . . . are . . . you?"

Yosef!

Yosef opened his eyes again. The dim form of a very tall fellow towered over his head. Yosef tried to move but could not make his arms or legs obey. "I can't move. You know I would hurt you if I could move."

You are dreaming.

"Then I can't hurt you. And you can't hurt her. Let me up."

In good time.

"Who are you, coming onto my roof and into my dreams uninvited?"

The intruder shimmered with faint light as he spoke. *I was called Zaphenath-Paneah, which means "Elohim has hidden from the mighty and revealed His face to the humble."*

"Very long name. Sounds Egyptian. Every Egyptian I've ever met has a long, unpronounceable name."

You have a good ear.

"But . . . what has an Egyptian to do with me? Who are you?"

Joseph. Son of Jacob.

"Yes, that's me. I am plain Yosef, son of plain Jacob. Yes, you've come to the right place. But . . . who are you?"

I told you. Elohim reveals His face to the humble.

"The meaning of your Egyptian name. Speak plainly, sir, or let me sleep."

I was born a Hebrew. I tended my father's sheep in these hills. Not far from here. Do you not remember the story you loved best of all when you were a little boy? In the Book of Beginnings*? The story about Yosef, son of Jacob?*[19]

"How do you know what story I liked best?"

We know many things. . . . How every night you begged your mother to tell you again how my father, Jacob, laid his head upon a stone and dreamed of angels ascending and descending on a great ladder from heaven to earth.[20]

Yosef smiled. Suddenly he could move. He sat up slowly and peered into the darkness.

The fellow remained obscured behind his cloak.

Yosef queried, "Your father? *The* Jacob? Jacob of Jacob's ladder?"

Yes. I am Joseph, son of Jacob. You and I share the same name. My name is your name. Everything means something. My father, Jacob, is the one written of in the Book of Beginnings . . . *Jacob who wrestled with the Angel of Adonai till daybreak . . . until Adonai blessed him and called him Isra'el.*[21]

Yosef frowned. "I remember the story. So, your father was Jacob the Great who wrestled with the Lord."

All men wrestle with Adonai and may only attain true greatness if they yield and are overcome by Him.

"My father was Jacob the ordinary. Your father died generations ago and is buried in the tomb of the patriarchs in Hebron. My father died three years ago and is buried not far from here."

I know your father well. A cheerful fellow. We have had many long talks about you beside the river.

"What river? You know my father?"

Of course. He told me . . . let's see . . . about you carving the whistles for Purim when you were only nine.

"How do you know about that?"

The being replied, *We who lived before you are not dead, but alive. We are a cloud of witnesses who watch you and cheer you on as you run your race here on earth.*[22]

Understanding flickered in Yosef's mind like the flame of a candlewick struggling to stay lit in an open window. "Ah. Then I'm dreaming about Joseph. The original. Joseph the redeemer of Israel. The one whose Hebrew name means 'increase' and 'cause great things to come forth.' And you are telling me now in this dream that your father is the patriarch Jacob, son of Yitz'chak and grandson of Avraham. But . . . are you . . . a dream? Or are you . . . ?"

The wind stirred the wind chimes. *I am the Dreamer of dreams.*

"Why should someone so great as you, Dreamer of dreams, visit my humble dreams?"

This is the season when the Ushpizin speak to the humble in Israel of miracles and wonders and reveal mysteries yet to come.

Yosef protested, "I'm a carpenter, not a prophet. Though my name may also mean 'increase' and 'cause great things to come forth,' I have to say that very little significance has come from me up to now. It is all I can do to pay my taxes and feed myself and Mary."

Joseph the Dreamer replied, *You are a dreamer like me.*

"True. A dreamer of dreams, that's true. I reason things out in my sleep. The way I'll build a table or a room. I draw the plans in my head while I sleep. Then I wake up and build it."

Just so. As it should be. Were you not expecting me to come to you? to help you reason things out?

"Expecting? No, I can't say that I was. I was hoping. Since the angel came awhile ago and told me about Mary. I go to bed each night hoping to learn more."

There was a smile in The Dreamer's reply. *There are hopes unspoken in the human heart that groan and sigh and rise to reach the ears of the Almighty as wordless prayers. This is one of those occasions. The Lord has heard your sighs, Yosef. The Lord loves your questions. Everything in Scripture means something! He longs to teach you the answers.*[23]

"I'm glad of it. I've been feeling very uncertain of myself, you see. So unworthy. I understand why he chose Mary . . . never was a heart more willing to serve the Lord than hers. But me? I am caught up in this great event with some reluctance. I wanted nothing more for myself than a humble life, you see. A house. A business. A wife and children."

And so humble lives are all a wonderful part of the Master's plan.

"So . . . *Ulu Ush-pi-zin.* Welcome, exalted wanderer. I'm glad . . . grateful you've come. Why don't you sit down, Joseph, son of Jacob, son of Yitz'chak, son of Avraham. Dreamer of dreams. Revealer of secrets."

The Ushpizin accepted Yosef's invitation and sank to the roof floor in a ripple of barely perceptible light. Suddenly Yosef could see his face. It was not transparent but glowing from the inside. He was handsome. Clean-shaven like an Egyptian. His dark eyes twinkled with amusement.

The visitor raised his hand. *Generations will call you Yosef the Tzadik, the Righteous Man. You who share my name and my gift of dreams are favored and beloved by the Lord.*

Yosef thumped his chest and bowed deeply. "You are the one who saved our people! I know all the stories by heart!"

But you still do not know the meaning behind all the stories.

"Teach me, then. I read about you as a child and loved the stories because you are the fellow I was named for . . . Joseph who wore the coat of many colors! Joseph sold into slavery by his brothers.[24] The same Joseph who became Zaphenath-Paneah, the right hand of Pharaoh. The mighty one who forgave and redeemed his brothers from famine when they came to appeal to Pharaoh for help."[25]

Yes. I am all of that and more. Firstborn son of Rachel. Beloved son of my father, Jacob, whom the Angel named Isra'el. Shepherd of my father's flocks. Hated and rejected by my half brothers. Slave. Prisoner. Prophet. Prince. Redeemer and savior to the same brothers who betrayed me.

Yosef gazed up at the stars. "Zaphenath-Paneah. Exalted one. Here with me. Who am I? A descendant of King David, yes . . . but through the cursed line of David's sons. A nobody when it comes to eternal things."

The being leaned closer and whispered earnestly, *Adonai hides His plans from the mighty but reveals His secrets to the humble.*[26] *Is this not the meaning of my Egyptian name? We will begin with that basic truth. All wisdom increases and grows and overflows from this fact: Adonai reveals His face to the humble!*

The Dreamer reached out toward Yosef, almost touching his brow. *Humble Yosef! You will see Adonai's face revealed on earth first of all men. You will carry Him in your arms. And after you, the sons and daughters of Israel will see their Redeemer and carry Him in their hearts! There is much more to come. It is written . . . much for you to accomplish. Yosef . . . young dreamer of dreams.*

Yosef asked eagerly, "Where will we begin?"

At the beginning. It is written: "Teach your children . . . when you lie down and when you rise up!"[27] *Torah—the Word of the Lord—will instruct you when you lie down and when you rise up. Listen for me. But now I must be gone. Look! Light rises in the east. The rooster crows. Dreams fade and the dreamer awakens.*

The Dreamer began to melt away. *Yosef! It is written . . . all . . . every detail foretold. Do not be afraid of the questions. Do not be afraid to ask.*

"I'm asking! Will you come back? When will you come back? Will you teach me?"

The rooster crowed again. Yosef's organized thoughts tumbled into an illogical heap. Exhausted, he slept more soundly than he had ever slept before.

Ecbatana, Kingdom of Parthia
Addendum to Journal of Court Astronomer Melchior
Late Summer, Year of Creation 3753

Apart from my official report on the New Moon and the wandering stars, I am adding these notes for my own benefit.

Old Balthasar tells me he is convinced we are nearing monumental changes in the world. He is no longer content to observe with me on New Moon nights alone. Ever since I reported the eclipse of Saturn (The Lord of the Sabbath) by the moon, Balthasar has forced his creaking knees to carry him up all seven levels of the city several nights every week. Even though he constantly cautions me against drawing hasty conclusions, his excitement is palpable.

Last night was no exception but was even more unusual because of the crowd. I was accompanied by two young royal offspring: Phrataaces, son of the king of Parthia and Queen Musa; and Aretas, son of the Nabatean princess the king divorced when he promoted Musa to queen. Aretas is fifteen. A fine, studious lad, quiet and observant. Phrataaces is two years younger and . . . not at all like his half brother. The rooftop platform of our observatory was crowded due to the full retinue of guards and servants.

I made my customary sunset observations, as I recorded earlier, then set about acquainting the princes with the night sky. I endeavored to make it both interesting and informative.

I fear I failed, at least as far as Phrataaces is concerned, since he several times complained that he was bored, that he was tired, that he was thirsty, and so forth.

On the other hand, Aretas seemed genuinely interested. I showed him Scorpius, perhaps the most easily recognized figure of all, with its claws and uplifted stinger. We spoke about how Mars, the god of war in many cultures, and The Adam (Ma'Adim to the Jews) were seemingly within the clutches of Scorpius.

What did this mean? he inquired.

Recalling Old Balthasar's warning not to suggest conclusions to the young men, I merely said that many races found significance in the signs in the sky. Some asserted that the signs present at the hour of one's birth affected a lifetime of fortune—for good or ill.

Aretas laughed and noted that then all men born at the same hour would invariably live identical lives, suffering success and failure in a kind of inescapable rhythm. Clearly this was not the actual experience of humans.

Phrataaces sniffed and announced he was cold, even though the air was warm and still. While all the servants and half the guards bustled about getting blankets and warm drinks and tidbits from the royal kitchen, Balthasar, Aretas, and I were left essentially alone.

Old Balthasar praised Aretas for his perception, and the prince, in his turn, knowing Balthasar to be an elder of the Jews, demanded his opinion on the subject of finding wisdom in the stars.

After staring at the rising conjunction of The Lord of the Sabbath and The Righteous for some moments, Balthasar said this: "There is one essential difference in the way we Jews approach knowledge—all knowledge, whether of the stars or other parts of creation—from the way most of the rest of the world examines knowledge. The Greeks and all who follow their precepts say the purpose of learning is gnothi seauton, 'know thyself.' We Jews teach rather that the proper object of study is da'ath Elohim, 'knowledge of God.' Because of these radically differing starting points, Your Highness, there will never be complete accord between the two ways. We say, 'The fear of God is the beginning of wisdom.'[28] The Greeks and all who draw from their philosophy—including both the Romans and the Parthians—hope to rise from studying man's higher nature to an understanding of God. It can never happen. Man's higher nature does not exist apart from a reflection of God. We say, 'Look at the stars and see the Creator!' Only on such a foundation will any study or learning have either sense or purpose."

Just then (and still well before the appointed conclusion of the lesson) Phrataaces demanded that he be allowed to return to the palace or heads would roll.

That was the end of the royal observing session, though Old Balthasar and I remained watching and talking for several hours more.

CHAPTER 7

The windows of the synagogue were ablaze with light as Yosef and Mary made their way to the Shabbat evening service. Men stood in knots outside the building, speaking to one another in hushed tones.

The couple separated at the door, Mary joining her sisters and mother to climb the narrow steps to the Women's Gallery. Yosef, wrapping his prayer shawl around him, found Heli near the steps. The expressions of everyone in Nazareth seemed particularly grim this evening.

"The latest news from Yerushalayim. Very bad," Heli confided as the two entered the synagogue.

"I was in the shop all day. Alone. I've heard nothing. What is it?"

Heli repeated the latest reports of arrests, torture, and executions. "It seems Herod has truly gone mad."

"We're safe here," Yosef remarked. "Who'll take notice of Nazareth?"

"There are reports that Herodian guards rode out to Beth Karem in search of Zachariah and Elisheba and baby Yochanan."

"They're safely across the river."

"Thanks be to Adonai!" Heli put a hand on Yosef's sleeve and pulled him to one side. "You and Mary. I fear for you and the baby."

"We are . . . I mean, Mary and I . . . we're so . . . obscure."

"The eye of evil must surely be searching everywhere," Heli warned. "Herod doesn't care who dies. He sweeps the innocent into the fires along with the guilty. Be careful."

"I will go only where the Shepherd leads," Yosef assured his father-in-law.

Heli nodded once, then covered his head as the cantor rose to sing the evening prayer:

"For in thy hand are the souls of the living and the dead. . . . You in whose hand is the soul of every living creature and the spirit of all human flesh. . . . Into your hands I commend my spirit! You redeem me, O Eternal God of truth![29] Our God who is in heaven, glorify your Name and establish your sovereignty forever, and reign over us forevermore."

Speaking in hushed tones in the darkened confines of his private apartment in Herod's royal palace in Jerusalem, Chief Steward Talmai completed his report. The only other person present was Herod's heir apparent, Prince Antipater.

"Within twelve hours after his father's fatal mistake, Tero the Younger and three hundred other army officers loyal—or thought to be loyal—to Prince Alex had been rounded up and imprisoned."

"Go on . . . go on!" Antipater urged.

"In two more days all three hundred were dead. Stoned at the hands of a mob angered by the report of their treason."

"Wonderful! Perfect! And my . . . brothers?"

Talmai lowered his voice even further, forcing Antipater to lean in closer in order to hear. "My lord, I must inform you that the princes Alex and Ari were transported to prison in Sebaste, and once there . . . strangled."

Antipater's narrow-set eyes glittered with glee. "We've done it, Talmai! Alex and Ari both gone! My other half brothers—Antipas, Philip, and the rest—all too young to be threats to me. We've won."

"The king, your father, is already suffering remorse. You must not act pleased," Steward Talmai warned.

Antipater snorted. "The king, my father, is ill and deranged. Don't you think I hear the reports? Nightmares? Headaches? Ghosts in every corner? We should suggest at once that I take over ruling . . . be made regent . . . so he can rest."

Horrified and fearing for his own life, Talmai spoke more forcefully than he ever had to a royal offspring: "No! That is exactly what you must *not* do! You still have enemies who will attempt to convince the king you have a plot to overthrow him."

When Antipater's pudgy face turned petulant, the steward hurried his explanation. "Instead, you must leave Judea. Express your sympathy to your father for the disloyalty of your brothers. Then suggest he send you to Rome, to convince Caesar that the executions were justified. Ingratiate yourself with Caesar; earn his support. If the emperor gives you his unqualified endorsement, you'll return here as the unchallengeable successor."

"And in the meantime my father will grow ever crazier and less able to govern. Caesar will see it and know it's time to replace him. I'll do it! Draw up the letters at once! My father and then me: No one else will ever claim to be king of the Jews!"

It was Yosef's favorite time of year. His favorite time of night. Quiet. Cool.

This night both he and Mary lay on their backs gazing up from the roof of their little house. The sky glowed with a broad swath of opaque light.

Yosef explained, "The Romans call it The Milky Way. The rabbis call it Jacob's Ladder."

Somehow, to Yosef, an angel ladder with starlit rungs fastened to the sky by comets seemed a more glorious and logical path for Messiah to descend to earth than by way of a virgin's womb.

Mary did not reply. Had she drifted off?

Yosef clasped his hands beneath his head. What was behind the veil separating heaven from earth?

"Mary?"

"Hmm?"

"You awake?"

"I love this time of year." She sighed in contentment. "Almost autumn, but still summer."

Yosef inhaled the sweet scent of hay growing in the field. Why were hay fields so much more fragrant at night?

"Mary?"

"Beautiful, isn't it?"

"What do you think about when you look at the stars? And then . . . when you think about *it*?"

"It? Yosef! You mean the baby?"

"I mean . . . when you think . . . what this means! Not just any baby. *Such* a baby! He'll know all the mysteries from the beginning of time. . . . No! *Before* the beginning! All that explained! Messiah. First Light. Think of it! We can ask him so many questions and he can tell us. What comes into your mind?"

"A baby." She hummed a moment. "I can't wait to hold him."

Yosef traced the outline of the constellation of The Virgin holding the infant on her lap. A shooting star blazed across the horizon. "A baby . . . he who sang the stars into existence . . . will be born."

"And now I'll sing him to sleep."

"Sleep. I hadn't thought of that. Will such a holy child sleep, you think?"

"Yes. In my arms."

Above their heads the stellar hours unwound slowly toward the west. "But the stars. Who will tend the stars while he sleeps?"

"He'll be a baby. Like any other. Babies sleep. At least mothers and fathers pray they'll sleep. At least some of the time." She smiled.

"But he won't be. Not like any other. Not like any other baby who has lived before now. Nor like anyone who will come after. *Immanu'el*, the angel said. 'God-with-us.' *Yeshua*, the angel said. 'Yahweh is Salvation!' The only Son of the Holy One of Israel! Mary? I have to ask. What do you think about when you think of him?"

"I want to sit beside his cradle. To be there for him."

"For him?"

"For him. Babies need that sort of thing."

"But think of who he is. Who he will be."

"I want to rock him and sing softly until he goes to sleep."

"But he's coming for all the world. To sit on David's throne, and all that. You know what the rabbis say about Messiah. To rule over Israel."

"I think he may be lonely. In a way."

"Lonely?"

She hummed, then replied, "Sure. He used to walk in the first garden with the first man and woman. Like a family. I'll bet he's missed it."

It was plain to Yosef that Mary had been thinking of this a lot too. Trying to reason it through. Yosef could not quite grasp such a concept. "The Son of the Most High . . . lonely for human company."

"He's a baby, growing in my womb like babies grow in their mother's wombs. He'll want me to love him just like a mother loves her children. And I already do love him."

Yosef peered hard into the southwest, searching for the outline he knew was there. "Look, Mary! Look! Do you see?"

"So many stars."

"So many. Yes. But before time on earth began, at the moment of creation . . . look! Adonai etched your part of the story into the line of the stars. The pictures that rise in the east and set in the west. There. You see? That point of light there: Kfar. The Star of Atonement. And that one: Messiah's virgin mother, holding the infant on her lap."

"I'm not much good at picking out constellations."

Yosef raised her hand and pointed it toward Virgo. "See? There. That bright star is her heart. That cloudy looking bit? That's the infant king, Messiah. The branch is in her hand . . . yes. The branch of prophecy. And . . . there. The star called Atarah. That's Messiah's crown."

"Oh! Yes! I see it. That one?" The picture seemed to please her. "It is . . . lovely, isn't it? I'll thank him one day for making the stars and writing his story in the heavens for everyone to see." Mary's voice was tender. "But first . . . my part is a small one. I'll be his mama. Rock my baby in my arms. No cold, distant stars to hold him. A mother's arms, warm and gentle. I'll sing him to sleep. Sit by his cradle and be there to love him and care for him when all the stars have vanished and he wakes in the morning."

Herod stormed up and down the throne room of his Jerusalem palace. With one blue-veined, age-spotted hand he waved the unfolded parchment of a letter. The missive bore so many red wax seals and purple ribbons of state it could only be an imperial communication. The fingers of Herod's other hand alternately plucked at his thin beard or gesticulated wildly at the document.

"See what you've done, Talmai? Do you see? Caesar himself writes to chastise me for the death of my sons. My boys, my boys! See where Caesar says he changed his mind about adding Nabatea to my domain. 'Cannot consider it,' he says!"

Though other courtiers were present, only Talmai occupied the center of the chamber and the bull's-eye of Herod's attention. Anxious to escape the monarch's wrath, Hermes and the other guards had backed into the tapestried walls, as if trying to mesh with the woven threads.

Talmai knew that any moment could witness an order for his arrest. His execution would follow shortly after. There was nothing to be lost by boldness. The chief steward, on his knees with his strained, pale features tucked low, nevertheless raised his voice. "May I see the letter, Majesty?"

Herod stopped pacing long enough to thrust the parchment into Talmai's grasp.

There was a slight pause while Talmai scanned the message, then offered, "Caesar says he 'regrets the decision about the princes,' Majesty, but he acknowledges that he left their fates up to you."

"But Nabatea! He doesn't trust me now!"

"Caesar expresses concern about the welfare of your state, sire. He hopes order and peace will be maintained." Talmai's tone was surprisingly confident.

"Then we must crush all rebels!" Suddenly manic in his level of activity, Herod strode about the room. He argued with the air, gestured toward unseen listeners. Sometimes he ranted and threatened, sometimes orated. Sometimes he wept that he was so unappreciated by his ungrateful, disloyal subjects. "Wretches! They even attacked the Temple and burned the genealogy scrolls!"

The scrolls under discussion were the Temple Mount family records burned by the king's express command. Was Herod merely acting a part, Talmai wondered, or had his madness progressed to the point where he genuinely believed his own invented plots? There was no way to tell . . . and certainly no way for Talmai to inquire.

Herod continued, "Pharisees are plotting against me. Won't acknowledge me as heir to David. The *am ha aretz* dreaming of their precious Messiah. Listen! Proclaim a loyalty oath! Make them swear allegiance to me and to Caesar! No one can escape it. No one. No records? Make them return to their ancestral homes to reregister! You see what the rebels caused? We must have new records! Administer the oath while they're there. Every adult male in the land must be witnessed swearing his allegiance to Caesar and to me, or . . ."

Talmai did not need the sentence's completion to know what was meant.

Carefully stalking diagonally across the room on only black squares of tile, Herod mused, "Just like the census and oath for Roman citizens last year. Time for Judea to fall in line."

Talmai knew that such a plan would uproot much of the country, disrupt trade, ensure an increase in banditry and ill will. He also knew that Herod, caught in the delights of his own scheme, worried about none of these things.

The king shook his finger at a wall sconce. "Finish the fall harvest, but make them fulfill this decree before time to be planting again. From the Holy Days to the Roman New Year festivities. That's when it must be. Register every male above the age of two. No more escaping taxes! We'll know them all! Otherwise they're rebels and must die!"

Talmai breathed a sigh of relief at his narrow escape.

But as days passed, he still wondered where this new upheaval would lead.

CHAPTER 8

It was nearly twilight. Gray sky melded with gray earth. Roiling dark clouds built towards the explosion of a thunderstorm. Men and beasts scurried to shelter in the caravansaries.

Only one remained on the mud-slick road. A ragged, pregnant twelve-year-old. A runaway slave whose time had come to deliver.

Rain now began to sluice down on the rocky hills surrounding Jerusalem, turning the road into a river.

Yet she struggled on.

Muscles contracted in a vise that wrapped around her back and squeezed her abdomen. Crying out, she stumbled and sank to her knees. Gasping for breath, she howled with confusion.

The words of the old woman in the Temple had come true: "*With the thunder will come your pain.*"

There was only one in all the world who could save the girl and perhaps the baby when the time to deliver came. The prophetess had instructed her that when the labor pangs began, she must escape from Jerusalem and find Rachel, wife of Zadok, in Beth-lehem.

As lightning forked and struck the earth and thunder caused the ground to quake, the girl understood the agony of childbirth. The fierce pain increased with the power of the contraction and, with it, her terror. Eyes wide in her ebony face, she stretched out spindly arms to no one and cried for her mother.

But her mother had been murdered when slave traders stole seven children from their Ethiopian village. The girl—a beautiful child, graceful, sweet tempered, black as obsidian—had been purchased by the house of the great King Herod. Kept with other slave children in the palace, she had been noticed by Hermes, Herod's chief bodyguard, and used for his pleasure. When her pregnancy was noticed, she had been sent back to the slave quarters.

Now her only hope was in finding Beth-lehem.

How far to this village that the Jews called the House of Bread? Could she survive the journey?

Blood pooled in the rain puddle. She endured forty-five seconds of crushing agony before the pain abated. Hours of experience had taught her she had only a few minutes before the fist would slam down on her once again. Only a little time to stagger forward toward her destination.

Mire sucked away the rags that wrapped her feet. She was so thin that her pregnancy at full-term barely showed beneath her clothes. Then she saw it. There on the opposite hillside, dimly glimpsed through the veil of rain, were the first glimmers of lamplight from the village.

"Rachel of Beth-lehem! Near the well of Beth-lehem," the old woman said!

One hope. No other hope. *Mercy! Cry mercy!* Cry for the mother she would never see again. Beg mercy from the stranger whom the old woman declared could save her!

The girl drew herself erect and staggered on. The remaining distance would have been no more than a thirty-minute walk on a normal day. But how many more times would the contractions knock her to the ground?

She wiped mud and water from her eyes and forced herself onward.

One hope: Rachel, wife of Zadok. The miracle worker! House of Bread. Beth-lehem Ephratha. The one merciful one would not turn her away!

It was an evening to celebrate. The letter from Alexandria arrived for Zadok of Beth-lehem with good news. "All is well. Safe arrival of two parcels. God be praised."

Zadok was one among a hundred shepherds who tended the sacrificial Temple lambs in the pastures of Migdal Eder.

His wife, Rachel, served as chief midwife for the territory of Ephratha. She was the daughter of a midwife, descended from generations of midwives. She had learned her ancient skill at her mother's side.

The eldest of five daughters, she was born to the famous healer Eliakim bar Rophi, who knew the secrets of medicinal herbs and whose duty it was to tend to the health of shepherds and their flocks in Beth-lehem. Thus Rachel became heir to the wisdom of both parents in bringing forth and preserving life.

Rachel had been born in a cottage within sight of the stone monument erected over the grave of the first Rachel, beloved wife of the patriarch Jacob. Ten centuries before, Rachel had died in childbirth on the road to Beth-lehem. For this reason bar Rophi, ever the romantic, had named his first daughter Rachel.

As an infant, Rachel in no way resembled her namesake. She was of dark complexion and had such a large nose that most who had stooped to chuck her chin and coo into her face assumed she was a boy.

Bar Rophi intended no presumption in naming his child for the matriarch whose beauty was of such renown in the annals of Israel. In his eyes the infant truly was beautiful.

And in the eyes of Zadok the Shepherd, Rachel remained truly beautiful. She knew every young family and each baby by name for miles around. The people of Migdal Eder were all her beloved family. The tidy garden beside their cottage was thick with sprouting herbs for blooming mothers and blossoming children. The rafters of their house were hung with bunches of lavender that all but eliminated the stink of the sheep pens when the wind shifted and blew toward the village.

This clean-swept, pleasant cottage was a place of much coming and going. Not a day passed without some neighbor, pregnant belly swelled to bursting, lumbering up the path to purchase tea to combat indigestion or sleeplessness. Those expectant mothers who lived more than a mile beyond the village and who Rachel suspected might experience a difficult delivery boarded the last week or so of their confinement. The birthing house was a nine-cubit-square, one-room building of white-washed limestone, situated on the far side of the herb garden behind the main house.

Rachel had delivered three baby boys over the last twenty-two days, but tonight the birthing room was empty. No babies due for at least another three weeks. A quiet evening.

Rain bucketed down, coursing from the funnel on the roof into the cistern. Their toddlers, Enoch and Samu'el, slept quietly on the soft fleece mattress in the corner. Zadok's best dog, a shaggy black creature named Bear Dog, slept at their feet. Zadok and his sister Havila's grandmother was spending the night with Havila. Rachel mended the frayed hem of Zadok's tunic while Zadok tallied the list of newborn lambs for the week. The couple scrupulously avoided discussing the horrific events in Jerusalem. They had not spoken of Onias since Zadok had returned from putting him on the ship. Even after good news, it was still too dangerous to mention his name.

"We needed the rain." Rachel pulled the needle through the coarse fabric. "Cool us off."

"Sheep in the pens are belly high in muck." Zadok did not look up from his accounts. "But I'll not be ungrateful for it. The pastures are bare from three years of drought."

"It's a good sign, this rain. Grandmother says so."

"I've had the lads move the ewes set t' deliver into the lambin' caves. So many lambs on the way. They're cheek by jowl, they are."

"You can add my little ones to your tally. You know how many babies in the last year?"

"You've been busy. Every other week it seems."

"Thirty-six. And do you know how many girls in the bunch?"

"No idea."

"Six. All the rest of them sons, including Lem and Sharona's baby. Now tell me it's not a portent of great blessing."

"So many sons usually means imminent war."

"Grandmother said she heard it's been a year for sons to be born all over Eretz-Israel."

Zadok cleared his throat. "The Almighty better send a few females along too, or the next generation will die off. Least that's the way I understand things work."

"A portent of blessing. Things have to get better."

"So many male children, there'll be no need of midwives in a few years. I'll have t' go to Moab t' buy a wife for little Samu'el. Then how would y' feel about it?" he blustered.

Pricking the fabric with her needle, she frowned down at her hands. “How can I talk to you about serious things, Zadok? Havila says she and Eliyahu talk about such things all the time.”

“Eliyahu is a rabbi. A fine man. Intelligent. A scholar. He discourses on the significance of babies. But you’ve married a shepherd. A practical man. What good is talk on such a night? I prefer t’ heed and put t’ practice with my wife the Lord’s command t’ be fruitful and multiply.”

“We’ll need a bigger house,” she shot back.

“We’ll leave the results of my obedience in the hands of the Almighty.”

Rachel smiled, shook her head, but did not reply.

His dark eyes brightened with amusement. It was his first smile in days, and she was glad to see it. He snapped shut the leather binder over the wax tablets, tossed down the writing stylus, and sank down beside her.

Bear Dog raised his head momentarily at his master’s movement, then sighed and slept again.

Zadok made a muscle. He was like a boy showing off for the girls in the market square. “Feel that. Eh? Like a stone. Look here, Rachel. Here’s the difference between a rabbi and a shepherd.”

Patiently she poked his bicep with her index finger. “Aye. A stone. Lovely.”

“Now tell me you don’t prefer strength over scholarship.” He thumped his chest.

She tapped his temple. “Stone right the way through. That’s for me.”

“I can heft a ewe off her feet and hold her on her back for shearin’ without effort.”

No response.

Zadok coaxed the mending from her fingers and kissed her lightly. A hint of desperation crept into his voice. “I feel like I’ve hardly seen you. Are y’ listenin’, woman?”

Rachel pulled away, retrieving the garment and attempting to resume her work. “If you want a frayed hem dragging in the mud, then persist.”

“Persistence has served me well.”

“Come morning, don’t ask me why it isn’t done!”

"If sons are all the Almighty sends our way, then we're on the swift road t' destruction. For what use are we strong fellows without the comfort of women? Give me a daughter, and I'll possess the greatest treasure in the territory. She'll grow up and look like you, and there'll be a line of suitors from here t' Yerushalayim."

Rachel laid aside her work. "Not like me. She mustn't look like me. My complexion. Too dark."

"And I say she shall look like her mother. Isn't it sung in the Song of Songs, '*How right they are to adore you? You are dark but comely, my love.*'"[30]

"How do you know these things, Zadok?" She sighed and leaned against his chest.

"I was a boy once. In Torah school we picked out the important quotes in Scripture and memorized 'em t' woo our women."

"Profane use of what's holy. So the rabbis would say."

"What do rabbis know about wooin'? Nay. Practical. I, as a shepherd, put the lessons of Torah t' practical use. The patriarch Jacob was also a shepherd and a practical man."

"Devious."

"True. But all turned out right for him in the end. Twelve sons he had."

"Too much rain has washed your brains clean."

"It follows, doesn't it, that if I stare into your beautiful brown eyes, Rachel, my ewe, our ewe lambs will be as beautiful as you?"

"Not the way of it."

"How can we know unless we test the theory?"

"Risky proposition, Zadok."

"A good proposition nonetheless. The babes are asleep. Grandmother's at Havila's. I'm home tonight. You've no business t' tend back in your lambin' barn. Nor prospects of anyone comin'. Ah, Rachel. The rain is fallin'. Listen. Let me gaze into your eyes all the whole night long." He kissed her gently. "Help me forget the world is such an unholy place."

She combed his beard with her fingers and whispered, "Zadok, you do have a way about you. But we shouldn't have a daughter. Though our hearts may be a garden, it's more than we can hope to think the Almighty could make a bouquet of our two faces."

"I am her father. She will be beautiful." He cradled Rachel in his arms. "Like her mother. And she will sing like an angel. Like her mother. Sing t' me, Rachel."

Rachel tucked her chin in thought. What song should she sing on such a night?

Rain drummed on the roof. Wind whined around the corner of the house. Suddenly Bear Dog leapt to his feet. A low growl rumbled in his throat as he stared fiercely at the door.

"Get by, dog!" Zadok commanded. "Back t' bed with you! It's naught but the wind!"

Then Rachel heard it: a sound, a cry, a wailing almost human. A premonition of evil coursed through her. She shuddered. "Wait, Zadok. Listen. Bear hears something. Do you hear it?"

"What?" Zadok grasped her arm. "What is it?"

"Listen." Rachel stood slowly, posed like a doe listening for danger. She wrapped the fleece around her shoulders.

"Nothin'. The wind."

Bear Dog slunk to his place. He crouched for only an instant before the desperate plea sounded again. Then, barking, the dog bounded toward the door.

"The beast's gone daft," Zadok grumbled.

Rachel raised one finger. "No, listen. Hear it, Zadok? A child. A human child. Crying."

Grudgingly Zadok rose from the soft fleece rug. Towering in the center of the room he cocked his head to one side.

Yes. There it was again. More distinct. Like the high-pitched shriek of a rabbit trapped in a snare. "Aye. Probably one of Lem's brats. Bad dream."

Nearer now. "Help . . . me . . . help . . . me . . ."

A child? A woman? It was the sound of human terror. Someone on the brink of death. Rachel had heard such a plea only once before, as a young girl when her mother had been unable to save the life of a woman who bled to death in childbirth.

"Zadok? Someone . . . dying. We must go see."

"Aye. Somethin' unnatural. Stay here, Rachel. Unnatural it is. Stay with the lads." Zadok tied his sandals, threw on his cloak, and grabbed his staff. Bear Dog on his heels, he stepped out into the gale.

Long minutes passed. Rachel paced before the door. The haunting keen faded into moaning winds.

Where was Zadok?

She thought she heard him call her name from the footpath.

As she threw open the door, wind and horizontal rain stung her cheeks. She held up the clay lantern but could not see him through the blackness. Bear Dog dashed into the pool of light, looked back, and sprinted away again.

"Zadok?" She held the lantern higher. "Where are you?"

His voice was gruff, almost angry in reply. "Rachel! I found a half-dead girl down at the well! Stir up the embers, woman!"

A moment later, carrying a fragile form wrapped in his cloak, Zadok pushed past Rachel into the house.

Yosef paused to shake the sawdust from his hair and beard. The last two days in the workshop had been feverish: An urgent order for a dozen winnowing forks had arrived the same week he had promised to finish a storage chest for Nachman the Butcher. Yosef had scarcely stopped to eat, and there had been no time at all for conversation.

So when his friend Tevyah, calling his name, puffed and panted up the hill toward the shop, Yosef could not imagine what was the matter.

"Yosef! Have you heard? What do you think?"

"Heard what? Think about what? Tevyah, stop and catch your breath!"

Tevyah's short legs never propelled his bulk rapidly. But such an effort this time had drenched his pale brown tunic with sweat. Plunging both hands into a water bucket, Tevyah splashed his round face, then brushed drips from his bushy eyebrows and thinning hair.

"The new census! Herod's ordered a census. It has to be completed by the Romans' new year."

Yosef shrugged. "So what comes next is new taxes. Is this a reason to get in an uproar?"

Shaking his head like an obstinate ox, Tevyah argued, "But there's more! A loyalty oath . . . to Caesar and to Herod! We are summoned to the synagogue. All heads of households are ordered to attend."

"When?"

"Now!"

By the time Yosef and Tevyah arrived at the Nazareth synagogue, it overflowed. Though only men were summoned to attend, the whole village was too anxious about the news to await a secondhand rendition.

Why? Yosef wondered. Numbering the people was not new. Herod had carried out one—when was it?—ten years back. Nor was a loyalty oath so unusual as to create such a furor. Herod had also implemented one of those before, at Caesar's behest. Because of their religious scruples, certain of the Pharisee sect and the desert-dwelling communes of Essenes had been exempt. No one had suffered for it so far as Yosef knew.

Still, the rumors flew.

Yosef shoved his way in to stand beside the side wall, shoulder to shoulder with Nachman on one side and Abner the Oil Merchant on the other.

"Yosef," Nachman acknowledged with a bob of his head. "Ten denarii for each man, five for a woman, two for each child. Is it fair, I ask you? Eh? Because a man is blessed by the Almighty to tax him up to the eyes?"

"What do you talk?" Abner challenged, leaning his greasy countenance across Yosef's chest. "It's not taxes! We must swear allegiance to Herod with an oath acknowledging him to be the messiah! It's blasphemy! It'll mean civil war!"

Had Herod truly gone so mad? Only a few months had passed since men were crucified throughout Judea for opposing Herod's will. If the king now thought himself to be divine, what would the aftermath be?

And what about Mary? How can I protect her and the child if the whole province goes up in flames? Blessed are you, O Adonai, who delivers us from evil!

"Shouldn't we at least wait to hear the news?" Yosef urged.

Nachman and Abner glared at each other, vying for the honor of delivering the worst bad news first.

Elderly and stoop-shouldered, Rabbi Mazzar stepped up to the bema. When he raised his knotted and trembling hands, the assembly fell silent even before the chazzan shouted for quiet.

An officer of the Herodian guard, wearing a bronze breastplate and green tunic and accompanied by a guard sergeant and three soldiers, flanked Mazzar. The rabbi did not introduce the man but merely beckoned for him to speak.

"Men of Nazareth," the captain intoned, "hear this royal decree. By commands of His Highness Caesar Augustus and Herod, king of the Jews, a census is ordered. Under pain of death, each head of household must register between today and the end of the Imperial Roman year. At the time of registration, each man must swear an oath of loyalty to great Caesar Augustus and to King Herod."[31]

"Roman calendar, Roman law, Roman taxes," hissed Nachman.

"Blasphemy!" Abner whispered.

"Silence!" the Herodian sergeant bellowed.

The captain continued, "Each man must go to the city of his birth, there to be properly recorded."[32]

No matter how much the sergeant yelled, the uproar resulting from these words increased as the meaning sank in.

"Leave Nazareth and go all the way to Hebron? What about my business?"

"Who'll tend my flocks while I'm off to Jericho? Who?"

Mary! My city to register is Beth-lehem! Six or seven days' journey. All the way to Beth-lehem, and Mary nearer to giving birth with every passing day? What does it mean? What to do?

The sergeant drew a multitailed whip from his wide leather girdle and swung it menacingly.

The crowd subsided.

"We will check the lists of names against those living here to see if any have failed to register," the captain warned. "No one should think they can escape this order. No one!"

When the soldiers had clumped noisily from the synagogue, Rabbi Mazzar led the congregation in the Shema, then offered this benediction:

> *"Blessed are you, O Adonai, who delivers us from evil. Deliver us, Lord, from every evil, and grant us peace in our day. In your mercy keep us free from sin and protect us from all anxiety, as we wait in joyful hope for the coming of our Messiah!"*

Yosef felt a jolt up his spine at the words. He looked around to see if anyone else noticed how he was shaking. The coming of Messiah! Yosef—as well as anyone else in the room—knew the longing those words contained . . . and even more about their immediacy!

But what sort of world was Messiah about to be welcomed into?

Part II

In those days Caesar Augustus issued a decree that a census should be taken of the entire Roman world.

LUKE 2:1

CHAPTER 9

It was early morning. Most of the Holy City was not yet awake. Even the Herodian guards at the gates did not bother to conceal their yawns as they admitted a pair of visitors from Beth-lehem.

Inside the Jerusalem home of Simeon the Elder, Zadok paced the tiled floor of the study. The shepherd's flashing eyes and deep scowl gave additional evidence of his agitation. His brother-in-law, Rabbi Eliyahu, sat beside Simeon. The two scholars shared a pot of warm, spiced wine as they watched Zadok stride up and down.

Zadok told Simeon about the arrival of the slave girl, then turned to the question of the oath. "What if it's a ploy? Aye, a census t' raise taxes—that's nothin' new. But another loyalty oath? What can it mean but a trick t' separate the sheep from the goats? Remember those students massacred when they pulled down the Roman eagle? And all the innocents killed in the panic after? My brother's wife trampled! My brother crucified! That was all Herod's doin'! I've not forgotten . . . nor has the rest of the country, I warrant. And now this new oath."

Eliyahu urged calm. "We haven't even seen the form of the oath yet, Zadok. It may be we can take it without blaspheming the Almighty. No panic, no trick. Just Herod's attempt to curry favor by following Caesar's census decree."

Simeon agreed. "Zadok, the Romans are keeping a close eye on Herod right now. He doesn't want—nor will they permit—a general uproar. You know that in all nations save Judea there are sacrifices . . . prayers *to* the emperor. Only here is it permitted to pray *for* him instead. Why would Herod upset the accepted practice now?"

Zadok remained unconvinced. "Because he's a bloodthirsty monster . . . or a madman! Take your pick. It's all one to the common folk . . . us of the *am ha aretz*."

Simeon countered, "I intend to consult the prophetess Hannah about the matter of the oath. She speaks for the Lord in all things. I've been selected to sit with others of the court of judges. Together we're to draft a form of the oath agreeable to our nation."

"Meanin' your neck is first on the block," Zadok commented wryly.

Old Simeon grinned. "No more than it is already! But remember this: At the same time the Levite Zachariah met the angel who promised him a son in his and his wife's old age—a vow that has been kept—a voice pledged that I wouldn't die without seeing Messiah.[33] Here! In the flesh! No matter what Herod—or the Romans—may do, I cling to that promise. You must also!"

"Aye," Zadok concurred grudgingly, but laying his hand over his heart. "The true King of the Jews! May he come soon and set all things right!"

Simeon found Hannah the Prophetess in her preferred location in the Temple's Court of Women. In the southwest corner of that plaza was a chamber set apart for the storage of oil and wine. Just outside this stood one of the four immensely tall, oil-fed menorahs that illuminated the Temple courts, also known as the Mountain of the House.

It was at the base of this lamp that Simeon encountered Hannah. Nearby stood a pair of soldiers and, feigning indifference, a pair of Herod's spies. A file of women waited to consult her. Sometimes the ancient prophetess gave counsel; sometimes she answered private questions, but often she preached as she was doing now.

"Hear the word of the Lord, O Israel: '*The Lord shall be king over all the earth: in that day there shall be one Lord and His name one.*'[34] *And the Lord says, 'Yet have I set My king upon My holy hill of Zion.*'"[35]

In that moment Simeon was worried that Hannah would go on to denounce Herod and get arrested. It was not safe to speak anything resembling a longing for the true King of Israel to come.

The women standing nearby looked perplexed. Some were impatient or frustrated. Their expressions suggested that nothing in Hannah's enigmatic words addressed their concerns about wayward husbands, recalcitrant offspring, or empty cupboards.

The throng drifted apart. None stayed to hear Hannah quote Scripture.

At her use of the word *king*, the ears of Herod's agents pricked up. But when she fell silent again, they appeared to lose interest . . . especially when they saw she had no following. No rebel band eager to respond to her. After a brief consultation between the spies and the soldiers, they also wandered away. The cleared space around Hannah gave Simeon the opportunity to consult her about the dilemma over the loyalty oath.

Hannah greeted Simeon with a smile and a nod, coupling his name with the words *yashar* and *tzadik:* "Greetings to you, Simeon the Upright and Just. I see concern in your eyes."

"Dangerous times, honored Hannah. I fear you're too bold. You may be in danger."

Hannah disagreed. "Ask rather how I could keep silent when the Lord urges me to speak! Didn't Jeremiah argue with God? Didn't he say, *'I do not know how to speak; I am only a child'*? And what was the Lord's reply? *'Do not be afraid of them, for I am with you and will rescue you.'*"[36]

After gnawing on his mustache, Simeon explained, "King Herod demands a new oath to express loyalty to Caesar and to him. How can we do those things without blaspheming? And yet, if we speak against the oath, hundreds or thousands will die. My concern is for the people. That we can find the right words to use."

Hannah retorted, "In the days of Babylon the Great, Nebuchadnezzar was a much greater king than Herod, yet after the Almighty disciplined him with madness and he recovered his wits, he said, *'I praised the Most High; I honored Him who lives forever. His dominion is an eternal dominion; His kingdom endures from generation to generation.'*[37] Nebuchadnezzar acknowledged a greater King than he. Herod has yet to do so."

Looking around and finding no one could overhear them, Simeon expressed his agreement, then added, "But if Herod won't accept the Lord's discipline, must it fall on the heads of the people?"

"Listen further to the king of Babylon: *'Now I, Nebuchadnezzar, praise and exalt and glorify the King of heaven, because everything He does is* yashar *and all His ways are* tzadik. *And those who walk in pride He is able to humble.'*[38] Tell me, Simeon the Upright and Just, which king you'll acknowledge."

"*'In all my ways I seek to acknowledge Him,'* the Almighty . . ."

"*'And He will direct your path,'*" Hannah offered, concluding Solomon's adage.[39] "Spoken by a king of the Jews who acknowledged one greater than himself. Listen again to the prophet Dani'el: *'In the days of these kings shall the God of heaven set up a kingdom that shall never be destroyed; and the kingdom shall not be left to other people, but it shall break in pieces and consume all these kingdoms, and it shall stand forever.'*"[40]

Simeon recognized Hannah's quotation but heard in the words something greater—an answer to his predicament. "It's all about *who* the king is," he muttered to himself. "An oath of loyalty to the King! That's the solution."

Hannah raised a hand in benediction. "Go in peace, Simeon the Just and Upright."

King Herod stopped his pacing to fling the parchment at Talmai's bowed head. After smacking against the steward's cheek, it fluttered to the floor.

"Preposterous!" Herod boomed. "How weak do they think me? *This* is what that rabble of pious fools suggests? This is what my father-in-law, High Priest Boethus, wants? Do the priests quake in their beds at night, fearing a return of the Maccabees? I'll show them who they should be afraid of!" When the king snapped his fingers, his bodyguard Hermes instantly appeared at the monarch's elbow. "Arrest them. Arrest all those who sat on this council."

"Majesty, if I may suggest . . ." Talmai offered. He knelt at the center of concentric black-onyx and white-marble rings on the chamber floor, like a sacrificial victim awaiting Herod's wrath. "Isn't the title the King of the Jews the same one used by your grandfather? By order of Caesar, no one but you is permitted to hold this designation. By coupling it with Caesar, are you not acknowledging your complete loyalty to him, and that of all your subjects?"

When Herod flicked his fingers toward the letter, Hermes leapt to retrieve it. On bended knee he offered it to the king.

Herod read aloud from the document:

"I will render unto Caesar what is Caesar's, and unto the King of the Jews what is His."[41]

"It doesn't even use my name!" Herod whined.

"No, Majesty," Talmai agreed. "But no one in all the world holds that title except you, and that right exists by the favor of Caesar. This wording avoids offending the more religious Jews while still linking loyalty to the emperor with loyalty to you . . . and whoever you designate to follow you. Anyone who refuses this oath is a traitor and can be put to death at once, yet no one can refuse it on religious grounds. And just as your census will please Caesar since it copies what he has already ordered for Roman citizens, so too this oath will please him with both its precision and its policy."

Herod's puckered, splotchy features looked as sour as a wizened, rotten apple. "All right, Talmai, make it so. But make everyone aware that it's because of my benevolence and mercy the oath is so mild."

"Naturally, Majesty. Of course, all your people already know it."

"No doubt, no doubt." Herod grunted. "Hermes, mark this: I want a trusted man at every registration table. Let any who refuse the oath be arrested. Let any who hesitate or mumble be noted, and their names reported to you."

Hermes' right fist smacked his breastplate just over his heart. "It shall be done, Majesty."

CHAPTER 10

Yosef assisted Heli in the older man's workshop. Sweat beaded on Yosef's forehead as he worked the bow drill. His nose wrinkled as the bit delved into the dense wood, releasing a feather of acrid smoke.

"Thanks for the help," Heli said. "Need to get the baby's chest finished before we leave for the census. You will carve it, eh? Something fit for a king."

Yosef shrugged. "Glad to. When you're back, it'll be me needing the extra hands. The census," he repeated with a grimace. "As if this autumn needed anything else to complicate it."

"That's true enough. Still, it'll be good to see the older girls again and the grandchildren. And we'll all be home before the weather turns foul." Then Heli added, "Have you seen the loyalty oath?"

"Aye," Yosef replied cautiously, pausing in his work to blow out a tiny orange flame caused by the friction. "Seems innocent enough."

"Swearing loyalty to Caesar and to Herod? Innocent?"

"You know what I mean. The rabbis teach that submitting to civil authority is no blasphemy so long as it doesn't violate God's laws. What we can't change we must endure, eh?"

"King of the Jews? Herod the Idumean?" Heli challenged.

Yosef made a shushing motion with his free hand. "Rabbi Mazzar explained it to me this way: It doesn't matter if Herod *thinks* we're swearing true faith to him. It harms no one if we speak the words, but in our hearts we hold that the true King of the Jews is no one but the Almighty himself."

"Then I'm not being disloyal to the baby?" Heli concluded in a hoarse whisper.

Yosef marveled at his father-in-law's words. The birth of baby Yochanan was a miracle that had changed the heart of Heli toward his daughter.

"We know who the true King of Israel is," Yosef stated firmly. "And our job is to protect him—and Mary—till his reign is announced to the world."

Yosef and Heli watched with amusement as Mary, surrounded by her mother and sisters, lay on the floor. The mound of her belly thumped and tapped beneath the delighted hands of Anna, Naomi, and Salome.

Mary held up one finger. "Wait. He really gets going when I lie on my back! There. There! Feel him! He's saying, 'Shalom, Naomi!'"

A great laugh exploded from Naomi. "Ahhh! And Shalom to you too, baby! I'm your aunt Naomi!"

"There! There it is!"

"Did you feel that?"

"Here—give me your hand!"

"Oh my!"

"An elbow? You think?"

"More likely his foot."

"Oh! Feel it? Mama! Feel him knocking?"

"Ha! He'll be a dancer, this one!"

Yosef could see bits of each sister within the others, and all possessed some resemblance to their mother. Expressions, facial features, tone of voice—alike though individual. Mostly he noted the overlapping of their souls.

He was grateful for Mary's sake that she had these three close at hand to stand as a wall of protection and support between her and the judgment of the village. It would be hard for Mary when they left Nazareth tomorrow to attend the High Holy Days in Jerusalem and register for the census.

Salome, her serious eyes wide in amazement at the infant's greetings beating within Mary, was contemplative and honored by the fact that an angel had appeared to Mary.

Nine-year-old Naomi, ever the clown, everyone's baby, simply accepted the miraculous events as inevitable. Of course the angel had come to Mary. Who in all of Israel but Mary was worthy of such an honor?

And then there was Anna. How would Mary have withstood the emotional assaults without her mother to stand by her?

Naomi leaned close and spoke directly to the baby. "You'll be huge by the time we get back."

"Huge," Salome agreed. "Nearly ready to be born."

"Oh, Mama!" Naomi shook her dark curls. "We'll be home in time, won't we? I wouldn't want to miss Mary's baby being born! In all my life there's never been anything . . . nothing at all so wonderful as this! We won't miss it, will we?"

"No." Anna wrapped her arms around Naomi and brushed her lips across her forehead.

"I could stay," Salome offered. "I could help with the cows. Milking and making cheese."

Naomi wailed a protest. "If she stays, I'm staying!"

Anna asserted, "You're going. Mary will stay and watch the livestock. When we come home, she and Yosef will travel to Beth-lehem to register."

Mary grunted as she sat up. "Naomi, I can't believe you want to stay home from Yerushalayim! You've only ever been once. I'll be fine. Yosef and I will manage."

Naomi stuck out her lower lip in a pout. "I just don't want to miss anything. I wake up every morning, and I can't wait to see how much fatter you are."

"It's true. Naomi says the same thing every morning. 'Let's go see how fat Mary is today,'" Salome agreed.

"Thank you." Mary grimaced.

"You'll be enormous by the time the Feast of Tabernacles is over and we come home." Naomi rubbed Mary's belly and glanced up at Yosef. "Don't let her do anything without me."

"I promise." Yosef laughed. "And you, Naomi, have safe travels and come back to your sister soon."

Yosef's heart was overflowing. *Blessed are you, O Adonai, who set your chosen mother like a jewel in the midst of such sisters! And in your wisdom you gave Mary a mother like Anna. See how their eyes shine with joy over the coming of a baby. No question of shame among them. The gossip of others is no more to them than rain falling on the back of a duck. Outside the light of their lives there is a darkness Mary could not bear without these steadfast ones.*

Too much to bear alone. Without the wisdom of Anna . . . the faith of Salome . . . the unfettered exuberance of little Naomi. The strength of these three together, added to Mary, are fortress walls high enough to hold back the condemnation of the whole village. Thank you, Adonai, for choosing this family to be born into when you chose Mary as your mother. Thank you that they are my family as well.

Rachel sponged the body of the unconscious girl in an attempt to bring her fever down. Zadok's grandmother, a widow of eighty who stayed sometimes with Zadok and Rachel and sometimes with Havila, had given up her bed in the small room attached to the back of Zadok's house.

The child of the stranger had been born missing his left arm. The mother was dying. Together with Grandmother, Rachel had fought for days to save the girl.

It was a losing battle.

"Her heart." Rachel took the girl's pulse as the old woman changed the baby boy. "So fast. Too fast. Unless I can bring her fever down . . ."

Grandmother cradled the ebony infant. "Has the mother spoken at all?"

"Not a word. Not her name. Never. I tried the barberry tea. Used the last of the frankincense oil. Nothing touches the fever." Rachel put the back of her hand to her own forehead.

"You haven't slept."

"I'm all right."

"You've milk enough for this one and your little Samu'el as well. That's a blessing."

"Grandmother?" Rachel winced. "I don't think . . . I mean . . . I've done all I can do. If only I knew her name. Sometimes when you say a person's name they hear and you can call them back from the darkness."

Grandmother remained beside the window. "Up there on the road is the tomb of the matriarch Rachel, wife of Jacob. Think of it! The mother of Joseph and Benjamin died right here bringing a baby into the world. No matter how important a woman is, eh? Childbirth is all the same for all."

Rachel shuddered and shook her head. Strangely, she had dreamed something similar: Rachel's tomb surrounded by hundreds of babies lying in open baskets. "I tried not to think of it. When the baby was born . . . when we cleaned him and laid him beside her . . . for just a moment I thought the dream meant something good. A happy omen for her. The baby, even crippled, would live and I hoped . . ."

"She's so young, eh? Should have her mother at her side. Poor thing. The Eternal knows her name. He may be calling her into the light, Rachel."

Rachel wrung water from a cloth and pressed it on the girl's brow. "Her baby. When he cried yesterday, I saw her stir. She senses he's alive somehow. But nothing since yesterday."

"Babies. So fragile, but stronger than their mothers sometimes. Their precious souls come from the Lord and travel such a hard road to life."

"He's healthy, even with only one arm. But look at her. Skin and bones. I've been trying to understand how she came to us here in Bethlehem. From where? Herod's palace, you think? Or Herodium? How could she walk so far in labor?"

"By the hand of the Lord. He directed her to you. She's brought you her child, Rachel." Grandmother brushed her lips on the infant's brow. "Sweet thing. He'll never know what she went through to give him life."

"If only . . . what more can I do?"

"Care for her son, perhaps. Nothing more. Nothing less."

Rachel held the girl's hand. Small and delicate, it was calloused from hard work as a slave, though Rachel guessed she was no more than eleven or twelve years old. *Blessed are you, O Adonai . . . who brought her here to our home.*

"Aye. Just a child herself. Never meant to give birth for many years. Who—what sort of animal—would make a child pregnant? This is what goes on in the household of Herod."

Rachel checked the pulse again. Like a frightened bird, it raced too fast not to burst. The breathing was rapid and shallow. Rachel knew the end was not more than an hour away. "Please, go find Havila. Ask her to send for Eliyahu at the synagogue."

"Yes. Eliyahu is a fine rabbi. The girl is past hope of medicine now, I fear. A rabbi is what she needs. Eliyahu will come."

Ecbatana, Kingdom of Parthia
Journal of Court Astronomer Melchior
15th of Elul, Year of Creation 3753

The golden boat of the setting sun towed the lesser vessels Mercury, Venus, and Mars— The Messenger, Splendor, and The Adam—after it. The last rays had barely disappeared behind the peaks of Mount Alvand when Old Balthasar thrust a bony forefinger toward the west and demanded, "Is it there? Spica? Can you see it?"

Squinting, I announced that yes, Spica—the star marking the wheat sheaf in the eternal seed in the constellation of Virgo, The Virgin—was in fact visible, though barely so, just above the horizon.

Balthasar sighed, apparently with relief.

"It's important?" I asked gently, already anticipating his reply.

"Since I can no longer trust my eyes, I must test my memory," the Jewish elder responded. "I know the date. I feel the air. I sense the seasons change. Then I reach into my recollections. On such and such a night, Spica is there, marking the last appearance of Virgo in the sky until spring." Whirling about, he waved eastward. "And there is the Full Moon, rising over the hills that separate Ecbatana from the plains of Media."

And, like a conjuring trick, it was so.

I expressed my admiration for his ability. He rejected the compliment, arguing that his was a lifetime of observation and not a special talent.

"Then I applaud your commitment," I corrected myself. With this he didn't argue and his granddaughter, Esther, expressed her agreement with a smile.

Old Balthasar elaborated further. "More and more I view the heavens as much within my mind as with my eyes. It makes it easy for me to imagine bygone observers standing in this same spot, watching, thinking, perhaps praying as I do for the fulfillment of the times."

Knowing he was reflecting on the promised coming of Messiah, I did not interrupt his reverie but waited for him to continue.

Soon enough Balthasar said, "I see Queen Esther—you know her name, in fact, means 'star'—I see her standing on this very rooftop. Did she wonder about the prophecy that a virgin would give birth to a son? Did she study Virgo and Spica and consider how the Almighty writes his message in three places: in his Word, in the sky, and in the longing hearts of men?"

Old Balthasar clearly had a lesson in mind for this night, and I was eager to receive it.

"You perhaps don't know that Queen Esther's son, who was later King Artaxerxes, is the very monarch who authorized the rebuilding of Yerushalayim."

I admitted I'd never thought about it.

Nodding without condemnation, Balthasar continued. "Think this through: Esther's faith and courage saved the Jewish people from the designs of their enemies. Then, because of her faith, the Almighty enabled her to aid them a second time, by having a half-Jewish child who would grow up to be a gracious Persian king. Nor is that the end of the story.

"Doesn't the prophet Dani'el begin the countdown of years leading to the appearance of Messiah from this very same event—the decree of Esther's son, King Artaxerxes, to rebuild Yerushalayim? All because Esther was a shining star of faith and obedience!"

It was stunning. Overwhelming. Events of five centuries earlier took on a present reality and even greater present significance. "And the count of those years . . . ," I prompted.

". . . is rapidly approaching completion," Old Balthasar concluded eagerly. "Just so. The history and the prophecy are as real as my granddaughter. As real as the fact that her name is also Star. As real as the fact that my name, Balthasar, is the Persian form of the prophet Dani'el's name in Babylon. Belteshazzar, he was called—and Balthasar am I!"

CHAPTER 11

Yosef secured the knot on the pack, stepped back, and observed the miracle of two donkeys dwarfed beneath their loads. "All right, Heli. It will hold. I don't envy you packing and repacking night and morning along the way."

Mary remarked to Anna, "Mama, you could buy supplies in Yerushalayim."

"At ten times the price? Not likely. It's no easy thing, this census; I can tell you!" Anna, uncharacteristically flushed by the effort of packing and loading, scowled at the two donkeys. "And during the High Holy Days! The worst time of year for travel! Pilgrim feast it may be, yet it's the time of year for any sane person to stay away from Yerushalayim. But they give us no choice."

The animals were nearly lost beneath their burdens—baskets of camping provisions, cheeses, a tent, rolled tapestry carpets, blankets, cooking utensils, water jugs, and clothing enough for Anna, Heli, Salome, and Naomi.

"Woman! We'll need another pack animal, or the rabbis will call us out for abuse!" Heli snapped. "You've carried away the entire house on the backs of these poor beasts!"

Anna clamped her fists onto her hips defiantly. "You're the one who said we should go for the Holy Days. Herod's census and the feasts, you said. Rosh Hashanah, you said. Yom Kippur. Sukkot. A month we'll be away! Camping out among half a million of our kinsmen in Yerushalayim. Tell me how we can manage with less? I'm too old for this."

Heli blustered, "Forty years in the wilderness, and our ancestors managed with two pots each and a bedroll."

"They gathered what the Almighty provided out of thin air and it was enough," Anna protested. "They came to the land of milk and honey and had everything. Now we've had forty years of Herod's taxes, and everything we own fits on the backs of two donkeys. Herod's Roman friends want to count our heads to be certain they're collecting every last copper. Bandits! We moved to the Galil to get away from them, and they hunt us down and command we be counted like cattle and sheep!"

"Mind your tongue, woman! You'll not be able to speak so freely when we're in Yerushalayim!" Heli shushed her and tested the rope that somehow held the provisions in place.

"Herod burns the records, then demands a census! And during the High Holy Days too." She put a hand to her head. "Did I pack the lamps?"

Heli spat. "When else can I take off from work? This is it. We go. We register. We celebrate the Holy Days. Two birds with one stone, eh?"

Mary soothed, "Mama, think of the grandchildren. Chloe and Shanna and the little ones. All of you together."

"All but you and Yosef. We could have been together very well right here. Nazareth. Without all this. Your elder sisters could have come home to Nazareth just as easily, and I wouldn't have to worry about lost grandchildren or sharing a well with half a million pilgrims." Anna touched Mary's cheek, then hugged her impulsively. "I'm worried about you. Leaving you here alone. I don't like it. Not one bit. We've never been apart during the holidays. I don't like leaving you alone."

"I'm not alone, Mama. Yosef and I will do very well. We'll take care of everything. The cows. And the house too, while you're gone. I'll teach Yosef how to milk and churn butter. You'll see. It'll be fine. Yosef will finish the work he has to do, and when you come back, Yosef can go register in Beth-lehem. By then everyone will have cleared out, and it'll be fine."

"Salome's heifer is due to calve any day," Anna fussed.

"We'll manage," Mary assured her.

Heli cupped his hands around his mouth. "Naomi! Salome! Get out here! We're leaving!"

Anna sighed and hugged Mary one last time. "I wouldn't go at all this year if it wasn't for the edict. You'll be able to manage? All this? Without us?"

"Go. I'm looking forward to the quiet," Mary answered.

Anna wiped a tear and pinched Yosef's cheek. "Work hard, Yosef. Take care of my girl, eh? Be well."

"I will, Mama," he promised. "*Shanah Tova.*"

"*Le-shanah Tova tikatevu!*" Mary added, hugging her sisters, who wept a little at their parting.

Heli, who already had the wild, exhausted look of one who had traveled far, hurriedly recited the baracha for travelers as they set out.

Mary stood beside the house for a long time, watching them go. She could still hear them singing as they vanished over the ridge.

"*Le-shanah Tova tikatevu ve-tehateimu,*" she whispered. "May you be inscribed and sealed for a good life."

"*It is far too soon.*" The neighbor leaned close to her elderly mother as Mary and Yosef passed on their way to market.

The old woman looked away. The young woman smirked and stared furtively after them.

Yosef felt her searing curiosity pierce his back. He blushed and rubbed his forehead nervously. The woman's voice seemed human at first; then it crackled like fire and changed into something else. What was it? Not human at all.

"*Count the months yourself, Mama. They was only wed at the end of summer harvest. You know what she's been up to. Poor Yosef!*"

Mary held her head erect. Her belly had blossomed beneath her dress. Anyone with eyes could see she was expecting. Anyone with a brain could do the math. Everyone with a tongue would have some opinion about it.

Heads turned to look and hands raised to greet them as they entered the bustle of the market square. Smiles flashed before faces hardened into masks of stone. Eyes of old friends became dark and cold above the grins.

Yosef stiffened and halted.

Mary turned to him, puzzled. "What is it, Yosef?"

He cleared his throat and patted his money pouch. "Nothing. Just thought I may have forgotten . . . money. That's all."

Sellers hawked their produce. It was ordinary, noisy. A market day like any other in Nazareth.

Suddenly, above them, to their right and left, and behind their backs, Yosef heard a hissing sound. Cruel words permeated the atmosphere like the stink of rotten eggs.

"See for yourself! It's true! You know what she's done! He could have had her stoned for it! Poor Yosef!"

Yosef and Mary stood before the apple seller's stall as Mary carefully selected six apples for Shabbat supper. Did she not hear the voices hissing like hot steam in a kettle?

"Count the months for yourself!"

"She was sick at the banquet."

"And pale as death after she finally came out of the house. And big as a water jug too."

Yosef turned loose of Mary's elbow and turned fiercely to glare at the source of the unkind remarks. But he could not single out any one person or group from the crush of shoppers. Men and women passed by in singles and twos, browsing and bargaining.

Knowing glances darted to Mary's bulging stomach and then back to the heaps of fruit.

Yosef seemed to hear their thoughts, though their lips did not move. So many voices!

But whose voices? Whose whispers?

"Can't abide the smell of her own cheeses. Her mother and sisters have taken over the dairy work."

"Nor fish. Can't abide the smell. Look at her . . . holding the hem of her veil over her nose. . . ."

Dozens of audible accusations with no human point of origin hammered Yosef's ears. Did Mary not hear them? Who was speaking? Who in Mary's hometown would dare slander her?

"Well, if she's not played the harlot, then no one ever has!"

"Thin in the face . . ."

"But look at that! Six months' bloom, or I don't know anything!"

"It'll have Yosef's name."

"Illegitimate though it may be!"

"Brazen."

"Bold as brass!"

"She doesn't give a copper about poor Yosef!"

"Was Yosef back from Yerushalayim?"

"You know she and her mother left for Beth Karem and the home of Elisheba the minute Yosef got home. And Mary didn't come back until he went to fetch her."

"There's something about this marriage."

"Poor Yosef."

"Lucky his mother isn't alive to see it."

Yosef's brow creased in consternation. Who was speaking? He searched passing faces without finding the culprits. Yet the verbal assault against Mary's honor continued.

Mary smiled up into his face. "Look, Yosef. These are good ones. Don't you think?"

"What? Eh?"

"Good apples. Nice big ones for roasting. For Shabbat."

"Fine." He scowled. "Though there's bad apples hiding here to be sure!"

The apple seller's lower lip jutted out. "Nay! Only the best! See for yourself!"

Yosef ducked his head. "Not these. Sorry . . . sorry. Not your apples."

"Are you all right?" Mary took his hands. "Cold as ice. What's wrong?"

"Nothing. Fine. Those'll do. Apples. Yes. Pay the man. Let's get home."

"But, Yosef. The shopping? The challah?"

"Right. Yes. Then pay the fellow and we'll move on."

The carpenter crossed his arms. He felt the weight of his concealed sword. He could defend Mary against a half-dozen stout fellows with weapons. But how could he protect her heart against the sword of gossip from friends and neighbors?

"Yosef?"

"Let's . . . go. Mary? Did you hear . . . ?"

"Hear what? Are you unwell?"

"Let's get the challah and . . . come on. The baker. Then home."

CHAPTER 12

Early sunlight glistened on rain-washed landscape. The earth sloped away, disappearing at the edge of the western sea. Already, barren rocky hillsides were dusted with the emerald tinge of new growth. For the next year lush pastures would fatten the Temple flocks under Zadok's care. For the first time in years, the land of Eretz-Israel, which the ancient Jewish patriarchs called "the navel of the whole world," would be green again. The sky was radiant sapphire fringed with retreating thunderheads.

It had been a long night. Rachel inhaled the fresh scent of the morning as she gathered a bunch of lavender from the rafters of the house.

Grandmother helped Rachel wash and prepare the body of the girl for burial. Wrapped in a winding sheet, she was placed upon a wicker bier and carried outside.

The sun had been up less than an hour. Havila held the newborn as Zadok spoke. "So, Havila. Eliyahu. Now you know everything we know. Now she, a stranger and an alien among us, has no one to mourn for her but her baby. Rachel and I will sit shiva for her."

"But . . . her name?" Eliyahu hooked a finger in his beard and peered down at the face set like a black-onyx jewel in the white shroud. "How can I say *kaddish* for someone who has no name?"

Rachel placed flowers across the girl's chest and took the infant from Havila.

Grandmother eyed the young rabbi sternly and croaked, "Her name is Eve."

Havila crossed her arms. "Yes, good. She mustn't be buried without a name."

Eliyahu seemed not to hear. "Are you certain you won't bury her in the potter's field, Zadok? She wasn't one of us. Not a Jew."

Grandmother flared. "She is one of *us*. A woman! Every woman's sister, daughter, beloved friend. Her name is Eve. We mothers of Bethlehem share her heart and understand her sorrow."

Havila also glared at her husband.

Rachel stood shoulder to shoulder with Grandmother and Havila. "You men would know that if you ever carried a little soul beneath your heart or felt it kick inside you or knew the pain of bringing forth life. But you're only men."

The pregnant Havila declared to Eliyahu, "How can you know what it means to be a girl of probably not more than twelve years and be laid in your grave because of what evil men have done to you?"

Rachel kissed the head of the newborn. "Havila and I will be counted as the poor girl's sisters."

Grandmother's lower lip trembled. "I will be the baby's grandmother."

Rachel agreed. "I will be his mother. We'll be his family. I'll raise the boy as my son. The girl was brought here by the hand of the Almighty for us to show her *chesed*. Mercy. She asked for me by name but came too late. Too late. And even if she had come sooner, there was nothing I could do to save her. She was such a tiny slip of a thing. Too young. Too small to give birth."

Zadok shrugged and replied gruffly to Eliyahu's question. "There. Y' see? Argue with three of them if y' like, but as for myself . . ."

Eliyahu raised his hand in surrender. "Look, I was saying . . . never before has something like this happened here."

Rachel replied, "It happens every day . . . everywhere."

Zadok clapped him on the back. "Enough said. The girl will be buried in our tomb, not the potter's field, eh? Rachel wants it. I agree. She will be Eve. Our sister. The boy will be ours. A shepherd. When he asks where his mother is buried, I'll not have to point to a field and tell him she's in an unmarked grave."

"So be it." Eliyahu raised his eyes heavenward. "The Eternal knows."

A mere handful of mourners made up the funeral procession. Six shepherd boys were paid a mite each to act as pallbearers. Rachel cradled the infant and led the way along the muddy path to the burial cave of the family of Zadok. Zadok followed after with his son Samu'el in his arms. Enoch gripped Grandmother's hand. They passed the ancient tomb of the Jewish matriarch Rachel. Havila walked solemnly beside Eliyahu, carrying their son, Dan.

The stone of the sepulchre was removed, and the body placed on a slab inside as Eliyahu intoned, *"Blessed are You, O Adonai! You give life and You take it away."*[42]

The farewell was a brief one. What eulogy could be spoken over one who had no name, no history, no life?

Grandmother spoke for all. "Only the Eternal knows her true name now. Her end shall be the same for each of us, no matter how long we live. The ages come and go, and we are but dust. Our names forgotten on earth. Our stories forgotten. The children we bear will follow us to the dust of the earth and will be forgotten by the living. Yet the record of our lives is written in the Eternal Book of Life by the very finger of Adonai. Eve, woman without a name, may the Eternal bless your memory through the life of this precious child. He is your legacy. May your child live long and know the One Eternal God and see his face on the earth. May your child grow up to become the best of what you had hoped to be. Omaine."

And so the day began.

Rachel embraced Havila and Grandmother.

Havila kissed the newborn. "He is beautiful, Rachel. Perfect little ears, eh? Black as an Ethiopian, whose king, they say, is a true descendant of Solomon and the Queen of Sheba. Perhaps this baby's mother was a Jew as well."

"It doesn't matter if she wasn't. We'll raise him to know the truth."

"Rachel, my dear," Grandmother advised, "you must pray before the *Bris*, eh? We'll all pray, for his name will be a sign for all who hear it spoken. Ask the Lord what his name should be. So much prophecy and blessing is in a child's name."

"I only know his survival is a miracle." Rachel traced his perfect lips with her finger. "If Zadok hadn't brought the girl in . . . five minutes more and we would've lost them both. I'm glad you understand, Havila."

Eliyahu stroked his beard and muttered, "And if the child had died, who can say? It might've been a mercy. What future . . . ?"

Every expression rebuked him.

"What?" he protested.

Havila glared at Eliyahu, raised her chin regally, and departed with Grandmother and the children.

Eliyahu waited until Havila was out of earshot. Then he quietly inquired, "Zadok . . . Rachel? What I meant. What I was saying . . . what'll you do with this baby?"

"He'll stay with us." Rachel held the newborn close. "Samu'el's nearly weaned. I have milk enough."

Eliyahu lowered his voice. "Zadok, we must speak privately."

Zadok laughed and dug at the earth with the toe of his sandal. "Give it up, Eliyahu. You're about t' be flogged. Wouldn't want t' face what you'll face when you go home. Privately y' say? Rachel will get it out of me no matter what you say. Won't y', Rachel?"

Rachel's eyes narrowed at the challenge. "I will. We have no secrets, Zadok and me, and you might as well know that."

Eliyahu harrumphed his disapproval. "You leave me no choice. Grim news from Yerushalayim. Zadok? Onias wasn't the only one arrested and punished. You know the stories. Madness! Herod sees enemies everywhere he looks. You don't want to draw attention to yourself. You'll have to think what you must do with this boy child. Clearly the offspring of a slave. Who knows who its father might be. Perhaps the girl was sent here with a purpose. And I don't mean she was sent by an angel, but by one of those devils who hovers round Herod's throne, eh? You take my meaning? Onias and his little daughter may be safe in Alexandria, but we don't want to draw the attention of Herod."

Zadok's eyes widened as the sinister possibilities occurred to him. "Aye. I take your meanin'."

This answer seemed to satisfy Eliyahu at last. "Yes. Then you see why you'll have to think on the matter of the child long and hard."

The first evening stars appeared in the clear skies above Beth-lehem.

Grandmother had tottered off to her room behind the house shortly after supper. Zadok braided rawhide rope and two-and-a-half-year-old Enoch stacked blocks. One-year-old Samu'el, gorged on his mother's milk and near to sleep, lay on his back on the fleece and with serious dark eyes observed his mother nursing the new baby by lamplight.

The newborn was healthy, eager for Rachel's milk. He clutched Rachel's finger as her own sons looked on. "Your baby brother," Rachel instructed Enoch and Samu'el.

Zadok cleared his throat as he laid aside his work and reached for his cup and a pitcher of ale. "The child's mother managed t' speak your name, Rachel. Your name only. 'Rachel,' said she as I knelt beside her at the well. Lyin' in the lee at the base of the well, she was. I suppose hopin' for some shelter. I know it means somethin'. Bear Dog found her with his nose or I wouldn't have seen her on such a black night. I wrapped her in my cloak and carried her home. Light as a feather she was. A feather. Starved. Arms and legs like sticks. I couldn't see her belly. Didn't know why she'd ask for you. It's clear enough now. Poor creature."

The baby continued to hold Rachel's index finger tightly in his fist. "The brand on her shoulder. Zadok? The brand."

Zadok nodded. "Aye. Herod's brand. Slave from the household of the Butcher King, sure enough."

"So now we know this is the use they put to female children in Herod's palace . . . that open pit of Hinnom."

"And worse if the rumors are true."

Rachel inclined her head toward the two boys at her feet. "Don't speak of it, Zadok."

"Aye. No need t' speak. The body of this infant's mother bears witness to the qualities of Herod's reign. Not that we needed more evidence. They're monsters who would use a young girl in such a way. This baby is the son of a monster."

"He didn't choose his father. And the Father of his soul is eternal and merciful."

"Herod's brand. You know what Eliyahu thinks. Of course, Eliyahu has an opinion on everything."

"Havila will keep him in line."

"Aye. A woman such as my sister keeps us males humble."

Rachel shifted the baby to her left breast. "Has Eliyahu convinced you there's a danger in this for us?"

"Thinks the babe is still someone's property. Legal, y' know."

"We should see to this baby's *Bris.* No matter his color. If he is circumcised, he's a true son of the covenant."

"Point taken. But the mother was most likely a runaway. We'll have t' find out the details."

"Who could blame her? No sane man, no righteous man. None who follow Torah could or would blame her for running away."

Zadok countered, "But we're discussin' the household of Herod, where sanity ran amok and anyone sane has been done away with over the last thirty years. And she spoke only your name, Rachel. Sent here, perhaps? One look at her, and it was plain she couldn't survive the birth. A runaway slave.

"We shepherds of Migdal Eder are the only ones who can trace our line back t' those who tended the sacred flocks in David's time. The last true high priest was murdered over one hundred years ago. Now we know that. They know that. They don't like it that we, the hereditary shepherds, know the truth of it.

"And that pitiful scrap of a girl who died in your arms could well be a snare for us shepherds of the Temple flock who oppose the Temple rulers who are bought and sold by Herod as surely as you're born." He jabbed the air with his finger. "And Boethus! That Egyptian dog Boethus as high priest. Herod's father-in-law. How can we not oppose his heresies?"

"But the baby, Zadok! We must keep him. He was sent to us from heaven. We must."

Zadok did not turn his gaze from the nursing child. "Civil law requires he be returned t' Herod. The offspring of the mother belongs to the master, though the mother dies."

Rachel's chin stiffened in determination. "I can't. I won't! For such a one as this, they would've left the cord uncut, unwashed. None would rub his body with salt. He would've lain polluted in his own blood until he died too. Then they would have thrown him into the garbage heap with his mother's body. That's what the ungodly in this land do with unwanted babies. It's a new form of human sacrifice. . . . You know it, and so do I!"

Zadok poured more barley ale, swirled the dark russet liquid as he considered his next words carefully. "There is a fine line between open rebellion—treason—and practicin' Torah. King Herod is not a Jew, and we've seen him kill members of his own family for less cause than he would have t' kill a buzzin' insect. If he took it in his mind that Zadok the shepherd of the Temple flock had stolen his slave girl and withheld his rightful property . . . Rachel girl, do y' see?"

"A baby isn't property."

"Well, legally. Now, don't get up in arms! I'm just sayin'"—he winced at her narrowed eyes and defensive posture—"what I'm tryin' to say is this: Eliyahu was tryin' to make a reasonable point. We'll have t' think through carefully how we handle this. There's the matter of my brother Onias. And it's possible someone among the royals or Herod's half-breed priest appointees at the Temple took offense that I was with Zachariah on the day of his vision last year. Some are still sayin' he made it up."

"Made it up?" Rachel's expression was incredulous. "And he struck dumb by the glory! Unable to speak a word. And then Elisheba having a baby! At her age!"

"Fannin' the messianic flame, they say, for political purposes. Zachariah went home. I'm in Yerushalayim twice a week, deliverin' lambs to the Temple. And when I'm asked about it, I can only say, 'Well, somethin' happened in there.' I can't deny it. And they could use this slave child t' have me thrown in prison. Discredit me as a witness. Say I am a thief. Or worse. We families of the shepherd clans don't follow Roman or Herodian law. Torah and tradition, that's for us. Till now, the authorities have left us to our old ways. It would be foolhardy to draw attention to ourselves with the students of Yerushalayim on the brink of open revolt and Herod a regular mad dog."

Bear Dog raised his head nervously to peer at Zadok.

"No offense, Bear Dog." Zadok scratched the beast's head. "We're speakin' of dogs who walk upright on two legs."

"If there was any justice in Israel, the master of that poor murdered girl would be taken out and given a taste of the lash for what's been done to her. I myself would braid the whip and wield the scourge."

Rachel's anger was not transmitted to the baby. He slept peacefully as the two discussed the death of his mother.

Zadok smoothed his mustache. "Eliyahu is right. We'll have t' think carefully on what we do."

"Do? Think? Do! Raise him as our own!"

"Be reasonable, Rachel girl! Look there! His skin is black as night, Rachel. Ebony black. Like his mother's. We can't claim he's an orphaned relative. Can't tell the neighbors that Rachel, the shepherd's wife, has thrown a black lamb in his flock of sons. And . . . why did the girl ask for you? only you?"

She frowned. "Because I'm the midwife of Beth-lehem. Why else? And I'm known by many round about as a skilled midwife. Who else would she ask for? Someone saw her condition and told her my name."

"But who? Who would send a runaway slave here?"

"Does it matter?"

"Aye, it well might. For the reasons I've given. Have y' forgotten? What's Herod's is Herod's. And what belongs t' anyone else is also Herod's, if he takes a likin' to it. Almighty Caesar Augustus has made it law."

"And the Almighty God of Israel has chosen to put this one fragile life in our care. He'll grow up to be a fine, strong man like you, Zadok. Even though he has only one arm. You, his father. I, his mother. A brother for Enoch and Samu'el. We'll redeem his life. Buy his freedom if we must! Zadok! Honestly. We tell the officials what happened. How she came to us. A few coins in the palm of Herod's steward to buy a newborn infant of no use to anyone. They'll take the money. Surely!"

Zadok twirled his beard round his finger. "Aye. There's the answer. Such a little bit of a slave as this lad can't be worth much on the auction block. Crippled as he is . . . no worth to them. I'll make inquiries. Ask Old Simeon at the Temple if Habib, that two-legged dog who oversees Herod's slaves, is part human. Who would be most reasonable to approach to redeem the baby? If there's no sinister intent toward us . . . if the girl was not sent to us as a snare, then they'll sell the baby to us. Aye. He's worth naught to them."

13 CHAPTER

The baby of the slave girl thrived on Rachel's milk and was presented to Rabbi Eliyahu for circumcision as commanded by Torah. Rachel and Grandmother had discussed and prayed about several choices of names. The importance and significance of the meaning were emphasized by Grandmother at every meal.

"See here!" Grandmother insisted. "Listen to an old woman, will you? A baby's name is a blessing or a curse all the days of his life. Against the height of his name he will measure himself and be measured!"

At the *Bris* Zadok, answering as his father, named the baby Gaddi, which meant "good fortune."

"No!" little Enoch protested. "He is my brother Obi!"

There was a pause punctuated with nervous laughter; then the ceremony proceeded.

Enoch, seeing the blood and hearing the unhappy wail of his new brother, cried out again, "No! No! Listen to Obi."

Thus, before the flint knife was washed or the cry of this newest son of the covenant fell silent, the name Gaddi was transformed into Obi, which sounded something like the Hebrew word for "storm cloud."

Owing to the dark color of the baby's skin and the healthy vigor of his squall, this seemed entirely appropriate. There was also the fact that the baby had arrived in the midst of the worst summer storm anyone remembered.

And so the small voice of Enoch was accepted as much as if an angel had appeared and pronounced that the Lord Himself declared Obi was the correct name. Obi must be the baby's heavenly name, the name of his soul.

With the formality of the *Bris*, Obi was surnamed bar Zadok, son of Zadok. The earthly name of Gaddi and the heavenly name of Obi were both on the document. Obi was officially a Jew. This fact alone would make it more difficult for the slave steward of King Herod to claim the child as property.

The first whispers of shock and disapproval that had circulated among members of the community fell silent. The infant was passed from hand to hand around the room, and all pledged to support and teach and protect this newest son of Abraham.

The afternoon of the *Bris*, young mothers of Beth-lehem who met often in Rachel and Zadok's garden took turns nursing Obi. Blinking up at each new face in what seemed like silent wonder, the son of the slave girl won the hearts of all. Over time, Rachel thought, he would grow fat and content on the milk of a dozen different mothers.

Yosef set out early this morning in search of the best straight-grained acacia wood with which to make the baby's cradle. Shouldering his axe and a satchel packed by Mary containing his lunch of bread and smoked fish, he led the donkey up the lofty hill behind Nazareth to where a grove of white oak trees grew.

He was grateful for hours alone to think and pray. There was no location in all of Galilee that Yosef favored more. It was to this lonely outpost that Yosef retreated when faced with momentous events. He had climbed the hill to pray the day before he asked for Mary's hand in marriage. He had come here to pray after his father died.

Today the donkey cropped grass contentedly. Tossing his axe and satchel to the ground, Yosef scrambled up the high, sunny perch of a boulder. From there he observed nearly half of Israel. Nazareth existed on a triangular plateau about twelve hundred feet above sea level. The village was twenty miles from the Great Sea to the west and fifteen miles from the Sea of Galilee to the east. The western road winding up a gorge from the Valley of Jezreel ended at the spring supplying water to Nazareth. There was his home—its white walls glistening in the sun. It was so small and ordinary.

Blessed are you, El Olam, the Ancient of Days, who would send Messiah, your Son and heir of all creation to live among us.

From this vantage point the village of Nain was visible some nine miles distant. Farther south were the mountains of Samaria, where the patriarch Jacob had built an altar to the Lord at Bethel. Not far from there rested the bones of Joseph the Great. Carried on the shoulders of the Hebrew slaves as they left Egypt, his body had been buried in the town of Shechem.

Blessed are you, O Adonai! May our eyes behold and our hearts rejoice, and our souls exult in your salvation and truth when it is said in Zion, "your God reigns!"

The rich green plain of Jezreel fanned westward with the blue thread of the Kishon River running through it. Close by, Mount Carmel ended abruptly at the sea. In the north the enormous snow-clad peaks of Mount Hermon shimmered against the azure sky overshadowing the Galil. Beyond Hermon was Lebanon, whose cedars had paneled the palaces of Israel's kings. Lebanon, where Herod, the non-Jewish Idumean who fancied himself king of the Jews, had placed his sons on trial for their lives.

That unbidden thought reminded Yosef that all was not well in the land of God's covenant. The land called Israel, which had once been promised by God to Abraham and later to King David, was now governed by a tyrant whose evil rivaled all the wicked kings ever recorded in Scripture.

Israel stretches out beneath me. What a world you have decided to enter, O Lord. El Shaddai. All-sufficient. Almighty. A baby? The plan that you would be my son as well seems flawed to my human mind. Yeshua will be called son of Yosef. Yeshua bar Yosef. . . . Who am I? Come then, Immanu'el! But what a terrible time you have chosen to be born as one so vulnerable. And how will I protect you?

Yosef worked through the afternoon, selecting branches from an enormous oak and cutting them and stacking them in a heap.

The wind from the Great Sea carried the hint of autumn with it. The seasons were changing. Yosef lay back on the warm table of stone. The breeze passed over him, cooling him, soothing him. It seemed a thousand half-formed questions swirled in his mind. Fragments of prayers so confused he no longer knew what he was asking.

Yeshua bar Yosef, son of Yosef . . . bar Jacob . . . son of . . . what does it mean? Why? Soon Yosef was asleep. . . .

The rushing wind stirred the wild oats. Oak leaves rattled as the sun sank low in the west and twilight fell. And then, on the breeze, Yosef heard the voice:

Yosef bar Jacob . . . Yosef, son of Jacob.

Constellations spun in the night sky above him.

Someone wrapped in a coat of woven blue, red, and gold in myriad hues sat beside him on the stone.

Yosef was not alarmed. "Here I am. And you . . . The Dreamer of dreams. Joseph, favored son of that Jacob whom God named Isra'el."

Yosef bar Jacob. The sun has set. Look! Look up at the sky! The Star of Jacob is rising in the east.

"I've stayed too long on this mountain and not gotten the answer to even one question. I'll be late for supper. Mary will be worried. I should wake up . . . out of this dream."

Yosef! Adonai has heard your question.

"Which question? I've asked so many."

How is it that the Messiah is called Bar El Olam—Son of the Eternal God—yet will live on earth and be called Yeshua bar Yosef?

"Ah. Yes. That question. All things seem to hinge on the answer." Yosef sat up and clasped his hands around his knees.

The face of his visitor was mildly amused as his eyes locked on Yosef's. *Shall I wake you?*

"No, please. If I should come home with fine wood and an answer to that question, I'll think it's worth missing supper. Where shall we begin?"

In the Beginning . . .

"In the Beginning. It is a very long time ago."

Before time existed, He existed. Listen to the Word of Adonai . . . "In the beginning was the Word, and the Word was with God, and the Word was

God. He was with God in the beginning. Through Him all things were created; without Him nothing was created which had been created. In Him is the life, and that life is the light of men. The light will shine in the darkness, but the darkness will not understand it."[43]

"You speak of Messiah. Of the baby Mary carries. Yeshua, who will be my son. Yeshua bar Yosef . . . Son of the mighty Elohim? Yeshua bar Yahweh? I still don't know how it can be or why."

He is within the first word of Scripture. Think, Yosef, of the first word in Torah. Six Hebrew letters: bet . . . resh . . . alef . . . sheen . . . yod . . . tav . . . *pronounced BeRESHiYT. What does it mean?*

"In the Beginning."

The very first word of Torah.

"I learned it when I studied for my bar mitzvah."

Yosef! Yet you have not learned that within that first word is contained the story of all creation and the Creator. The visitor produced a scroll from beneath his cloak. He handed it to Yosef and commanded, Open it.

Yosef obeyed. Before him was the parchment, and on it was written the first line of Torah, which told of creation. The Hebrew letters glowed with a blue fire that illuminated the darkness. The letters vanished until only one word remained.

Yosef? What is this you hold? the visitor asked.

"Only the first word. Six letters: *bet . . . resh . . . alef . . . sheen . . . yod . . . tav*. Six Hebrew letters that mean "in the Beginning" in Hebrew. The Greeks call this scroll Genesis."[44]

Correct. But this is not a Greek document. It is Hebrew. Dictated to Mosheh by the Angel of the Lord as they met face-to-face. Look carefully at the letters. These six letters contain the clue to all creation. Read it in Hebrew. Only two letters at a time. Begin, "In the very Beginning."

Yosef did not touch the Hebrew letters of the scroll as he began to recite. *"Bet Resh."*

Stop there. Now tell me what small Hebrew word is spelled by Bet Resh.

"Ah!" Yosef gasped as the first two letters of Scripture flamed up from the scroll and burned into his mind. He blinked at the illuminated word glowing on the ancient document.

His visitor grinned broadly. *Yes, Yosef! Your mind does not deceive you. Say it. The first two Hebrew letters of "in the Beginning" are* Bet *and* Resh . . . *the exact same spelling as the Hebrew word for . . .*

"*Bar*! Son! *Bar*! It means 'son'! *Bet Resh* spells BAR! And this not only means 'son' in Hebrew. It indicates the 'heir apparent, a ruler coequal with his father.'"

Correct. Now please speak aloud the next two small Hebrew letters of the Hebrew word for "in the Beginning."

"*Alef. Sheen* . . . of course! How could we have missed it? It's the word *Osh*—"

Stop! Let your heart shout its meaning to all of Israel and the world, Yosef!

"This spells the Hebrew word for 'foundation'!"

Correct. There are small words with enormous meaning that are plainly visible within the larger Hebrew word. Now you begin to comprehend the depth of Holy Scripture and the vast storehouse of God's love for us from the foundations of the world. Say the next two Hebrew letters and you will grasp the sleeve of truth as it passes before you.

Yosef could hardly breathe as the reality of what he was seeing filled his mind with light. Was he dreaming? There were the words before him! "The next two letters *Yod! Tav!* The word is *Yath!* This means 'who'!"

Read on.

Before Yosef's eyes the next three letters of Genesis flared from the sheepskin in blue-white flame. "*Bet . . . Resh . . . Alef*—the word is *Bara*. This means 'created'!"

The coat of many colors glowed with tints so luminous there were no names for those hues on earth.

Now, breaking the Hebrew sentence into these smaller words, what eternal truth do the first nine letters in Genesis explain?

Yosef began to read the illuminated letters as they flashed before him in rapid sequence. "*Bar* . . . son . . . heir of the Father. *Osh* . . . from foundation. *Yath* . . . who. *Bara* . . . created."

Go on! One with Elohim, He created . . . the heavens and the earth. Yosef's visitor stood and bowed deeply as he finished his proclamation. *The Word of the Lord. This amplifies the truth of eternity. It does not contradict it. So, you see, within the Hebrew word* In the Beginning *is also the identity of the Creator. He is The Son. He is The Heir. He has existed From the Foundation. He is The Word. The Creator. The Son and Heir is one in being with Elohim. And there is much, much more. So very much more eternal truth woven into these nine letters . . . if only we had time.*

"I can't remember all of this as it is! I'll awaken and it will be gone! My mind is too small to comprehend the Living Word of the Living God! Please! Write it down for me!"

Joseph of the Coat of Many Colors, Revealer of Truth to the Humble, smiled and patted Yosef the Carpenter on his shoulder. *It is written. And think of it! This tiny glimpse of the Holy Scripture's depth and majesty is found after only one quick look at the first nine letters.*

Comprehension of the enormity of his task pressed Yosef onto the hard cold stone of earth. "Yeshua is the Son and Heir . . . the Word . . . the Creator. And I am to be his father? I? I will carry Bar Elohim—the Son and Heir of Eternal God—on my shoulders? Rock him to sleep? He who has never slept? Teach him his *alef–bet*, though his is the story of the Scriptures and the word that spoke worlds into existence? Teach him to pray who is Lord of the Sabbath, existing in equal power and glory with Elohim from the foundation? Yeshua bar Yosef, the son of a carpenter? It's too big for my mind to comprehend! This dream brings so many unanswered questions. . . ."

The coat of many colors began to fade. *This is only . . . the beginning of wonders. . . .*

"Wait! Don't go! Don't leave me feeling so . . . so . . . small!"

It is written. Soon! Soon! He is coming soon! You will behold him face-to-face. Immanu'el . . . God-with-us.

CHAPTER 14

Zadok, his red-haired assistant Lem, and a teenage boy were responsible for a flock of three hundred sheep and lambs destined for the Temple, but Bear Dog did most of the work. Whenever the shepherd spotted a wayward ram or an obstinate ewe, a sharp whistle dispatched the canine like a streaking four-legged arrow. Snapping teeth and a few urgent barks, and the prodigal was soon trotting back to the others.

Lem and Zadok occupied their journey discussing the inscrutability of their wives and the sometimes blockheadedness of their children. Lem spoke as the senior statesman, by virtue of his five boys to Zadok's three.

The drive had begun at Beth-lehem's Migdal Eder, the Tower of the Flock, before sunup. Now, some six hours later, it was nearing its conclusion. They emerged from the Kidron Valley at the stock pens on the northeast corner of the Holy City.

Given the numbers of pilgrims who would crowd Jerusalem during the High Holy Days, this quantity of sacrificial animals would not even supply one day's need. Several other flocks were on the road at the same time, as well as herds of goats and one of bullocks. Pigeons kept in great pens on the Mount of Olives just east of Jerusalem made their shorter journey into the city in wicker cages.

Zadok loved the grandeur of the Temple—perched on its platform and visible for miles around. He enjoyed listening to the singing of the psalms. He was proud of the fact that many people besides Jews came to see the place where the One True God, God Almighty, was worshipped. It was one of the wonders of the world.

But as much as Zadok, a pious Jew and a hereditary Levite shepherd, approved of the worship of Yahweh, delivering the lambs always made him irritable. Perhaps it was just an emotional response to the overfed, greasy, obsequious Temple official who accepted the transfer and offered a notched stick as a receipt.

Mostly, Zadok reasoned, his distress was caused by the fee collected from worshippers in exchange for their lambs. Arriving pilgrims were allowed to bring their own animals, but then each creature had to be inspected and approved as suitable for sacrifice. The inspecting Levites charged a payment for this service. Sometimes it was exorbitant; sometimes it amounted to a bribe.

Purchasing from the preapproved flocks guaranteed acceptance . . . at a price. The excess funds were devoted to Temple services, but a portion of each transaction lined the pockets of High Priest Boethus and his friends.

The result was that, after each commission was fulfilled, Zadok was relieved to turn back toward home. The shepherd boys aiding a senior herdsman were often disappointed to draw Zadok as a companion. He seldom wanted to enter the Holy City and sample the delights of the marketplace. This occasion was no different. "Too much work still to do."

Lem agreed. "If we hurry, we can be back at Migdal Eder before the middle of the afternoon watch."

Just as they passed the Sheep Gate, a peremptory voice called, "You, shepherd!"

"Aye? What?" Zadok boomed, caught off guard in his haste. He swiveled to see the speaker. It was one of the gate sentries.

"Your name Zadok?"

Zadok sized up the guard. Samaritan. Armed with spear, shield, and helmet. A no-nonsense look on his face.

"What of it?"

"What's become of your brother, the traitor?"

The horrifying nightmare of seeing Onias nailed to the wall of his house leapt to Zadok's mind. The tortured claws remaining of his brother's hands and feet. Rage and hot bile threatened to choke Zadok.

Lem, seeing the tension building, laid a quieting hand on Zadok's shoulder.

With great effort Zadok bit back an angry reply but could not help hefting the staff of his shepherd's crook as if in preparation for striking a blow. "You ought to know. Some of your . . . breed . . . crucified him."

"There's talk he didn't die . . . maybe escaped."

Zadok remembered again his wife and children before answering. "I thought King Herod demanded his men always be thorough about their work."

The soldier eyed Zadok suspiciously, then retorted, "You'd best remember that yourself."

Grimly, Zadok replied, "I will."

On his way from his office in the Temple complex to his palatial home in the southwest part of the Holy City, the *cohen hagadol*, High Priest Boethus, swept through the Court of Women. Followed by a procession of scribes, assistants, lackeys, and other relatives on the Temple payroll, Boethus found himself face-to-face with Hannah the Prophetess.

Everyone else in Jerusalem bowed and stepped aside when he passed.

She did not budge.

Boethus would gladly have avoided the confrontation, but showing reluctance to face a crazy woman would undoubtedly get reported to Herod. Demonstrating weakness in office had caused the removal of many previous high priests. Better to give the talebearers something good to carry back.

"Woman," he said sternly, lifting bejeweled hands in admonition, "you must confine yourself to family matters and to praying for the poor and widowed. Your meddling in politics is wrong. You must stop speaking against the king."

Her response was swift. "Didn't the prophet Jeremiah say, '*So the word of the Lord has brought me insult and reproach all day long. But if I say, "I will not mention Him or speak any more in His name," His word is in my heart like a fire, a fire shut up in my very bones. I am weary of holding it in; indeed, I cannot.'*"[45]

"Yes, well . . . ," Boethus sputtered.

Hannah continued. "Nevertheless, perhaps you've been given false reports of me." Her eyes blazing, Hannah's gaze made a circuit of the entourage, during which several faces fell away from meeting hers. "Listen to the Word of the Lord: *'The days are coming when I will raise up to David a righteous Branch, a King who will reign wisely and do what is just in the land. In His days Judah will be saved and Israel will live in safety. This is the name by which He will be called: The Lord our Righteousness.'*"[46]

At that moment Hannah pointed an accusatory finger. It was first directed at the gold ring on Boethus' thumb, given him by King Herod, then shot upward till it was directed at Boethus' turban.

Unconsciously Boethus' fingers flew to his forehead, where they touched the gold plate or Ziz. Belatedly he jerked his fingers back, as if the words *Holiness to Yahweh* had burned him.

Temporarily stunned and unable to reply, Boethus had no choice but to listen to Hannah conclude: "And with what oath did Mosheh's successor, Joshua, Yeshua bar Nun, challenge the people? *'If serving the Lord seems undesirable to you, then choose for yourselves this day whom you will serve. . . . But as for me and my household, we will serve the Lord.'*"[47]

With that Hannah made her exit, without waiting for the high priest to offer either benediction or dismissal.

Yosef opened his eyes as the first call of the shofar shattered the stillness of the morning. Golden sunlight gleamed in the west.

Mary, her back to him, was dressed in her best sky blue dress and wrapped in a red shawl. Chin in hand, she leaned against the rooftop parapet and gazed out over the hilly streets of Nazareth.

Yosef cleared his throat. "*Shanah Tova!* A good year, Mary."

She turned to him, beaming. "*Le-shanah Tova tikatevu*, Yosef! May you be inscribed for a good year in the Book of Life."

From the platform on the synagogue roof the trumpeter raised the ram's horn to his lips and blew a second time. *Tekiah*, one long blast. *Shevarim*, three short notes. *Teruah*, nine rapid notes, followed by *Tekiah*, one long note.

The cry of the ram's horn seemed to Yosef to send the longing of Israel's heart hurtling across time and space to the heart of *olam haba.*

Yosef sat up. *Blessed are you, O Adonai, King of the Universe, who commanded us to blow the shofar on this day as a reminder that you are the King who was, who is, and who will be.*

"Shalom, Yosef. It's still early," Mary remarked quietly.

Yosef felt the truth of her words. "Have you already milked the cows?"

"And churned the butter. Your breakfast is ready downstairs. But sleep awhile longer if you like."

"I'm up." Yosef wrapped a blanket around his shoulders to ward off the morning chill.

Blessed are you, O Adonai, who proclaimed Rosh Hashanah as a day of rest. On such a day I would not have complained if you had ordered that the shofar be blown at noon instead of before sunrise, however.

Mary touched her stomach and smiled wistfully. "He's awake now, Yosef. *Tap. Tap.* Listening to the sounds of the world celebrating creation. Quickly, give me your hand."

He sprang to her side. She guided his palm to the bump that was a tiny elbow or knee or foot. *Tap-tap-tapping.* The lively signal of the infant king seemed to Yosef a miracle surpassing the sunrise.

Since ancient times, the shofar had awakened the people of Israel every year on this date to remind them of the prophetic promise that one day the shofar would announce the coronation of the Messiah King. How long had the blast of the shofar been only a tradition, a holiday? When had the expression of a distant hope become an excuse to sleep the day away?

Yosef counted the notes of each sequence to the number fourteen. Fourteen, the number of King David's name. Fourteen, the number of Messiah, the one called "The Sit at the Right Hand of Yahweh."

How many in Israel lay awake and waited for the shofar to fall silent so they might roll over and go back to the business of sleeping?

O Adonai, they do not know! They do not realize this is the last year before the prophecies are fulfilled! Just another Rosh Hashanah, they think. Just another holiday. Do not hold it against your people that they have grown weary waiting for you to come! Blessed are you, O Adonai, who keeps all your promises and gives us reminders that the future is yours.

Yet now, on this very day, the trumpet announced the reality of what had been promised from of old.

Blessed are you, O Adonai, King of all the universe. King of the world and of our lives! Today we celebrate the creation of the world and you, whose word spoke it into existence.

"He hears the shofar," Mary said. "Yes, baby . . . for you. Listen: the herald announcing Yeshua's coronation as king over all the earth! *Tap. Tap. Tap.* And we're the only ones who know how soon he is coming indeed!" Her eyes met Yosef's. "I love it when he dances." Then a pause. "No one knows he's coming, Yosef. Every synagogue in Israel and in all the world . . . the shofars touch the ear of every son and daughter of Avraham, but they don't know. They don't realize."

"No," Yosef answered, not wanting to take his hand away from the friendly rapping. "And I don't think they're meant to know, Mary."

"No. Not yet. Not even an army could keep the baby safe if Herod knew."

"Mary?"

Did she not realize that she was in danger as well? Herod would have no second thoughts about giving an order to have her heart run through—pinning her to the ground with a Herodian spear.

She seemed to read the fear in his eyes. "No, Yosef! *Le-shanah Tova,* Yosef! *U-metukah tikatevu!* You and me, Yosef, are inscribed in the Book of Life for a good year this year! The angel promised it. Blessed are we. This is meant to be a year of blessing and joy for all of Israel. Whether they know it or not. And it's sure to be a sweet year for us. For you and me."

Obscurity . . . hide us beneath your wing, O Adonai!

"Mary, we must pray for a quiet, hidden life until the child is old enough to ride into Yerushalayim at the head of an army. Obscurity! That must be Yahweh's plan for us and for him. I mean, Herod would hurt you if he knew the truth of what the shofar proclaimed this year. So—" he put his finger on her lips—"we must remain careful. I'm sure of it."

Ecbatana, Kingdom of Parthia
Journal of Court Astronomer Melchior
First New Moon after the Fall Equinox
1st of Tishri, Rosh Hashanah, Year of Creation 3754

Tonight it was my privilege to observe and report the sighting of the New Moon that marks the inauguration of the Jewish civil New Year.

The seasons have advanced far enough that the days are noticeably shorter and the sky was perfectly clear. For this, the most significant New Moon of the year, not only was Old Balthasar with me as witness but so was Shadrach, eldest son of Rabbi Misha'el of the Ecbatana synagogue.

It was the thinnest sliver of moon I have ever viewed—almost lost in the western glare and often disappearing for moments into the west. Yet with my sighting confirmed by two others, the word instantly spread throughout the Jewish Quarter. Immediately cries of "Shanah Tova!" sprang to everyone's lips, and the ringing of trumpets resounded across the city.

Because of my official duties for the court of King Phraates, it was not possible for me to join the synagogue service then about to begin. Before he and Shadrach made their way downward, Balthasar gripped my hand warmly and offered me a blessing for the New Year. As he left the observatory platform, he added, "It's going to be an extraordinary year. Mark my words!"

During the first evening watch, as darkness fell, Jupiter and Saturn were already above the eastern horizon. Mercury settled into the west, followed by Venus and then Mars, at almost precise hourly intervals . . . as if the heavens themselves marked the time of the New Year festivities.

It dawned on me after an unpardonably long reflection on my part that the order of the moon and the wandering stars in tonight's sky was the same as at the dawn of creation. The same as is demonstrated by the order of the menorah candles.

Except for the sun, which is at the center of the candlestick, the orders were identical: The Holy Spirit within the sign of The Virgin; The Messenger, Mercury, in The Balances; the Splendor of Venus by the left foot of The Snake-handler; Mars, The Adam, under his right heel; and finally, much later, Righteousness and The Lord of the Sabbath in Pisces!

MOON-MERCURY-VENUS-SUN-MARS-JUPITER-SATURN

Holy Spirit ***Sabbath***

Messenger Star ***Righteous***

Splendor ***The Adam***

Holy Fire

Inspired by this revelation, even though I could not hear the worship from my lofty perch, I loudly recited the psalm for the evening service to myself: Psalm 29.

> *"Ascribe to the Lord, O mighty ones,*
> *Ascribe to the Lord glory and strength.*
> *Ascribe to the Lord the glory due His Name;*
> *Worship the Lord in the splendor of His Holiness."*[48]

By the time ruddy Mars had disappeared, Jupiter and Saturn stood well up in the southeast. Their conjunction is once again extremely close. The greater light was above the lesser, but by no more than half the width of my fingernail held at arm's length.

Old Balthasar says they will grow closer still over the next week; then, he says, we'll see. If this pairing is truly a sign, after this second close approach within the sign of The Two Fish, Righteousness and The Sabbath will separate only to reverse direction and reunite once more.

May it be so!

Jupiter and Saturn remained visible all night, only dropping out of view as hazy blue enlightened the eastern sky.

Around midnight Shadrach reappeared. He brought me a roasted chicken and some wine as compensation for my being unable to attend the celebration below.

Balthasar's granddaughter, Esther, came with him. She prepared the food for me but of course could not traverse the city at such an hour by herself.

She's such a beauty; it's no wonder the rabbi's son volunteered to escort her.

CHAPTER 15

"Shanah *Tova*, Yosef." Mary bowed her head that evening as he kissed her brow.

"May the Lord inscribe a good year for you, Mary."

Yosef retreated to his bed beneath the stars. Each passage from tonight's readings at the synagogue had elicited a flood of new questions that Yosef had never wondered about before now. How many times had he heard these Parashahs read aloud? As a child in Torah school. In the academy studying for his bar mitzvah. Every year of his life the complete five books of Torah had been read and exposited by some rabbi or teacher. Yet Yosef had never thought to examine the depth and significance of the Hebrew words beyond what he heard read aloud.

Was Torah more than the single thread of Hebrew history? Was Scripture rather a tapestry of many threads woven together to create a unified and living picture of Adonai's plan for mankind?

Never had he wondered what the stories meant to him personally. If it was true what The Dreamer had said, that every word of Torah meant something, there was so much to learn before Yosef could be guardian father to the Anointed King.

How could he sleep? But if he could not sleep, how could he dream? His thoughts whirled. He sighed and smiled as he eagerly lay on his back and fixed his eyes on the panoply of stars stretching above him like the flames of a menorah. After only a minute he spotted the pattern of The Two Fish and the two gleaming gems of Tzadik and Shabbatai, which seemed each night to swim ever closer to each other across the celestial sea.

He mentally considered the catalogue of queries gleaned from his search of Torah. So much was left unexplained. Surely it would take many dreams in order for all his questions about Messiah to be answered. Where would his teacher begin?

Yosef slipped into the heavy darkness of deep sleep with many questions in his mind. How long did he doze before the dream began?

How long before he knew he was not alone on the rooftop?

In the distance Yosef heard the echo of a shofar in the hills. Incense wafted through the night air. The rustle of feathers seemed very near, as though the wing of a great eagle covered him.

He lay very still, hardly daring to breathe.

Yosef? The voice was a whisper, not a shout.

Was it an angel?

Yosef?

Yosef tried to speak but could not. What was it the boy Samu'el had answered when the Lord had called him from his slumber?

"Here . . . I . . . am," Yosef stammered.[49] He became aware of the live covering of a giant wing spreading above him like a tent. No stars, no light, except for a glimmer through the mottled pinions.

The voice, deep and mellow, resonated from the darkness. *Shanah Tova, Yosef.*

"Welcome to my roof. But . . . who are you?"

Yosef! Don't be afraid. We have met before. I am Gabriel, who stands in the presence of the Lord.

There was a long pause. The air hummed. The flick of feathers rustled around Yosef. Like the feathers of a mother bird protecting her young beneath her wing.

Yosef, son of Jacob . . . son of David . . . your prayers have been heard.

"I've prayed so many prayers. I can't keep track. So many questions . . . about everything. I'm worried about Mary. I wish her mother were here. This is a small town, and every woman has turned against Mary."

Not one of your requests has fallen to the ground.

"I have so many questions. So many. It will take a lifetime to answer them all."

There was the glimmer of a smile in the reply. *Longer than one lifetime. Do not be afraid.*

Yosef was afraid in spite of the command to be fearless.

Light shimmered like lightning flashing on a distant hill.

Sit up, Yosef, son of Jacob.

Yosef obeyed.

You have asked for wisdom. No earnest prayer for wisdom ever goes unanswered. You asked tonight, on the anniversary of the birth of creation, why it is ordained that Israel read about the birth of Avraham's son, Yitz'chak, and the birth of Hannah's son, Samu'el the prophet.

"I don't mean to be impertinent, but it seems if we're celebrating creation, then we ought to think about the heavens and the earth and the stars and the sea and . . . the seven days. Instead we read about two baby boys?"

And two mothers. First Sarai, wife of Avraham, who did not believe the promises of Adonai.[50]

"And the other reading tonight?"

The mother of the great prophet Samu'el. Hannah, who lived in Ramah with her husband. Hannah, whose heart was dedicated to Adonai. When her rival mocked her because she had no children, Hannah carried her broken heart to the house of Adonai. There, with tears, she prayed without speaking. She made a vow that her son would serve Adonai all the days of his life. And her prayer for a son was answered. She called the baby Samu'el, which means "Heard of God." The child's name also contains the command of the Shema within it: "Hear, O Israel!"

A warm wind passed over Yosef, rolling back the darkness. He stood on a high hill overlooking a valley. Suddenly he saw before him a young woman walking up a long road to the ancient Tabernacle. Somehow Yosef knew he was seeing Hannah in the hour she fulfilled her vow to the Lord. In her arms she carried a child, a little boy of about two. So young!

She brought her boy to Eli, the high priest. Eli was an old man.

Hannah smiled. Her lips moved as she spoke to Eli, yet Yosef could not hear her words. She kissed her son one last time and put him down. The tiny child fell to his knees and bowed before the priest as his mother turned and walked away, leaving him in the care of another. Hannah's face was resolute, though tears streamed down her cheeks. How could she leave this one so small, so longed for, and so loved?

The shrill cry of a hawk sounded above Yosef's head. He glanced up, then back down. This time he saw Hannah sitting under a tree. In her hands was a child's coat. She looked at Yosef as if she were speaking directly to him. *"For my little boy, my son, Samu'el. It is written that Jacob made a coat of many colors for his boy Joseph to wear. Every year I make Samu'el a little coat and bring it to him to wear in Shiloh, where he serves the Lord."*

"You never stopped loving him," Yosef said to her.

"Never." Hannah stroked the fabric of the garment. *"You never stop loving your children, though they may not be with you. In the end you have to give them back to the One who gave them to you."*

"To give up your son," Yosef replied, "seems like a very hard thing for a mother."

"Yes. Very hard. From the beginning my life is a mirror of Mary's life. Like me, she will be mocked and slandered. She will have a son who will live at the center of her heart. And she will give him to the Lord. He will wear the coat she makes for him with her own hands, and one day it will be stripped from him and worn by another. . . . Yet after sorrow joy will come."

As Hannah laid her cheek upon the fabric as though she were embracing her infant son, the image began to fade.

Darkness surrounded Yosef. The flick of feathers sounded above him and around him.

Yosef whispered, "You are still here?"

Yes.

"None of this is the way I imagined it. The virgin who will give birth to the Messiah. Who would think that old friends would gossip about her? or that she would suffer? If a person is chosen to serve God—I mean, out of all the women on earth—shouldn't everyone recognize how special she is?"

The angel did not reply for a long time.

Yosef took the silence as a negative answer.

Yosef approached with another question about the reading at the synagogue. "And why has the Lord begun his work of salvation with the birth of a baby?"

The angel answered, *Yosef, have you forgotten the reason the heavens and the earth were created? Each baby carries within its heart the story of God's love. Mankind was not created for the sake of the world. No, the heavens and the earth were created for the sake of mankind.*

The story of creation begins with the word Bar . . . *son. And the spirit of Adonai brooded over the waters . . . like a hen above her nest.*[51] *All of creation was covered by His love. When the nest was finally perfect, man and woman were created last of all. Created to have fellowship and share in the love of Adonai every day. He walked with them in the garden until the children He created and cherished turned from Him and followed their own way.*[52] *There is no greater sorrow than the fall of man and the entry of death into a perfect world.*

But here is the good news! All of Torah points to this hour in history and to the birth of the One by whose word all of creation came into existence. If the Lord created all things because of His love for His children, does it not stand to reason that He would come personally to save everyone who calls upon His name?[53]

And the Savior must come first as a long-awaited baby to reign on earth on the throne of King David, just as the prophet Samu'el predicted. This baby will be born to Mary, who, slandered and reviled like Hannah, has said, "Lord, may your maidservant find favor in your eyes."[54]

Yosef was troubled by the reality that even righteous men and women did not go through life without sorrows. "Will it always be this hard? Will there always be gossip? slander? opposition?"

The angel replied, *Even in her joy at Samu'el's birth, Hannah sang these words about the Messiah: "The Lord brings death and gives life; He lowers to the grave and raises up."*[55] *Life follows death! Eternal resurrection follows the grave! Though you cannot see it now, one day Mary will cling to Hannah's song like a survivor from a shipwreck clings to a plank that floats upon a wild sea.*

For the sake of love—to save even one . . . to save only you—for this cause the Son of God is born into the world. One day, as Samu'el prophesied, Messiah will sit upon David's throne.

But first there are stormy seas ahead. Yosef! Be strong and be a man! Be strong for Mary! Stand by her. Comfort her. You also were chosen from among all men from the dawn of creation! For this moment you were born. "It is not by human strength that one prevails. Those who oppose Adonai will be shattered. He will thunder against them from heaven. Adonai will judge from the ends of the earth. He will give strength to His king and exalt the horn of His Anointed."[56]

"How can I know what to say? how to help her?" Yosef pleaded. "I wish her mother were here."

This is the message of the Day of Remembrance. Like Hannah, Mary must say of her son, "So now I give Him to Adonai. For His whole life He will be given over to Adonai."[57] *After death comes life. . . .*

CHAPTER 16

nlike other underlings who endured public humiliation by Herod, Boethus was taken to task in private, with only Talmai and Hermes as witnesses.

"It's an outrage!" Herod stormed. "The courts are your responsibility. The guards are under your direct control. Yet you say you can do nothing about someone who openly speaks treason? How long must I endure daily reports on how brazenly this Hannah woman preaches?"

"Majesty," Boethus entreated, looking at Talmai for support but finding none, "she's an old crazy woman. No one pays her any heed."

"So? If that's true, no one would care if she disappeared, eh? Is that your plan?"

Boethus backed up literally and figuratively. "That is to say, Majesty, reasonable people, sensible people, know she's mad. But among the *am ha aretz*, she's regarded as . . . almost as an institution. She's over eighty. She has seen the Temple desecrated twice. She saw the Temple in its most dilapidated state—long before your magnificent reconstruction began."

Clearly Boethus hoped a little flattery would redirect the king's attention. "She's also honored by the people for her husband's memory," he added, "since he fell defending the Temple."

This was a misstep.

"In an ill-advised struggle against the Romans," Herod shot back. "Rome, our ally. Rome, master of the world."

"Just so, Majesty," Boethus hurried on nervously. "As I say, sensible people know better. But—"

"But what? Is she to be allowed to continue attacking me? Listen to the words that came from her mouth just yesterday: '*Be sure to appoint over you the king the Lord your God chooses. He must be from among your own brothers. Do not place a foreigner over you, one who is not a brother Israelite.*'[58] Do you hear? She preaches rebellion! She asserts that I am not properly the king of the Jews."

"Majesty," Boethus said helplessly, "that's a quotation from Holy Scripture. The book of Deuteronomy. It was spoken by the lawgiver, Mosheh, to the people, before they ever entered this land."

The king exploded with derision. "Who is Mosheh? What is Scripture? Used against me?"

No sooner were the words uttered than Herod was seized with spasms in his face and neck muscles. His eyelids twitched horribly, and he made gagging sounds. Hermes sprang forward to offer assistance, but Herod waved him away.

While the king struggled to regain control and to eliminate the panic from his eyes, Talmai and Boethus studiously avoided looking at him. Nevertheless, Boethus could not help noticing the foam on the corner of the king's mouth or the spittle in his beard.

When Herod resumed speaking, it was in a quieter, less mocking tone. "Should anyone be able to twist the words of the great lawgiver into political intrigue and sedition? Is that proper? Is it allowed anywhere else in my realm, except here in my own capital? By my own . . . by the high priest?"

Boethus remained silent, hoping the question was rhetorical. But when Herod repeated the query, he was forced to answer. "Majesty, that passage is . . . just part of history."

"Meaning?"

There was no escape. "Meaning, it's part of Parashah Shoftim. It's read in every synagogue in the land, every year."

Herod slumped against the back of his chair. "Every synagogue?"

Talmai at last spoke. "The high priest is correct, Majesty. The old woman may be crazy, but she's also cautious. She confines her remarks to quoting Mosheh and the other prophets. All my agents agree on this. She never speaks her own opinions but only recites from the Tanakh."

"You too, Talmai? So we can do nothing?" Herod challenged.

"It is to your advantage, sire. We keep our spies in place . . . add more of them perhaps. Send agents to bait her into making treasonous remarks. But even if she doesn't, she's still a magnet for dissent. We have only to watch who listens and nods approval to know where the real traitors are. Mixed in with the housewives and fishmongers, there are bound to be real rebels. By watching Hannah, we'll catch them."

The Beth-lehem caravansary was a large, open space surrounded by a wall of mud bricks. The fence nearest the highway sheltered nothing but the inn's single gate and a well with a watering trough. The other faces of the square supported a two-story-high inn. The rooms comprising the upper floor were built over arches used as stables.

During the months of good weather, from late spring to early fall, as many as three caravans at a time might shelter within its borders. When one of the three annual pilgrim feasts rolled around, as was now approaching, the overflow of Jerusalem's visitors lodged there as well.

Family groups dotted the courtyard, perching on their piles of belongings.

The caravansary also sold grain and hay. Once a month Zadok went there to buy fodder for his livestock. Hailing the innkeeper, he announced his needs, only to be met with a shake of the head.

"What do y' mean?" Zadok asked.

"Look there." The innkeeper pointed to a cleared space in the center of the courtyard. At a table sat an official dressed in Herod's livery. Behind him, lending weight to the clerk's official character, was one of Herod's soldiers, a Samaritan guard. A single file of men waited to register for the census and swear allegiance to Caesar and to Herod.

Zadok was even more curious about the two other men flanking Herod's clerk. Both Imperial officers were clean-shaven—foreigners, without doubt—and their robes were of finer cloth and brighter dye than Judean workmanship. They managed to convey both superiority and boredom.

"Romans," the innkeeper muttered. "Here to observe the oath taking and report back to the governor in Syria. Herod's idea."

Zadok scowled. "So? What's that got to do with grain for my chickens?"

"Everything. I mean, they've taken everything. All my rooms are reserved for them and their servants. All my provision is set aside for their horses. Even if they don't need it all, I can't sell to anyone else. Herod's orders."

"And Herod's lackeys spy on you?"

"And everyone else," the innkeeper hissed. "If the fat, bald one recording names thinks you have an extra shekel in your pocket he makes a signal to the soldier. The Samaritan guard lets you know that unless you want to see your name on a list of traitors and rebels, you better cough up that coin."

"Extortion."

"So this is new?"

"New to Beth-lehem." Zadok grimaced, hoping that no whisper of his brother Onias came to the attention of Herod's bullies.

"They've been coming and going. Going and coming. Bringing their women in from Idumea. I've sent my wife and daughters to stay in Beth-Anyah until the census is over. Ah, Zadok! You're lucky you don't have girls. Such a worry! So many strangers in town. What to do?"

Zadok crossed his arms across his broad chest and thought of Rachel and the other women in the village. Often they were alone at night as their men drew lots to tend the Temple flocks in the fields. "Perhaps we'll shelter the ewes together, eh? No one out after dark for fear of wolves."

"Spoken like a shepherd," the innkeeper fretted. "Beth-Anyah for my girls. And even that is not far enough."

It was the smallest sparrow from a nest of four fledglings in the rafters of the barn. Puffed into a ball of half fluff and half feathers, it cheeped miserably on the ground while the mother sparrow fluttered frantically above it.

Yosef, rough-hewn planks over his shoulder, paused midstep to take in the scene. Mary called him to breakfast.

"A minute!" he replied.

No doubt the barn cat was lurking nearby. It was a very large and efficient gray male who every day presented Mary and Yosef with a dead rodent. The sparrow family had built their home in a niche out of reach of the hunter, but even so it was within the cat's territory.

And now there would be a price to pay.

"So, little one. You've taken a tumble, have you? Where is the cat?"

Yosef leaned his burden against the wall and stooped to have a look. The baby bird, cheered on by Mama, hopped toward the hayrick.

"You're spry enough. No damage. Too ambitious, eh? Trying to get away from your brothers and go it alone before you're ready? I know how you feel."

The mother bird fluttered desperately over an empty stall.

"Mama? You've found the cat? The cat, Mama? Keep him distracted for a bit, and I'll do what I can."

Yosef sang under his breath, *"Blessed are You, Adonai, who sees when even a sparrow falls."*[59]

Yosef emptied grain from a woven basket and, in a swift motion, clamped the yellow-and-red wicker vessel upside down over the chick. "Don't be afraid. You're beneath your mother's wing, eh? Just a moment in the dark, my friend, while I get a ladder."

Jogging to his workshop, Yosef chose his longest ladder and hurried back to the rescue.

The mother sparrow danced tantalizingly near the cat. She flitted from fence post to woodpile to beams and back, continuing her diversion.

How do they know how to fight for their children, Lord? Yosef braced the ladder against the rafter. *Blessed are you, O Adonai, who made even very small mothers very brave.*

Yosef crouched and lifted the basket. "Keep it up, Mama." The fledgling closed its eyes in terror as Yosef cupped his hand around it and slipped it into his pocket. He could feel it tremble through the fabric of his tunic as he climbed the ladder.

The mother turned her attention to Yosef. With a shrill cheep she spread her wings and swooped toward him in warning.

Blessed are you, O Adonai, who made the heart of even such a tiny creature so fierce for her little ones.

A moment only until Yosef could see into the feather-lined nest. Three siblings huddled within. They blinked up at him in astonishment. *What is this enormous creature?* their expressions seemed to say.

"Here is your brother."

With one deft move, Yosef replaced the fallen chick in the nest and clambered down the ladder before the mother could attack again.

He stood, grinning, as the mother sparrow, exhausted, settled among her brood. Yosef had a sense of deep accomplishment. Certainly, he thought, out of all proportion to the deed. *Blessed are you, O Adonai, who let me rescue the baby bird.*

Mary entered the barn. She was smiling curiously. "Yosef? Breakfast is ready."

The cat, defeated in the game of advance and retreat, strode out of the barn. His ears were back in distinct disgust. He sat in the sunlight and licked his forepaw.

"Sorry I'm late." Yosef laid the ladder lengthwise against the interior of the building.

"Yosef? Everything all right?" Mary glanced at the nest and then at the cat.

"Yes. It was nothing. Nothing at all."

CHAPTER 17

Zadok and Rachel purchased two turtledoves from the bird seller to offer in memory of Obi's mother. Then they carried Obi across the Court of Women to pay the Redemption of the Firstborn.

Obi was wrapped in a blue blanket for the occasion as was the custom for all firstborn male children. This bright color always ranked first in order of blue, purple, and scarlet some twenty-five times in the book of Exodus. Each color represented some attribute of Messiah. Blue, *tekeleth*, symbolized heaven. The word sounded like *taklith*, which meant both "completion" and "perfection." So it was written that Messiah, the perfect firstborn Son of the Most High God, would descend from heaven to redeem the earth. He would rule as king over all the earth from Jerusalem and through Him all things would be complete.[60]

"Is Hannah there today?" Rachel attempted to see over the heads of the multitude in the court.

Zadok, head and shoulders taller, reported. "Aye, the prophetess is there. She sits on the steps of the Treasury, beside the chamber of oil and wine. At the base of the great menorah, where the redemption offering of the firstborn son is given. There's a great crowd about her.

Temple guards stand watching. Listening to her. No doubt the ears of High Priest Boethus. Just as Simeon told me. Spies. Herodian scribes. Every day, he said, it's the same."

The couple inched forward toward the box with the trumpet-shaped opening, where Obi's redemption money could be offered. Hannah rose and turned her eyes as Rachel and Zadok moved forward.

When they were within a few feet of Hannah, she looked at Obi. "So, she found you . . . Rachel, the shepherd's wife. Her son and yours will be counted among the first of Messiah's lambs. He and all the little sons of Beth-lehem. They will be the first beneath the throne who cry, 'How long, O Lord, until you take vengeance?'[61] And as for you, Rachel, wife of the shepherd who guards the flocks for sacrifice, your heart will be the first heart among all mothers who understands the cost of our redemption."

Cost of redemption? The words chilled Rachel.

Hannah closed her eyes and appeared to sleep. Zadok took Obi in his arms and recited the baracha for the firstborn of Eve. Then Rachel, Zadok, and Obi left the Temple Court and Jerusalem for home.

Today Yosef missed the good company of Heli. Wrapped in his prayer shawl, he felt very alone among the men of Nazareth in the synagogue. Together they recited at the end of the morning service:

"The Lord is my light and my salvation;
Whom shall I fear?"[62]

Yosef felt the probing eyes of his friends on him this morning. Thoughts hung unspoken in their looks.

"The Lord is the defense of my life;
Whom shall I dread?"[63]

Yosef closed his eyes as Nachman the Butcher seemed to direct the words of the psalm toward him.

"When evildoers came upon me to devour my flesh,
My adversaries and my enemies, they stumbled and fell.
Though a host encamp against me,
My heart will not fear."[64]

Yosef lifted his hands to embrace the words. *Hear me, O Lord!* Yet even as he prayed, he feared the disapproval of his friends.

"Though war arise against me,
In spite of this I shall be confident."[65]

He had no confidence in himself that he could carry this off. Challenges to Mary and to his marriage were on every tongue in Nazareth.

"One thing I have asked of the Lord, that I shall seek:
That I may dwell in the house of the Lord
All the days of my life,
To behold the beauty of the Lord
And to meditate in His Temple."[66]

This verse Yosef considered each morning, and it comforted him. To think that the Lord would dwell in his house! Sup at his table! Work beside him in the workshop! Of all men, Yosef was most blessed. Why could he not believe it?

He raised his head as the shofar called an end to worship. The blast was a reminder to all present of the sin of the golden calf while Mosheh was on Sinai receiving the second set of tablets. Yosef recognized how quickly his heart, like all human hearts, could slip from the heights of divine revelation to the depths of disbelief and idolatry. How changeable he was—longing to serve the Lord who had called him out but also desiring the approval of men.

Yosef bowed and removed his tallith, folding it neatly and placing it in its bag. He emerged into the courtyard and blinked into the morning sky.

Behind him, his best friend, Tevyah, called, "*Shanah Tova*, Yosef! Good year!"

Nachman the Butcher and Yuri the Baker were at Tevyah's side. "*Ketivah tovah*. . . a good inscription, Yosef!"

But Yosef saw reservation in their expressions. As there was in his. "*Gam le-mar*. . . also to you."

Tevyah pulled him to the quiet courtyard of the synagogue. Like Yosef, Tevyah was a member of the carpenters-and-stonemasons guild. With Yosef he had gone to Jerusalem to serve out his apprenticeship. Yosef had no closer ties outside his brother in Bethsaida.

Tevyah slapped him on the shoulder. "Yosef, old friend, every year it's the same, eh? Since our bar mitzvah. You and me and Nachman and Yuri. The four of us. This morning is our *hatarat nedarim*."

This was the customary practice of one person asking three others to serve as a *bet din*—a court of friends who would answer honestly two questions about his character:

What do you see when you look at me?

What did you see me do this year that I should regret?

How could Yosef answer his judges if they spoke honestly? And yet it was unthinkable that he would proceed through the Holy Days without this yearly ritual.

It was a pleasant day. They found a quiet place beneath an oak tree on a hill. Yosef sat in his circle of friends. Tevyah at his right. Yuri at his left, and Nachman across from him.

Yosef had been last to be judged last year. So, from this court of four, he was first to be judged this year.

He smiled nervously and looked off toward the village and the little house where Mary waited for him. *Adonai, help me to be faithful.*

Drawing a breath, he began, "What do you see when you look at me?"

His judges did not look at him as they contemplated their answers.

Yuri began first. "A weak man."

Nachman added, "Yes. A man whose righteousness is ruled by a woman."

Yosef gazed steadily at Tevyah. "And you, Tevyah? What do you see when you look at me?"

Tevyah shrugged slightly. "I agree. A man being badly used. Ruled by a woman rather than by good sense."

Yosef inhaled deeply, drinking down their criticism like a draught of scalding tea. "So, is this my *hatarat nedarim*? Or is it Mary's?"

"I was with you in Yerushalayim, Yosef." Tevyah wrapped the fringes of his prayer shawl nervously around his calloused fingers.

Nachman rubbed his cheek. "You were faithful to Mary, though there was plenty of opportunity to do as you liked."

Yosef, confounded by this evaluation of his morality, shrugged. "What of it? With a woman like Mary to come home to, I thought of no one else. Wanted no other woman."

The friends exchanged glances. "That's what we wanted to speak to you about, Yosef." Tevyah looked him straight in the eye.

"Yes? So?" Yosef clenched his fists, suddenly comprehending.

"You were faithful to your betrothed. Tevyah is witness to that." Yuri leaned nearer and looked over his shoulder.

Tevyah hissed, "Yosef? Is the child yours?"

A rush of anger surged through Yosef. He grasped Tevyah by the neck of his tunic. "What are you saying? What sort of question is this!"

Tevyah coughed and tried to pry Yosef's fingers loose. "You . . . you're supposed to ask what we saw you . . . do this year that you should regret!"

Nachman grasped Yosef's arm hard, holding him back. "Yosef! Calm down. Please, Yosef! Friend . . . old friend . . . brother. You know us. Tevyah asks a good question. A fair question. A question a true friend must ask in such a case. What did we see you do that you should regret? You married a girl who was unfaithful to you."

"You say such a thing about my wife?" The volume of Yosef's voice decreased as his fury increased.

Yuri inched nearer the oak, as if seeking refuge. "A question, Yosef! What sort of friend would I be, eh? Eh? Look at her! What is she? Seven months along in a pregnancy—even six—and only a couple months married? I have to ask you, Yosef. If the baby is not yours, make your charges and be rid of her! We'll support you!"

Tevyah shook his head. "You weren't home when she became pregnant; that's certain. You know us, Yosef. Would we say such a thing if we meant to harm you?"

Yosef growled, "I've known you all my life. And what do I know? I know you, Tevyah, by your foul tongue! And you, Nachman and Yuri, by your evil thoughts."

Tevyah protested, "We're . . . we . . . all of us! Your friends. Trying to help you. This is . . . every year . . . I am your *bet din* and you are mine!"

Yosef flung him away.

Yuri urged, "*Mutarim lakh*! Yosef! You are released from your oath to her if you wish to be!"

Nachman, a big man and a match for Yosef, extended his hands, palms up, pleading peace. "Yosef! There is a way out of this marriage!

Yosef! You'll find another wife. A true wife. Not a harlot with a bastard child for you to raise."

Yosef covered his ears with his hands. *Adonai! I won't speak to them. I won't be in the same space with them. I will not hear it. I will not have it.*

"Steady, Yosef. We . . . tell you this. You must bring charges of adultery against her for your honor. To clear the air."

Yosef raised a hand as if to silence them. "Your words poison the air. I can't breathe the same poisoned air created by your breath. It is a shame to Israel that such men enter the synagogue and pretend to pray!"

Tevyah argued, "Is it your child? It's only justice. Her condition is too plain to hide or pretend any longer. It is what it is!"

Nachman asserted, "We have done what we have done—taken you aside—said what we have said, only for your sake."

"Leave my presence at once! Or I will break you in two."

Tevyah and Yuri formed a unified wall. "Hold fast, Yosef! We are your true friends. She's summoned a demon to bewitch you!"

Yosef raised his fists. "A demon? Well, may the Lord rebuke the demon who accuses her and the innocent child! As for you! Here are my hammers. I'll not smash your faces here and now. But this is my warning. Never speak a word to me again. And if you approach her with one word of accusation—if you so much as whisper such slander about her to any other human—I will tear you apart."

CHAPTER 18

Yosef did not come in to supper. He remained in his workshop, carving the pattern of a menorah and vine leaves on a chest by lamplight.

He heard Mary before he saw her, still not knowing how to face her. He could not admit to her what had happened this morning after services, yet he knew she would realize something terrible had gone on.

A soft rapping sounded on the door.

Yosef did not put down the chisel. "Enter."

The door swung open with a groan.

"Still working." It was a statement, not a question.

"Yes. I want to finish this."

"Beautiful! Oh, Yosef! So beautiful. Mama and Salome and Naomi and I will fill it with baby Yeshua's clothes. But stop for a moment. I brought you some supper." Mary placed a tray on the workbench, where he remained seated.

He did not reply. His stomach rumbled, giving away his hunger. "Sorry I missed supper. Thanks."

She gave him a glass of buttermilk. "I didn't eat much anyway."

He downed the cool, tart liquid. "I had so much to do. Forgot to eat. Sometimes I forget to eat."

Mary took the cup from him, hesitated, then leaned down to peer into his face. "You are glum tonight. Do you want to tell me?"

Yosef shook his head and resumed chipping at the pattern. "Sorry."

She did not budge. Her face was half concealed in shadow and her rounded form illuminated by the lamplight. It was as though the person who was Mary was entirely encircled and engulfed . . . lost within the presence of the infant she carried.

"Yosef? I don't mean to interrupt you."

"It's all right." He plucked at wood shavings and studied his work.

"Please. Put down the chisel, eh? I have to say you've done a lovely job of taking out your anger on the chest. You'll finish early."

He set his tools aside.

She stepped into the light. Her eyes, warm but sad, met his.

Yosef asked, "You know, eh?"

"Well—" Mary sat beside him—"I don't know all of it. But I know something happened today. Today was the day of *hatarat nedarim*, wasn't it?"

He nodded. "Tevyah . . . my dearest friend . . ." He faltered.

She patted his forearm. "He just doesn't know," she consoled.

"No."

"How could he? Did you finish?"

"I . . . left them. All three of them. Friends since we were boys and . . . I nearly took Tevyah's head off. No, I didn't finish."

"Well, then?" She kissed his hand. "Yosef. Husband. Brother. Friend. I will be your faithful *bet din* if you will be mine."

"Yes." His shoulders ached. He wiped his brow with the back of his hand. "Yes."

She urged him to speak. "You may ask me the questions about yourself, and I will answer honestly."

Yosef took her hand and met her frank gaze. Her brown eyes wrapped him up, bound his wounds, accepted him as he was . . . and forgave him utterly that he had not come in to supper or trusted her enough to share his heart with her.

"All right then. Mary, my *bet din.* When you look at me, what do you see?"

She did not answer immediately. Her face reflected sober thought, the responsibility of deep and honest consideration. "It will take all our lives for me to answer all the things I see in you, Yosef. But I'll try to sum up. So far . . ."

His thirsty soul panted for her reply. Perhaps she really knew him better than he knew himself. She could tell him who he was, what he was destined to become. Mary would not lie to him. "Just tell me . . . please."

"I see Yosef the gentle. I saw you put the baby sparrow back in its nest. In the rafters of the barn. You found the ladder, and not many men would."

Yosef smiled for the first time all day. "Not a great deed in the scope of all eternity."

"Oh? I thought it was a very great deed. It was at your feet at that moment, and you stopped and did something about it. That makes it great in the eyes of God, I think. And says something great about you."

"Then . . . thank you."

"That's not all." Mary intertwined his fingers with hers. "I see a man of such strength. I see a warrior, who loves and defends me and the baby. My truest friend. Most faithful protector. Do I need to explain that?"

"I'm glad." He sighed with relief.

"And I see Yosef the righteous. Yosef the Tzadik."

At this he balked. "Well . . ."

"But you are, Yosef. Righteous! How your heart longs to know the Lord. The psalm you sing morning and night:

"Hear, O Lord, when I cry with my voice.
And be gracious to me and answer me.
When you said, 'Seek my face,' my heart said to you,
'Your face, O Lord, I shall seek.'"[67]

Yosef repeated, *"Your face, O Lord, I shall seek."*

A gentle smile played on Mary's lips. "Yes. You see? Righteous. Yosef. Have you forgotten so soon? Chosen from all men in all the world! You will be the first man to see his face. The first man in all of Israel to embrace him. You, my Yosef, kind and gentle man, The Lord of All the Angel Armies has put his safety and mine in your hands. He has trusted you above all men. Guardian of the infant king. Oh, Yosef! Can you doubt his judgment of your character?"

"It's not the Lord that I doubt. I doubt only myself."

"If you doubt that he has chosen you . . . if you doubt that he will give you the strength to accomplish whatever task he sets before you . . . if you doubt that even so small a thing as rescuing a baby sparrow is important . . . then you doubt him."

Yosef nodded once, accepting that unbelief was his natural inclination, but true faith in God's mercy and love was his great desire. "Am I forgiven for this failure of faith, my compassionate *bet din*?"

She embraced him. "Yosef, our beloved and chosen guardian, *mutarim lakh*, you are forgiven and released from this failure."

"Omaine," he said and repeated the final verses of Psalm 27:

"I would have despaired unless I had believed
That I would see the goodness of the Lord
In the land of the living.
Wait for the Lord;
Be strong and let your heart take courage.
Yes, wait for the Lord."[68]

Thus ended the *hatarat nedarim*.

CHAPTER 19

Shortly after sunrise Zadok, Rachel, and Eliyahu hiked back to the tomb to say kaddish and mourn for Eve, the slave girl, as was the custom during the Holy Days. Grandmother stayed at home to watch Enoch and Samu'el. Rachel carried the girl's son, so that even the infant could pay respects to his mother.

"Look!" Eliyahu directed Zadok's attention to a mounted party of six Herodian soldiers approaching on the road from Jerusalem.

As if summoned by death, the soldiers spotted the small cadre of mourners and turned onto the side road leading to the tomb.

No one spoke as they drew up their horses, blocking the road back to Beth-lehem. The members of the troop were dressed in Herodian livery of yellow and red. The captain of the guard was clearly Samaritan with black hair and eyes that seemed to burn with hatred.

"You there!" the captain beckoned Zadok. "We were told we would find Zadok, the shepherd of the Temple flocks, at the tombs."

"Why do y' want him?" Zadok steadied Rachel, who had blanched immediately at the guard's words.

The soldier replied, "And Zadok's wife is the midwife?"

Zadok replied, "Aye. Who's askin'?"

"I am Hermes. The personal guard of Lord King Herod."

"I am Zadok. Here is the midwife of the territory of Beth-lehem Ephratha. And what would you be wantin' with us? We're after payin' our respects to the dead here. Can't y' see?"

"We're after a runaway slave," the captain challenged. "Her skin is black as a starless night. She can't have gotten far. She was due to calve. It has taken a while, but the truth is out. An old, crazy woman sent the girl to Beth-lehem. Sent her to the house of the midwife. Have you seen such a slave?"

"Aye," Zadok admitted.

"We've come to fetch her back." Hermes' horse danced impatiently beneath him.

"And what will you do with a runaway slave? Little bit of a girl that she is?"

Hermes shouted from the restless horse, "She'll be made an example of so others will not think they can leave the palace of the king at will."

Zadok challenged, "And the old woman? Flog her too?"

Hermes spat at Zadok's feet. "That's no business of yours."

Zadok stepped aside. "Then take the girl. And welcome. She came uninvited. No reason for her t' sleep another night among us."

"Well? Where is she?"

Zadok jerked his thumb toward the tomb. "In there. I reckon a floggin' won't do her any harm since she didn't survive childbirth. Go ahead. In there. See for yourself."

"Roll back the stone," the officer instructed Zadok. Stepping from his mount and passing the reins to a junior officer, Hermes strode toward the entry. Stooping, he covered his nose and mouth against the stench and peered in. Without perceptible emotion, he said, "Dead. And the slave's pup?"

Rachel stiffened.

Zadok placed a hand on her arm in warning. "We have it here. The child . . ." Zadok inclined his head in a signal that Rachel must show the officer the baby.

She obeyed reluctantly.

The soldier glanced at the face of the infant and yanked the blanket away. His lip curled in disdain. "Black as my horse. A crippled male? Property of Lord King Herod even with only one arm, eh?"

Rachel blurted, "Very fragile. He'll die if you take him now."

The soldier mounted his horse. "The mother was a valuable slave. Her whelp may be of some value as well. You'll have to take the matter up with Habib, steward of slaves. Bring the thing to Yerushalayim. The palace of Lord Herod. At the end of your Holy Days. Be there."

It was already a harried morning for Zadok. Two of the other shepherds were sick, as was Lem. Zadok was asked to drive two hundred sheep into Jerusalem with only teenage helpers and his dog.

Already getting a late start with so many animals to gather from three widely separated folds, Zadok was annoyed to hear his name called from Migdal Eder.

"Ho, Zadok," the Chief Shepherd shouted. "Package for you."

Zadok was not expecting anything, but accepted the small bundle without comment as a way to avoid conversation and get on with his day's task. The cloyingly sweet aroma that rose from the linen-wrapped container made the shepherd think it was a shipment of medicinal herbs for Rachel that his wife had forgotten to mention. As such he dismissed it from his mind.

It was not until the sheep were safely delivered to the Temple attendants and Zadok was eating a belated meal of bread and dried fish that he unwrapped it. The outside of the package was addressed to Zadok, shepherd of Beth-lehem, but there was no indication of the sender's identity.

The sack contained two pounds of dried Egyptian dates, moist and sweet, the fruit almost as long as Zadok's little finger and milky white in color. "Why'd Rachel order these?" he wondered aloud, passing out a handful to each of his assistants and munching on one himself.

Egyptian dates?

Zadok's heart skipped a beat. Mustering his calm, he suggested to the two boys with him that they take the rest of the afternoon to visit the Jerusalem bazaar. After exchanging an incredulous look, the pair departed hastily before their chief changed his mind.

Buried in the center of the sticky mass of fruit was a small folded scrap of parchment. Though the handwriting was unfamiliar and the message used no names, Zadok knew instantly who had sent it: his brother Onias!

It read:

Fourteen generations from Avraham to King David, fourteen from David to the Exile. Another fourteen are now complete.[69]
Dani'el's calculations confirm this: The time is now.
So do the stars!
The place is as near as your heart . . . keep watch and pray. He will come soon; I know.

That was all. Onias was afraid to say more, for fear of endangering Zadok and his family. But Onias had not stopped cherishing the study of prophecy, the longing for Messiah's birth, even though it had led to his crippling at the hands of Herod.

Shoulders hunched, Old Simeon, Zadok, and Rabbi Eliyahu huddled around Simeon's study table like birds in a rainstorm. On the planks a heap of partially unrolled scrolls crisscrossed each other: from the prophets Isaias, Dani'el, Micah, and from Torah, Genesis and Numbers.

Atop the stack was the anonymous note from Onias.

"The Almighty preserved your brother's life and the knowledge in his head," Simeon observed. "No one else has put it all together like this. Except . . ."

"Aye?"

"These are the same things Old Hannah, the prophetess, preaches at the Temple."

"She had better be careful," Eliyahu warned. "There are some who say she's crazy and no concern to anyone, but others fear for her life . . . afraid of what Herod will do to her."

Simeon nodded. "Like Onias. So, the testimony of two witnesses." Then he repeated, "If she's put it all together."

"But put what together?" Zadok's bass voice growled. "Fourteen generations? Dani'el's calculations? Near as my heart?"

Eliyahu interjected, "The fourteens! That's plain enough. A third set of fourteen generations is now complete. The full time period since the Exile is finished. Counting the years mentioned by Dani'el the prophet leads to the same conclusion. Something must be about to happen!"

"Seein' how Herod kills the righteous and promotes the greedy and profane, I don't need mathematics t' tell me that," Zadok challenged. "Aye, we need another Judah Maccabee t' cleanse the Temple and drive out Herod. But where is he—the one who can do all this?"

"Don't make the same mistake as others," Simeon warned. "They read of what Messiah will do as king—defeating Israel's enemies and purifying the worship of the Lord—and fail to understand that he comes first as a child." Simeon clapped one aged hand on Zadok's shoulder and the other on Eliyahu's. "And you, my friends, may be the first to greet him!"

"Beth-lehem's no fit place for a king t' be born," Zadok complained. "There's naught but shepherds' babies born there . . . *am ha aretz*, every one. There's no palace there, no grand houses. Shepherds and sacrificial lambs—that's Beth-lehem."

"And kings . . . David!" Stabbing a crooked finger down on the scroll of Micah, Simeon argued, "Yet it is clearly so: Beth-lehem, birthplace of King David, who received the promise that the future King Messiah would be of his descent."[70]

"So a child born in Beth-lehem," Zadok mused. "Could it be he's already there?"

Simeon and Eliyahu shook their heads in unison.

"Possibly, but unlikely," Eliyahu intoned.

Simeon added, "Mystery upon mystery. The Son of God, whose origin is from forever past, coming to earth as a man."

Zadok grunted. "Mystery indeed! And it better remain so. After Herod went t' all the trouble of prunin' his own family tree, he won't allow anyone else t' be proclaimed 'branch of Jesse,' eh?"[71]

"Surely the Almighty will send legions of angels to protect his Son," Eliyahu suggested.

Simeon raised watery blue eyes from the parchments. "Son of God, but also Son of Man . . . a human infant. Perhaps he'll need human assistance too."

Ecbatana, Kingdom of Parthia
Journal of Court Astronomer Melchior
7th, 8th, and 9th of Tishri, Year of Creation 3754

Tomorrow night, at sunset, begins the Day of Atonement.

Though it has been more than a week since the New Moon and we are well into the Ten Days of Awe, I find it impossible to leave off making nightly observations of Saturn (The Lord of the Sabbath) and Jupiter (The Righteous).

As Old Balthasar predicted, the two bright lights grew ever closer together during this, the first week of the New Year. This conjunction is every bit as compressed as the one last spring.

It has taken me nine nights' watching to be sure, but now I can report with certainty that the two planets passed their closest union two nights ago and are separating in the sky.

As Balthasar reminded me, it is not that a single conjunction of Saturn and Jupiter is unusual. These two wandering stars approach each other in this fashion every twenty years or so.

But for them to do so twice in a single year is remarkable.

And that they have remained for most of a year within the sign of The Two Fish, or the nation of Israel, is still more significant.

If they continue this swirling dance to bring on yet a third combination . . .

Two months after the first conjunction, after drawing farther apart, by high summer it was plain that The Lord of the Sabbath and The Righteous were again approaching each other, culminating in the grand sight of two nights ago.

The next two months should tell the tale.

Then what?

CHAPTER 20

Herod threw the basket of bread at the serving women. "Get out!" he bellowed. "You offer me stale bread? Get out!" Sniffing his wine suspiciously, he asserted, "Probably poisoned. Bring me a condemned criminal to test it on."

"Majesty," Talmai soothed, "your taster has already sampled the wine."

Herod's eyes glittered dangerously. "So he's in the plot too, eh? Didn't we recently hear of Caesar narrowly escaping death by poisoned figs?" The king overturned the basket of fruit at his elbow. Grapes and late-harvest figs spiraled across the floor. "Or someone may put a serpent in the basket?"

The steward attempted, without success, to reassure the king.

"The very air is poison!" Herod complained. "The stench is unbearable. Why does Yerushalayim stink so badly, Talmai?"

"The city is crowded," Talmai conceded. "Many of those going to register for the census decided to combine their journeys with a holy-day pilgrimage. All the inns and caravansaries are occupied. They say Yerushalayim has twice as many visitors this year as last season. And . . . they say there is sickness among the people."

Ordering incense burners to be lighted in all corners of the room, Herod clamped a perfume-soaked linen to his face. He bellowed for his chief bodyguard. "Hermes, the town is filled with rebels and assassins! Plague and fever! Their very breath poisons me. Staying here one more night will kill me! Hermes! Prepare the caravan at once."

"With what destination, Majesty?"

"I'm not well enough to travel far. We go to Herodium, just southeast of Beth-lehem. That's it! I'll be safe there. We must leave today!"

It was pleasantly warm. Rachel sat outside, nursing Obi under the turning leaves of the grape arbor. Grandmother, Enoch, and Havila's boy, Dan, fed pigeons with dried bread crumbs. Samu'el solemnly plucked grape leaves from the vine, presenting each newly detached bit of foliage to his mother.

Havila rested beside Rachel, both hands on her stomach. "There's sickness in Yerushalayim. So crowded. So many pilgrims this year."

Grandmother crooned, "Like flocks of pigeons. Yes, there you go. Everybody hungry. Everybody crowding and pecking one another, eh?"

Rachel nodded. "The census and the Holy Days. I'll be glad when they all go home. They all want to see Rachel of old's tomb and the pastures where King David watched his sheep."

Grandmother mused, "Take a drink from David's Well."

"Yerushalayim overflows into Beth-lehem, and every time the sickness comes with it. I'd best make certain we have enough herbs to deal with it." Rachel stared off into the sky, then announced, "There's flaxseed oil enough. Plenty of dried mint. But Zadok'll have to gather more hyssop, mallow, rue, and milk thistle."

Grandmother clucked her tongue. "Just like his grandfather when we were young. Poor man! A lamb for every pilgrim family at the Temple."

Rachel shifted the baby in her arms. "Droves of lambs this year. He hardly ever gets to stop running for more than an hour at a time. Up before dawn and off to Yerushalayim. Won't be home till late."

Havila nodded, "Eliyahu's gone too."

In the distance, on the ridge where Rachel's Tomb overlooked the valley, a trumpet blared a warning.

"The royals?" Grandmother screwed up her wizened face. "I was wondering how long it would take for old Herod to run for Herodium. The same every year. Every year, when the pilgrims come, he shelters in the fortress."

A second and then a third brass voice joined the discordant chorus.

"Yes. Herod," Rachel declared firmly, "wanting us to turn out and wave as he passes. Let's just stay home."

Havila looked worried. "Stay if you want, but someone in the village is sure to report it. You know the edict. Herod must have his praise from the citizens even if it's beaten out of us."

Rachel sighed. "You're right."

Grandmother scattered the remaining crumbs. "Come on, then. We'll bow to Herod and pray to Adonai that the plague passes quickly, eh? Eh?"

A stream of villagers, mostly women and children from the outlying cottages, assembled by David's Well. They were joined by several hundred visitors, all of whom knew Herod's trumpet was a command to cheer the Butcher King along his route. The head of the procession was already in view: a half-dozen mounted trumpeters, followed by a cavalry troop in red-and-gold livery.

Rachel recognized Hermes, captain of Herod's guard, in the lead on his black horse. Protectively she covered Obi's face with the corner of the blanket and looked away, lest she catch his eye.

"Herod. Going up to Herodium." Lem's wife, Sharona, flock of sons in tow, made her way to Rachel's side. "Where the vulture can keep an eye on us mice from his perch."

"Long as he doesn't breathe on us," Grandmother muttered.

The crowd made a show of waving and cheering—most without enthusiasm. Rachel, bile rising in her throat at the nearness of evil, stood with her head bowed. Havila held Enoch and Dan while Rachel juggled Samu'el on one hip and Obi on the other.

The king's palanquin passed with its curtains tightly drawn. It was near enough to touch. Rachel shuddered and held the baby close. The sound of coughing, like a growl, emanated from within the conveyance.

"Won't ever even know who came and who didn't without someone telling him," Havila whispered.

Grandmother added, "He knows what demons whisper to him."

Suddenly Hermes' black horse whirled from the procession and trotted back to where Rachel, Havila, and Sharona stood. The lifeless black eyes of the Herodian guard bored into Rachel. "You there."

Rachel did not look up. The horse was shod with iron meant to trample and kill anyone foolish enough to stand in the way.

Grandmother and Sharona herded children back from the road.

"You! Yes, you with the big nose and broad hips! You! I'm talking to you!"

Rachel raised her eyes and fixed her gaze on the gilded sheath of the short sword bearing the emblem of Herodian rank. Was he among the guards who had crucified Zadok's brother and executed so many innocent men at Herod's whim?

"Sir?" Did her expression reflect her revulsion?

Hermes cleared his throat and spit at her feet. "Yes! You! I remember. You're the midwife, eh? The midwife of the territory of Ephratha? Yes?"

Havila and Sharona, wide-eyed, backed away even farther.

"Yes." Rachel swallowed hard. Her heart raced. She put down Samu'el and motioned for him to move toward Havila and Sharona.

"I remember. I saw you at the tombs. You had a baby from the dead slave. The runaway."

Rachel cradled Obi's head and pressed the sleeping infant protectively against her breast. "Yes."

"Well? Is that it? Did the creature live?"

As if to prove the point, the infant's large hand reached upward, fingers spreading wide.

The officer leaned over in his saddle. "I remember. One hand! Should have let the thing die."

Rachel looked the officer full in the face. "Sir, he is a good baby."

Hermes' lower lip jutted out. His eyes narrowed with some indecipherable thought. Then he snorted and sat back, like a wild animal confronting something threatening. With a jerk of the reins, he pulled the warhorse around and galloped to his place at the head of the troop.

Ecbatana, Kingdom of Parthia
Journal of Court Astonomer Melchior
11th of Tishri, Year of Creation 3754

After the close of the final Day of Atonement service I hurried to the observatory. Clearly Old Balthasar has communicated his excitement about this year's significance to me. Like him, I now believe this time to be one of enormous importance and promise.

Therefore, on a night as momentous as Yom Kippur, I felt it absolutely necessary to study the sky.

Venus (called Splendor by the Jews) was amazingly bright in the west as I ascended the circles of the city. Many people, recognizing me as the court observer, stopped me to ask what it was, even though they must have seen it many times before in their lives.

Old Balthasar calls this "the difference between seeing and observing, just as there is a difference between hearing and listening."

I know exactly what he means, though in a different context. I have been around Esther since she was twelve, but have only lately realized how I care for her. Yet will her father permit the match? permit me to become her betrothed? I'm still afraid to ask.

But I digress.

As twilight faded, Venus brightened and other stars appeared. First I recognized the outline of Scorpius.

Soon I could make out the constellation called in Hebrew Afeicus and in Persian Affalius, both meaning "The Snake-handler." I remembered that the shape now identified as a scorpion has, in ages past, been called a serpent.

It's odd, but I'd never before noted how the scorpion or serpent appears to have stung Afeicus in the heel, even as he is crushing its head.

Seeing but not observing?

When I asked Old Balthasar about the possible meaning of this, he reminded me of the curse laid upon mankind in the Book of Beginnings, after Mother Eve and Father Adam succumbed to the temptation presented by that old serpent, Satan.

There is found written not only the curse but also the answer. The Almighty addressed the serpent, saying, "I will put enmity between you and the woman, and between your seed and hers; he will crush your head, and you will strike his heel."[72]

Balthasar reminded me that the phrase "the woman's seed" is the first reference to our Redeemer being born of a virgin. He concluded by noting that the story of creation was barely begun before both the need for the Redeemer and God's plan to provide Him were already in motion!

Part of the reading for today's Day of Atonement service involved a recitation of what was taking place at the Temple in Jerusalem. What must it be like to actually witness the once-a-year entry of the high priest into the Holy of Holies, and to lie prostrate in the Temple court while the high priest speaks aloud the Shem meforash . . . the never otherwise uttered Name of God!

To be in the very presence of the Almighty and to speak His Name! What a powerful, almost overwhelming, thought for a lowly scribbler like myself.

The waxing ten-day-old moon rose in the sign of The Waterbearer, washing out much of the sky's other sights. It was not strong enough to erase the stars Lord of the Sabbath and The Righteous, just east of The Waterbearer in The Two Fish and remaining impossibly close together. They stood almost exactly due south at midnight.

I watched until moonset—about halfway through the midnight watch. When I left the platform, the figure of Orion (The Hunter), known in Hebrew as Coming Forth as Light, was rising in the east. As I descended toward home I pondered the journey Orion would make over my head into the west tonight. That notion in turn reminded me of today's prayer: "May it be your will, Lord our God, to lead us in safety, guide us to our desired destination, and bring us safely home."

Since I expect to make no journey longer than from the bottom of Ecbatana to its top, why this plea should replay itself in my mind I cannot say.

CHAPTER 21

Mary brought her sewing to the carpentry shop, where Yosef worked to complete the baby's cradle.

"Mary?" Yosef laid down the chisel and took the tiny baby coat from her. He held it in his broad, calloused hands. "A tiny coat of many colors. Like Jacob gave to Joseph. Like Hannah made for Samu'el each year. Will he fit in a coat so small, you think?"

"For his circumcision. Eight days. Babies are very small. And for the Redemption of the Firstborn at the Temple. Blue, because he is the firstborn of heaven. Purple, the blending of blue and scarlet, because he will be both God and man. Scarlet, the color of Adam." Mary traced the pattern of the lion and the lamb that Yosef was carving into the panel of the cradle. "What is the verse? The lamb and the lion and . . . and his place of rest will be glorious? Isaiah, is it? In such a bed his place of rest will be glorious."[73]

"I wanted to do something special for him."

"Yosef! Your finest work. Perfect. Every detail. God chose an artist when he chose you."

"And you"—he returned the garment to her so she could finish the embroidery—"a treasure."

For the first time he saw a flicker of doubt in her eyes. "I'm just . . . I . . ." She looked down at her work. "I miss Mama. Really miss her and Naomi and Salome. So much, you know."

"I'm not much comfort. The sour women of Nazareth . . . if your mother were here, I don't think they'd be so bold about the way they're treating you."

"It is hard, Yosef. So hard sometimes. But I can bear it. All of it. All of them. So angry, they are. Because they don't understand. What they're saying . . . I can bear it because I believe what we do—you and I—will make a difference. But how will we live here and raise him, I wonder, with their evil tongues wagging?"

"They'll forget in time. It will become easier," Yosef replied. "Mary, you were my *bet din*. Judged me kindly. With mercy. But I was afraid to be your judge. Afraid to tell you what I see when I look at you because . . . maybe I wasn't sure about a lot of things. But now . . ."

"Now?"

"Are you afraid to ask me what I see when I look at you?"

"Sometimes it all seems so big. I think about Aunt Elisheba. Uncle Zachariah. Herod searching for them. Herod so afraid of a baby that he would kill it. Afraid of the message of an angel because he is so evil. And I wonder about our safety too. The great events of the world and I am so small. I think about the angel, and it hardly seems it can be real. Then the baby moves and I know: Nothing is too hard for God."

"I've been dreaming. Good dreams. Answers to things . . . to questions I never asked. Answers about who you are, Mary. Ask me. I'll be your *bet din*."

She sat opposite him and leaned her cheek upon her hand. "Tell me. Help me put the pieces together. What do you see when you look at me?"

He answered without wavering. "You are our second beginning. Our second chance."

"You mustn't be obscure. I'm not clever. Speak plainly."

"All right. All right." He pressed his lips together and tried to put his thoughts and dreams in logical order. "Like Avraham you offer your miracle child to the Lord.[74] And the salvation your son brings the world will forever free us from the curse of sin and death. The chains forged in Eden will be broken at last. You are the virgin, the second Eve, who is obedient to the voice of the Lord. Because you trust—completely trust the Lord's promise to you—because you have said you would obey.

"Obey! It's more than a word with you. Because you really meant what you said the night the angel spoke to you. You believe whatever God does in your life is all right with you! Even if you hurt. Even if people are cruel. You trust the Lord! Because of your faith—a faith like Avraham's yet found in a woman—the chains of sin and death that bind us all will somehow be broken forever."

It was a good talk. The couple returned to their work. Yosef finished carving the lion on the cradle, and Mary embroidered the words of Isaiah 11 on the hem of the tiny garment: *And a little child shall lead them.*[75]

It was written in the Song of Songs that all a man had he would give for love. This thought was on Rachel's mind as she watched Zadok striding toward the house from the lambing cave with Enoch perched on his shoulder.

The boy spread his arms wide and raised his face to the sky. "I'm flyin', Papa!"

Zadok laughed. "Aye! That you are! Enoch, my son! An eagle! That's what you are, Enoch!"

All Rachel had—all her possessions—what were they when weighed in the balance with Zadok and her three sons? She checked Obi and Samu'el, who slept side by side. Samu'el's two hands were square and strong like Zadok's. Obi, though he had only one hand, would grow strong and straight like Zadok. He, too, would be a shepherd one day like his father.

How grateful she was that Obi's mother had come to Beth-lehem so the child could live and be loved in a real family!

Rachel caressed his cheek and kissed his curly hair. Yes! Obi had become her son just as much as Enoch and Samu'el.

What would Rachel give to keep them safe? What price could she put on love? Compared to her boys and Zadok, nothing in all the world had any value.

It was very late. The moon had long since sunk into the western clouds. Zadok and Rachel had been asleep for hours.

The male voice calling, "Ho, in there! Is this the house of the midwife?" was unfamiliar, but there was no mistaking the urgency of the tone.

Zadok, having been out all the night before retrieving some lost lambs, was irritated. "Why'd they wait so late to come for y'? Which of your mares is due to foal?" he grumped.

"None," Rachel replied. "Must be a traveler who asked for me in the village. Go back to sleep. I'll see to it." Throwing a shawl around her shoulders, she rose from the bed, lit an oil lamp, and went to the door.

More pounding on the entry made the door panels jump. "Hurry up in there!" the gruff voice demanded.

Zadok was suddenly wide-awake. "Wait, Rachel! Don't—"

But Rachel had already thrown back the bolt and flung wide the door. Facing her was a Herodian captain and a pair of soldiers. They forced their way into the cottage. "Are you the midwife of Beth-lehem, wife of Zadok the Shepherd?"

Closing the door between the front room and the sleeping children, Zadok was at her side in an instant. "I'm Zadok. What do y' want?"

"You have a brother named Onias the Tutor?"

Out of the corner of his eye Zadok saw Onias' letter lying on the table. In the shepherd's mind it flashed a dull red, like a guilty blush. He struggled to keep his face turned away from it. "Had. He's crucified."

"Then you are the Zadok who was in the Temple when a crazy priest named Zachariah claimed he saw an angel?"

"Aye, I'm that Zadok. What of it?"

"And you saw this angel too?" the captain inquired with a sneer.

"Never said I did," Zadok retorted.

"Or heard him speak?"

Zadok shook his head. "All I know is what Zachariah made signs to explain . . . same as everybody in Yerushalayim knows by now, 'cept you, it seems."

"Keep a civil tongue or I'll cut it out," the officer threatened. "Lord Talmai, chief steward to the king, is seeking news of this Zachariah. Stories are around about a miraculous birth. High Priest Boethus wants to talk with him."

"Stories!" Zadok repeated with a snort. "Y' know how old that Levite and his wife are? Next story will have a crucified man back from the dead."

The captain nodded thoughtfully. "So I think too. But Zachariah and his wife are missing. Moved away somewhere. You know where?"

"Haven't seen him since—" Zadok paused and pondered—"not for over a year. Never did live hereabouts. Doesn't now."

"If you hear anything about him . . . or a child of his . . . you come to Lord Talmai and report it, you understand? There might even be a reward in it for you."

Rachel blustered, but Zadok squeezed her shoulder and she subsided. "I understand," the shepherd responded. "Is that all?"

"For now," the captain concluded suspiciously. "For now."

As soon as the door was shut and bolted again, Zadok swept Onias' letter from the table. Thrusting it into the remaining coals on the hearth, he stood over it until it was entirely consumed.

Ecbatana, Kingdom of Parthia
Journal of Court Astronomer Melchior
15th of Tishri, Year of Creation 3754

This month's Full Moon marks the beginning of Sukkot, the Feast of Tabernacles. In keeping the tradition of remembering the years the ancient Hebrews wandered in the wilderness, Jews and Yahweh followers build rooftop shelters of palm branches.

Because my small home is built into Ecbatana's city wall, I have no rooftop on which to build. Old Balthasar and Esther invited me to their home to help construct their sukkah. Esther and I laughed a great deal at my clumsy engineering efforts. The resulting booth is decidedly not watertight and has a distinct lean toward the southwest. Old Balthasar tried to relieve my embarrassment by commenting that it's a very pious booth, since it inclines its head toward Jerusalem like a good pilgrim!

With the fall season now almost a month advanced and given the altitude of Ecbatana, several blankets will be needed to make sleeping in it comfortable. And pray to God it doesn't rain for the next eight nights!

The Full Moon, emblem of the Holy Spirit, rose in the sign of Aries (The Lamb) about a quarter hour after sunset.

I want to note here that at midnight the constellation of Andromeda was directly overhead. Her name in Hebrew, Sirra, means "The Chained."

I asked Old Balthasar about the significance of the name.

His instruction sent me back to the Book of Beginnings. Then he explained, "The celestial figure of Sirra reminds us that all humanity has awaited the coming of the Seed of the Woman—he who will finally break the chains of the Curse."

Then he pointed me to verses in the book of the prophet Isaias that promise that the coming Messiah will be sent "to proclaim freedom for the captives and release from darkness for the prisoners. To proclaim the year of the Lord's favor."[76]

Would that it could be this year!

CHAPTER 22

The Sukkot feast Mary had prepared—fruit and cheeses and sweet pastries—was heaped onto platters positioned all around the leafy hut.

The honorary chair of the Ushpizin was decorated with the finest purple woolen cloth and woven palm fronds. So many beeswax candles were lit that the shelter glowed from within like a lantern on the rooftop of Yosef and Mary.

Twilight faded as Yosef, wrapped in his prayer shawl, recited the prayers over wine and bread. Grinning with expectation and pleasure at the bounty they would share with their friends, the couple sat down to wait for the arrival of their guests.

Yosef and Mary heard the happy shouts of welcome from the streets. Then the familiar voices and laughter of visiting neighbors moving from house to house in celebration.

An hour passed. No one came to the hut of Yosef and Mary. It became clear no one was coming.

The couple sat in silence for a time, listening, waiting, pretending nothing was wrong.

"Are you hungry, Yosef?" Mary ventured as singing commenced from the rooftop of Yosef's friend Tevyah.

Yosef was not hungry, but he lied. "I've been hungry for days. Since you rolled out the first pastry and I smelled it baking."

"We shouldn't wait, I think. Don't you think we should eat?" For the first time he heard forced cheerfulness in Mary's words. "So the food isn't wasted?"

He blinked at the mound of pastries. Thirty-six layers of pastry beaten until it was as thin as parchment. Layer upon layer filled with chopped dates, walnuts, and honey. At great cost from her cheese money Mary had purchased the ingredients and made enough for every member of the synagogue to have a piece.

Yosef scowled. "Yes, I suppose we should begin." And then, "Mary?"

"It's all right," she soothed. "But please . . . don't be too nice to me. Not now, Yosef. I can't stand your pity. It will make me cry."

"Then I'll say it plainly: they aren't coming."

"They'll miss the best sweets in Nazareth."

"In the house of the sweetest lady."

"No, Yosef, not so nice . . . please."

"Then I'll say it plainly. There's a cruelty about this . . . this shunning."

"It's all right, Yosef."

"It's not all right. Look! Look! All your work. You've been at it for days. I could hear you downstairs as I built the sukkah. Singing around the house like a little girl."

"My favorite holiday." Mary's voice cracked. "Camping out under the stars. Neighbors and friends."

"I built it big enough." It seemed very empty with just the two of them and so much food.

"It's lovely. The prettiest sukkah I've ever seen." She brushed the foliage with her fingertips and turned away. "I do wish Mama and Papa were here . . . and my sisters. Here to see." Her lower lip trembled.

He stooped to look at her face. Her eyes brimmed in the candlelight.

"Oh, see what they've done!" Yosef fumed as a round of song rose and fell from the neighbors' huts. "You're crying!"

Through the branches Yosef looked up at the stars. *Blessed are you, O Adonai, but . . . do you see how they break her sweet heart? Do you not see how they steal her joy?* Clumsily, Yosef reached for Mary and pulled her against him.

She wept quietly in his arms. "I don't mean to feel sorry for myself. I do miss . . . Mama."

"It's not right."

"But even so, I'm all right." She wiped her cheeks with the back of her hands, then began to heap a plate for him. "You see? This is not about me or you. It's about the Lord. About the true King coming to Israel. About his coronation." She caressed her bulging middle. "I almost forgot who our guest is. I almost let it be about me. But it's not about me. See? I almost forgot the One who has come to our house to stay with us."

"But you cried, Mary. I didn't think you . . . ever cried."

She laughed and shook her head. "That shows what you don't know about women! Pregnant women cry. Always. Even when things are perfectly fine. Mama and Aunt Elisheba warned me that I might feel like crying sometimes and that I should just go ahead and cry! So—" she shrugged—"come eat. The glory of the Lord fills our little tent." She patted her tummy. "Think what blessing our dear friends are missing when sweet baby Messiah is so near, and they don't even know who he is."

Yosef nodded and took the plate from her as distant laughter seemed to mock their little assembly. "Mary, I'll never leave you alone."

"I know. The Lord knows too. And I'm glad—so glad—that he chose you to watch over us."

Blessed are you, O Lord, King of the Universe! Blessed are you, unwelcome and slandered even as an unborn baby! Blessed are you, who has come this night to share our lonely exile.

"Yosef? Are you awake?" From inside the rooftop shelter Mary's voice sounded almost childlike, very small and sad.

Yosef lay across the entrance of the hut. Even now, hours later, he fumed at the cruel slight of their neighbors. "I'm awake. Do you need anything? anything at all?"

"Yes. The stars. I'd like to see the stars tonight. And you've made the roof too sturdy."

"I thought it might rain." He rose and removed a half-dozen branches from the supports. "How's that?"

"Thanks. There they are, still together. Oh, look, Yosef!" she exclaimed with wonder, as though she were seeing stars for the first time ever. "The two bright ones there. Still together. The rabbis say their dance means something. It is a sign for Israel, like the one that came the year Mosheh was born, they say."

Palm branch still in hand, Yosef searched the skies and found the sight that stirred so much speculation in Galilee. Jupiter—Tzadik, The Righteous; and Saturn—Shabbatai, The Lord of the Sabbath—remained side by side in the constellation of Nun, The Two Fish of Israel.

Blessed are you, O Adonai, King of Heaven and Earth, who foretells your plan with signs and wonders in the sky! You who move the stars, why will you not soften the hearts of those who have known Mary her whole life?

There was no answer.

"Can you see them now?" he asked.

"Yes." A long pause and then, "Yosef?"

He leaned the palm branch against the side of the hut. "Yes?"

"Can you see the stars too?"

"I'm outside. Of course." He tried not to let irritation at his neighbors creep into his voice, but it was difficult.

"What I mean is . . . are you able to really look at the stars? And understand?"

Yosef sank down on his mat and craned his neck. Two gleaming jewels hung upon the starry rope that bound the celestial fish together. He did not reply for a time as he attempted to focus on her question. "I heard a Syrian in the marketplace telling another fellow that in Damascus people think the stars shine for Herod's sons. The Roman governor has taken the conjunction as related to the doom of the Herodian princes. The last male descendants of the royal Maccabee line, they say."

"The stars have stayed so close since the first night the angel spoke. And since your dream too, Yosef."

"Well then, it must have something to do with what's happening. But I'm no astronomer. And if the Lord ever asked my opinion about his methods, I would tell him there never was a more dangerous time on earth for a baby to be born. Never a world more filled with danger for Jews than this time. Thirteen hundred years ago Mosheh led our fathers from Egypt with the coffin of Joseph at the head of the procession. And look at us. Once a year we're still sleeping out beneath the stars in little huts, remembering our wandering in the wilderness and still looking up and wondering what it all means."

Yosef lay back slowly and gazed at the cold white points of light. "Ah, Mary. Every day and night I ask God why. Why now? Why Israel? Why must you endure this? And why put you in the hands of a fellow as weak inside as me?"

He had wanted her to reassure him that he was strong and able, but Mary was silent. Had she gone to sleep?

The soft night breeze sprang up as lights around the village winked out one by one. But above the hills of Galilee and all the world, the two wandering stars continued to shine—like beacon lights to a fleet of fishing boats.

Blessed are you, O Adonai, who told us all that the heavens declare your glory night after night.[77] *I look up and believe you are and that nothing is impossible for you. And yet . . .*

In the midst of Israel there shines Saturn—Shabbatai, The Lord of Sabbath. And there is Jupiter—The Tzadik, The Righteous One. Blessed are you for creating pictures in the heavens so that every language reads your message when they look up. But, Lord, I confess I don't understand all the writing. And is this night part of your plan? How they have pierced her heart by their gossip and coolness! I don't understand why sweet Mary, blessed and chosen by you above all women, should suffer for her obedience to you? Is suffering part of your glory?

CHAPTER 23

There were only a few short hours left in the night when Yosef finally fell asleep. Exhausted from anticipating heavenly revelation, only to be disappointed by the absence of The Dreamer, Yosef had eventually collapsed in a heap.

The nagging realization that he would wake up worn-out and just as ignorant as he had been the day before was his final conscious thought. Perhaps he would not dream a conversation with The Dreamer again. Perhaps he would be left to parse out the meanings of Torah without heavenly assistance.

Yosef did not know how long he slept before he felt a soft tapping on his shoulder.

Yosef.

He heard bells. Felt the cool breeze of a presence. "Not now. Not tonight. I'm too tired."

Open your eyes.

Yosef was no longer on his rooftop. Instead he lay on the cold stone floor of a rich man's courtyard. The space was surrounded by a wide-pillared portico with a fountain in the center. The square was open to the night sky. The constellation of The Two Fish was directly overhead.

Yosef could not see his host, only the house, foreign and beautiful.

Yosef. Sit up. The voice was familiar. It was Joseph the Great, the Dreamer of dreams.

"Where are you?" Yosef asked.

Look up. The stars. A great multitude of stars. The Two fish. Can you not see my father Jacob's blessing? the blessing of my two sons, Ephraim and Manasseh?

"No. Only stars."

The Dreamer instructed, *Your question was heard. Why are these stars, The Two Fish, the sign of the nation of Israel? Since every night the sign grows stronger you should understand what it means. Stand up. Come with me.*

"Where are we going?"

Time is nothing. Walk.

Yosef obeyed. He entered the house as though he knew where he was going. Floors were polished marble. The roof was open to the sky. Pillars that reached up and up into the stars were topped with gold capitals, yet supported nothing.

The Dreamer spoke again as Yosef walked into a room where an old man lay upon an ornate bed. A wealthy young fellow, an Egyptian ruler by appearance, with two boys on his knees, sat opposite him.

The Dreamer said to Yosef, *There is my old father, Jacob, in his bed. The* Book of Beginnings *called him by the name of Isra'el when this moment was recorded in Torah. He was no longer just a man named Jacob. He was about to become the great nation God had promised to Avraham. So God called him Isra'el.*[78] *And there . . . that is me, myself as I appeared when I was the right hand of Pharaoh in Egypt. And those are my two boys. Manasseh is seven. He is my firstborn. Ephraim is five.*

Jacob, the wrestler of the Angel of the Lord was propped up on cushions. As Isra'el he was ancient, small, and frail. His long beard was yellowed and stained. Gnarled hands and crippled feet, unable to stand the weight of a blanket, protruded from the bedclothes. His ragged breath was shallow. Eyes were marbled blue with cataracts. He was blind and dying!

Yosef said to The Dreamer, "I see you and your sons are saying farewell to your father. I shouldn't be here."

The Dreamer replied, *Stay. Sit there on the steps. They don't know you are watching. Time is nothing. Together we are looking back at a moment in my earthly life and finding Truth. It is important for you to understand why the constellation of The Two Fish is the eternal sign of the blessing of Israel. Listen. Observe.*

Yosef remained silent as the final drama in the life of Isra'el played out before his eyes.

The old man wheezed as he spoke to his son. *"Joseph, El Shaddai appeared to me in Luz in the land of Canaan and he blessed me. He said to me, 'Behold, I will make you fruitful and numerous. I will make you a congregation of nations, and I will give this land to your offspring after you as an eternal possession.'*[79]

"Joseph, my son, you were the firstborn son of my beloved wife Rachel . . . and so your two small boys who were born to you here in the land of Egypt shall become mine. It will be as though Rachel, your mother, had two more children by me. Ephraim will be my son and partake in my inheritance. And Manasseh will be my son and partake in the inheritance. Thus you, through your two boys, are given the double portion of blessing traditionally reserved for the firstborn. It will be as if you who were her first child were born first of all of the others . . . before any of my twelve sons."

"My father . . ." Joseph bowed low to his father in gratitude of the honor. *"Mother would have loved having grandchildren."*

"Aye. That she would. I never dreamed I would spend the rest of my life without Rachel's good company."

"How lonely I was for Mother after she died, even though you were always good to me, Father. When my brothers sold me, I tried for many years to forget about my family. But God had another plan in mind. Though I was hated and betrayed, I know now I was led by Yahweh's hand here to Egypt. He raised me to power so I could save my family from starvation in the famine and forgive the brothers who betrayed me."[80]

"Your mercy has saved the whole house of Isra'el."

"Though in this land of Egypt I have great wealth and honor, the only blessing and inheritance worth having are the blessing you give, my father. I long for the blessing God gave you."

"Some may look at me and think old Isra'el is only a poor refugee. Of no use to the world anymore. Blind and dying. But I alone carry the covenant blessing of El Shaddai, the Almighty! We know the truth of what that means, eh?" Isra'el smiled from behind his whiskers. *"Blessed be the Name of the Lord."*

Isra'el inclined his head toward the little boys, as if noting their presence for the first time. With a gentle voice he addressed them.

"Well now. Who is here? Who are these?" Isra'el stretched his hand toward his grandsons.

Joseph replied, *"Father, these are my boys, whom God has given me here."*

Isra'el opened his arms wide. *"Bring them to me, and I will bless them."*

Joseph took his boys from his knees and brought them to Isra'el's bedside. The old man embraced the little ones and kissed them. Then he wiped away tears of joy and told Joseph, *"I dared not accept the thought that I would ever see your face again, and here God has shown me even your offspring."*

Joseph the Great, though he was the highest official in the land of Egypt, bowed and prostrated himself with his face to the ground before his aged father. Still on his knees between his two boys, Joseph placed Manasseh on Isra'el's right hand to honor the firstborn. Ephraim, the second son, was on Isra'el's left. But the old man extended his right hand and placed it on Ephraim's head, even though he was the younger child. He placed his left hand on Manasseh's head.

Then Isra'el proclaimed the great blessing upon them. *"O God, before whom my forefathers Avraham and Yitz'chak walked—the God who has been my shepherd all my life until this day—may the Angel of the Face who redeems me from all harm bless these boys! May they be called by my name, ISRA'EL, and by the names of my fathers Avraham and Yitz'chak, and may they increase abundantly like fish within the land."*[81]

In that instant Yosef the Carpenter dreamed he saw the two stars within the constellation of The Two Fish blaze with light! It was as though heaven had heard Isra'el's blessing and burned it into the night sky for all the world to see.

The image began to fade as the carpenter strained to see it through a mist. Old Isra'el, the two little boys, and their father vanished. . . .

Then Yosef was somewhere else, striding through stars and spiral galaxies. Which way was home?

The voice of The Dreamer of dreams broke into Yosef's thoughts. *Do you understand your dream?*

"So much to take in."

This is the true story of why the nation of Israel is symbolized by the con-

stellation of The Two Fish. In Hebrew the exact words are 'May they increase abundantly like the fish.'

God's blessing of Israel is an eternal covenant. God does not lie or break His Word. Never before have the wise men of the nations looked up and seen the wandering stars shine so brightly within the boundaries of Israel's sign. Now consider one more truth regarding The Two Fish. Within the constellation are two stars—two fish—that symbolize the blessing of Israel. The first represents Manasseh, the elder brother—the physical descendants of the seed of Avraham. The second represents Ephraim, the younger brother—the Gentiles who by faith will become the adopted spiritual children of Isra'el's blessing. Men of all nations will see the Light of Messiah and follow Him, yet the Gentiles will never take the place of the nation of Israel, their elder brother. It is written in Isaiah: "The Gentiles shall come to Your light, and kings to the brightness of Your rising."[82]

"How will the Gentiles know whom they seek?"

"The heavens declare the glory of Adonai. Day after day they pour out speech; night after night they display knowledge. There is no speech or language where their voice is not heard. Their voice goes out into all the earth, their words to the end of the world."[83]

The heart of every man longs to hear Adonai's true voice. Philosophies and false religions will come and go, but only the Word of Adonai recorded in Torah is eternal, and the Spirit will draw them to the truth. The stars remain a steadfast witness of the glory of their Creator and clearly speak of the story of redemption.

"We've all been watching for a sign," Yosef said. "The people look at the stars. There. Up there. In The Two Fish. So many months the stars of The Righteous and The Lord of the Sabbath have been shining, moving together and apart. And people know something unusual is happening. Everyone is hoping the sky will crack open and the Messiah will descend on a white horse and flood the world with light and righteousness and hope. Few are expecting a baby to be born as king. *I* wasn't expecting it."

Is it not written plainly in the Book? And for those who do not have Torah to guide them, there in the stars, a great event is proclaimed to all mankind.

"How can mortals understand the meaning unless heaven speaks to us?"

Heaven has spoken. Plainly. The truth of Yahweh is like a pearl a man drops in the sand. The wise man sifts the sand and throws the grains away and finds the pearl. Torah is the pearl bearing Messiah's identity. That truth is often buried in the shallow sand of man's arrogance, hypocrisy, and ignorance. Every word in Holy Scripture is Truth. Everything in Torah—from the first letters of the first word to the last words—points to Yeshua, our Redeemer. All else is shifting sand.

"I pray the Lord will teach me so I'll follow what is truth and throw away what is sand."

Tonight you have dreamed of the smallest pearl in Torah, Yosef. Yet it explains the symbol of fish used throughout all Scripture. It serves as a reminder of God's eternal covenant with Israel.

"Understanding even such an obscure fact seems important."

Well spoken.

"Thank you. Now . . . I'm tired."

Thus ends the lesson. If you forget all else, remember what was promised long ago in the book of Numbers: "There shall come a Star out of Jacob, and a Sceptre shall rise out of Israel."[84] *The star of the coming King has risen within the sign of Israel. No future generation can ever accurately claim that these wondrous sights did not appear in the heavens in this age. This sign within the constellation of the two fish may be a small pearl, hidden in the sands of time, but it is an important one. In the last days, proof of this celestial event will be remembered and discovered again. And this is only the* beginning *of the wonders the world will witness.*

"No! Keep away! Keep them away from me!" Herod shrieked as he fled from his chambers to the top of the tallest of the four towers at Herodium. His bare feet and bony shins appeared below his nightshirt as he stood, wild-eyed, his back to the parapet.

Jutting from the Judean countryside, Herodium warned Nabatea against invading from east of Jordan. But Herod's palace loomed most threateningly over Beth-lehem. Herod the Builder had named many projects to honor his Imperial patrons, like Caesarea Maritima and Agrippa's Gate, but this—his personal retreat, prize palace, and stronghold, constructed some fifteen years earlier as a conical fortress both within and atop a manmade hill—he had named for himself.

Even so, Herod the Butcher King had no peace here. Hermes and the other bodyguards who chased after the king spoke soothingly to him, but without success. So Hermes summoned Talmai and begged the steward for assistance. "We searched his rooms. There's no one there!"

"Of course not," Talmai hissed. "He's had another nightmare . . . seen ghosts! He thinks Mariamne, the wife he had executed, comes to accuse him."

Unexpectedly, as if he had been listening to their conversation, Herod shouted, "They came with her! Alex and Ari . . . the three of them together! One out of each wall of my chamber . . . surrounding my bed!"

"Calm yourself, Majesty," Talmai urged. Snapping his fingers, the steward took a cloak from one of the guards and placed it around the king's shoulders. "A dream."

His lips clamped together, the steam of his breath spurting like smoke from his nostrils, Herod nodded slowly. Lifting his chin, he stared into Talmai's face. "Or a warning?"

"Majesty?"

"All this talk of Messiah! We round up troublemakers, execute them, disperse them, and still I hear it! We burned the genealogy records, yet the claims persist: the rightful King, the true King of the Jews. But I am the king of the Jews, Talmai! No one but me!"

"Of course, Majesty. Deluded men, all of them. Puppets of rebel Pharisees and the like."

"But what if someone comes with an army? What if one of my enemies—Nabatea or Parthia—what if they support his claim?"

"You are ready to meet any threat, sire. Your army. The backing of Rome. You alone are king."

"That old priest," Herod said abruptly. "An angel spoke to him. Something about a miraculous child."

"Rumors and myths."

"But one my enemies might seize on—use against me!" Herod's eyes swept the horizon from Nabatea, around Hebron, and then across Beth-lehem to where Jerusalem lay to the north. "Double your spies! Send out more patrols! If the child exists, find him before an invading army can proclaim him king!"

Ecbatana, Kingdom of Parthia
Journal of Court Astronomer Melchior
8th to 12th Cheshvan, Year of Creation 3754

It is scarcely possible for me to record the unemotional record of these nights' observations. Indeed, my hand trembles as I write this, adding unwanted flourishes and squiggles to my usual precise notation.

Briefly, the cause of my excitement is this: Four nights ago I made record of the fact that Jupiter (The Righteous) and Saturn (The Lord of the Sabbath) were no longer getting farther apart within the figure of The Two Fish. After separating one month ago tonight, they lately appeared frozen in place in the sky, as I compared both to each other and to the other stars.

I almost held my breath with anticipation. I did not even share my thoughts with Old Balthasar, lest I be overeager and hasty in reaching a conclusion.

But now I can speak: After three additional nights' careful watching, constantly measuring the apparent separation of the two bright lights with a pair of very thin, silver-tipped calipers held at arm's length, my conclusion is proven. The Lord of the Sabbath and The Righteous are once again drawing closer together . . . coming to yet another conjunction of these two bright lights within the sign of Israel!

While not entirely unthinkable, such a thing has never been seen within the memory of living men, nor have I found any record of this exact circumstance being recorded before . . . ever!

When I brought the news to Old Balthasar, he first bowed his head and prayed, "Thanks be to the Almighty, who has permitted us to live to see this day!" Then with barely suppressed excitement he confided, "I too have watched the lights in the sky, but I was afraid my old eyes—and my desire for it to be true—were deceiving me. But now, my son, the final confirmation has been presented. He who is The Tzadik, The Eternally

Righteous One. He who is The Lord of the Sabbath has been—or is about to be—born in the land of Israel. Born to be King of the Jews. I am certain of it!" Then he said, "We must go to him. I must carry the word to my brothers in Israel."

At this announcement not only did I hold my breath, but I felt my heart almost stop beating. "Go to him? to the land of the Jews, ruled by Rome? Leave Ecbatana?"

Esther also protested, "Grandfather! At your age? The journey is too hard and too long, and winter is coming on."

"Nevertheless, I must go," Old Balthasar asserted firmly. "Will you come with me, my son?"

With more assurance than I felt, I agreed, saying firmly, "Of course. So long as King Phraates gives his consent. I cannot leave my post here without permission."

Esther looked from one to the other of us males with consternation. She bit her lip, but when she finally spoke she said, "Then I'm going too! No argument, Grandfather!"

"So it's settled," Balthasar affirmed. "Tomorrow we prepare for the journey, and the day after tomorrow we go to seek an audience with the king!"

Two things I noticed: So certain was Old Balthasar that he would go worship the newborn king that he said we would get ready for this pilgrimage before the king's permission was obtained!

Also, again he called me "my son."

Part III

There were shepherds living out in the fields nearby, keeping watch over their flocks at night.

LUKE 2:8

CHAPTER 24

Pilgrims returned to Nazareth after the autumn feasts in Jerusalem. Everyone was home, it seemed, except for Anna and Heli and Mary's two sisters.

Birds flying south darkened the skies above Nazareth in advance of a fleet of clouds. It was clear storms were coming. Yosef knew the season had turned by the lonely feeling that crept in on the fall air . . . and by an unexplained sorrow in Mary's eyes.

Mary was a summer person at heart. A woman who preferred long days of sunlight and walking barefoot in tall grass. As the inevitable signs of winter encroached, her perpetual smile was replaced by longing for her mother's homecoming.

"I'll be glad when Mama and Papa are back." She stirred the embers.

With a fragment of broken pottery Yosef scooped coals into a jar that he would carry to the rooftop room where he slept each night. "Maybe tomorrow. Soon they'll be home."

"Seven days' journey from Yerushalayim. Ten days since the Feast of Tabernacles ended. I thought Mama would be home."

"Only a few days late. Maybe they stayed on with your older sisters."

"Everyone else from Nazareth has returned. I asked Rivka, the rabbi's daughter. She's the only one who doesn't turn her back on me when I speak to her. Rivka and her family arrived home three days ago. I asked her if she had seen Mama and Papa and my sisters in Yerushalayim. She said not since before Yom Kippur. So many people this year, Rivka said. Everyone expecting Messiah. Hoping, she said. Every day more terrible rumors. Buzzing like a beehive. Every Jew from everywhere gathered around their campfires looking at the stars and waiting for King Messiah to arrive on his great white horse and destroy Herod and the *cohen hagadol* Boethus and the false rulers of the Sanhedrin in the Temple. And she said they also hoped Messiah would cut down the Romans with a flaming sword."

Yosef passed his hand over the warmth of the coals. "They've forgotten what is written by Isaias the prophet: *'Every warrior's boot used in battle and every garment rolled in blood will be destined for burning, will be fuel for the fire. For unto us a child is born, to us a Son is given, and the government will be upon His shoulders.'*"[85]

Mary recited the Scripture they both had memorized. "*He will be called Wonderful, Counselor, Mighty God, Everlasting Father, Prince of Peace.*"[86]

Yosef closed his eyes and remembered the promise of the great angel who had appeared to him in a dream. *Of the increase of His government and peace there will be no end. He will reign on David's throne and over His kingdom, establishing and upholding with justice and righteousness from that time on and forever.*[87]

The fire crackled. The two sat silently contemplating their holy secret.

At last Mary sighed. "Instead, Rivka told me, there was sickness that spread through the camp of the pilgrims in Yerushalayim."

"Every year there's sickness," Yosef replied. "So many people."

"When Messiah the King didn't come and the Holy Days ended, all the pilgrims left the city disappointed." Mary sat back and clasped her hands. "That's what she said."

Yosef tested the warmth of the clay pot and added a few more coals. He remarked cheerfully, "They're right to look for Messiah, eh? Every righteous man in Israel is reading the signs of the times. They just don't know where to look. And it's a good thing they don't know."

"Yes. Herod."

The image of Herod's retribution clouded Yosef's mind. "No one can know. Not yet. That's the idea. Let the neighbors think the worst. Of you. Of me. It's all right."

"Oh, Yosef. I miss Mama. I would like to talk to her. Every day I have more questions about . . . well . . . the practical side of things. I've helped in delivering calves and lambs. I suppose it's all the same. But still, I wish Mama were here. What if someone got sick? Naomi or Salome?"

"If they got sick, then they'll rest a few days and recover and start home. Don't worry."

But it was plain to Yosef that Mary was indeed troubled. For the first time since he had known her, a shadow seemed to stand at her back and plague her with imagined fears. He could see the pain of betrayal flickering in her eyes as they walked to market. Only a few would even talk with her. Most just made her the fodder of their gossip.

And in the months since their marriage, Yosef had seen, with sadness, those barbs of betrayal hurt Mary deeply. She seemed so strong yet was so vulnerable. Were her frequent, unexpected tears simply part of pregnancy or the result of her pain? Perhaps it was because she had become so alone in her hometown—so rejected by all who had known her since infancy.

Blessed are you, O Adonai, who will someday set all women free from the tyranny of emotions! Blessed are you, that one day you will smile into the eyes of your mother, and at your command she will no longer be fettered by the dark and ancient curse of worry that rides on the back of love.

As if Mary heard his prayer, she looked up and smiled. "Yosef? I think it may rain tonight. Will you be all right? Sleeping on the roof?"

Outside the rattle of the dry leaves on the trees and cows bawling in their pens confirmed her opinion.

Yosef stood and stretched. "My room is fine. A fine solid roof on it. I've come to enjoy sleeping up there. I'll be fine even if it rains. And if I wake early in the morning, maybe I'll look out on the road and see your mama and papa coming."

"Well, then. You'll wake me if you see them?"

He stooped to kiss her forehead. "Of course. Sleep now. Rest. They are in the hands of Adonai. Remember: nothing is impossible with him."

He placed his right hand on her brow and recited the Shema and Psalm 91, the evening psalm: *"Under His wings you will find refuge. His faithfulness will be your shield and rampart. You will not fear the terror of night."*[88]

Havila, Rachel, and Sharona sat beneath the arbor as their children played.

"Listen, Rachel," Havila volunteered. "Old Simeon in Yerushalayim knows Habib, the slave steward, well enough to know he's a dangerous and corrupt fellow. Yesterday Simeon told Eliyahu that when you present the baby to Habib, you must act as though it means little to you if you keep him, one way or the other."

Rachel plucked a broad grape leaf. "I know. That's what Zadok told me. 'Act like you don't care *this* for him.'" She offered the leaf to Sharona. "But it must be in my eyes. What I'm feeling, I mean. How can I hide what's in here?" She tapped her heart.

Sharona accepted the leaf and wiped milk from Obi's cheek as he drifted off to sleep. "Obi. Such a name. Storm Cloud. It doesn't seem to fit, does it?"

"As easy tempered as any child you'll ever see," Rachel agreed. "Slept all night last night. Didn't wake up until Samu'el and Enoch clattered in to demand breakfast. Never such a temperament! All babies should be so easy!"

Sharona sighed. "Obi. Such a name. If Habib decrees the baby should remain at Herod's palace, you must remember it may be for the best. For the sake of your own boys. I mean . . . such a name! Obi! Out of the mouth of babes."

Havila agreed. "Too late. Look at Rachel. She loves the wee thing like she gave birth to him herself."

"His mother died in my arms." Rachel shook her head as though that explained everything.

Havila shrugged. "He's Gaddi Obi bar Zadok now—legally Zadok's third son. Eliyahu wrote a *ketubah* of adoption."

Rachel took Obi as Sharona's toddler staggered a few steps, then dropped to hands and knees and crawled to where Rachel sat with the baby on her lap. "I can't imagine Habib will reject our petition. As Simeon instructed, we'll take two silver denarii for the transaction. One to redeem the child from slavery—the price of a newborn slave—and the other for Habib to line his own pocket. I hardly think he'll argue the matter. All Yerushalayim is talking about the census. Something as small as a baby? Who'll care?"

Sharona hefted her toddler onto one knee. The baby woke and started to cry. "Habib is a cruel fellow, they say. Think of the poor girl who gave birth to Obi."

Havila put a hand to her brow as though thinking of that made her head ache. "What she must have gone through . . . and what if . . . ? Rachel? What if Habib blames you for her death?"

"You're a lamp on a dark night, Havila," Rachel replied sarcastically.

"You can't blame me. It's the naming of the baby. Gaddi. Good Fortune. That was a good name. But then little Enoch shouting out the other: 'Obi! Storm Cloud.' You can't help but wonder if it is a bad omen . . . if there's something bad on the horizon. The whole country is stirred up about the census. What if Habib refuses to agree to the adoption?"

Rachel held Obi facedown across her knees and patted his back gently until he burped. "I think Habib couldn't. Wouldn't. There'd be riots if Habib refused to allow a newborn Jewish baby to be redeemed for the price. Obi bar Zadok is now a son of the covenant. Habib the Slave Steward is the son of an Idumean pig farmer, and he'll think twice before he claims a circumcised Jewish baby as a household slave for his master."

Grandmother emerged from the house and headed toward the arbor. Sharona's four older boys grew bored with their game and congregated beneath the shade. Grandmother seemed not to notice that all conversation halted when she appeared. "Nicer out here. I've not been restin' well. It's my back, you see."

Rachel patted the empty place beside her. "Here. Nice."

Grandmother plopped down with a sigh and cocked one eye at Obi. "Sleeping is he? Well then. And what do you think? Not Good Fortune but a Storm! What a name! The Lord named him Obi. That's certain."

Havila frowned and made the sign against the evil eye. "Do you think? A portent, Grandmother?"

The old woman smacked her gums. "Can't be anything but a sign. Enoch crying out the name 'Obi . . . NO! Obi!' so plain-like."

Sharona's eyes grew serious as she stared at the sleeping infant. "Bad fortune? A storm coming to Beth-lehem?"

Grandmother slapped her knee and howled as Sharona's sons gawked at the infant as though he were a thing to be feared. The old woman played to them. "Obi? Bad fortune? I think not. Every baboon in shoes I've ever met has been named Gaddi. Gaddi? What's that? That's the name of a marketplace juggler. Nay! Obi—there's the name for an Israelite. Obi the Shepherd. Obi the Storm Cloud. Black as night. Ohhhhh! Strong as . . . strong as an ox. Smart as a . . . as clever as . . . well . . . he'll be one to reckon with. Obi bar Zadok will be a man no fellow will try to cheat. Picture him all grown up. Picture him with nothing but his shepherd's stick coming up against a lion." She acted out the part of Obi in a fierce battle using his shepherd's staff as a weapon. "I'd want a man like him on my side, eh?" She mussed the hair of Sharona's middle child. "What do you say? Eh? Eh? Well, I forgot your name."

"Matthew," the boy replied.

"Well, I put it to you, Matthew. What name would you rather walk beside in a dark alley on a black night in Yerushalayim, when bandits were about? Eh? Gaddi the Juggler? Or Obi the Mighty?"

"Obi," the boy asserted. He sat with his mouth open as he imagined having a friend like Obi.

The old woman grew more animated as every eye turned on her. "Or yet, suppose you have a heavy load you must carry uphill and can't lift it on your own. Eh? Who do you want? Gaddi? Eh? Or Obi?"

"Obi!" the four brothers cried in unison.

The old woman spread her hands in a broad gesture, indicating she had made her point. "So, there you have it. Out of the mouth of babes, as it were. It is written. Obi. A good name. A great name. Now we're all in agreement."

Ecbatana, Kingdom of Parthia
Journal of Court Astronomer Melchior
14th of Cheshvan, Year of Creation 3754

I suspect Old Balthasar's eyesight is more reliable than he lets on. I marveled at his calm assurance that a journey of a thousand miles to Jerusalem could be undertaken with two days' preparation.

How little I then understood his commitment to meet and pay homage to the newborn King of the Jews!

I thought I was the one who broached the exciting news about the third conjunction and set all this flurry of activity in motion.

Incorrect.

Balthasar, it seems, had already made plans for our departure.

The winter court of King Phraates and his present location are at Ctesiphon, west of the Zagros Mountains. It happens that Ctesiphon is on the most direct highway from Ecbatana to the nation of Israel! Even obtaining the king's permission will not delay us one moment from the route we must follow anyway.

Before I last reported to him, Old Balthasar had already determined that a caravan of silks and spices was preparing for the journey westward and would be leaving today.

A lesson: Never underestimate the wisdom, the cunning, or the determination of an elder. They can be surprising in all those character traits.

Ecbatana is the point at which the so-called Silk Road runs east to the lands of Bactria and beyond. As such, it is the confluence of many caravans. Because of the danger from bandits, all travelers practice a belief in safety in numbers.

Old Balthasar spoke on my behalf to the governor of Ecbatana, explaining our mission and that we sought an audience with the king. He stressed that the enterprise would someday bring lasting fame to the king. That perhaps it would be celebrated in song.

The governor, impressed by Balthasar's sincerity and commitment and having no complaint about my previous work, agreed and gave his consent. Old Balthasar next laid out a considerable sum of money for supplies and for the purchase of two donkeys for the journey. One of these he would ride. The other would haul our provisions.

Esther and I will walk.

So, joining ourselves to one hundred other traveling companions, we set out over the mountain passes. For some time the road climbed, more or less continuously. Strung out over a mile of steeply ascending road, the caravan covered no more than eight miles of our journey before stopping for the night. We made our camp, pitching two tents beside a rushing mountain stream.

The night was crystalline in its clarity. But for once I was too tired (and too aware of the exertion required tomorrow) to remain awake for observing the stars.

CHAPTER 25

It was evening. Yosef was alone on the roof, praying and searching for the first three stars in order to welcome in the Shabbat day. From the parapet of the roof he spotted Anna and Heli and Salome at a distance as they led the donkeys up the steep road toward home.

Only those three.

Where was little Naomi?

The answer came with the next thought.

Heli and Anna carried themselves in the posture of grief, as though some terrible burden was on their shoulders. Salome, grim, almost angry, stared at the familiar world of Nazareth with unabated hostility.

So Naomi is never coming home. Naomi is dead. O Adonai! Blessed are you who gave Mary's sister life and who gave us all so much joy through her. And blessed are you who have taken Naomi away from this world to live with you in joy forever. But how will I tell Mary? How will I comfort her?

He descended the steps. Mary sat beside the window, claiming the last light of day for embroidering the sleeve of a dress for her mother. Tiny red roses, perfect images on a twisted vine, circled the hem.

Smiling, she glanced up at him. Then the smile faded. It was clear to him she knew in an instant. Her hands dropped to her lap. "Yosef? Yosef? What . . . no, who?"

O Lord, how do I tell her? How?

"Your mother and father are coming up the road. And Salome."

Mary nodded once. She breathed, "Naomi." This was not a question but a statement of fact. The acceptance of some unconfirmed tragedy she had sensed for days.

"Maybe she's stayed behind with one of your sisters. Maybe . . . maybe it's nothing at all."

Mary laid the sewing aside and stood silhouetted against the window. Her voice trembled. "No, Yosef, please don't. Not even a moment of false hope."

She put her hands to the small of her back as he watched. Her rounded form proclaimed the contradiction of new life and joy in the face of death and sorrow.

Mary whispered, "Naomi was the youngest. Mama's baby. Ours too. My baby sister. All of us loved her. How could we not? The favorite of us all. Mama will need me to help her."

Outside, Anna's voice rose in keening as she neared the gate. Mary's expression changed from resignation to surprise, as if she had just been slapped. It was real. Her fears were not unfounded. It was real.

"Mary! Oh, Mary! Naomi is gone! Gone!" Anna cried.

Mary shook her head and said, "Eve."

So there it was. Spoken. The name of the woman who had by her pride brought death upon all her children. This curse of death that came to all through the disobedience of the first woman must now somehow be broken with the help of another woman. Mary! Mary, the cheerful young woman whose name in Hebrew meant "bitter."

It was in that instant that Yosef's soul understood. *Training. The greatest test yet to come. Even this. Even this! Even sorrow so profound is meant to train her for the years ahead.*

Joy was Mary's natural instinct—her truest self. Praise and thankfulness were her first unprompted responses to each morning. Kindness to others and righteous submission to God's will were maxims that dictated all her actions.

But in such a bright and happy soul, what training could prepare her for the crushing sorrow that must somehow accompany the ultimate battle to break the curse of sin and death? Rejection and slander by old friends had only been the beginning. And now the death of little Naomi, so sweet and young. Never did dying seem so undeserved as this.

A chill coursed through Yosef as holy comprehension flooded him.

Joy was her instinct.

Longing to serve God was her heart's desire.

Sorrow and grief were the long and arduous lessons Mary must learn in order to survive what was to come in her life.

Blessed are you, O Adonai, who must give her strength to bear what she must bear for all our sakes.

The stone benches ringing the anteroom belonging to Habib, King Herod's Idumean steward of slaves, were packed with merchants. Some had been waiting for days.

Zadok and Rachel were the newest petitioners and, as such, were required to stand. Rachel nursed the baby as Zadok, shepherd's staff in hand, stood between her and the other supplicants. He towered beside the window that overlooked the packed streets of the city. The herdsman passed the note containing his information to a thin, officious attendant, along with a silver shekel.

Two hours later Zadok's name was called. Rachel and the infant remained behind in the chamber. Every head turned to stare in resentment as Zadok was ushered into the small but opulent, gilt-furnished room that served as Habib's office.

Habib was seated in a red-and-gold-overlaid Egyptian chair no doubt obtained on some military campaign or other. He was an old soldier who had served under Herod through Roman wars and civil rebellions. The scars of battle on his face and his rank of honor testified to his loyalty to Herod. Three fingers of his right hand were missing. Doubtless all his body was marred with old wounds concealed beneath robes of royal blue Oriental silk. Gray eyes set beneath grizzled brows were iron hard; the crooked line of his mouth fixed in a permanent snarl. He held the papyrus containing Zadok's petition between the thumb and forefinger of his mutilated right hand.

Zadok snapped his staff against the mosaic-inlaid floor and bowed deeply from the waist. "Lord Habib."

"You are Zadok of Beth-lehem?"

"Aye, Your Honor."

"So, you found our runaway slave."

"My dog found her. She was beside the well. Near death."

"She survived?"

"No, Your Honor. She was in labor. A mere child herself. But you know all that."

"She died?"

"Aye, that she did."

"The infant?"

"Alive, Your Honor. My wife is a midwife. Managed t' save the little one, though there was naught t' be done for the mother. She perished and we buried her."

Habib's eyes narrowed slightly. The paper fluttered almost imperceptibly in his fingers. "The child. It thrives?"

"Aye. My wife has cared for the poor thing herself."

"What gender?"

"A boy, sir."

Habib shifted uneasily at this information. "And you. Zadok, is it? Shepherd? Eh? Why did you not come to us with this information before now?"

"We didn't know if he would live. He's circumcised."

Habib leaned forward slightly and frowned at the news. "Circumcised, you say? The child of a black runaway slave, and you circumcised him?"

"Aye. As the law of Mosheh requires."

Raising his chin, Habib challenged Zadok. "No such requirement is made for the child of a slave. You attempt to change his legal status from alien slave? You make him a Jew?"

Zadok lowered his gaze to the floor. He sensed danger here. Danger in the fact that the child had been circumcised. "Aye. By my poor lights, I believed it was a mitzvah. Religious duty. Followin' the example set by our Father Avraham and all his household, Your Honor. Even slaves born to Avraham's household were subject to the Lord's command. Only followin' the strict letter of the law as I was given t' understand it. I apologize, Your Honor, if my ignorance in such great matters as the legal status of a Jewish slave differin' from all other kinds of slaves has caused offense. Well, there's no puttin' back what has been cut away now."

Habib seemed somewhat placated by Zadok's manner. "Is the infant black? His mother was black. Black as ebony, with ivory teeth."

"Aye. The lamb is black."

"And you've made the thing a Jew."

"To a simple shepherd a lamb is a lamb, sir, whether black or white."

"I repeat," Habib stated, waving a lapis-ringed forefinger, "this religious ceremony does not change the creature's legal status as a slave. It does not alter the fact that it is the son of a slave and the property of King Herod."

"Of course not, Your Honor. Never such a thought entered my mind. Though the rabbis might differ with you on the issue—you know the law."

With an uplifted, suggestive eyebrow, Habib noted, "Lord Herod's captain of the guard, Hermes, was particularly fond of the slave girl. You should have brought the infant to our attention immediately."

Zadok suppressed a cringe. So the girl was the toy of the most favored of Herod's own sadistic bodyguards . . . though such fellows fell in and out of favor regularly. Hermes had a reputation for cruelty and perversion.

Habib continued, "Clearly it has survived and is the property of Lord Herod. Therefore it must be returned to the household of Lord Herod."

"He's still fragile. But my wife is nursin' him, Your Honor. Her milk is what's keepin' him alive."

"There are wet nurses in the household of Lord Herod. It will be seen to."

"But, sir—my wife, she delivered the baby. He would have died if it hadn't been for the skill of my wife."

Habib let the paper flutter to the ground. He muttered, "Perhaps it would have been better if it had died."

Zadok smiled and spread his hands as if it mattered little to him. "You know women, sir. Out of pity now she's taken a fancy t' him. Aye. Just like a woman. Find a stray. Says he's been heaven-sent."

"Heaven-sent? The girl was a runaway. A valuable household slave."

"We'd like t' buy the little thing."

"Buy yourself one of Lord Herod's slaves?"

"No. Redeem him, as it were. You see, raise him, a freeman . . . with our boys. Raise him up t' be a shepherd."

"A shepherd." Habib appeared suddenly bored by the audience. "Well, then."

"Aye. Though he's worth less than a lamb at market, I'll pay the price of a pregnant ewe for it."

Habib gazed at the silver coin in Zadok's palm. "Why did you not bring the thing with you?"

"My wife has come with me, sir. She's in the antechamber, ready t' return the babe if Lord Habib requires it."

Habib clapped his hands and the attendant appeared. "Bring the woman and child."

Moments later Rachel, bearing Obi in her arms, entered the office. Zadok nodded, indicating that the interview was proceeding well.

She kept her eyes on the floor. Light streamed through the high windows and pooled upon her.

"Woman," Habib commanded, "bring Lord Herod's slave to me."

Rachel's lower lip trembled at the command. She advanced to the chair of Habib, lowering Obi for him to examine.

Habib flicked the blanket from the infant's face and peered down at him. He exclaimed, "It is black! As its dam was black. Curious that it bears no resemblance to the father. And missing its left arm! Like one of Lord Herod's pet monkeys."

Zadok saw the muscle of Rachel's jaw twitch with anger at the comment. But she remained mute as Zadok had warned her she must.

Habib began to laugh. He threw his head back and gulped the air in great bursts of laughter. Tears of amusement came to his eyes. At last he sat back and wiped his nose with the back of his hand. "So! Zadok of the Temple flock! Two silver denarii? Is this a fair price for something of so little value that cost the life of a female slave?"

He laughed again. "Make the son of a Samaritan bodyguard into a Jew! Make the illegitimate child of an ebony slave into a shepherd of Migdal Eder! It would be the highest insult to the priest and Levites. I'll warrant that having something so black and ugly and crippled call itself a Jew and herd the hallowed sheep into the Temple pens will cause a stir. I might pay to see such a sight! I will consult with Talmai on the price and send word."

At this he snapped his fingers and commanded that Zadok, Rachel, and the baby be escorted from his presence.

The Silk Road, Behistun, Kingdom of Parthia
Journal of Court Astronomer Melchior
22nd of Cheshvan, Year of Creation 3754

After traveling for more than a week, we have finally reached the caravansary at Behistun. I have been told (and fervently pray) that the worst of the Zagros passes are behind us. At times we crept along the flanks of mountains, with giant overhanging cornices of stone threatening to plunge down and wipe out all trace of the narrow trail and us along with it.

At other times our path followed the windswept skyline of a knife-edged ridge. On such occasions the powerful gusts, veering from west to northwest and back again, seemed eager to lift us bodily into the air and carry us into the depth of the canyon beyond.

But tonight we are within a palisade of brush and brambles that encircles a dirt plain trampled as hard as rock from thousands of hooves over hundreds of years. The fence of thorns almost always keeps out the wolves, the proprietor told me.

Looming over the caravansary are the bare, jagged spearpoints of a rocky outcrop. Since ages beyond counting, this rock face of Behistun has been used to celebrate gods and men. There is an altar to Heracles here, sacred to the Greeks, and an image of Ahura Mazda, the supreme god preached by Zarathushtra.

Part of the space is devoted to an inscription ordered by King Darius. On it he recorded his triumphs in civil wars and against invaders from the North.

These carvings—executed by long-dead men who lived and worked here, extolling their heroes and gods—made me feel very small indeed. But Old Balthasar, hearing me say this, reminded me how the One God directs all the affairs of men, great and small, kings and shepherds. He added the reminder that gods whose image can be recorded in stone are just that: stone. The Almighty twists even the plans of kings to His own purposes.

Over the past week the weather has turned steadily colder. Also, with the turning of the year, the days are much shorter and the temperature drops with the sun.

At twilight we sat close by the fire talking, waiting for the bawling camels and braying donkeys to subside for the night. Then Balthasar excused himself for sleep. He permitted Esther to sit longer with me if she wished.

I pointed out to her where the constellation of Heracles—or Hercules, as the Romans style him—was descending into the west. I showed her where his foot rests on the head of the dragon. Together Esther and I recalled her grandfather's teaching about how the promised Messiah will crush the head of the serpent;[89] *a message so important that it appears in the sky more than once.*

Looking eastward, we watched The Lord of the Sabbath and The Righteous rising together as Mars (The Adam) skimmed the mountain peaks to the south of us. I mentioned to Esther that, as the year progresses, Jupiter and Saturn will move farther into the west when studied at the same time each night, almost as if they are going before us on our journey.

A couple hours passed in pleasant conversation. We were watching the rising of the figure of Orion (The Hunter) when suddenly an arrow of light lanced between the stars Rigel and Betelgeuse. "A meteor," I said idly, with no special thought.

Then a second rose out of the east, followed by a third that streaked directly overhead.

Soon it was clear that a fan-shaped arch of shooting stars was rising in the east. Every moment brought greater numbers of brighter trails. We watched, awestruck with the display, until it culminated in a fireball so brilliant that it dazzled the eye, eclipsing even Sirius (The Guardian) in intensity. It flashed overhead, traveling completely across the sky from east to west, even leaving what appeared to be a trail of smoke behind. Then it was as if a dam had broken. Suddenly the night sky was alive with blazing bits of light and streaks of fire.

Strings of camels stirred and flocks of sheep reacted nervously. All around the caravansary drovers appeared from their shelters to quiet their charges, then stayed to marvel at the sky.

In this interval Old Balthasar emerged from his tent. Standing behind us, he murmured this question: "Do you know the radiant for these? From what portion of the sky are they launched?"

I examined the paths of the shooting stars, following them backwards in flight—back past Orion, back past the Great Sheepfold, back from the outline of the Great Dog, till they arrived at . . . "Aryeh!" I announced.

Old Balthasar nodded. "The Lion. He who will be The Lion of the Tribe of Judah will also fulfill the prophecy: 'And a star will come out of Jacob.'"[90]

"It is another sign?" I inquired.

"It is another reminder," he replied.

We continued observing together until the appearance of the waning half-moon at the shoulder of The Lion obscured the amazing brilliance of the meteors.

Even then the brightest still sparkled overhead.

CHAPTER 26

The thirty days of mourning for Mary's sister, who had succumbed to one of Jerusalem's rampant diseases, came to an end. By then cold weather had settled over the hill country of the Galil in earnest.

The tragic death of Naomi had caused a delay of Yosef and Mary's departure to Beth-lehem from Nazareth. Daylight hours grew shorter as the season of Hanukkah, the Feast of Dedication, neared. Carpentry work was at a standstill. It was a good time to leave Nazareth.

A herd of livestock consisting of eight milk cows, four calves, sixteen goats, and twenty-two sheep followed Mary to her parents' home on the outskirts of Nazareth. Yosef, shepherd's staff in hand, brought up the rear of the procession, in case there were stragglers.

It amused Yosef that he was not needed in the journey from his house to that of Mary's family. The creatures that combined his meager holdings and the flocks of Heli and Anna followed close by Mary, as though she held each one bound by a length of invisible rope. At the sound of her voice ears pricked up and the pace quickened. Mary's faithful bovine, Rose, strolled with nose adoringly plastered against her mistress's back.

Turning from the lane onto Heli's property, Mary stepped aside and called, "Hey-up!" Each animal knew her voice and her meaning. At Mary's command the cows continued directly toward the barn and their stalls, sheep and lambs separated into the right-hand pen, and goats to the left.

Salome appeared at the door, then joined Yosef and Mary in securing the gates and feeding and watering the animals before twilight.

The sisters spoke little to one another as they worked. It was as if the absence of Naomi's unbridled laughter had chained their joy, Yosef thought.

Now the sisters stood together beside the water trough of the sheep pen.

"Look, the ewes are bunching together beneath the shelter. Standing close with their backs to the north," Mary observed.

"A storm coming," Salome confirmed.

"By midnight," Mary agreed.

Unlike Mary, Yosef knew little of animal behavior foretelling the weather. He glanced toward the thunderheads gathering on the far northern horizon.

"Will you stay in Nazareth until it passes?" Salome seemed hopeful.

Yosef shook his head. "We're too near the deadline as it is. Census has to be finished by the end of next month, the royal edict said. Everyone. No exceptions. And after that, there'll be penalties. Arrests. Punishment for those not on the registration lists."

"I wish you weren't going, Mary." Salome rubbed her temples.

"It's all right," Mary reassured her. "Yosef and I . . . we'll find Naomi's grave and say *kaddish.* I'll make sure the stonecutter put her name on the monument like he was paid to do. And we'll offer the sacrifice at the Temple. It's good we're going now. It will be a comfort to Mama, knowing that I can see to the details for Naomi." A long pause. "How is Mama today?"

"About the same. Only thirty days of mourning prescribed . . . but I don't think she'll ever get over it."

"It's all out of the proper order. A child dying." Mary leaned against the fence rail and gazed toward the clouds. "How small are all the things we wrestle with every day until this immense enemy comes to wrestle with us. We're busy in our gardens, and we look up and see the storm clouds gather. But always in the distance. We never believe it will reach the place we stand. Never believe it will sweep away everything. Everyone.

"Then suddenly here it is. The Curse, unbroken since Eden, finds us. It crouches on our doorstep. It knocks. *Death.* It calls on us to pay the debt of sin. The wind is always swirling. Gathering. Blowing. Changing everything . . . and leaving an empty place none can fill. It makes everything else we fuss about in life seem petty and insignificant, doesn't it?"

"Small. So small." Salome exhaled slowly.

Then Mary suggested, "Or maybe . . . instead, death makes the small things about our life *holy.* Details we think are insignificant are . . . truly sacred."

"I like that thought. So, will you and Yosef stay for dinner? It's not much. Papa's measuring for a door. And Mama has a headache. The smell of cooking, you know. It's a cold supper, but you're welcome."

Yosef smiled at Salome's small response to Mary's great truth. *Blessed are you, O Adonai, who requires us to get on with the petty details of our lives even in the midst of grief.*

As if confirming the truth of this, Mary replied, "We have to finish packing. We're leaving tomorrow at first light."

"Mama's sleeping. I made her a tea of valerian herb and willow bark. But I know she'll want to see you both."

"We'll stop by in the morning on our way south," Mary promised. "If she wakes up this evening, tell her I was here. Tell her I love her. Papa too."

A drizzle had fallen steadily throughout the day and into twilight. Zadok did not attend synagogue nor return home for supper.

"Must be trouble at the lambing cave," Grandmother noted as she and Rachel ate at home after the service. "It was Zadok's turn to eat at home tonight, and there's trouble. Well, it's lambing season. Trouble. Men with big hands. What can you expect? Takes a woman with a touch. I'll watch the babes tonight. You'd best be on your way, Rachel."

Rachel nursed Samu'el and Obi as Grandmother gathered enough food to last Zadok through the night.

Rachel dressed warmly, then loaded five loaves of barley bread, a crock of stew, and freshly pressed apple cider into a basket.

The light of her lantern, diffused by the rain, barely fell two steps ahead of her on the narrow path. A faint glow shone from the lambing cave where forty-eight young ewes, pregnant for the first time, were kept in individual stalls.

Rachel shook the rain from her fleece cloak as she entered, then took in the scene with one glance.

Lem shared the lambing watch with Zadok tonight. Each man was in charge of twelve ewes selected and bred for their perfect conformation in hopes of producing the ideal lamb. All of the firstborn males from this group would be declared korban, set apart for sacrifice at the Temple. One of these might be selected as the perfect Passover sacrifice.

The ewes were restless.

"I've brought supper." Rachel set the basket on a sack of grain and waved to Lem, who was busy cleaning a newborn lamb at the back of the cave.

Zadok glanced over the top of the stall but did not stand. His face was haggard. He was stripped to the waist, and his right hand was bloody. "Rachel girl! We would've sent for y' but as y' can see . . ."

Zadok's ewe, sides bulging, panted as a contraction gripped her.

"She's in a bad way." Rachel laid aside her cloak and knelt beside the terrified animal.

"Aye. We've already lost one male lamb. A big handsome thing he was. There he is. Dead. Aye, over there. His poor mother won't let anyone near him." Zadok jerked his thumb toward a frantic ewe who paced and bleated at her lifeless offspring, trying to make it rise. "We've bred the ewes to a great handsome ram the high priest received from the governor in Damascus, and now we've got . . . well, look at them. The lambs are a full two pounds heavier than usual. Hard for these first-time ewes t' deliver such big lambs. The shoulders! It was a mistake. I said it at the time, but y' know Yerushalayim! They're always wanting bigger, better lambs for the sacrifice."

Rachel ran her hands deftly over the straining ewe's sides. Bulges and bumps told the story. "Twins."

"Aye, so I thought. Well?"

"Tangled."

"I couldn't get so much as two fingers into her. She's too small,

Rachel." Zadok wiped sweat from his brow. "What say you?" He drew a short curved knife from his belt. "She's not going t' make it. We might save the lambs if I kill her and cut them out."

"Let me try." Rachel rolled up her sleeve and washed her hands in the bucket by the gate. Slathering soap onto her arm, she knelt behind the tortured creature. "Hold her steady, Zadok."

Cheek against the ewe's back, Rachel worked her hand gently into the birth canal.

"What? Can you find a foot?" Zadok asked.

"No . . . not . . . yet . . . not . . ." Rachel closed her eyes and held her breath as a contraction tightened around her hand like a vise. And then, "A knee! If I can . . . straighten the leg . . . I've . . . hooked my finger round it."

Firmly Rachel pulled until the lower leg of the creature was straight. First one . . . and then the other. A tiny hoof emerged, followed by a foreleg, then a shoulder and another foreleg. A nose protruded. A strong contraction pushed the baby out with a gush of water and blood. It was a male—extremely large for the size of the ewe.

Rachel laid the baby in Zadok's arms. He peeled away the cowl membrane and began to rub the wet body with straw. "He's breathin'. Aye, he's a good one!"

Rachel again turned her attention to the ewe. The animal's head drooped, and her eyes were glazed with agony. "One more to go, sweet thing. Hold on! You can . . . you can . . ."

Another contraction clamped down on Rachel's hand as she grasped two hooves of the second lamb and tugged. "He's on the way. Hold her head, Zadok . . . almost . . . and . . ."

The second, a smaller lamb, black and scrawny, emerged into the world with startling ease. "Second-born. A male."

Rachel exhaled and began the task of rubbing down the baby. The mother turned her attention to the stronger newborn, nudging it and cleaning it.

Zadok scowled at the second-born. "Might as well kill him now. He'll be no use t' the Temple. Take milk from the ewe and stunt his elder brother's growth." Again Zadok's knife was produced.

Cradling the little one in her arms, Rachel scrambled to her feet. "No." She turned from Zadok, refusing to give him the baby. "Look there." Rachel inclined her head toward the pen where the grieving ewe nudged the dead body of her firstborn. "All these months she carried life, and now it's come to nothing. She'll grieve to death. You know how it is. Look, Zadok! We'll give her the black lamb to raise as a substitute!"

"She won't let us take her baby. Dead as he is, she won't give him up."

"She'll die of grief."

"That may be. But why do you think she'd accept such a pathetic little thing as this as her own? Look at the size of the dead one! Perfect, if ever I've seen perfection. These ewes know their own lambs. No, she won't be fooled."

"It's a shame to kill him, Zadok. Not to try."

"There are rules for the Temple flock. We'll have t' cull the scrawny one out, Rachel. Slit his throat and be done with it. It's no use, I say. Put him out of his misery. We'll slaughter the ewe as well."

Rachel walked slowly toward the pen, where the grieving sheep bawled and circled the body of her offspring. "Zadok! Let me try."

"Rachel, if you offer her the black lamb, she'll kill him, mark my words. Stomp him t' death."

Undeterred, Rachel stepped over the barrier into the pen with the bereaved mother. "Look here. Look, girl." Slowly she knelt and held the tiny lamb out. "That's it. He needs you." The ewe sniffed the stranger and backed away with a snort. She lowered her head to attack. Hissing and stamping, she chased Rachel from the enclosure.

"I told y'," Zadok chided. "Sorry. Sheep know their own and will not accept another as a substitute. There's only one solution. I'm sorry. Go home now. I'll kill blackie, and then tomorrow we'll slaughter this ewe. She's past savin'. No redeemin' either of them."

Rachel was determined. "Wait. Zadok? Wait. I have a plan. Joseph's Coat, Zadok! We can try it. Come on. I'll go to the side of the pen. I'll show her the black sheep and distract her. You fetch the dead lamb."

"How am I t' do that?"

"Put him in the manger. Lift it out of the stall when she's looking at me."

"You are stubborn, woman. But, aye, 'tis worth a try."

Rachel continued to rub the black lamb with straw as she walked slowly toward the stall. Zadok hefted the dead lamb and placed the limp carcass into the makeshift bier. Stooping, Rachel extended the black lamb toward the frantic mother, drawing her attention and fury as Zadok removed the manger.

"Got it!" Zadok cried as the mother, wild with grief, whirled and charged him. She threw herself against the wooden fence.

"All right, then. Hurry!" Rachel knelt beside Zadok. He skinned the dead lamb with a few deft strokes, removing the coat in one piece.

"A shame about this lamb. Perfect. Perfect lamb, he was." Zadok presented the one-piece skin to Rachel. She covered the black lamb with the hide, slipping it over his head and legs. Within moments he was entirely concealed by the substitute fleece. It was a trick shepherds used to fool a ewe into accepting an orphan.

"Now, then—" Rachel stood—"shall we give it a try?"

Lem joined them, gazing at the flayed body of the perfect lamb for a moment. "A pity one so fine as this died and now this little worthless black sheep will live because of it. Not a fair exchange. I'd rather see a hundred black lambs perish than lose one so fine as this one lamb. But the will of the Almighty, eh? My way is not his way."

Zadok replied, "What's done is done. All right, then."

"Lay the baby in the manger," Rachel instructed.

Zadok obliged. Positioning the live newborn where the dead one had been, Zadok hefted the feed trough easily over the barrier. Then he and Rachel and Lem stepped back to watch the result.

Crying with an almost human voice, the ewe circled the pen twice.

"Come on, girl. He's there. Look there. In the manger," Rachel urged.

Lem was skeptical. "She'll notice the switch right off. And reject the cull."

Zadok encouraged, "Come on! Have a look, girl. Your baby is alive after all."

Catching a whiff of her dead lamb's fleece as she passed the manger, the ewe halted and sniffed cautiously.

Rachel urged, "Yes. That's him. And he's not dead!"

The lamb in Joseph's Coat stirred and raised its head. It gave a timid bleat. The black mask of its face was the only thing exposed. He bawled loudly.

The ewe responded, nuzzling him affectionately. She licked his face as if to ask him why he had slept so long. And why was he in the manger?

"Well!" Zadok stepped over the barrier again, lifted the lamb to the ground, and positioned him to suckle. "Will she let him nurse, do y' think?"

Rachel laughed with joy. "Look at her, Zadok! She doesn't see him as he is! She sees her own lamb instead! She's accepting him as her own!"

The ewe blinked in contentment as the lamb eagerly latched on for his first meal.

Rachel spread her hands wide. "I'm filthy."

"Worth it."

"It's a bit of a walk home and it's raining."

Zadok kissed her. "Aye, a good rain."

"There's your supper in the basket. Send word if you need me again."

Khanaquin, Kingdom of Parthia
Journal of Court Astronomer Melchior
30th of Cheshvan, Year of Creation 3754

By my calculations this was the last day of the month of Cheshvan. Sunset should have shown the New Moon and with it the first of the month of Kislev. Instead, beginning yesterday and increasing all through today, heavy clouds rolled in, obscuring the sky.

Unexpectedly the west brightened toward the end of the day. A thick band of pink-and-orange peaks and turrets lay on the horizon at sunset, resembling the lighted battlements of an immense fortress.

At this season and from this location the sun sets considerably south of west. At the last possible moment the glowing molten orb of the sun appeared across the plains, like a beacon hovering over where I imagine the Holy City of Jerusalem to be.

In the past week our caravan passed through Kermanshah, finally leaving behind the last of the canyons and ridges of the Zagros Mountains. I am heartily sick of up-and-down travel. Perhaps now we'll make better progress than the ten miles each day we have managed so far. For three days we had no more than what water we carried because the springs were dry, and this year's rainy season has not yet begun. Once we reached the Qara Su River at Kermanshah, our difficulties with water ended. From the oppressive look of tonight's sky, water will not be a problem after this.

Khanaquin marks the beginning of the lowlands of Mesopotamia. This is the so-called Land between the Rivers, named for the Tigris and the great Euphrates. In a week we hope to be in Ctesiphon and at the court of King Phraates.

I watched for hours, hoping for breaks in the cloud cover, but was without success until after midnight. At that time the southwest cleared just enough to reveal The Lord of the Sabbath and The Righteous, well on their way toward setting for the night. They are noticeably closing the gap again toward their third conjunction.

What an amazing year for signs in the heavens this is: the appearance of The Adam (Mars) next to The Atonement Star at the heart of The Virgin; three conjunctions of these two most significant wandering stars, all in Israel's sign of the two fish; an awe-inspiring display of shooting stars; an eclipse or encompassing of The Lord of the Sabbath by The Holy Spirit . . . has there ever been such a year of visions?

Question: If Old Balthasar believes the conjunction of Jupiter and Saturn in Pisces means the birth of the Promised One of Israel, what will happen now that Saturn and Jupiter are setting earlier and earlier? If we have not succeeded in our quest before their appearance in the heavens is over for this year, what will we then do? What will lead us farther?

No wonder Old Balthasar was in such haste to depart from Ecbatana once he was convinced of the truth of the signs!

An hour past midnight the sky closed in completely, and it grew distinctly colder. A light rain mixed with snowflakes descended, which means the passes we lately crossed must be receiving even heavier snowfall.

A Manzandaran drover herding wild ponies from his homeland to sell in Ctesiphon paused in his prayer to his god. He explained to me how fortunate we are to be west of the mountains. "Likely the highway is closed till spring. Likely we're the last caravan of the season."

27 CHAPTER

Anna's eyes were covered with a damp cloth as she lay on her bed in the dark bedchamber in the early morning. Fierce and unrelenting, Anna's headache had not eased.

Yosef hung back, framed in the doorway as mother and daughter said their good-byes.

Mary sat beside Anna and whispered, "How can I help?"

Anna answered haltingly. "Mary? When the white lights came and I couldn't see . . . I had a dream . . . about . . . about you. I think."

"I'm here, Mama. Should I stay with you?"

"You must go . . . must . . ."

"How can I leave you like this?"

"Don't be afraid." Anna squeezed her hand.

"Not for myself. It's you."

"Fear nothing."

"Yosef and I . . . we'll do what we must; then I'll come back."

"I dreamed . . . such a dream, Daughter! When the white lights came . . . I understood."

Mary glanced up at Yosef with a look of helplessness. "Yosef? How can I leave Mama now? Like this? So sick?"

Anna breathed, "You must go, Mary! Go now. This . . . my illness . . . is meant to keep you from your purpose."

"I'm afraid to leave you. How will Salome manage?"

"You must."

"I've always been happy here. I'm afraid. Afraid I'll never be back . . . somehow . . . suddenly afraid I won't see you again."

"I dreamed . . . Jacob's Rachel dying on the road to Beth-lehem. I heard her voice, weeping for her children . . . and I understand why. She failed. I know why . . . helpless. Helpless in the end to change anything. I can't make it easy for you. Can't. I couldn't save Naomi. Couldn't set it right even though I prayed that God would spare her life and take mine. The Curse must end with your sorrow."

"What ends, Mama? Don't you need me to stay? I could take care of you until you're well. Then Yosef and I will leave."

Anna wagged her head, though it was clear that even this slight movement caused her pain. "I need you to . . . go! Now."

"What about you?"

"The burden of helpless love—helpless to change anything—it is yours to carry. A love so great . . . you carry him for . . . for all of us. Have courage, Mary. For the sake of every mother's heart and every mother's child, you must! No other way to put an end to it. You must . . . follow the story of Redemption inscribed in the stars of the heavens by the finger of Elohim."

Anna raised Mary's fingers to her lips. "Mary . . . your name means 'bitter'; I chose that name because of your father's unhappiness that you were not a son. Yet there is no bitterness in you. Only in me. You have been my greatest delight."

"I'll send word. We'll send word to you and Papa. You'll know all is well." Mary wept.

"Don't cry for me, Mary."

"I'll pray for you. And when we get to Yerushalayim, I'll pray for you to get well. Two turtledoves . . . and I'll pray the headaches stop."

"Yes. Yes. Your prayers. A better gift than tears."

"You and God will have both. Each tear my prayer."

"Mary's tears. Yes. Farewell, then. My blessing goes with you. Dear daughter . . ."

Morning broke through the bank of clouds as Yosef and Mary headed southeast on the winding road that led from Nazareth to Nain, nine miles distant. Nain—or Na'im, which meant "Pleasant"—was a well-named village nestled at the foot of the Hill of the Moreh, which meant "Teacher."

Yosef remembered the story in the second book of the Kings when Elisha had raised from the dead the only son of a woman of Shunem who had befriended the prophet and offered him lodging.[91] In honor of Elisha's ancient miracle, the countryside around Nain had become renowned in the Galil for its hospitality. It was dotted with private homes and a great inn at the crossroads that offered shelter for weary travelers.

The drizzle that had threatened to become a torrent did not materialize. Though snow glistened on the distant peaks of Mount Hermon to the north, the stiff wind on the heights of the Galil died away by midday.

Mary, snugly clad in heavy layers of blue-and-white-striped woolen fabric, walked without speaking beside an aged female donkey named Hyacinth, which had been Mary's pet since her tenth birthday.

It was clear to Yosef that even with favorable weather, the ninety-mile route south to his hometown of Beth-lehem was likely to be a slow journey.

The road was damp from the recent rains, but the downward grade was not difficult to traverse.

It was midafternoon when they paused at the Nain caravansary inside the gates of the village to eat and rest awhile. A welcoming fire blazed in the pit of the courtyard. Dozens of travelers and their animals were journeying south to Jerusalem for the Feast of Dedication at the Temple and for the census registration in the surrounding towns. A serving girl of about nine carried a tray suspended from her neck and sold bread still warm from the oven.

The child approached Mary and smiled. She bowed slightly and addressed Mary alone. "Shalom. May the Spirit of Adonai bless you and your child with the miracle of Elisha."

"And may the blessing he gave to the Shunammite woman be upon you," Mary replied.

On the Mountain of the Teacher lightning blazed at her words. The faint jingle of bells echoed in the thunderclap. Time and sound and motion froze for an instant. Had past and future meshed somehow within the brief exchange between the two? Were their words more than mere pleasantries?

Yosef blinked as the image of a woman weeping in front of a funeral procession flashed before him. Then a whisper resonated in the air: *Don't weep.*

The babble of the caravansary resumed. The little girl nodded and stooped to display the contents of the tray. "Bread? My mother saw you and your husband enter the gate. She told me that, since you are expecting, you are eating for two. She said to offer it two for a penny for you."

Yosef thanked her and paid for the hot rolls and a small crock of butter. But Mary only picked at her meal. She gazed solemnly into the flames and answered with cursory replies when other women asked what she and her husband were doing traveling at such a time and with her in such a condition.

"You're tired?" Yosef inquired.

"I didn't sleep much last night."

"We'll shelter here tonight."

"I can go on. We could make another two miles."

"We'll stay. Rest. Better to sleep here than camp along the road. You'll feel better in the morning if you have a night's rest."

Without waiting for Mary's reply, Yosef found the innkeeper's wife. She was heaping bread onto her daughter's tray.

"My wife is . . . ," Yosef began.

The woman's glance was a rebuke. "She's weary, I'll say. You men. Always in a hurry. Life can wait. You've no doubt walked her feet off. Where are you bound, sir?"

"South. Yerushalayim. Beth-lehem."

The woman grunted in disgust. "The census! They have no pity, them Herods. A pregnant woman! No pity! Well, you'll be wise to travel slowly, sir. And wise to stay the night. She looks as though she's ripe. Done up, she is. A woman knows such things."

"What is the cost?" Yosef dug into the leather pouch that hung at his waist.

"A penny for your donkey's stall and fodder. Your woman blessed my child with the blessing of the great prophet. I'll not take money after that. Before the Eternal, I accept her gift in exchange for a room for yourselves. Upstairs in the corner. Fresh straw to sleep in." She pointed to a door at the top of the steps above the arcade of the stable.

When he returned to the fire pit, Mary was solemn and alone in the midst of a laughing crowd.

"Are you all right?"

She glanced up at him, pained. "You heard it too. The voice. I saw it in your eyes."

He nodded and slipped his warm hand around hers. Her fingers were like ice. "'*Don't weep,*' he said."

"Was he speaking to me? What does he mean?"

"He means . . . don't weep, Mary. . . . Come on, then. There's a quiet place. Clean straw. You need to sleep."

Leading the donkey to her stall, Yosef unloosed the pack and shouldered it. Their sleeping chamber was small but clean with a basin for washing near the door. Spreading a double sheep fleece over the straw, Mary sank down with a sigh and rubbed her stomach. Yosef covered her with a blanket.

For the first time all day she smiled. "Shalom, little one. Did I wake you?"

"Glad to be lying down, is he?"

"He's been quiet in there all day. Letting me rock him to sleep. The motion. Side to side."

"Like a ship at sea."

Mary laughed. "A wide, slow merchant ship lumbering to Nain."

"And now that his ship's in port . . ."

"He's dancing." She tugged Yosef's sleeve and pulled him down beside her. "Here, Yosef. Say Shalom." Positioning his hand on the exact spot, Yosef felt the tapping feet of the infant Son of the Most High.

"Shalom . . . Yeshua." Yosef whispered the name the angel had given the Holy Child.

Blessed be the name of the Eternal God, the God of Israel, who alone performs miracles! The name of the Eternal shall be blessed from now and until forevermore!

Yosef lay back and stared at the patch of sky through the window. "Mary, you've hardly said a word all day."

"I am . . . I was remembering something Mama said to me."

"You mustn't worry about her if you can help it."

"Not worried about Mama. Praying for her. No, I was thinking about the baby. Mama mentioned the ancient story of Rachel this morning. Rachel on the road to Beth-lehem." She began to drift off. "If . . . the time should come . . ."

She did not finish the thought. No need. Yosef understood her concern. *If the time comes and we're traveling. If Mary's time comes to deliver as it did so long ago for Rachel, wife of Jacob. Rachel went into labor and gave birth to Benjamin along the road to Beth-lehem. And Rachel died and was buried there.*[92] The terror of the tale recorded in the *Book of Beginnings* made him shudder.

What had Anna been thinking? Why had she talked to Mary about the ancient tragedy of Israel's greatest love story, which had left the baby Benjamin without a mother and the patriarch Jacob without his beloved wife?

Yosef frowned and closed his eyes. Would angels come as midwives to attend to Mary and deliver the Holy Child? Or would Yosef be left to deal with it on his own? Would Mary survive? Were Anna's words a warning that Mary, like Rachel, would die somewhere along the road and he would be left to raise the child?

Don't weep.

He turned his head and studied Mary's profile as she dozed. Pretty girl. He had always thought so. Thick brown hair fell loose on the sheep fleece. Her cheeks were rosy from exposure to the cold. Her lips were curved in a half smile. Her face was serene, like a little girl's. So young. She was strong enough, yes. And Mary knew more than he did about the birthing of calves and lambs and such. The Lord had prepared her well for the task. She did not seem to fear what was happening to her.

Yosef was more afraid than she was. He was more afraid than he had ever been in his life. Mary was a long way from home. A long way from her mother. He hoped they would be back home in Nazareth in time.

Ctesiphon, Kingdom of Parthia
Journal of Court Astronomer Melchior
8th of Kislev, Year of Creation 3754

As of today we have been in Ctesiphon only three days—and one of those the Sabbath—yet Old Balthasar chafed at the delay in seeing the king. On our arrival he contacted kinsmen who are important merchants in this city, telling them we brought stunning news of fulfilled prophecy as seen in the stars.

Such is Balthasar's standing as an elder of Israel that they believed him without question, instantly exerting great effort to fulfill his request. Despite their assurances that the necessary contacts were made and bribes paid, Balthasar acted impatient, as though King Phraates should drop everything and see us immediately.

When Hanan'el, Balthasar's cousin, explained that a royal audience might take weeks to arrange, my mentor stormed about, lamenting even a single day's delay.

Only after Esther's reassurance that the Holy One of Israel had not brought her grandfather to this moment in the history of the world only to exclude him now did Balthasar relent and relax . . . somewhat.

In any event, the summons came this afternoon, surprising everyone (except Old Balthasar) at its promptness. A royal guard of six soldiers called at Hanan'el's house, where we were lodging. Old Balthasar and I, together with Hanan'el, were summoned to an immediate appearance before King Phraates. Esther remained at home with Hanan'el's wife and children.

As we were escorted through the streets of Ctesiphon, I could not help but experience fear mixed with excitement. This capital of Parthia is truly huge and magnificent. If Ecbatana is a large city at a mile in circumference, Ctesiphon is enormous. It is said that Ctesiphon, together with Seleucia across the Tigris River from it, combine to possess over one hundred thousand inhabitants! While Ecbatana is justly famous as a stop on the Silk Road, Ctesiphon is at the convergence of the Silk Road and the Royal Road leading south to Babylon and to the Great Sea beyond.

Here you meet caravans of silk merchants, truly, but also dealers in peppercorns from India, exquisitely carved white ivory brought from Africa by Ethiopian traders with skin black as midnight, brown-hued travelers bearing a pungent red bark said to come from far-off islands, and even beautifully formed, gleaming porcelain from regions so far away that their language of origin is completely unknown here.

There are even merchants here dealing in balsam from King Herod's Judea. The news from Judea is all bad . . . more sons of Herod imprisoned or murdered, it seems, and all the Jews there are fearful some spiteful neighbor will denounce them as traitors.

No matter what variations of speech, skin, or style, all people, it seemed, stopped their business dealings to stare at us and comment as we were ushered past. Hanan'el whispered to me that this is the way condemned prisoners are marched to execution. His explanation did not comfort me.

Fortunately, the true reason for the peremptory summons was not long in coming. As soon as we arrived at the palace—a grand building with a great arched entry and a vaulted hall within—we were introduced to a swarthy-skinned man wearing a snow-white turban. His name was Gaspar, he said. He is a magoi of the ancient religion of the Medes. He acted overjoyed at encountering Old Balthasar and me. Gaspar had also read the signs in the heavens. Leaving Barygaza on the coast of India, he had sailed first to the peninsula of the Arabs, then northward to Charax, then come overland to Ctesiphon. His express purpose was to journey to the land of the Jews to acknowledge a king whose birth he saw written in the stars.

He had arrived only a few days before we came, making the same assertion, which clarified why the audience was arranged with such alacrity.

The king's seneschal led us into the presence chamber, where we four lay facedown on thick crimson carpet until King Phraates gave us leave to stand.

The king looked just as he is depicted on the coins minted in

Ecbatana. That is, he was clean-shaven and wore a short braided wig. On his forehead was the royal wart. His face and body were fleshy, but evidence of the once-youthful warrior was revealed in his eyes and jawline.

At the king's command, Gaspar reviewed the sights in the heavens of the past year, explaining to the king their special significance to the Jews and the meaning beyond Israel to all worshippers of the One God.

At several points the king asked me to elaborate on certain technical aspects of the apparitions, nodding his understanding and asking perceptive questions about whether finding deep meaning in this year's celestial events was real or imagined.

Next Old Balthasar amplified the meaning by references to prophecies of the Jews, citing many sources, such as the prophets Isaias and Dani'el, to confirm both the sign of the virgin giving birth and the imminence of the prophesied event.

King Phraates listened carefully but remained cautious. "We are at peace with Rome—for the moment—though Caesar still covets our western lands, as does King Herod. Herod has had enough trouble with his own heirs. I do not think he will welcome one he is certain to regard as a usurper. If he thinks I am interfering in his affairs, he will complain to Caesar—or use it as a pretext to start a war."

"Nevertheless, sire," Old Balthasar said firmly, "we must honor our God."

"It is nearing sunset now," King Phraates said, "and the storm has passed. Show me the stars."

With that, we—the king, the guards, Queen Musa, and the two young princes we had met earlier—ascended to the rooftop.

At sunset the waxing half-moon stood almost due south, but it was not this unremarkable sight that excited comment. As darkness increased, the divine selection of this night to approach King Phraates became apparent. As if inscribed on the night by the single stroke of a pen, the line separating light from darkness on the moon's face ended exactly at the twin beacons of Saturn and Jupiter, all in a row. They were so placed that, even though the moon was many times brighter, it did not wash away the beauty of the other starry messengers.

"You see, Highness," Old Balthasar explained, "for my people this is significant. The moon of the Holy Spirit supports The Lord of the Sabbath and The Righteous, as all rise together in the sign of the Jews."

Bowing deeply, Gaspar added, "While I do not have the detailed knowledge of my brother, here, even among my people there is a tradition of One who is to come, bringing light to the darkness and signifying the end of an age. I too believe his sign in the sky and wish to worship him."

When two hours had passed, the king was convinced. "I have never seen such a sight. Jupiter and Saturn appear to draw the moon after them as if all are bound together. And you say this is just one among many unusual sights this year?"

It was then my place, as the king's astronomer, to confirm what a string of rare occurrences the sky had presented within the last nine months.

King Phraates made up his mind. "I will give you a writ of safe passage through all Parthia and letters requesting the same from the Roman governor of Syria and from King Herod. You cannot travel as official envoys. I will not risk that. But I won't hinder you from going."

It was then that Queen Musa made an unusual request. "My lord, why not send your son, Aretas, as your representative? He can bring you a report. The journey will be educational for him, yet his very youth will be proof of your peaceful intent."

"And why not send Prince Phraataces?" the king asked, an eyebrow uplifted. By reputation the queen would never let her son be away from her influence and protection for more than an hour at a time.

"Unfortunately, his health is too delicate; otherwise I would have suggested it."

And so we not only received permission to go to Judea but had a royal prince accompanying us.

CHAPTER 28

Zadok and Lem and six other men of Migdal Eder herded the flock of four hundred lambs through the Sheep Gate and onto the Temple grounds, where they would be washed and prepared for sacrifice during the Feast of Dedication. Coins in his pocket, Zadok made his way onto the Temple Mount to make an offering and pray that favorable news would soon come about the redemption of Obi.

Striding across the stone courtyard toward the Temple treasury, he spotted Hannah the Prophetess, sitting once again on the steps, surrounded by Herodian lawyers. The old woman fixed her eyes on Nicanor Gate. In spite of the stream of questions, she did not speak directly to her interrogators.

"Old woman! Who do you claim this child of the priest Zachariah is?"

Her lips pressed together tightly.

"Well, then, what do you say he is?"

No reply. Hannah's chin stubbornly raised, as though the trio of lawyers did not exist.

Zadok chuckled as he covered his head with his prayer shawl and paused before the offering trumpet. He whispered a baracha for Onias and one for Hannah as he tossed two silver shekels into the box.

"Have you nothing to say about this matter?" Hannah's interrogators continued.

Zadok peered toward Hannah. She closed her eyes and inhaled deeply. "It is written. Thus says the Lord: '*Behold, I will send My messenger, and he shall prepare the way before me: and the Lord, whom you seek, shall come suddenly to His temple, even the messenger of the covenant, whom you delight in: behold, He shall come, says the Lord of hosts.*'"[93]

This was not answer enough for the Herodian inquisitors. "Then are you saying Zachariah is the messenger spoken of by the prophet? Or his son is the messenger?"

Zadok knew this was an important distinction for Herod. If the son of Zachariah was the fulfillment of the prophecy, then Herod would have nothing to worry about. After all, it would be many years before the baby could open his mouth to announce the coming of the true King of Israel.

Hannah answered again with a prophecy concerning the forerunner of the Messiah. "Listen! The voice of him that cries in the wilderness: '*Prepare you the way of the Lord! Make straight in the desert a highway for our God! Every valley shall be exalted and every mountain and hill shall be made low. And the crooked shall be made straight and the rough places plain. And the Shekinah glory of the Lord shall be revealed, and all flesh shall see it together; for the mouth of the Lord hath spoken it.*'"[94]

"You speak to us in riddles, old woman! Tell us plainly who the child of Zachariah will be!"

Hannah smiled enigmatically and remained silent.

The lawyers put their heads together. "She's a clever old bag. If all she does is recite Scripture in the Temple, how can we charge her? What can High Priest Lord Boethus—or, for that matter, even the king—say if all she does is quote Scripture?"

It was a good point, Zadok thought. Hannah had taken refuge in the fortress of God's promises.

The chief lawyer probed, "Are you saying that Zachariah . . . or his son . . . is the Messiah?"

Hannah replied, *"Behold! I will send you Elijah the prophet before the coming of the great and dreadful day of the Lord."*[95]

Now they had her! Their eyes glinted like wolves. "You claim he . . .

someone is the Elijah? Who? What terrible day? Are you predicting the ruin of the kingdom of Herod? Are you saying Herod is not the true king of the Jews? Are you saying someone will overthrow King Herod? take his place? rule over his kingdom?"

Hannah closed her eyes. Her lips moved in prayer as though she waited for the correct answer.

Zadok, suddenly aware that he had caught the eye of one of the three officials, remained concealed beneath his prayer shawl.

Hannah whispered, "*Thus says the Lord: 'A shoot will come up from the stump of Jesse. From his roots a Branch will bear fruit.'*"[96]

Zadok knew the prophetic meaning of this Scripture that concerned his hometown. Jesse was the father of the shepherd-king, David of Beth-lehem. Though the kingdom of David had been cut down like a great tree, David's descendants, the stump of the great tree, still survived. From one of those lines of descent it was prophesied that Messiah, the Son of David, would be born.

Hannah did not stop there. "*The* Ruach HaKodesh *of the Lord will rest upon him. The Spirit of wisdom and of understanding. The Spirit of counsel and of power. The Spirit of knowledge and of fear of the Lord—and He will delight in the fear of the Lord.*"[97]

"Speak plainly, old woman! Do you say that one more wise than King Herod will usurp the Herodian throne and rule over Israel?"

"*He will not judge by what His eyes see. Or decide by what He hears with His ears! But with righteousness He will judge the needy. With justice He will give decisions for the poor of the earth . . . with the breath of His lips He will slay the wicked.*"[98]

The trio covered their ears and cried, "Treachery!"

Hannah smiled again. Zadok knew she was pleased that they had recognized themselves in that last Scripture.

She stood and raised her voice, turning the heads of all in the Court of Women toward her. The lawyers, stung as though they had been struck with a whip, backed away as a crowd gathered to hear Hannah's prophecy. "It is written in the book of Numbers: '*The oracle of one whose eye sees clearly, the oracle of one who hears the words of God, who has knowledge from the Most High, who sees a vision from the Almighty. . . . I see Him, but not now! I behold Him but not near. A star will come out of Jacob; a sceptre will rise out of Israel!*'"[99]

Fearless, Hannah raised her hands toward the sanctuary. Her voice resounded from every portico and chamber. "Hear, O Israel! Listen to the oracle of the prophetess! Thus says the Lord to you who live here and now! You will see him, and very soon! You will behold him, and he is very near! The Star has indeed come forth out of Jacob! The Sceptre soon will rise from Israel!"

Hannah claimed that the prophecy was on the cusp of fulfillment. The Star rising from Jacob was close at hand?

Everyone knew this could not refer to Herod or his offspring. There was not a drop of Jewish blood in Herod. And as for his children, they were a muddle of every mix and ruling power in the empire of Rome.

So, there it was. She had spoken plainly enough.

Hannah fell silent. With a sigh of weariness she groped for her seat and sat down heavily. She closed her eyes in repose as everyone in the Court of Women buzzed about the meaning of the encounter. Would the Herodian faction now have enough to convict the old woman?

Zadok thought of Onias, crucified for merely studying the records in search of the identity of Israel's coming King. He feared for Hannah.

A beggar boy about eight years old approached Zadok as he stood by the gate of the Jerusalem sheep pen and finished the final tally on the flock.

"You're Zadok, sir?"

"Aye."

The child held up a small parchment scroll bearing the red wax of Simeon's seal. "The old gentleman said Zadok'd pay two pennies if I found Zadok and gave him this message."

Zadok tossed the child a two-penny coin and read two words: *MY HOUSE.*

"A penny a word." Zadok shrugged and pocketed the scrap. He called to Lem, who waded through the shaggy herd, "Tell Rachel I'll not be home for supper."

CHAPTER 29

It was too late to return to Beth-lehem. The gates of Jerusalem had closed long ago.

Simeon provided Zadok with clean clothes. The two men sat in Simeon's windowless basement with the scroll of Genesis open before them to the story of Rachel's death in childbirth on the road to Beth-lehem.

Simeon rolled up the scroll. "Zadok, I'll tell you plainly: The word of the Lord has come to Hannah. She told me this morning that this is a matter for the shepherds of Beth-lehem first. She mentioned you by name. Your wife also. She made it clear we are to study together the Torah reading Parashah Vayishlach before the third watch.

The story of the birth of Rachel's second son Ben-Yamin. Zadok knew it well. He was uneasy hearing that the parashah of death in childbirth should somehow mean something to him. "Why me?"

"I make it a habit to listen when Hannah speaks. You'll know. You'll see." Simeon carefully wrapped the document and placed it in a cupboard.

Zadok's mind was heavy with exhaustion. He'd had little sleep the last few weeks. He yawned and hoped Simeon would soon offer him a quiet corner to curl up in. He looked longingly at the stone bench built into the opposite wall. It was covered with sleeping cushions and long enough even for someone the size of Zadok.

"Set me in a field watching a thousand sheep, and I can count the stars and stay awake. But here, in a closed room, I'm nearly done up, Simeon."

"Stay awake, my friend," the old scholar instructed as he slid the bolt of the door closed.

The distant call of the watchmen on the walls indicated the change of the watch.

"All right, then," Simeon announced. "There it is. I'm bound to show you, by Hannah's instruction, the secret your brother Onias learned. It is a secret for Levites, of which you are one . . . and for prophets."

In a few quick movements Simeon tossed the cushion from the stone bench onto the ground. Sliding his fingers between two joints, the top slab of the bench opened, sliding back into the wall. A shallow tray cluttered with plates and cups and spoons was within.

"That is clever." Zadok rubbed his eyes. "But I'd rather sleep on it."

"Take out the tray," Simeon instructed.

Zadok obliged, revealing another layer of linens beneath.

Simeon, betraying some impatience, scooped out the contents and heaped them on the table. Then he lifted the lamp, revealing the hollow interior of the storage space. Simeon slid his hand along the lower joint of stones and pressed inward. The stone bottom groaned and slid open with a whoosh, revealing a steep, almost vertical set of stairs that vanished into darkness.

"What's this?" Zadok peered in.

"A cistern from the days of Solomon. At first glance nothing out of the ordinary . . . yet. Come." Holding the lamp in front of him, Simeon stepped into the space. "Still tired?" he asked Zadok, who leapt after him.

The same terror and curiosity Zadok had felt as a boy exploring the caves around Beth-lehem rushed through him now. What mysteries were beyond the light? Zadok's broad shoulders barely fit through the narrow passageway. His head brushed the roof.

Simeon waited for him at the bottom of the cistern. He held up the lamp, displaying the raised carving of a seven-branched candlestick at eye level on the far wall.

Zadok shuddered. All sense of weariness vanished.

Simeon touched the flame of each branch of the candlestick from right to left and spoke the Hebrew names of the wandering stars of the heavens.

Holy Spirit ***Sabbath***

Messenger Star ***Righteous***

Splendor ***The Adam***

Holy Fire

The wall yawned open. The flame of the lamp was extinguished. The blackness was absolute.

Zadok's heart raced as he touched the cold stone. "We all heard the legend. The prophet Jeremiah and his scribe Baruch hid the Ark when Yerushalayim fell."

Simeon chuckled. "Not a legend. Now raise your three fingers against the wall. You will feel three distinct patterns in the stone, yes? Grooves that are one, two, and three fingers wide. Place your fingers into the slot that is three fingers wide and hold on. That's it. Hold on to the back of my tunic with your other hand. Step neither to the right nor the left."

"What is to the right and the left?"

A pause. Then Simeon murmured, "You don't want to know. Just hold tight. It's a long way."

They set out through the pitch-black tunnel.

Zadok hooked his fingers in the back of Simeon's belt and shuffled after the much shorter man. His right hand aloft, he slid his fingers along the course of the downward trek. To his right and left at various intervals he felt a waft of air, which was a signal that there were many openings along the way. Water dripped. The soft whistle of a breeze told his senses that the rock upon which Jerusalem was built was a honeycomb of secret passageways, caverns, and rooms.

"Where do the other trails lead?" Zadok asked.

"Other places."

"Other than where?"

"Other than where we are going."

Legend said that the labyrinth beneath the holy hill had been built by the masons of Solomon. Over a thousand years had passed since the first Temple of Yahweh had risen, stone by stone, on the very mountain where Abraham had offered his firstborn son as a sacrifice to the Lord.

How had Old Simeon become guardian of such a secret?

The groove above Zadok's head came to an end. Simeon spoke for the first time since leaving the house. "A good long walk, eh? A Shabbat day's walk."

Zadok did not remove his fingers from the slot. "Will there be light?"

"Hmm. Stay here."

Zadok heard the sound of stone grinding against stone in tortuous movement; then light escaped from the crack of a portal, causing him to shield his eyes. The scent of spices filled the air.

Simeon recited the Shema: "*Hear, O Israel: The Lord our God, the Lord is one.*"[100]

Zadok joined him as the two moved forward into a chamber that looked very much like the windowless room of a house. An oil lamp burned on a table. By its light, Zadok saw old Hannah sitting in a chair, carefully copying down text from the scrolls of Isaias.

She looked up and smiled. Her cot, unmussed, was evidence that she had not slept.

"Shalom, Hannah," Simeon said. "Here he is. I've brought him as you asked."

The old woman placed her quill pen on a dish and indicated that the two should sit on the bed.

"Welcome! Welcome! Sit down, Zadok, shepherd of Migdal Eder. I've been hoping for a word with you in private. No opportunity in the Temple. In the open. Herod's spies all around. Sit! Sit! My, you are a large fellow to fit indoors, eh? Much larger indoors than outside in the Temple court."

Hannah was very much like Grandmother in private, Zadok thought. Who would think from looking at her that she was the prophetess of Jerusalem? Who back home in Beth-lehem would imagine that he, Zadok, an ordinary shepherd of the Temple flock, could journey beneath the Holy City and in the end meet the prophetess face-to-face?

"What is this place?" Zadok blurted.

"My home," the old woman replied, her eyes twinkling with amusement. "Nearly sixty years. The Romans drove me underground. Beneath the Temple Mount. Ah, the people I've met in this chamber!"

Zadok gulped and looked around nervously at the old woman's belongings. A worn coat hung on a single hook. A water jar in the corner. This rope cot against the wall. A blanket. One lamp. One table. One chair. An open cupboard filled with scrolls of various shapes and sizes.

"They say you live in the cinnamon closet in the Temple."

"Half true. Beneath it. As you can see." She pointed up. "But Simeon and I must swear you to secrecy. None above are old enough to know what is beneath. What is below the Temple ground is yet undefiled by Herod's hogs rooting about. So we keep the secret, eh?"

Zadok nodded. "A very clever passage from one part of the city into the Temple walls. I heard as a boy that Hebrew soldiers used such a tunnel to escape the Assyrians. And that the Maccabees themselves knew the way in when they came t' win the Temple from the Greeks. So, now I've trod the path of warriors."

"It may be of use in the future." Hannah put her writing implements away. "No one else may know."

"He's trustworthy." Simeon lowered himself onto the floor and stretched out. "It's been a very long day." He closed his eyes and was almost instantly asleep.

Hannah continued. "Zadok, you've come from Beth-lehem."

Zadok replied, "Aye. Brought the lambs in from Migdal Eder. A big delivery to the Temple. The pilgrims, you see. So many. Because of the census the whole countryside is filled up."

"Even little Beth-lehem, eh? Crowded with strangers?" Hannah asked.

"Aye. To the brim. Them as come t' register often have relatives. Some come t' visit David's hometown. Drink from David's Well and pray at the tomb of Rachel. That sort of thing. Aye. The inn is always full these days. The whole land is burstin' with folk from all over. Never seen so many."

"The very subject on my mind." Hannah inhaled with satisfaction.

Hands on her knees, she leveled her gaze at him. "You watch the Temple flocks by night."

"Aye. We shepherds draw lots for time and day. It's a fair system. I spend my fair share of nights sleepin' outdoors. It's an honor . . . so they say. Watchin' over the lambs that are korban, set apart. I don't mind it."

"You've seen the stars. I mean, the signs."

"Aye. We've wondered what it foretold. The death of Herod's sons, most believe. But I've given it some thought. My brother Onias told me they portend the end of Herod and the comin' of Israel's true King." He laughed. "There! I've said it aloud. I can say it straight out and in the open since we're underground and can't be heard."

"Your brother was right. And he who is to come will come first to Beth-lehem." Hannah patted Zadok's big hand.

"I've heard the Scripture. Aye. It comes up from time t' time when folk discuss the Messiah."

Hannah quoted the passage from Micah: *"But you, Beth-lehem Ephratha, though you be little among the thousands of Judah, yet out of thee shall come forth unto me One that is to be ruler in Israel; whose goings forth have been from of old, from everlasting. Therefore Israel will be abandoned until the time when she who is in labor gives birth. . . . He will stand and shepherd His flock in the strength of the Lord, in the majesty of the name of the Lord His God."*[101]

"Aye." Zadok remembered he was in the presence of one who knew many more secrets than the one about the tunnel. "That is the very one I meant." He chewed his lip. "I am a fool. This is important, isn't it? I mean, you've summoned me here t' tell me."

Hannah patted his hand again. "You are no fool. The Lord reveals his secrets to the humble."

"I am that. My brother Onias is the clever one. I never cared much for studies. Lambs—that's my line. My wife. My sons. They're my life. The rest of it . . . well, I try t' stay out of the way of politics and care for my own. I'd die for those in my care if it came to it. But there's not much else concerns me."

Hannah looked away and clutched her heart, as though a pain had coursed through her with his words. "You are a shepherd. And understand a shepherd's heart. How hard it must be to give up your lambs."

"Here's the way of it. Since David was a shepherd . . . all the firstborn males in the flocks of Beth-lehem are set aside for sacrifice at the Temple. Every lamb that's perfect. Only the best lambs. It's my job t' see they're well born and cared for till the day comes I lead them through the Temple gates. Then I turn my back and leave them there—the place where my lambs must die as an atonement for a stranger's sin. The blood of my beloved lambs pays the redemption for another fellow's sin."

Zadok dropped his head and stared at his fingers. "If I think on it much, I don't like the system. That's the truth. I don't like savin' them so they can die. Poor wee things. Not that I understand it. It's just the way it is."

He spread his hands and studied his palms. "But, honored lady—Prophetess—you summoned me here for a reason. And I'm doin' all the talkin'."

"That's why I asked you to come. So I could understand. I saw you and your wife the day you redeemed the life of the slave girl's firstborn. I saw your heart. A good heart. And, you see, there was something I didn't understand. An image of slaughter that seemed beyond comprehension. But it must mean lambs and . . . I think I know what the vision means. You have explained it."

"What?"

"Why Beth-lehem? I asked myself. True, the Son of David is the Shepherd of Israel. Messiah will be our shepherd. Well, yes. But then I read, he will also be the lamb. Firstborn. It is written: '*He was oppressed and afflicted yet He did not open His mouth. He was led like a lamb to the slaughter.*'"[102]

Hannah shook her head in sorrow and muttered, "So, Lord, I see it clear enough now, why the Redeemer of our souls must be born in Beth-lehem. Firstborn Son, perfect and without blemish. He will be delivered among the firstborn lambs of the flocks of Beth-lehem that by law are set apart for Temple sacrifice. Firstborn. Korban. Set apart for holiness unto the Lord."

She lifted her eyes heavenward. "I must yield to this if it be true, though I wish it could be different. So . . . it is the echo of the sacrifice of the firstborn son that Avraham offered to God upon this very mountain.[103] Now God provides his firstborn Son, the perfect atonement sacrifice for the sins of the world.[104] This is the Word of the Lord."

Zadok still had no idea as to what Hannah was talking about or why she had wanted to converse with him. Yet she was a pleasant, seemingly ordinary old woman in the privacy of her own surroundings. Was there more?

Hannah roused herself. "Simeon! Wake up. It must be nearly morning. The gates of the city will open. Zadok the Shepherd must go home to his flocks! To his sons! To his wife!"

Pumbeditha, Kingdom of Parthia
Journal of Court Astronomer Melchior
14th of Kislev, Year of Creation 3754

The weather having remained clear, our caravan has made good time. After leaving the Tigris River at Ctesiphon, we journeyed across the lowlands of Mesopotamia. Today we reached the Euphrates, called in Holy Scripture "the Great River," at a village named Pumbeditha.

It was here that I, for the first time, got a true sense of being on a journey to Eretz-Israel, the land promised to God's chosen people. Many times I have heard Old Balthasar speak of how the Almighty pledged that the Jews will occupy all the region from the river of Egypt to the Great River Euphrates.[105]

Will this all come true when the new King comes into power? For surely the Jews of Judea, under Herod, under Rome, occupy no such possession today. Nor have they ever in their history, except perhaps in the days of King Solomon.

In any case, watering our donkeys in the Euphrates set me to pondering. Many weeks' travel still lie between us and Jerusalem. It makes me wonder if He whose heavenly signs we have been studying will at last forge this promised expansive kingdom.

Pumbeditha is home to a large settlement of Jews. Their forebears were part of those carried away captive to Babylon. After Babylon fell to King Darius of Media, not all returned to Judea. The great-grandparents of these in Pumbeditha elected to remain here.

They have preserved the faith of their ancestors, but they no longer look for a literal fulfillment of the prophecies, either about the land or about the coming of Messiah. Though Old Balthasar spoke with them at length, they countered with a superior attitude and the reply that "proper philosophy will bring in an 'age of Messiah.'"

This sentiment they may truly believe, or it may be that seeing Judea under the rule of Herod the Idumean has just filled them with permanent despair! Old Balthasar reminded them that it was in this month, Kislev, about 440 years ago, that Nehemiah received permission from King Artaxerxes to rebuild the wall around Jerusalem.[106] *He further pointed out that this is also the month to celebrate the cleansing of the Temple carried out by Judah Maccabee some 160 years ago. His message was this: Since the Almighty caused real miracles to happen for His people by way of earthly kings and heroes, why not expect Him to literally fulfill a miracle of even greater significance—namely, the coming of Messiah?*

They remained unconvinced.

Prince Aretas is an eager student and a pleasant companion. Though his father provided him with servants and a palanquin to carry him, he prefers to walk alongside Esther and me, discussing both prophecy and astronomy, as well as history and politics. Our new companion, Gaspar, participates as well, though he and Balthasar are continually discussing something. It is comical to watch the two of them—Gaspar leaning down from his camel and Balthasar craning his neck upward from the donkey.

One hour after sunset I was able to show Prince Aretas the conjunction of The Lord of the Sabbath and The Righteous as they stood due south of us. It is well we saw them then, because the rising Full Moon soon flooded the sky with silvery light. By three hours past sunset Jupiter and Saturn were sinking low in the southwest.

This, their third conjunction within seven months, fills me with awe and wonder . . . and also concern. What will happen now? Are the signs in the sky over? We are here, just halfway in our journey between Ecbatana and Jerusalem. Will the memory of what we have seen fade?

Old Balthasar is not afflicted with any such doubts. His eagerness continues unchanged.

I rose again before daylight. Just as the moon's disk sank and the sky darkened perceptibly again, Virgo was rising. Seeing again The Atonement Star at The Virgin's heart reminded me of what I have been allowed to experience this past year.

And then I was refilled with eagerness and excitement too.

CHAPTER 30

It was early morning when a rider dressed in the red-and-gold livery of Herod approached Beth-lehem from Jerusalem. He cantered slowly through the village, dismounting at David's Well to demand water for his horse from Sharona.

She refused, then abandoned her water jug and corralled her boys, taking refuge among a handful of other women who had come to draw water.

"I have an official message for Zadok, shepherd of the Temple flocks, from Habib, master of Herod's slaves."

Though his words seemed to be directed at her, Sharona did not reply. The fellow was a Samaritan, after all.

He remounted his horse, cursed all Jews and Jewish women, and galloped to the synagogue to get directions to the house of Zadok.

"What does it mean?" Sharona whispered. "From Habib, master of slaves?"

"Baby Obi," someone muttered. "He's come to demand the price. Should we warn Rachel?"

"No. Let's go get Havila."

"It can't be good news."

"Though what Habib would want with a one-armed baby as a slave I can't imagine."

Like a flock of birds, the women of Beth-lehem, young and old, moved together through the village toward the house of Rachel's sister-in-law, Havila.

Grandmother came to the door and cried out, asking who had died. Havila hung back, trembling at the sight of her friends and neighbors gathered around her front door.

Within seconds Eliyahu came running from the synagogue. The crowd parted for him.

"Havila!" he cried. "Come quickly! Rachel will need you! Herod's man has come to collect Obi or the redemption price!"

Zadok blocked the door of his house from the Herodian messenger. Rachel, Obi in her arms, stood behind him. Bear Dog, ears back as though ready to fight a wolf, crouched at Zadok's left.

The crowd of Beth-lehemites swelled as word passed from one to another that Herod's man had come to take Obi away. They halted, silent, at the gate of the low stone fence that circled Zadok's cottage.

Resolute, Zadok towered above the messenger. He held the paper in his hand as though it were a sentence of death for the child.

"The price is what it is, Shepherd!" the messenger demanded. "I didn't set it. As you can see, there's the seal of Talmai's signet ring. Lord Habib presented the case to Talmai, and this is the judgment."

"Thirty pieces of silver!" Zadok growled. "The price of a thirty-year-old male slave fit for fightin' in the arena. Whoever heard of such a thing? He's a babe!"

"A slave to King Herod's household, nonetheless. And, as you see, judgment includes the cost of his mother's life. She died in your care."

Zadok's eyes narrowed threateningly. Rachel put a hand on his arm in warning. To strike a blow now would mean death. "Thirty pieces of silver!" Zadok scoffed.

The messenger looked past him toward Rachel and Obi. "That's the price. You have three days to pay the redemption or he goes back to the palace. That is the will of Lord Herod. Defy it at your own peril." He whirled and strode from the house.

Mary and Yosef traveled the road through the hill country of Ephraim toward Sychar, which had been called Shechem, a city at the foot of Mount Gerazim. Shechem was known as the place of Yahweh's witness to Israel. The stones of ancient monuments and the tomb of Joseph the Dreamer bore mute testimony to the importance of Shechem. From Abraham to the present day, the history surrounding Shechem confirmed God's steadfast love for His chosen people.

Yosef and Mary recited the stories as they journeyed on a path etched by two millennia of history:

"It was at Shechem Avraham built an altar to the Lord who appeared to him and promised all the land to his descendants forever.[107]

"Two generations later, Avraham's grandson Jacob returned to this place from Paddan-Aram with his wives, Rachel and Leah, and a family of eleven sons. At Shechem, beneath the great oak, Jacob buried the idols Rachel stole from her father. Then the Lord appeared to Jacob at Bethel, reconfirming the Covenant of Avraham with him. Jacob built an altar there and called it El Elohe Isra'el—'God, the God of Isra'el.'[108]

"Several years later, at the age of seventeen, Joseph the Dreamer, Jacob's beloved firstborn son by Rachel, went in search of his father's flocks and his brothers in Shechem.[109]

"Joseph's last fond memories of his homeland were of the hill country surrounding Shechem. He named his firstborn son Manasseh, hoping to forget what he had left behind.[110] When at last Joseph lay dying, he commanded his children, 'You shall carry my bones up from here.'[111]

"Four hundred years later Mosheh the Deliverer led the descendants of Jacob out of the slavery of Egypt.[112] The bones of Joseph were carried before them through the Red Sea.[113] Then for forty years Joseph's coffin was with them as the people of Israel wandered through the wilderness.

"When Mosheh died, Joshua, son of Nun, became the leader of Israel.[114] Joshua, known in Hebrew as Yeshua bar Nun, was a chief of the tribe of Joseph's son Ephraim. Yeshua's surname, bar Nun, meant 'Fish.' Thus Yeshua bar Nun was identified with the blessing of abundance that old Jacob had given to Joseph's children, Ephraim and Manasseh.

"Under Yeshua bar Nun's guidance, the tribes of Israel crossed the Jordan with the Ark of the Covenant and the coffin of Joseph at the forefront. Yeshua bar Nun led the tribe of Manasseh into the city of Shechem. Finally, in Shechem, the bones of Joseph the Dreamer were laid to rest.[115]

"On Mount Ebal, Yeshua bar Nun built an altar of uncut stones and carved a copy of the Law upon a pillar. The Ark of the Covenant was placed in the valley between two mountains. From Mount Gerazim half the tribes shouted the blessings that would come from God if they would obey the Law. From Mount Ebal the other half shouted the curses if they disobeyed.[116]

"In Shechem Yeshua bar Nun set up a large pillar as a memorial for Israel. *'Behold, this stone shall be for a witness against us, for it has heard all the words of the Lord which He spoke to us. Thus it shall be for a witness against you, lest you deny your God.'*" [117]

This afternoon, shadows lengthened as Yosef and Mary continued to walk.

Mary remarked quietly, as if reading Yosef's thoughts, "How far our people have strayed since those days."

Yosef scanned the rocky slopes of Mount Gerazim, where Samaritan shrines had replaced the altars and memorial pillars of the patriarchs. How desolate and evil the place seemed. Yet these very stones had heard the rumble of God's voice! The Ark had passed over this very highway. Why did the stones of witness not cry out "Hosannah!" as the mother of the unborn King of Heaven and Earth rode through the Valley of Decision? How miraculous it seemed to Yosef that *all* the hopes of *all* the patriarchs and prophets for two thousand years were contained within the womb of one young woman riding humbly on the back of a donkey.

Surely Herod sensed Messiah's coming and trembled. Why else would the Butcher King send soldiers out to scour the land in search of Zachariah and Elisheba and their baby? Indeed, the whole world seemed to be waiting—some with dread and palpable hatred, others with hope and breathless anticipation. Like those who once shouted the blessings and curses from the slopes of Mount Gerazim and Mount

Ebal, both camps watched for the arrival of the Righteous One and a shining angelic host.

Blessed are you, O Adonai, who has kept your incarnation a mystery from the darkness! You have hidden your Son from those spirits of unseen darkness who roam the land seeking to destroy your plan.

A cold wind sprang up. Yosef tugged the fleece around Mary's shoulders. "Are you warm enough?"

"I feel them all." Her voice was hushed as though they had walked into the synagogue. "Ten thousand thousand who walked this road before us . . . and those who will come after. Yosef, it's as though no time has passed."

The hope and light of Israel and of all the world seemed a very heavy burden for one as young as Mary to carry. Yosef remembered the prophecy in Lamentations: *In His winepress the Lord has crushed the Virgin Daughter of Judah.*[118]

Shadows deepened. The sun hovered above the horizon.

"Sorry. We're later than I thought we'd be." Yosef scanned the countryside for shelter. "It's nearly Shabbat. We won't make it to the inn at Shechem before nightfall. Better find a place to camp."

Mary nodded. Her cheeks were chapped from the wind. Her eyes watered with the force of the gale howling down from the heights onto the road. They were on the loneliest, most dangerous stretch.

Yosef's thoughts were darkened by memories of evil Israelite kings who had divided the land with civil war and turned from the One True God to worship demon gods. The reality of the failures of the nation of Israel to keep their covenant with God somehow seemed tangible in this pass. The ancient oak of Shechem where the idols had been buried was now the heart of idol worship.

Above the storm Yosef thought he heard the wails of infants offered up as human sacrifices on the altar of Molech. Such memories mingled in his mind with the present threat of bandits who haunted the road and preyed upon Jewish pilgrims. Yosef regretted his decision to travel through Samaria.

"Yosef!" Mary's teeth chattered as she raised her hand and pointed toward three men, their features shrouded in heavy cloaks, striding purposefully toward them from the direction of Shechem. What were they doing out so close to nightfall? They could only be up to no good.

Too late! Too late to hide behind a boulder and wait for daylight!

Yosef led the donkey to high ground, a knoll beside the road. He positioned himself in front of Mary and grasped his staff in both hands. The weight of the sword against his hip was little comfort against three attackers, but perhaps his size and obvious prowess would deter them.

The three strangers did not hesitate at Yosef's warlike stance. Tucking their heads against the force of the gale, they strode forward.

"No matter what, stay behind me, Mary."

"Yosef! The Lord is with us!" Mary answered so quietly Yosef barely heard it.

Still, it was a reminder. Yes, the Lord was with them. As surely as if the Ark of the Covenant and the pillar of fire and all that signified the power and protection of the Lord traveled with them, Mary carried that presence within her.

"Yosef," she instructed, "lower your staff."

He blinked at the approaching enemies and turned to look at her. She was smiling. "What?" he asked.

"You don't see them?"

"Them? Yes."

"All of them?"

"Yes. Three scruffy fellows who look as though they would slit our throats, shove us into a ditch, and steal what little we have."

It was sunset. The men were barely thirty cubits away.

"Yosef? That's what you see?"

"Why . . . yes. Yes."

"Don't be afraid." Mary shook her head and slid from the donkey.

"Don't . . . don't . . . ," he stuttered.

What was wrong with her? Her face was beaming, as if she were greeting old friends.

"Don't be afraid." Standing beside Yosef, Mary gently took the staff from him and laid it on the ground.

The men drew nearer. Yosef thought he saw swords—hilts protruding menacingly from beneath their cloaks.

Don't be afraid, Mary said? But I am *afraid! O Lord! I am afraid for her! Afraid for the baby!*

The three men, in perfect step, almost a march, raised their right hands in unison. *Shabbat Shalom!*

Mary whispered, "O Adonai, open the eyes of Yosef, and let him see."

Suddenly Yosef heard wind chimes and voices—many voices—speaking in harmony, *Hail Mary, full of grace . . . Adonai is with you!*[119] *Blessed are you, and blessed is the fruit of your womb, who is Yeshua, the salvation of Yahweh.*

Yosef gasped as the appearance of the three brigands was transformed into a cohort of shining soldiers dressed in silver battle gear. Their swords and shields were upraised as an emblem of protection and honor. All eyes were on Mary.

Mary knelt, pulling Yosef to his knees. "My soul praises the Lord."[120]

Yosef covered his face. He glanced up, thinking the vision would be gone. Was he asleep? Was he dreaming?

The captain of the host, a fellow twice the size of Yosef and bathed in light, stepped forward. An angel, yes, with many angels behind him.

Then the image of many faded. Once again only three men stood before the couple.

They spoke. Yosef felt a voice rumble in his chest.

Mary, highly favored by the Lord. Yosef, honored guardian of the Ark and the Word she carries. We have been sent from Shechem, where we watch over the tomb of Joseph day and night. Many years ago the rabbi of the Academy of Joseph was told by the prophetess that you would come to his door. A faithful servant, he believed that the virgin bearing the Son of the Most High would rest in Shechem, just as the Ark of the Covenant rested there. He has remained in Shechem through trials and persecutions, though all others have fled and deserted the tomb of Joseph. The rabbi, a Tzadik, has made ready for your arrival every Shabbat night for many years. And now we must hurry.

CHAPTER 31

Baby Obi easily fit into Zadok's large hand. "You're a wee thing, Obi. And no use at all as a shepherd or a slave. But the fact is, I've grown t' love y' as sure as if you were born t' me." Zadok gazed into Rachel's worried eyes. Coins were spread out on the table.

After paying so much to smuggle Onias out of the country, not much was left. A year's savings and only a few coins. How could they pay the price for Obi?

"Thirty pieces of silver," Rachel whispered hoarsely. "Zadok?"

"I know. I know." The big man's lower lip trembled. He kissed the baby and shook his head. "Lad, I'd sell everything I own for you, and still it wouldn't be enough. Talmai and Habib have chosen to punish us for the death of your poor mother, though it was Herodian brutality that killed her."

A single tear splashed onto Obi's brow. "Ah, Rachel! I had such plans for the lad. Yes, I know. It would be hard for him at first with only one arm, but I dreamed I'd teach him how t' tend the flocks as good as any man. I knew a fellow once who lost his left hand to a lion. He did well with the flock with his right hand and his teeth."

"What can we do?" Rachel rocked Enoch to sleep. "Oh, Zadok!

I've come to love him. Enoch and Samu'el love him. He's part of our family. But thirty pieces of silver, Zadok! How?"

Warmth without fire. Fire without flame. Light without lantern. Yosef and Mary walked in the center of the three figures on the Road of the Patriarchs. Every detail of the countryside was vivid to Yosef's eyes, though he knew the land was shrouded in absolute darkness. The gates of Sychar were closed. They paused beside Jacob's Well. On the stone parapet above them Samaritan guards leaned on their lances and talked about women. They did not seem to hear or see Mary and Yosef.

The angel in the center was undeterred. He passed through the wood of the locked portal as if it were not there. Moments later the smaller pedestrian gate swung open, and the angel appeared, beckoning Mary and Yosef with a nod. The other two angels followed. Once they were inside the city, the gate locked behind them.

They passed the inn of Shechem, a dilapidated structure whose filth was evident by the stench of animal waste and human sewage in the street. Inside, drunken men and women cursed one another and God as they brawled.

This was the great city that Jacob had given as a blessing to his son Joseph the Dreamer? This was the city of blessing where Joseph's bones rested?

Yosef silently recited a prayer of thanks that they had not arrived in time to take lodging in such a place.

They walked uphill and through a labyrinth of stinking lanes for ten minutes. At the end of a twisted alleyway they came to a tiny gatehouse. It was joined to a larger structure that Yosef guessed was the synagogue. Feeble light beamed from two high windows. Except for this, the place seemed abandoned.

The three angels bowed deeply. *He is waiting. He has waited a long time. Hail Mary, full of grace. The Lord is with you. Peace be unto you.*

"And also with you."

Yosef, a voice whispered as the trio melted into the darkness. *Fear not. Yosef, son of Jacob, son of David.*[121] *Greater is He that is with you than he who is in the world.*[122]

The echo of raucous laughter sounded from somewhere in the

quarter. A dog yipped, returning Yosef's awareness to the present reality of a dark night in Samaria. He swallowed hard and knocked on the door.

It flew back, flooding the street with light. An elderly man, extremely plump, with a long, grizzled beard, squinted at them. "It is you!" he cried, reaching out to grasp Yosef's hand and tugging the couple and the donkey into the single room. "Quickly. Come in, children! Shabbat Shalom! Hurry! Off the street now before they see you!"

He slammed the door and shoved the bolt into place. "Shabbat Shalom! Welcome to the Academy of Joseph! Welcome! Welcome!"

The man cackled and stroked the nose of the donkey. "I'm Rabbi Yismah. 'He will rejoice!' So my father named me. Ah! And your names? She didn't tell me your names. Only said that you would come here where Joseph the Dreamer sleeps through these centuries. We sleep and dream and wait for the Redeemer, and now you bring him within you! I dreamed of the two of you and the donkey but never remembered your names. Always woke up before I heard the names. Unless . . . is it Yosef? Eh?"

Yosef answered, "I'm Yosef bar Jacob of Nazareth."

"Aye! You would be. Yosef. Like him. He was also called son of Jacob. Of course. And from Nazareth . . . aye. It is written that Messiah shall be called a Nazarene! So it is written!"[123]

"My wife, Mary."

"Mary. Aye! 'Bitter' is your name. Bitter sorrow will come through the night, but there will be joy in the morning.[124] All the bitterness of the human heart will be turned to joy. I've been awaiting your arrival for quite a long time. Over thirty years since the Roman caesar placed Herod the Idumean on the throne and called him king of the Jews. Many righteous men have died since that day, holding to the truth and hoping to see the hour of our redemption. Now you've come. Shabbat Shalom! Water to wash your feet. Water drawn from Jacob's Well. Bread on the table. Fodder there in the corner for your beast. Aye, waiting here . . . expecting you. Quite a long—very long—time!"

There was no bread to be seen. No table. The room was as sparse as a gatehouse stable.

Yosef recited the blessing for washing, then washed Mary's feet in the warm, fresh water. How he longed to talk about what they had seen!

The angels. But no hope of that. Rabbi Yismah would not be silent. It was as though he had not had anyone to talk to in years.

"I know! I know! It seems I am the last Jew in Shechem. All others have fled the Herodian persecution. He places Samaritans and Syrians over us to govern. So the others are gone. Dead mostly. But I am the rabbi of Joseph's tomb. The guardian. When the pagans scrawl obscenities upon the walls, I paint them over the same day and say a baracha."

Mary said, "We've heard of the guardians of the holy sites. Heavenly beings. Even in Samaria they say. Along the Patriarch's Road they stand watch near the holy places of Israel's blessing."

"You've heard?" The rabbi put a finger to his lips.

"We were shown the way to your house," Yosef replied, uncertain of how much to say. "Escorted."

"You saw them as well, then?" The old man wagged his head and lifted a lamp, illuminating the corners of the room. "Light and peace the angels bring. Fill the corners. But I'm the last of the human sort. All gone. All gone. Everyone has forgotten. Forgotten to honor Joseph's house as it is written by the prophet Amos. In the last days, it says, they will forget the destruction of Joseph's house.[125] Herod sent a troop of fellows to drive us out from the main hall because we preached that Messiah's coming was near. Killed my brothers. Desecrated the synagogue. But they didn't know about the other . . . now I'm the last. The last."

Rabbi Yismah tapped his temple. "I hid myself and hid the Torah. Hid the writings of the prophets. The scrolls. I came out after some weeks. Herod's soldiers have left me alive because they think I'm mad. No harm in a madman. The Samaritans hereabouts think I'm a conjurer because of what happened to the Herodians when they entered Joseph's tomb ten years ago to steal. Looking for money."

He hissed conspiratorially as he removed the pack from the donkey. "Lepers . . . all of them. Struck down with it. The Syrians worship demons and practice fortune-telling down at the old oak where Jacob buried the idols Rachel carried away from her father's house. It still goes on. It's the little failures that seem to take the worst effect, eh? Demon worship down at the oak after all this time."

Mary stared at the light. "The angels were . . . beautiful. Have you seen them here?"

"The Gentiles imagine there are no angels standing guard round

Joseph's tomb. They laugh and say Messiah will never come. But I told them, 'The Ark of the Covenant came this way and so the Daughter of Zion who carries in her womb the fulfillment of all Torah will rest one Shabbat day in Shechem. She will rest here in this house.'"

Rabbi Yismah sighed. "I have spoken truth . . . this was the prophecy of Hannah bat Peniel. So the people of Shechem call me mad. But I've been waiting here. Waiting for you to come. Every Shabbat. Everything ready."

His mouth spread wide in a toothless grin. He grasped Mary's hand and led her to the far wall of the room, revealing a door set so low in the stone that a man would have to kneel to pass through.

Lifting the latch he swung the door open on groaning hinges. Inside seemed to be a storage space. He dropped to his knees and indicated that Mary and Yosef must follow him.

At the back of the cupboard was another door. Rabbi Yismah opened it with a key. Beyond was a labyrinth of corridors and doors that seemed to lead nowhere. At last he opened an ordinary door.

Mary gasped in delight as she entered a room.

Yosef came after her into a tiny synagogue about fifteen cubits in width, depth, and height. By the light of a menorah Yosef could see the space was inlaid like a jewel box. It was richly decorated with deep blue-and-gold tapestries on the walls. The ceiling shone with stars in such accurate re-creation of the heavens that Yosef wondered for a moment if they were outdoors. There was an ark containing Torah scrolls on the wall facing Jerusalem. A bema was at the head of the room, and three rows of long benches on each side faced one another. In the center of the room was a table, where candles blazed. A complete Shabbat meal of wine, bread, lamb, cold chicken, and vegetables had been prepared.

Rabbi Yismah made a baracha. Yosef and Mary recited the Shema with him.

So many questions!

"You've traveled far." The old man escorted Mary to the cushions surrounding the low table. "Sit. Sit. *Ulu Ush-pi-zin!* Exalted wanderer! Honored guest! This is Beth Joseph. House of Joseph. The Herodians did not find it. And though Shechem was a Levitical city, no Levites remain but one. Only me. The last. The last. We've been waiting for you."

Yosef sank down beside Mary. The warmth of the room and the food arranged in front of them made him suddenly ravenous.

Mary asked, "How did you know we would come tonight?"

"Tonight?" The old man spread his hands over the table. "I have been preparing this very table for you every Shabbat, as I said, for something over thirty years. And before me there were others who made the Shabbat meal ready. And before them others . . . and before them, eh? This is the year he must come." Rabbi Yismah pointed up to the panorama of painted stars.

For the first time Yosef noted that the image was of Israel's constellation of The Two Fish and the wandering stars of Tzadik and Shabbatai, together in tight array. "I've seen such a sky!" Yosef exclaimed. "Every night for most of the year."

The rabbi answered by reciting the ancient family blessing of sons: "May the Lord make you like Ephraim and Manasseh." Then Rabbi Yismah made the blessing over the bread and broke it. He spoke another for the wine.

Mary dipped the crust in the hummus. "But . . . all this!" She gestured toward the feast.

"As it should be," Rabbi Yismah said, eating his hummus tucked betweens slabs of barley bread.

"Enough for a king," Yosef remarked, licking his fingers.

"Since those first days when our fathers crossed over Jordan—came out of the wilderness with Yeshua bar Nun at the head—Shechem has been a city of Levites," Rabbi Yismah explained. "Faithful servants here beside Joseph's tomb have been preparing the Shabbat meal in expectation of the Lord's coming since ancient times."

The rotund rabbi smiled and spread his arms, as if embracing the Sabbath feast. "Each Shabbat we lay aside worries. Put down our work. Is it a burden to pause for one day a week? to invite the Lord of Heaven to enter and share a meal with us? I look back at the meal Adonai shared with Avraham.[126] I look forward to the meal Adonai will someday share with all his people.[127] Though I don't see him with my eyes, I see you, Mary, blessed of all women, and know the ancient promise will be fulfilled. Soon."

A thrill of expectation coursed through Yosef. Was this day not proof that everything would go well? If such a beautiful place of worship could be preserved, hidden away and forgotten in the midst of the violence and corruption of Shechem, perhaps it was possible Mary and the child could go on their way unnoticed.

Rabbi Yismah talked eagerly between mouthfuls. "He comes to those who call his name. He abides with those who long to know him. I've felt his nearness. I'm nearly one hundred and twenty now. The generations have come and gone. Rulers and kingdoms. The Maccabees. Now Rome and Herod. Troubles. Striving. Politics. Corruption. Murder. All of it. Come and gone. But on Shabbat, for me the world does not exist. Never on Shabbat. Avraham would have rejoiced to see you both sitting at this table. You were barely a whisper of promise to our fathers. Now here you are, Mary. Real. Living. Perhaps Avraham does see you . . . you on your way to—"

He raised a crooked forefinger and jabbed the air. "To Bethlehem? The city of David, eh? Eh? I am blessed to see with my own eyes the virgin predicted from of old: she who will give birth to the Redeemer of Israel."

"But you know so much about us," Yosef said. "Our destination."

"Every detail—who you are, Yosef son of Jacob—is recorded in the Law and the Prophets. Your steps on this journey are ordered by the Lord from the foundations of eternity. Many years ago Hannah the Prophetess of Yerushalayim caught me by the sleeve and told me that each Shabbat I must never cease to watch and wait and prepare for the virgin Daughter of Zion and Yosef, son of Jacob. I thought she meant, somehow, that the Joseph of old would rise from the dead and come dine. The Dreamer who sleeps in the tomb."

He jerked a thumb toward the wall. "But no. He'll rise and come to supper when the Lord calls us all to supper, I suppose, and not before."

He scowled down at his plate. "Where was I? Ah! When I heard your name, Yosef, and the name of your father, Jacob—the same as the Dreamer and his father—it all became clear."

The rabbi patted his rotund girth. "You can see I've never failed to prepare for you. Though I didn't know what to expect. I've eaten many fine Shabbat meals since my youth."

Yosef scanned the ornate detail of the room. Clearly it had been built by skilled artisans. Perhaps even by the men who had crafted Solomon's Temple itself. "How has this room remained a secret?"

"It's a fortress. Enclosed on all sides. There. That wall. This space shares a wall with Joseph's real tomb. They've tried to find it. Tried to find the secret of it. The Assyrians. The Greeks. The Romans and the Herodians. But they didn't find it. No."

Rabbi Yismah blinked with satisfaction. "It's well disguised within a warren of rooms in the larger, public Academy of Joseph. Walls and corridors. This way and that. Shechem was a City of Refuge through the time of Israel's judges. Though we Jews in Shechem have fallen on hard times, the true Word and those who carry him have found refuge in the House of Joseph. Aye. As Joseph of old gave his brothers food and refuge in Egypt, so you now take refuge in Beth Joseph at Shechem."

The rabbi swirled his cup. "You're safe. Safe tonight. All tomorrow you must rest. An army of angels all around you. The journey is too great for you unless you rest. Shabbat rest for you both. And rest for the Son of David—the One whom heaven has proclaimed will soon be born King of the Jews."

CHAPTER 32

Zadok warmed his hands by the fire. His prayers were like the smoke drifting up through the hole in the roof.

Rachel, Obi at her breast, had cried herself to sleep. Obi would die of neglect in the palace of Herod. Such a little one, maimed as he was—how long would it be before he was put out in the cold night to die?

Zadok had learned early that the strength of a man consists of finding the direction God is going and setting his course on the same path. But tonight, loving Obi freely, which was God's course, was exacting a terrible price. The pain of love for this child, whom no one else would love, had thrust a spear deep into Rachel's heart . . . and his own as well.

Zadok considered the black lamb in the lambing barn. Still covered in the fleece of the dead lamb, he grew and thrived on his adopted mother's milk. If he was taken from her side for even a few moments, she stamped and bawled and grieved for him as if he were her own.

Well, Rachel's milk had nourished little Obi. Her breath on his cheek made him smile. He did not know she had not given him birth. She had forgotten he belonged to Herod's household.

Zadok closed his eyes and murmured a stumbling prayer. "Lord,

I'm a simple man. I've no great words like Eliyahu or my brother Onias. I'm not wise like Simeon at the Temple. But it seems to me that it would be a very good time for you to redeem us all. Aye, I know. That's a large request. So I'll scale it down, eh? Thirty pieces of silver. The price of a fine male slave. That's what Herod requires for the life of this innocent babe. It's said you own the cattle on a thousand hills . . . lambs, too.[128] Lord? All we need is thirty pieces of silver to buy his life."

Sleeping within the confines of Shechem's hidden synagogue, Yosef was not surprised to hear a voice whisper his name. His response was eager: "*Ulu Ush-pi-zin* . . . welcome, exalted guest. Joseph the Dreamer?"

Yes.

"Near this place where you—your bones—are buried, and which was part of your life many times, well, I've been expecting you."

We have much to talk about. Tonight you must learn more of your responsibility and why the time has come for Messiah to be born.

"I'm already so aware how small and powerless I am and how important is the birth of this child."

Yosef the Tzadik, your great gifts are your humility and your faith. But you are not so powerless as you suppose. Did you not learn today how your steps are ordered by the Almighty?

"True," Yosef admitted. "And you, Dreamer, are best equipped to say so."

So you have been rereading my life? Yes, my steps were ordered by the Almighty, but if I had doubted that truth at any point along the way, I might have missed the fulfillment. Listen: betrayed by my brothers, sold into slavery, falsely accused, cast into prison . . . who, hearing my tale, would not have advised me to "curse God, and die"?[129] *But then: raised to glory and power, still lonely for my family until at last able to save, deliver, and forgive them. Finally to see my sons receive the blessing of my father as his own children and heirs of the promised covenant.*

"Yes! Yes! A great mystery a long time unraveling."

Joseph nodded. *My story is one containing many shadows of things to come. But that is not what I came tonight to speak of. Tonight we must talk of mothers and trees.*

"Mothers and . . . ?"

Suddenly in Yosef's dream there were no synagogue walls or roof. He was outside, but it was day instead of night. The weather was warm, not cold. Across a small valley, near a pool of water, was a beautiful tree. The surroundings were lushly green, as on a day in late spring. The fragrance of many exotic fruits and flowers overwhelmed Yosef's senses.

When Mother Eve was tempted by the serpent, she was offered the fruit of a tree that would make her like the Almighty. She didn't need the tree for food. She could eat of all the other trees. The Lord fed Adam and Eve by His own hand. Why did she taste the fruit, knowing God had forbidden it?[130]

"Because she wanted wisdom enough to be in charge? She wanted to possess the power of God?"

She was unwilling to let God be God in the lives of her husband and her future children. In her love for them, she believed she could act better for them than the Almighty Himself. This has been the curse of mothers ever since.

Yosef understood.

The Dreamer continued, *The plan to redeem all creation from the curse of sin has been waiting ever since that day for the woman who would not repeat the error of Mother Eve.*

Abruptly it was high summer. The hot breeze smelled of dust and wheat ready for harvest and a calf roasting on a spit. The tree across the valley had metamorphosed into a grove of mighty trees. Beneath them, in the shade, rested a trio of men. An elderly man bustled about, attending their needs.

Yosef heard the sound of barely stifled, mocking laughter.

The Dreamer explained: *Avraham's wife, Sarai, was also given the opportunity to be humbly obedient. When The Lord of All the Angel Armies appeared to Avraham under the great trees of Mamre, Sarai listened to but did not believe the promise. Though Avraham told her to bake bread, she did not. Her offering of bread was not presented at the Lord's table. Even so, God gave her a son.*[131] *Even though she received the son of promise, heir to the covenant, she could not correct Mother Eve's mistake.*[132]

"Yes! I understand. Go on."

Now the grove of trees was replaced with a single oak. Its gnarled trunk was sturdy, but its limbs stretched eastward from many years of fighting the wind. Dark green leaves, tinged with red like drops of blood, fell from the branches as the gales of fall whistled through them.

Without being told so, Yosef somehow understood that the scene he now viewed was near where they really were.

The Dreamer drew a deep breath and sighed heavily. *Now we come to the part of this tale I know the best yet is the hardest for me to tell . . . because it concerns my own mother, Rachel.*

"Ah," Yosef murmured.

Do you recall how my father, Jacob, fled from his father-in-law, Laban?

"He was afraid Laban would not let him leave, or that Laban would cheat him out of his flocks, or that Laban would take Rachel away from him."[133]

My mother was also afraid. Not confident in God, the God of her husband, she stole Laban's idols of carved wood. Did she think they would bring her luck? Did she think possessing them would protect her from her father's anger? Perhaps she did not believe my father was heir to the promise of Avraham and Yitz'chak. She wanted my father to be the heir of Laban, and possessing the idols was the proof. But her motive for stealing the idols doesn't matter. The point is, she didn't have enough faith in the Almighty to let His plan unfold in her life and in the lives of Jacob, her husband, and me, her child.

"Again, just like Mother Eve," Yosef interjected.

Just so. I was there—a child of eight years. I saw her take the idols. I saw her hide them inside the camel's saddlebag and sit on it. I saw her lie to her father, claiming she could not rise because she was on her period . . . even though she was already pregnant with my little brother.

And I heard what my father told Laban: "If you find anyone who has your gods, he shall not live."[134] *In that moment my father pronounced my mother's doom.*

Yosef was shocked. As many times as he had heard the story of Rachel stealing Laban's idols, he had never made that connection before.

When my father was at last back in the Land of Promise, when it was time to reaffirm the covenant, he ordered his household to purify themselves.[135]

The Dreamer stretched out his hand and gestured toward the oak. *There, under the oak of Shechem, every one of my brothers and all our servants, buried their golden earrings, charms of good luck and the like, and the wooden idols brought back from the foreign land. And I saw my mother secretly throw Laban's idols into the grave as well.*

But it was too late! We moved from Shechem to Bethel. From Bethel we were on our way to see my grandfather Yitz'chak when the days were accomplished for my mother to be delivered of my brother, there in the lambing cave of Beth-lehem—House of Bread. And there she died.[136]

Yosef saw the image of a young boy standing beside a newly dug grave. The boy's shoulders shook as sobbing racked his thin frame. Busy cradling a newborn infant, the boy's father could not even interrupt his own agony to comfort his son.

Ben-Oni, my mother named my brother with her dying breath. Son of Sorrow. Son of my Sin. Son of my Failure. Son of my Wasted Effort. Yet my father called him Ben-Yamin, Son of My Right Hand.

There was a long pause in the narration, which Yosef did not interrupt.

So my mother, Rachel, given the opportunity to resist the sin of Mother Eve, also failed. She abandoned the false gods under the tree, but it was too late to escape the consequences of the Curse.

"I . . . I'm sorry," Yosef said, feeling in The Dreamer the lost and abandoned grief of a little boy whose mother was snatched away by death.

At last Joseph the Dreamer resumed. *The years come and go; the seasons repeat, but not endlessly . . . not without hope. Winter is coming, Yosef the Tzadik, and with it another woman who will face the choice to resist or repeat the sin of Eve.*

This time is different. This time the outcome will forever change the lives of men. This time at the House of Bread, Living Bread from heaven will be offered to all who are hungry.[137]

A breeze tickled Yosef's ears. He shivered as if a drip of water had run down his spine.

There is a tree in Mary's future as well, The Dreamer predicted. *Another mother of the promise . . . but also another tree.*

"Wait!" Yosef demanded, though Joseph's outline had gone wavery and his form translucent. "Wait! I'm afraid for her!"

I did not say there would not be sorrow, Joseph warned. *But remember my story. Don't give up hope in the tale before reading the ending. Keep reading, Yosef the Tzadik. Keep reading.*

The dreamer awoke, but The Dreamer had gone.

CHAPTER 33

Sunup came too soon, since Zadok had not slept. Distant hooves announced the return of Herod's messenger to take Obi away.

Zadok pulled back the curtain and glimpsed six riders pass the ancient tomb of Rachel on the way to the village.

Rachel, Zadok's wife, sat up. Her eyes reflected the terror of a dream from which she could not awaken. Obi stirred beside her and opened his eyes with a tiny bleat. Enoch and Samu'el likewise roused.

"He's here." Zadok spread his hands in helplessness. "He's brought several more besides, in case there's trouble."

"No, Zadok!" Rachel snatched up Obi and held him close. "It's not yet time. Another hour!"

"Rachel. One hour or one hundred. What can we do? I've prayed all night. All night. Feed the wee thing one last time. I'll not have so much money all in one place unless I become a bandit."

Fists banged on the door.

Rachel froze like a rabbit in the lantern light. "I can't. He'll . . . you know what will happen to him! Zadok?"

Outside came voices, urgent.

Eliyahu and Havila.

Grandmother.

Lem and Sharona.

"Zadok! Rachel! Hurry! They're coming! Herod's men are coming!"

Zadok threw back the door to reveal a hundred faces, maybe more. Friends and neighbors crowded into the yard. Eliyahu, wearing his prayer shawl, was at the head of his congregation.

"We've come," Eliyahu solemnly declared. "All of us."

Zadok warned, "If there's a fight, there'll be bloodshed. Go home. Go home."

Eliyahu, ever the rabbi, raised his finger to instruct. "If they take him, the blood of Rachel's heart will be on our hands. It is written in the Ten Words—we are commanded—*Ve-ahavta le-re'akha kamokha ani Adonai: 'Love your neighbor as yourself. I AM the Lord.'*"[138]

Grandmother nodded vigorously as the riders approached. "Thus ends the lesson. Get on with it, Eliyahu!"

"Yes, just so. Neighbors, it is written: 'All a man has he will give for love.' The word for *love* comes from *e hav*, which means 'I will give.'" Eliyahu presented a leather pouch, jiggling it loudly. "The price of firstborn redemption. Given by every son born this year and last in Beth-lehem. It's enough to purchase freedom. Count it."

And so it was that the life of baby Obi was redeemed from Herodian slavery by every infant son in the village of Beth-lehem.

Eliyahu advised, "Make them give you a receipt, eh?"

Hanukkah, the Feast of Dedication, brought with it the coldest weather of the year. On the seventh day of the festival, Yosef and Mary neared the end of their journey.

The Road of the Patriarchs ascended to Jerusalem from the north. Yosef and Mary, two days' journey south of the ancient village of Shechem, were within a few miles of the great city. Yosef led the donkey. Mary, wrapped in fleece blankets, rode.

She pointed. "Oh, look! Yosef!"

"It is beautiful from a distance," Yosef agreed.

The newly hewn stone of the Temple crowned the mountain like the snow of Mount Hermon. Yosef, who had worked on the edifice for several months, plainly saw that an additional layer of stone had risen on the northern wall of the Temple platform.

"It's different now than last time I saw it. I was just a little girl." Mary's voice betrayed her excitement.

When Herod's engineers and the army of builders completed the rebuilding of it, Yosef thought, the structure would be among the great marvels of the world. From the perspective of a few miles' distance, it was no surprise the city of Jerusalem had been the object of conquest for thousands of years. The holiday of Hanukkah was a perfect example of the violent history of Zion.

All the Near East, including Israel, had been conquered and occupied by Alexander the Great and his Greek armies three hundred years earlier. After Alexander's death, his kingdom had been divided among his generals. Israel and Jerusalem had eventually come under the control of the Seleucid dynasty ruling from Syria.

The religion of the Jews had been outlawed. Sabbath keeping and circumcision were banned. The sacrifice of pigs on the altar in the Temple and the worship of Greek gods were established. Though many Jews in the land exchanged their faith in the One True God for political safety, some stayed loyal to Yahweh.

One of these was an old priest named Mattathias, who had lived in the village of Modi'in one hundred and sixty years earlier. He had five sons, including Judah Maccabee, who rebelled and drove the pagans from the Temple, from Jerusalem, and from the land. When at last Jerusalem was liberated, Judah and his brothers reclaimed the Temple from the Greeks. They found only enough purified oil to light the Temple lamps for one day. However, when they lit the Temple menorah with it, the seven-branched lamp burned for eight days. It was a miracle—and the light remained long enough to purify the Temple and send word to the priests and people throughout the land. Once again Jerusalem was the Holy City, where the Name of the One God was worshipped.

Every year since that time, Israel had celebrated the Feast of Dedication. It was the most terrible irony that once again a foreign king ruled in Jerusalem, Yosef thought, as he and Mary approached the city. Though Herod might pretend to be a Jewish convert, the alliance with Rome that established his reign proved otherwise.

Once again, no matter how white the stones of the Temple Mount glistened, there were moral filth and corruption within the walls.

"One night in Yerushalayim," Yosef remarked. "Then we'll press on to Beth-lehem to register. And then home to Nazareth."

Mary agreed. "In the morning I want to visit Naomi's grave. Say *kaddish*. Offer two doves at the Temple. I promised Mama. Naomi's buried just outside the eastern walls."

Her expression fell. "I hadn't thought till right now that this view was one of the last things Naomi ever saw. Mama said she was so excited. Nearly the same age I was the first time I remember making aliyah. Oh, Yosef! She was so young. Her life hardly begun. I didn't think I would miss her so much."

Yosef nodded. His gaze fell on a procession of a company of one hundred horses surrounding slaves bearing royal litters. The banners of Herod fluttered in the wind. The king's entourage emerged from the city gate to the sound of trumpet flourishes.

"Herod," Yosef said. "Too cold for him in Yerushalayim. Last year he stayed in the city through Hanukkah, then moved to Caesarea. They say he hates the cold."

Mary's brow puckered in a frown. "Then he picked a bad day to travel."

A rider galloped toward them, shouting, "Make way for Herod, the king of the Jews! Make way for King Herod! Off the highway, scum! Get out of the way!"

Yosef led the donkey off to the side of the road as the parade rapidly approached. Prancing horses and uniformed lancers projected the warning that none should dare block the way of the great King Herod.

Yosef stroked the donkey's nose and observed Mary's expression. Her eyes narrowed. When a trooper stared at her face, she looked quickly down, riveting her gaze on a clump of sagebrush.

The curtained litter of Herod drew close. Yosef heard a ragged cough from within.

Mary blinked as if the human sound had startled her. She shuddered. Yosef shared her apprehension. It was as though some very dangerous and evil animal stalked them. And they were too near . . . literally within a few yards.

Yosef thought of Herod's sons, strangled at their father's command. Words like *murderer* and *demon-possessed* raced through Yosef's head. He turned away lest somehow the Butcher King peek through the curtain, read Yosef's revulsion, and leap shrieking from his lair to rightly accuse Yosef of treasonous thoughts.

Blessed are you, O Adonai, who hides the true King of Israel where evil cannot think to find him. Blessed is the Son of David, who will one day truly purify your Temple with his Light.

34 CHAPTER

Yosef and Mary spent the seventh night of Hanukkah at a small inn just inside Jerusalem. In the morning, after prayers, they found Naomi's grave.

"It is a storm. A terrible storm." Mary stared at the stone with Naomi's name carved on it.

"I'm sorry." Yosef knew she was not speaking of the weather.

"Death blows in like a wind from who knows where and tears our lives apart. Nothing will ever be the same."

"Your mother. She'll be glad we found the grave," Yosef said.

"Can there be anything so terrible . . . ever . . . for a mother as watching her child suffer and die? Helpless. And then to have to go on living . . ."

"No, I suppose not." Yosef sat down beside the grave. "No pain like the pain of loving someone more than your own life and not being able to take your child's suffering on yourself."

"Poor Mama. Naomi was her baby."

"I'm sorry," he repeated lamely.

Mary's fists were pressed tight against the sides of her head. Tears brimmed in her eyes and threatened to cascade down her cheeks. "The

Lord picks us up in the palm of his hand and moves us to higher ground, but it's *never* the old familiar ground we loved. *Never* the same as before. Something is gone forever now. I've lost something. Believing that everything would always be easy, I suppose. I've lost . . . what is it?"

"Death came to the world by the loss of innocence." Yosef could not bear the sadness of her expression. He had to look away from her as he spoke. "Now when death comes, it seems to take our innocence with it. A great and terrible enemy, death is. Maybe he will change everything. Put the world back right. Restore our innocence."

"We'll all be like babies again. Yes." Mary sighed. "It would be so fine, wouldn't it, Yosef? But too late for my little sister. Mama says Naomi talked about the baby. How happy she was that he was coming soon. Last of all, that's what she talked about. Just before . . ." Mary's head bowed in her grief. Then she continued in a soft voice, "Mama says Naomi wanted to hold him so badly. But now she won't."

Yosef studied his rough, calloused knuckles and wondered if he should say aloud what he had been thinking ever since they heard that Naomi had died. "Mary? I think—I *believe*—that Naomi must have got her wish. I think maybe *he* held *her* . . . you know?"

Mary nodded slowly as his words sank in. "I'll tell Mama. It's a good thought. I will tell her."

Blessed are you, O Adonai, Yosef breathed, *who will someday conquer the storm. Our sorrow is immense—a wave that threatens to wash us overboard. Blessed are you, who will not be conquered by the force of the gale.*

The road from Jerusalem to Beth-lehem was far longer and much harder than Yosef ever expected. Unsuccessful at holding back dusk and cold, the sun had already given up for the night. Now their progress was even slower.

And Mary was in labor.

How could this happen? Just over halfway from the Holy City to the City of David her water broke. The baby was on the way, and all that remained to be decided was where he would be born. It was farther to go back than to press on. There was no other shelter nearer than Beth-lehem.

Sensing the trouble they were in, Yosef hoped he did not communicate his worry by either his words or the tension he felt in his face and shoulders. Urging the donkey to move faster, at times he seemed to be dragging it.

Mary was in pain. Successive waves of contractions gripped her, making her gasp and bite her lip. Her hair escaped from her scarf and hung in tattered, damp clumps around her strained face. When she was gripped by the agony, Yosef walked beside the donkey that carried Mary, steadying her.

As each crushing spasm passed, Mary hauled herself upright, smiled through gritted teeth, and nodded to show Yosef she was all right. Her look communicated trust. She relied on him to get her to a place of safety.

She trusted him. Yosef was supposed to be her protector, yet here she was, in the middle of nowhere, about to give birth. She had no mother or other woman to comfort and guide her through the ordeal that was now just beginning. She did not even have a warm room and a secure space.

"Yosef!" Mary gasped. "It . . . will be . . . all right. Don't worry."

Not able to speak without railing in anger and frustration, Yosef gave a wave of his hand and kept trudging forward into the growing dark. Why could Mary not be home in Nazareth, surrounded by her family?

Still on the main north-south highway, they passed the dark bulk of the ancient tomb of Rachel.

Yosef, convulsed with fear, silently fretted: *Oh, God! You can't mean that as a sign to me! It won't work! Your Son cannot be born into the world at the expense of Mary! No!*

A reddish star hung low in the southwest, and over it, a two-day-old moon. The pair formed a bow launching an arrow toward where Beth-lehem lay. In Yosef's memory, the village was only behind another low range of hills. "Nearly there, Mary. Hold on."

Over the summit Beth-lehem and the surrounding vale of Migdal Eder sprawled across their view. The windows of small white houses glowed with lantern light. In the courtyard of the caravansary a fire sparkled. Yosef kept his eyes averted from Herodium, only three miles away to the southeast. The night was full of terrors enough already.

The evening rang with raucous laughter and general revelry.

Camel drovers and herdsmen drank and sang during the last night of Hanukkah celebrations.

But where there was a caravansary, Yosef reasoned, there was also an inn . . . and help.

As they entered the gate of the caravansary, Yosef glanced back at Mary. Her eyes were closed, shut tightly against the vise that she said clamped around her middle. She swayed on the donkey's back, barely managing to hang on. Yosef jumped to her side, helping her down beside the watering trough.

"Let's get you inside," Yosef said.

"I . . . not just now, Yosef. Let me sit still a moment. You see to the room."

The central square was crammed full of animals and people. The fire Yosef had glimpsed from afar resolved itself into a dozen campfires. Travelers were packed all around them, pushing and shoving to get nearer the warmth. Nearby a fight broke out. Yosef had to push through a ring of spectators encircling a battle where two men battered each other with cudgels.

Yosef took the steps to the second floor of the inn two at a time. He had to hammer on the door to get it open. When at last it swung inward, the way was barred by a heavy, jowled man in wine-spattered and grease-stained robes. Waves of odor and sound rolled past the blockade—soured wine and too many bodies, debauched laughter and coarse humor.

"Need a room! Quickly!" Yosef ordered.

The innkeeper shook his head and snorted. Moving one shoulder aside, he let Yosef peer inside. There were so many occupants it was not even possible to see across to the other wall. Jugs of wine were passed over the heads of the mob, contents sloshing and spilling. Three men fought over a girl. A serving man standing in a corner flung loaves of barley bread into the mob, as if afraid to step into its grasp.

"But you must have a room. At least one!" Yosef demanded.

"Not a prayer of one. Four caravans stopped here tonight. Two companies of Herod's soldiers. A Roman centurion on his way from Egypt to Syria. Courtyard full. Rooms taken. Houses all spoken for. There's nothing at all."

"But you must help! My wife's having a baby!" Yosef pleaded.

The innkeeper pressed his bulk outward and Yosef backward with it, as if afraid Yosef would try to force his way inside. From the landing the innkeeper pointed toward where a streak of limestone showed as a bright gash on the dark hill opposite. "Try there. Lambing cave. Kind of a stable, but out of the night air. That's all."

And he slammed the door in Yosef's face.

Tadmor, Kingdom of Parthia
Near the border between Parthia and Roman province of Syria
Journal of Court Astronomer Melchior
1st of Tevet, Year of Creation 3754

Tonight was the New Moon, marking the first of the new month and the beginning of the last day of the Feast of Hanukkah. I record this with both certainty and joy because today was the first time in two weeks we have seen sun, moon, or stars.

Since the last time I viewed the heavens there has been constant rain. The roads are sloppy, sometimes impassable by day. Our beds are soggy by night.

Old Balthasar grew stiff in every joint and his breathing labored. Esther worries about him constantly. Prince Aretas and Gaspar have combined to extend every comfort their equipages could provide. Prince Aretas donated his pavilionlike tent to Balthasar and Esther, while he moved into the much smaller one belonging to his guards. His guards, meanwhile, sleep outside or take turns huddling two at a time under an awning barely big enough for one. I have heard them muttering, complaining about "the old Jew."

Gaspar produced a saddlebag full of the hardened yellowish tears of resin called lebanah, or frankincense. He caused his servants to place a quantity worth a month's wages in a cauldron of boiling water. Every night this steamed the interior of Balthasar's lodging with sweet fragrance. It did relieve his chest and help him to sleep.

Now we are in the village called Tadmor, or by some, Palmyra. We wait here while a paid courier travels to the Roman legion post across the border with our request to proceed into Roman lands. The transaction could have been speeded up with a few well-placed bribes, but all of us can use the rest. For once, even Old Balthasar wasn't urging haste.

CHAPTER 35

"Where is the miracle of Hanukkah?" the people asked Hannah the Prophetess as they gathered in the Court of Women for the final night of the holiday. "You told us Messiah would come before Hanukkah came to an end. Where is he then?"

As was her custom, the old woman sat beside the storage room for wine and oil at the base of the giant menorah that towered to the height of the Temple walls. This Festival of Lights, also called the Feast of Dedication, commemorating the cleansing of the Temple, was her favorite feast. After all, it was pointed out that Hanukkah contained the name of Hannah within its first letters.

She who had lost a husband defending the Temple against the desecration of Rome often spoke the Scriptures that said the Anointed One would come suddenly to the Temple and cleanse it. She prophesied that His Light would shine so even the blind of Israel would see it and rejoice.

"He must come among us tonight exactly as the Haftarah Shabbat reading for Hanukkah proclaims! *'But I will dwell among you—then you will realize that The Lord of All the Angel Armies has sent Me to you. Yahweh shall take Judah as a heritage to Himself for His portion upon the Holy Land,*

and He shall choose Yerushalayim again! Be silent, all flesh, before Yahweh, for He is aroused from His holy habitation!'"[139]

The torchbearers touched flame to the eighth bowl of the great light.

Whispers of amazement swept through the Temple courts. The pilgrims looked up at the blazing lights of Hanukkah. They gazed expectantly at the stars in the heavens, but heaven seemed very distant from Jerusalem.

"What is the old woman talking about? Is she saying Messiah is coming tonight? coming to earth this very night to save Yerushalayim?"

Hannah spoke again. "'*Behold there will come a time! And the light of the moon shall become like the light of the sun, and the light of the sun shall become sevenfold, like the light of seven days, when the Lord binds up His people's wounds and heals the injuries it has suffered! . . . In that day, there shall be neither sunlight nor cold moonlight, but there shall be a continuous day, of neither day nor night, and there shall be light at evening time. . . . Your sun shall set no more, your moon no more withdraw; for the Lord shall be a light to you forever! . . . Cause a new light to shine upon Zion and soon, soon, may all of us be worthy to enjoy its light!'"*[140]

She stood up and cried out to the multitude, "People of Israel! People of Yerushalayim! Listen to what the Lord says to you tonight! This very night! Yes! This is the miracle of the Light that shines forth for us on the eighth day of Hanukkah! '*The light that burns, though there is no oil! On this very night, the people that walked in the darkness have seen a brilliant light! On those who dwelt in a land of gloom, light has dawned!*[141] *Tonight heaven proclaims to all in Yerushalayim and the waiting world: "Arise, shine, for your light has dawned; the Presence of the Lord has shined upon you!"'"*[142]

Herodian scribes marked down Hannah's words and discussed if any of them might be taken as treasonous against King Herod or Rome. All these sayings were gleaned from the readings for each night of Hanukkah. Was this treason? Was she rousing the people in Jerusalem to look for a Messiah who would never come?

High Priest Boethus stormed with his entourage into the Chamber of Hewn Stone. "Let her live! Let her speak nonsense to the people. Her predictions of Messiah never come true. By her word, all Yerushalayim and all the people were expecting him tonight! Expecting him to ride in on a white horse and slay us all and cleanse the Temple. But Messiah didn't come, did he?"

Boethus laughed and snapped his fingers. "And he isn't coming. The legend of Messiah will die. Who will listen to Hannah and her Hanukkah promises after this night, I ask you?"

The eighth and final candle of Hanukkah burned low. Wax dripped on the table of Rachel's tidy house. The embers of the fire glowed softly. Smoke and dried lavender mingled in a pleasant wintertime aroma.

Rachel, Havila, and Grandmother were alone with the children tonight. Supper was long over. Plates had been cleared from the table. The children slept like a pile of puppies on the sheep fleece.

"Has there ever been a night so cold?" Havila asked.

"And our men out in it too. It was very fine of Eliyahu to stand Noah's watch on the last night of Hanukkah," Rachel said. Once an hour a pair of herdsmen walk the circuit of the slumbering sheep, and tonight the shepherd Noah was sick. So Rabbi Eliyahu, himself the son of a shepherd, had offered to fill in for the man. Rachel fetched another fleece to lay across the three boys—Enoch, Samu'el, and Dan. Baby Obi slumbered soundly in his cradle.

Grandmother brought mugs of hot cider. "It has always been the lot of a shepherd. Freezing nights. Hard ground. Little sleep. Holy Days, feasts, and what does it all matter to a shepherd? The sheep don't care it's the last night of Hanukkah, eh?"

Grandmother lay down on Rachel's bed and closed her eyes. "My own Boaz—that was your grandfather, may he rest in peace—died on such a night as this, watching the flocks. I can tell you this . . . the sheep never mourned his passing, though Boaz—may he rest in peace—gave up most of the Holy Days for the wooly brutes." Grandmother sighed and drifted off to sleep.

Rachel winked at Havila. "Well, there it is. My Zadok, your Eliyahu, and Sharona's Lem, too, are guarding the ungrateful sheep of Migdal Eder."

Havila sipped her cider. "We should have invited Sharona and her boys for supper. She's alone since Lem's lot was drawn for the watch tonight."

"Sharona! Alone!" Rachel snorted. "Never. You and I delivered all her sons. She's the least alone of any woman in Beth-lehem. And I wouldn't have wanted such a pack in this little house tonight."

The drink warmed her as she sank down beside Havila and patted Havila's tummy. "Oh my!" Rachel felt the movement of the baby. "She's wide-awake in there."

"She?"

"A girl. You're carrying her high. And besides, so many boys delivered in Beth-lehem this year. We're due for a few ewes in the flock."

"I'm ready. You know, Dan was born in the summer. I thought that was bad. But the cold. My bones ache."

"You're getting along. A little peace. That's what you need. And you don't need such a rowdy herd as Sharona's boys hanging from the rafters."

"True." Havila smiled. "A quiet night. I haven't minded at all, to tell the truth. Eliyahu is no doubt enjoying the camaraderie of Zadok and the other men."

"They don't seem to mind the nights away from home. They talk politics and spin yarns about lions they've killed." Rachel laughed. "More like rabbits they've snared."

"This little one is spinning . . . spinning. Maybe it'll grow up to be a shepherd too, eh? My back. I'll be glad when this pregnancy is done and I can bend down to latch my shoes again."

The two sisters-in-law cradled the mugs in their hands and stared at the coals in silence. Rachel thought about other Hanukkahs, when the house had bulged with visitors and Mama had been alive. She never missed Mama so much as this time of year. Papa too.

Havila murmured, "I miss my mother."

"You've read my mind."

Havila bit her lip. "What is it about Hanukkah? I'm always so . . . let down when it comes to the final night and the candles burn out and . . . nothing has happened. I mean . . . nothing really."

Rachel nodded, understanding the vague feeling of disappointment. "Yes. I had hoped . . . felt that something . . . something wonderful would happen this year before Hanukkah came to an end."

Truth be known, Rachel had hoped and prayed that Messiah would ride onto the Temple Mount with His army behind Him. It was not the sort of thing the wife of a Temple shepherd could speak aloud. "Ah, well. Next year, eh? Maybe next year?"

"It will be the same next year." Havila drained her mug. "It's always the same. Only more so."

Rachel rose and went to the window. Opening the shutter a crack, she gazed across the terraced hills and little houses of the village into the valley of Migdal Eder. The distant watch fires of the shepherds gleamed. The sky was especially bright.

Which were the fires of earth and which the stars of heaven? On this, the longest night of the year, the line seemed blurred. *Beautiful. If only! If only!* It was as if there were no separation between the two, yet, Rachel knew, the gulf between heaven and earth was vast.

36 CHAPTER

This was not the way it was supposed to be! Was it? Yosef's senses reeled as he led the donkey toward the mouth of the cave.

Mary's breath caught as yet another contraction slammed her. She leaned forward over the neck of the beast. "Yosef?" she panted. "Yosef? How . . . soon?"

"I'm sorry, Mary. So sorry."

"Where . . ." Her words, punctuated by agony, came seconds apart. "Where . . . is . . . it? I . . . can't . . . Yosef? Need to . . . lie down . . . the pressure . . ."

"Wait. Not yet, Mary! We've got to find shelter." He tried to pray. Hollow, terrified words seemed to fall to the ground. *Blessed are you . . . O Adonai! Help me! Help her! O Adonai!* Yosef tugged harder on the lead rope. *O Lord! What do I know about delivering a baby? It wasn't supposed to be like this! Why does the donkey move so slowly?*

Faint lamplight shone from the opening of the cave.

"There, Mary, I see it! Hold on! Right there. And I'll find help."

"There. Better." Her voice was almost strangled. "Better. Oh! It passed. Yosef! Please hurry!"

He could go no faster. He called toward the lamp in the stable. "Shalom! Anyone within?"

A sleepy boy of about ten appeared framed in the doorway and squinted into the blackness. "Aye. I stand the watch on the ewes tonight."

With each step Yosef explained, "I need help, boy! My wife is in labor. Having a baby. You understand? No room for us at the inn. They sent us away. Sent us here. Clean straw. Water. A stall." They entered the circle of light.

The boy gawked at Mary. "But, sir, this is the lambing stable. You'll be needin' . . . someone else."

"No time." Yosef could plainly see now that blood dripped from Mary's foot. He lifted her from the donkey and carried her in his arms across the threshold of the cavern. The animal, at home with the scents of the barn, followed them into the shelter.

The boy jabbered with excitement. "We're full up too, sir. Lambin' time. I'm to fetch my father, Lem, and the shepherds if a ewe begins her labor. A quiet night tonight till you came."

Mary buried her face against Yosef's shoulder and groaned as agony closed around her. "Oh. Another one." Her breath was shallow. "This time . . . oh!"

Yosef felt the warmth of blood and water through her clothes.

"Lord . . . have . . . mercy . . ." Mary panted.

"Hold on, Mary! I'll find help."

The stableboy picked up the lamp and hurried ahead of them, looking from pen to pen for one empty stall. All were filled with ewes, sides bulging with lambs soon to be born. An ox knelt next to the only vacant cubicle.

The boy held up the lamp. Light fell on a mound of clean fodder that overflowed from a manger. "Here, sir! Will this do? This one. Bring the lady in here, sir! Aye. That's it. Lay her down here."

Yosef gently lowered Mary onto the soft bed of hay. Her face was ashen. Sweat streamed from her in spite of the cold. She was trembling. "Boy! Hurry! Fetch my pack from the donkey." Then to Mary, "Mary? Mary, can you manage? I'll find help."

Mary nodded. The contraction passed. She smiled, caught her breath, placed one hand on his cheek. "Yosef. So good to me. Always . . . I . . . never thought . . . at home . . . my cows . . . they make it look much easier than it is."

Yosef swallowed hard and shook his head. "Not supposed to happen like this. I thought, you know, your mother would be near."

"Me . . . too." Her teeth chattered with the shock of blood loss. Another pain gripped her . . . crushing . . . crushing. "Pray . . . Yosef! Please . . . pray for me. . . ." Mary squeezed her eyes shut and curled into a ball. This time she said nothing.

Clearly the pains were accelerating in time and intensity. Blood stained the straw beneath her. Too much blood, Yosef noted. *As if she were crushed in a winepress.*

The stableboy rushed to bring the pack. He halted midstride at the sight of Mary. "Is she dyin, sir? I've seen ewes die in this very stall. It's said Rachel herself—I mean the first Rachel, wife of Jacob—died in this very same cave. Bringing forth Benjamin, so they say."

"Hold your tongue," Yosef commanded as he daubed perspiration from Mary's brow. Her eyes reflected agony. Was it supposed to be so hard?

Yosef rubbed his head. *What to do?* He barked, "Boy! Is there a midwife in this town?"

"Aye, a good one. Named Rachel, wife of the shepherd Zadok. Brung me and my brothers forth, as my mother would say. Every one of us."

"Go! Go get her! Hurry, boy! Tell her . . . tell her . . ."

The child stood blinking down at Mary an instant too long. "Tell her . . . the lady's in a bad way, sir? She is, isn't she?"

Yosef roared, "Just go! Run! Fetch the midwife back!"

The boy, jarred from his stupor, wheeled and bolted from the cave.

In the distance Yosef heard an echo from the amphitheater of Bethlehem's hills. It was the treble voice of a child crying out the name of Rachel.

Young Jesse stood wide-eyed and trembling outside the door. "The man says you've got to come quick, Rachel! She's in a bad way. She's very young, I think. And he's scared."

"But the lambing cave?" Havila questioned as Rachel pulled on her fleece boots and coat and checked her leather midwife's bag for supplies.

Jesse repeated what he had gleaned from his brief encounter. "No room at the inn, the fellow said. Someone at the caravansary sent them up to the cave."

"Had to be Mordechai. Must have been drunk," Rachel fumed. "Sending a woman in labor to the lambing cave. Some joke. No heat."

Jesse rubbed his nose, which was red from the cold. "Mother never looked so bad when she brought forth my brothers."

Havila remarked, "'Brought forth,' is it, Jesse? Your mother drops sons like apples fall from a tree."

Jesse frowned. "Lots of blood. I don't know. Maybe she's dying."

Rachel and Havila exchanged a sober glance. Havila muttered, "If only Mordechai had sent her here."

Rachel shouldered the midwife's kit. "Get the birthing room ready. Light the fire. Warm it. If I can, I'll move her down. Maybe there'll be time. If not, I'll send Jesse back for coals to build a fire. And heated water."

Havila kissed Rachel on the cheek. "I will. I'll wake Grandmother. She can watch the boys. Send Jesse."

"Just stay warm and pray. No good you making yourself ill. I lost Obi's little mother this year. One death is one too many for a lifetime."

An inexplicable sense of dread filled Rachel as she glanced over her shoulder at her sons. Some weight—an unseen danger—crackled in the air. "My lambs," she whispered. "Such a hard world they've been born to."

A blast of frigid wind bit into Rachel's cheeks as she and the boy set out for the cave.

CHAPTER 37

"Wait here," Rachel instructed Jesse as she entered the cave. Only one dim lamp glowed at the back of the space. Except for the faint stirring of the livestock, it was very quiet. An untethered donkey munched the hay.

As Jesse had said, a trail of bright red was spattered on the ground. Too much blood. It was clear to Rachel that the woman was hemorrhaging. Had she already died in the time it had taken Jesse to find Rachel? Rachel glanced at the lamb covered in the skin of another. Too often death walked beside birth.

"Shalom," Rachel called softly as she hurried to the stall. She took in the sight. The pregnant woman lay on the ground, pale as death. A brown wool blanket covered her. Her husband knelt beside her, his hands clasped as if imploring her to live. He looked at Rachel, acknowledging her presence.

Rachel climbed the gate and knelt beside the woman. Checking her pulse, she said, "Passed out."

"Her name is Mary. I'm Yosef the Carpenter . . . of Nazareth."

Rachel crooned, "Mary, sweet . . . Mary? It's Rachel. I've come to help you. Can you hear me?" A faint flutter of eyelashes acknowledged

Rachel's voice. "Good. I'm going to help you now. I'm going to help you, but you'll have to work with me."

"Will she live?" Yosef asked in a stricken voice.

"How close are the pains?"

"Very close. She swooned during the last one."

Rachel hissed, "What were you thinking, Carpenter? Taking a pregnant woman anywhere . . . this late in her confinement? Her first? And riding a donkey? Are you insane?"

"What . . . what . . . can I do?" The husband sat back on his heels as if Rachel had struck him.

"You're no use to me or her here. Go back to my house with Jesse. Your wife can't be moved now. My sister is preparing water for washing. Warm water. Salt. Warm oil. Bring a jug of coals to build a fire to take the chill off. And a basin. Hurry! Run! The baby is in the birth canal."

She scowled as Yosef bounded from the stall. "Men! Idiots! No idea what a woman goes through to bring life into the world."

Mary opened her eyes and gave a weak smile.

Rachel grinned and sat at Mary's feet, grasping her hands. "You agree with me, eh? Men, eh? That's the girl. You may think you're going to die, but you won't. Now, listen to me. Stay awake. When you feel the pain, I'll pull you up. Sit up. Push when I say. Push hard. Do you understand? You'll have to work at this. First baby. Always the hardest. You want a boy or a girl?"

"A son," Mary whispered and squeezed Rachel's hands in understanding. Then she grimaced as a contraction clamped down.

"All right then. Yes, good, strong contraction. That's good. He's positioned right. Now to business. We're nearly here. I see the crown of his head. Such a head of hair! Come on, then! Ah, his eyes are open, looking all around! All right. I'm going to let go of you so I can support him. He needs my hands. That's it. Push, Mary. Harder! . . . Here he comes! Such shoulders. He'll carry his father's beams, I warrant. A strong one he'll be. Push! No wonder you had such a hard time. There you go, Mary! Look at those big hands. Must be a boy with such hands. They're wide-open. See? He's reaching out to the world. Once more—yes, that's it! Now push. Harder. One more time! And . . . there! Yes! A son, Mary! A baby boy!"

The last night of Hanukkah was crystal clear over the fields of Migdal Eder, the Tower of the Flock. There was more than a hint of frost in the air. The shepherds of Beth-lehem—Zadok, Lem, and a dozen others—sat with Rabbi Eliyahu, close to their campfires.

Everything was perfectly still and at rest.

It was nearing midnight.

The slender, waxing crescent moon and Mars had gone to bed long before. The Adam was keeping The Holy Spirit company in the sign of The Waterbearer. Just now The Lord of the Sabbath neared the western horizon with The Righteous only minutes behind, still keeping their yearlong occupancy of The Two Fish.

Gesturing toward Jupiter and Saturn, Zadok remarked to his companions, "Been quite a show these many months past, Lem. Have y' noticed how those two are moving farther apart now? Sorry t' see it end without . . ."

"Without what?" Lem demanded. "Without somethin' happenin', you mean? Got your hopes up we'd be rid of old Herod and the Romans? Best not to hope like that. Never disappointed is my motto."

"You're too cynical, Lem," Eliyahu said. "He will come, eh? When it's right, when it's time, Messiah will come. That is the certainty that feeds our hope."

Zadok sighed. Lem was probably right. Anyway, what right did Zadok have to be downcast on such a beautiful night? His Rachel. His boys. All was as it should be, at least in Beth-lehem. At least for tonight. Old Hannah. Simeon. Hadn't they always cautioned that Messiah would come when men least expected Him?

Casting up the account of the year in his memory, Zadok ticked off the number of times he had really expected the Lord's Anointed to arrive: At the turn of the year at Rosh Hashanah. On the Day of Atonement . . . many had been expecting Him then. Throughout Sukkot and all the discussions of the Ushpizin's stories . . . all of them, those long-dead men, waiting for a fulfillment they had never experienced either. The census and the loyalty oath had been really good reasons for Messiah to come and deliver Israel, in Zadok's opinion. Still there was nothing. Now the last night of the Feast of Dedication was almost over.

What had been the Hanukkah readings this week at Shabbat? The Parashah was from Numbers—listing all the offerings brought to the Lord for the original dedication of the altar by all the clans of all the tribes. So many bulls, so many goats, so many rams, so many sheep. Zadok looked over his charges in the field, multiplied that by the number of years he had been a shepherd, multiplied that by all the shepherds back to the time of Moses.[143]

It was staggering! All those sacrificed animals, all that blood poured out. When would it ever be enough? Would it ever?

It made the Haftarah reading for the Shabbat of Hanukkah all the more poignant: *"Shout and be glad, O Daughter of Zion. For I am coming, and I will live among you," declares the Lord.*[144] If the Lord really, truly lived among men, suddenly all the deferred hope would be resolved. All the centuries of sacrifice would be evidence of faithfulness—not just rote obedience.

Zadok's back was getting stiff. "Come on, Lem, Eliyahu. Let's take this round."

Away from the glow of the campfire the stars were brilliant pinpoints of light on a solid black veil. "Like a giant curtain with a great light shinin' through pinpricks. What do y' suppose the other side of the curtain is like?" Zadok questioned.

Lem grunted, hunching his head deeper into the cowl of his robe and thrusting his hands into his pockets.

"See where Aryeh, the Lion of Judah, leaps out of the east!" Rabbi Eliyahu remarked.

Raising his staff to point directly overhead, Zadok guided their eyes to where Sirius outshone all the other stars. "How bright The Guardian shines tonight. Urgin' The Lion to join him at the peak of the sky."

"Oh?" questioned Lem, jerking his chin toward the west. "Your Guardian fellow may be bright now, but just wait till yonder star comes up. The horizon is already glowin'."

It was true. Between the paired Jupiter and Saturn a third iridescent gleam appeared. Already outshining the two wandering stars and dimming the outline of The Two Fish, the radiance increased like the rising of a Full Moon.

"But . . . it's not possible," Zadok protested. "That's west, not east, and the moon set hours ago!"

Shepherds and sheep both rose to their feet as the new point of light grew to a flame, then became a shimmering, blazing bowl, like the top of the bronze menorah lampstand on the Temple Mount.

Some of the men cried out in fear. Others stood mute or drew swords.

Zadok planted his staff in the ground and grasped it with both hands.

The light increased in size as it approached, until its radiance engulfed them, as if they had all been transported into the center of a furnace. There was no odor of burning or heat. Rather there was the aroma of sweet incense. The atmosphere was no longer winter night but spring morning.

A gleaming golden figure stood with them in the midst of the light. In form and features he was a man, but twice normal size, and his outline glittered like starshine.

Zadok sank to his knees; his legs had lost their strength. Without turning his head to look, he knew Eliyahu, Lem, and the others had all done the same.

In a voice that rang in Zadok's ears and vibrated in his chest, the angel—for so Zadok knew he must be—spoke: *Do not be afraid. I bring you good news of great joy that will be for all the people. Today in the town of David a Savior has been born to you; He is Messiah the Lord. This will be a sign to you: You will find the babe wrapped in swaddling cloths and lying in a manger.*[145]

Something like a thunderclap assaulted Zadok's senses. It was not thunder, nor had the angel shouted. It was the abrupt inrush of the meaning of the angel's words. *The Savior! Born today! Born in Bethlehem!*

Zadok found himself humming deep in his throat, or rather joining in as the air around him droned. But it was not just the air. The very earth beneath Zadok's feet groaned . . . the long, protracted reverberation of an impossibly deep resonance. It was the sound of a city gate opening. The entry to an embattled fortress being thrown wide to welcome its Deliverer; the creaking unfastening of the rusted-shut cell door to an imprisoned world being offered its freedom at last.

The hinges of creation revolved. Stars and earth and men held their collective breath and listened to the resounding chord echoing with the lifting of the Curse.

Then the interior of the glowing orb was full of angels—rank upon rank ranged in semicircles up and up until disappearing into the sky. How had they all appeared, and from where? Had all the stars in the sky become angels? Or had the angels simply stepped through the pinpricks in the curtain?

It was as if the angels were in the stands of a great arena, and the shepherds were on the arena floor. Like an audience witnessing the climactic moment of a play and spontaneously rising to their feet to cheer, the angels chanted in unison: "*Glory to God in the highest, and on earth peace to men on whom His favor rests.*"[146]

The aura surrounding them was dazzling, but it was also resplendent with every shade of the rainbow. Blue meshed with purple, flowed into scarlet. On all sides of Zadok the night-become-day sparkled with colors that had no names. The breath of holiness that caressed his cheek trembled with music that had no counterpart on earth.

And beyond the colors and the golden orb?

The glare was too brilliant. Zadok could not make it out clearly, but through squinted eyes he perceived a great city, streets thronged with people, walls that towered into the heavens, a mighty river, an enormous tree. Past the city were mountain peaks and valleys and soaring eagles.

Then the angels sang their *Gloria*—a swelling chorus of praise and amazement. How long had they been the spectators to all the dramas enacted on earth? If angels cheered, then what did this night's announcement mean for mere men?

At some point Zadok, in his rumbling bass, took up the song. Eliyahu's uncertain tenor did the same, as did Lem's increasingly confident baritone. All over the fields of Beth-lehem Ephratha human and angelic voices joined in an unending hymn of praise. Even as he sang, Zadok thought, *Holy, holy, holy, Lord! Heaven and earth are full of your glory! Hosanna in the highest!*

Zadok scarcely noticed when the angelic host departed, or when the shimmering orb dimmed, or when it shrank away entirely and the sky returned to darkness and stars. By then he and Lem and all the rest of the shepherds were on their feet, babbling to each other. "Let's go to Beth-lehem!"

Rabbi Eliyahu capered like a child: "Let's go and see this thing that has happened, which the Lord has told us about."[147]

"Can you believe it?" Lem chattered as they ran, stumbling and laughing, across the fields. "Angels! Angels came to us shepherds! Why us, Zadok? Why poor shepherds like us?"

"And why not?" Zadok demanded exuberantly. "Avraham. Yitz'chak. Jacob. Joseph. David. All shepherds. Five heirs of the promise. Five seals of the covenant. Every one of 'em. All hopin' for this day. And here we are, their shepherd descendants, alive t' see it!"

Tadmor, Kingdom of Parthia
Journal of Court Astonomer Melchior
JUST PAST MIDNIGHT!
Year of Creation 3754

Around the evening meal tonight all Old Balthasar and Gaspar could ask was "Has he been born yet?"

And tonight's sky may have provided the answer!

At sunset Mars (The Adam) and The Holy Spirit moon were both in the sign of The Waterbearer. At that same moment, as the sky darkened, Jupiter (The Righteous) and Saturn (The Lord of the Sabbath) appeared due south of us.

Pleased to be able to fulfill my sole function on this journey, I stayed up hour after hour, recording sights and impressions.

Then, at about five hours after sunset, it happened!

Low in the southwest, Jupiter and Saturn were near to setting for the night when, between them, a third, evanescent light appeared! Whether it was a phantom star generated by the combined light of The Righteous and The Lord of the Sabbath or a real but previously unknown star, I cannot say. All I know is that one moment it was not there and the next a golden glow occupied the space between the other two lights, increasing in brilliance until it eclipsed them both—brighter even than the moon!

In my excitement I cried out, and soon Gaspar and Prince Aretas joined me in staring at the golden glow.

Unbeknownst to us in our concentration, Old Balthasar also arrived. When he coughed, we turned to see him wrapped up to the chin in furs and fending off Esther, who was trying to shepherd him back to bed.

"Wait," Balthasar insisted, croaking. "Hanukkah! Listen! Here was the reading for tonight: 'To Joseph were born two sons . . . Joseph called the firstborn Manasseh . . . and the name of the second he called Ephraim.'"[148]

The sign of The Two Fish, yes? The blessing linking the two celestial fish and the nation of Israel. But there is more!"

Wheezing, Balthasar stopped for air, but now no one dared interrupt him. "There is more. Tonight do we not also read: 'When Mosheh entered the Tent of Meeting to speak with the Lord, he heard the voice speaking to him from between the two cherubim above the atonement cover on the Ark of the Testimony. And He spoke to him. The Lord said to Mosheh: "Speak to Aaron and say to him, 'When you set up the seven lamps, they are to light the area in front of the lampstand.'"'[149] Don't you see? Between the two cherubim! The Lord is speaking! The heavens are God's true lampstand! A light! A new light has come!"

We kept our places, hardly able to utter any more sounds. The ball of light did not fade for perhaps half an hour. When it did, the others retired while I reentered my tent to record these thoughts.

This wonder is so powerful and unexpected it leaves me filled with reverence and a little anxiety. Was this the most important sign? Have we missed His birth? Have we come too late?

Nevertheless, we will press on. Surely now His coming will be announced to the whole world! We will doubtless find Him in Jerusalem, King David's capital, honored and acknowledged by all!

CHAPTER 38

Between the fields and the village, Lem asked, "How will we find him?"

"In a manger," Eliyahu reminded them. "The angel said in a manger. Must mean they took a manger from a barn to use as a cradle."

"Aye, but which manger? Whose house? How many stables are there in Beth-lehem? How'll we know?"

Zadok clapped his hands, making Bear Dog jump. "Nothin' easier! Isn't my Rachel a midwife? And Eliyahu's wife another? One of the two of them was surely called to assist."

Since Zadok's home lay on the outskirts of the village, they directed their steps there first. Mindful that a new mother might be within—and even more aware of approaching a baby announced by an angel as Messiah the Lord—Zadok loudly shushed the others.

Even though it was his own door, he knocked diffidently and called softly, "Rachel. Rachel girl?"

Havila answered Zadok's summons. "She's been called away. To the lambing cave." Then, seeing her husband and a double rank of shepherds hovering outside, she demanded, "What's all this?" Her expression suggested she thought they had all been drinking or that some prank was afoot.

Everyone tried to speak at once, babbling of golden light and heavenly choirs and visions beyond imagination, while Bear Dog barked and barked.

Through about half the jumbled explanation Havila frowned with disbelief, but she knew her husband too well. He could never lie to her about anything or play a trick with a straight face. "Eliyahu," she said sternly, "tell me the truth."

"An angel came to us," Eliyahu said in calm, deliberate answer to his wife's inquiry.

"Hundreds of angels—maybe thousands," Lem corrected.

"But the news is this: the Savior! Messiah is born! Here! Tonight! In Beth-lehem!" Zadok concluded.

"In little Beth-lehem," Rabbi Eliyahu confirmed. "Just as the prophecy foretold."[150]

Havila, lost in amazement at what she heard, suddenly came to herself and seized her husband's arm. "You don't suppose . . . ? A young couple, the stable lad said. The mother not much older than himself."

"What's this?" Zadok demanded.

"The birth Rachel was called out for. The lambing cave, Jesse said. Travelers with no place to stay and the mother in a bad way, the lad said. Rachel sent the husband to fetch supplies. Oh, go, Eliyahu . . . Zadok! Go quickly, but send me word."

Running across Rachel's garden, up the slope to the ridge, and along its length to the limestone crevice took no more than five minutes. Every man in the group, save Eliyahu, knew the lambing cave intimately, had labored there many times, yet all hesitated outside in the pale starlight.

"You go in," Lem urged. "You're husband to the midwife."

Just inside the entry Rachel met Zadok. She was pleased and excited to see him. "I'm glad you've come. The most wonderful thing has happened—"

"I know," Zadok interrupted. "But tell me first. . . . Are they . . . is she . . . is he . . . ?"

"All well," Rachel confirmed, "but it was a difficult delivery." Then she asked, "What did you mean, 'you know'?"

So Zadok told the story of the angels over again.

Rachel stood with arms crossed, rubbing them. "Yes. There was something, Zadok . . . but I can't speak of it." Taking Zadok's big, rough hand in her small one, she led him toward the back of the cave.

Beside a lambing pen Zadok saw a strong man hovering protectively. Propped up on a mound of clean straw on which blankets had been spread was a young woman. Her face showed exhaustion, but it was radiant.

Near the new mother stood a rough-hewn, acacia-wood manger, lined with sheep fleece. From within it came the thin, mewing sounds of a newborn baby. Zadok unwound his scarf from his neck and stood gazing at the scene. A small donkey grazed contentedly in the hay, sharing it with a placid ox.

Stepping forward, Zadok twisted the scarf in his hands until it was a single, tightly wound knot. "Please, ma'am. Sir. Do you suppose . . . ? Might I see the child?"

The mother nodded and leaned over the manger to raise a fold of swaddling cloth that had fallen across the baby's face.

Zadok stepped forward, then knelt. He clasped his hands in front of him as his mind reeled at the implications of what had happened.

It was all so . . . so ordinary seeming. This was not a palace or a fortress; it was a cave. The air was warm and moist with the breath of sheep and lambs and smelled of wool and manure, not incense and costly perfume. The teenage mother was not dressed like royalty. Her protector was clearly *am ha aretz* . . . one of the people of the land.

And yet . . . and yet . . .

There was the baby, wrapped in cloths and lying in a manger, even as the angel had foretold.

The accuracy of that fulfillment could not be doubted, which meant . . .

Head bowed, tears streamed down Zadok's furrowed cheeks. "My Savior and my Lord."

Silently Eliyahu and all the rest came in twos and threes to witness the miracle that had come to pass. Tough shepherds, they were used to living rough and dealing every day with life and death. Still, all of them knelt. All of them wept.

They would have stayed and continued worshipping if Rachel had not called a halt and shooed them out. While the rest returned to the flocks, Eliyahu hurried off to tell Havila. Lem went to inform Sharona.

Even then, though it was past the middle watch of the night, the shepherds gathered again around the campfires, swapping recollections and making mental lists of who all they would tell on the morrow.

And often, until daybreak, each stole glances toward the western horizon when he thought no other was watching, to see if the golden flame would reappear.

Yosef sat on the shadowed ground beside the manger, out of the way. Despite Rachel's encouragement for Yosef to go to her home and sleep while she tended Mary and the baby, the carpenter refused to leave the lambing cave.

Rachel had sternly pronounced that Mary could not be moved. The idea of taking her out into frigid air and transporting her over rough terrain was foolish and dangerous. There had been too much bleeding to take any risks. Mary needed to regain some strength first. Lying on fleece-covered straw and wrapped in layers of blankets, Mary was as well-off as she could be anywhere for the moment.

Mary's face, once pallid enough to frighten Yosef, had regained some color. Lines etched into her cheeks by pain and exertion had begun to smooth. Another woman, Rachel's sister-in-law Havila, bustled into the cavern with a clay jug from which wisps of fragrant steam arose. Rachel knelt beside Mary and spooned broth into the new mother's mouth, after which Mary dozed again. Yosef was handed the remaining soup, which he gratefully devoured.

Firelight flickered outside the cave's low entrance. Occasionally a shepherd's dark silhouette eclipsed the glow. Rotating their other duties amongst them, some of the herdsmen guarded the newest mother and her lamb. Yosef had heard no consultation on the matter. Apparently a silent consensus had been achieved to see that Mary and the newborn were not disturbed.

Nor were the shepherds the only ones keeping watch. Ox and donkey still maintained their vigils. Yosef recalled the words of the prophet

Isaias: *The ox knows his master, and the donkey his owner's manger, but Israel does not know, My people do not understand.*[151]

Yosef could not quite grasp it all: In the scarred and stained acacia-wood box by his right hand lay the angel-announced baby. The one to be named *"The Lord Saves," because He will save His people from their sins.*[152]

But who in all His people Israel knew it? A handful at most were aware of the miracle. And right now a majority of those were Temple shepherds! Inhaling, Yosef sampled the air in proof of the fact that *Immanu'el*, "God-with-us," had actually been born in a stable. Nearby, a lamb, wearing a second fleece as a jerkin over his own skin, poked his black nose through the slats and bleated softly. The baby turned his face toward the sound.

Who could take everything in? Yosef wondered. Apart from more proclamations by heavenly heralds, how would anyone else accept it?

Baby Yeshua, Eternal Word of Yahweh, the One True and Living God, pursed rosebud lips and made sucking noises. Inside the feed trough, wrapped in swaddling cloths and cocooned in a blanket that was tucked over His head and around His shoulders like a prayer shawl, the Son of God blinked unfocused eyes at the lamp's flame.

"Shalom, little one," Yosef whispered. To the carpenter, who had little experience with newborns, the infant looked for all the world like a partially unwrapped Torah scroll. When a synagogue's ark was opened to deliver the Word of God to a reverent, adoring congregation, the scroll's royal covering of blue, purple, and scarlet was first laid aside, revealing the humbler, inner wrapping . . . just like now.

Yosef the Tzadik, a worshipful congregation of one, adored what he saw and rubbed the corner of his eye on his robe's sleeve.

Chathal, the baby's Uncle Zachariah had said. "Swaddled." How very near in sound to *Chatham*—a sign, a seal, like the mark of a king's signet ring on an official proclamation. What message had the shepherds related from the angel? *This will be the seal of truth for you: You will find a baby swaddled in cloths and lying in a manger?*[153]

Four babies sealing the covenant: Yitz'chak, Avraham's son of the promised family; Mosheh, born to be the molder of a nation; Samu'el, who anointed God's king and inaugurated the kingdom; and Yochanan, the herald of the King.

And now . . . Yeshua the King. The Fifth Seal.

With a bit of wiggling and squirming, Yeshua freed one hand from the confines of the swaddling. A tiny fist emerged and went to His mouth.

Instinctively, Yosef reached his own calloused hand toward the child's. Partway there, struck by sudden hesitation, Yosef paused, but the baby's eyes had already spotted the motion.

A moment later baby Yeshua's right hand closed around Yosef's little finger. Yosef's eyes overflowed onto his cheeks and down into his beard.

"Shalom," he whispered again. "Welcome to our—" Stopping, the carpenter corrected himself. "Welcome to your world. You are loved."

For to us a child is born,

To us a Son is given,

And the government will be on His shoulders.

And He will be called

Wonderful Counselor, Mighty God,

Everlasting Father, Prince of Peace.

ISAIAH 9:6

Digging Deeper into FIFTH SEAL

Dear Reader,

Take a moment to step into Mary's and Yosef's shoes.

Although the newlyweds were just beginning their life as a couple, they already have a baby on the way. Because the timing of the pregnancy is suspicious, all their neighbors intently watch the bride's waistline . . . and count the months prior when the groom-to-be was out of town. Vicious gossip swirls around the new bride and groom. Gossip that isn't true, but there is no way to defend themselves or the bride's honor without giving away a precious secret or endangering the life of the baby.

Then news comes that the madness of the evil king Herod—the Idumean who shouldn't even be ruling the Jews—is increasing daily. And the people wonder, *When will the long-hoped-for Messiah come to bring peace and righteousness to our tumultuous nation?*

Let's face it. It was not a good time to walk the earth. And it was an even worse time for a child—any child—to be born. Yet in the midst of this upside-down world rife with injustice, prejudice, and betrayal, God was sending a miracle. The greatest miracle of all time.

Yosef was a simple carpenter, thrust into a situation beyond his control and his understanding. Mary was an innocent young woman filled with undoubting faith. Yet there were times when the gossip broke her heart . . . and her spirit.

Both Yosef and Mary seemed so ordinary—salt-of-the-earth kind of folks. They lived in a small, ordinary home in a tiny village in the middle of nowhere. Yet they were uniquely chosen by God to play pivotal roles that would impact not only *their* generation, but all generations to come—throughout the world and for all eternity.

At times, you may feel "ordinary" too. You may wonder what God has in store for you, or if He's even thinking about you. But take heart:

> *"I know the plans I have for you," declares the Lord,*
> *"plans to prosper you and not to harm you,*
> *plans to give you hope and a future."*
> —Jeremiah 29:11

That means God is preparing *you* for a unique role too. How will you respond?

Following are six studies. You may wish to delve into them on your own or share them with a friend or a discussion group. They are designed to take you deeper into the answers to questions such as:

- Why does God allow suffering?
- How bold should I be about what I believe and hold dear? (You'll meet three gutsy women who won't back down . . . and for very good reasons.)
- How can an "ordinary person" like me make an impact?
- What's the difference between *accepting* life and being *content* with life?
- Who is the real Messiah?
- When the future seems scary or unclear, how can I look ahead with expectant hope?

Through *Fifth Seal*, may the promised Messiah come alive to you . . . in more brilliance than ever before.

1 TURBULENT TIMES

> "There never was a more dangerous time on earth. . . . Ah, Mary. Every day and night I ask God why. Why now? . . . Why must you endure this?"
>
> —Yosef (pp. 162–163)

Have you ever asked God why? in the midst of a turbulent time? Tell the story.

____

____

____

____

Imagine that you have one night to make a crucial decision: Should you leave your childhood home and travel into the unknown or not? What would you choose?

____

____

____

____

Now add this information to the scenario: It is highly possible that within the next few days soldiers may come to question you, to put you in prison, or to silence you—permanently. Would your decision change? Why or why not?

____

____

____

The little village of Nazareth had been peaceful—relatively untouched by the maniacal purges of King Herod and the deadly politics of Jerusalem and Rome. After all, why would a king care about an unknown town in the middle of nowhere? Then Herod's madness and evil begin to spread. Herod's own sons—Alexander and Ari—are condemned by their father for treason (see pp. 13–14) and are executed. Righteous teacher Onias, brother of Zadok the Shepherd, is crucified on the wall of his own home "by order of King Herod for complicity in an imaginary plot" (p. 4). Two hundred others are murdered. Spies are everywhere—even at the Temple, which should be safe ground (see p. 127).

It's no wonder that Zachariah and Elisheba decide to flee the Galil with their miracle baby, Yochanan. And it's no wonder that Mary and Yosef realize they must hide the identity of the baby in Mary's womb.

READ

Thus far the brutal purge in Jerusalem had resulted in the arrest and trial of Herod's sons and the murder of over two hundred others. This had prompted Aunt Elisheba and Uncle Zachariah to rent out their vineyard in Beth Karem to tenant farmers. East of the Jordan the couple could live in obscurity and raise their child in safety. The angel who had appeared to old Zachariah in the Temple had spoken treason against the Herodian dynasty. The miraculous birth of Zachariah's baby boy nine months later was a very real threat to the aging monarch. . . .

Jerusalem still reeled from Herod's attacks on imaginary enemies. Might Herod wake up some morning and remember an aged priest, an angel, and a baby boy? Like Pharaoh of old, was it possible that Herod could consider a newborn his rival and seek to destroy him?

Zachariah and Elisheba could not take the chance.

—p. 16

The image of Herod's retribution clouded Yosef's mind. "No one can know. Not yet. That's the idea. Let the neighbors think the worst. Of you. Of me. It's all right."...

It was plain to Yosef that Mary was indeed troubled. For the first time since he had known her, a shadow seemed to stand at her back and plague her with imagined fears. He could see the pain of betrayal flickering in her eyes as they walked to market. Only a few would even talk with her. Most just made her the fodder of their gossip.

And in the months since their marriage, Yosef had seen, with sadness, those barbs of betrayal hurt Mary deeply. She seemed to strong yet was so vulnerable. Were her frequent, unexpected tears simply part of pregnancy or the result of her pain? Perhaps it was because she had become so alone in her hometown—so rejected by all who had known her since infancy.

—pp. 178–179

ASK

Which situation would be the most difficult for you to handle?

- Someone threatening *you* physically.
- Someone threatening your *family*.
- Having someone think the worst about you or a family member.
- Being alone and feeling lonely.
- Seeing a loved one's tears and knowing she/he has been treated poorly emotionally by others.

Explain.

___

___

___

___

READ

Blessed are you, O Adonai, who told us all that the heavens declare your glory night after night. I look up and believe you are and that nothing is impossible for you. And yet. . . . Lord, I confess I don't understand. . . . Is this night part of your plan? . . . Is suffering part of your glory?

—Yosef (p. 163)

Under His wings you will find refuge; His faithfulness will be your shield and rampart. You will not fear the terror of night.

—Psalm 91:4-5

The three angels bowed deeply. . . . *The Lord is with you. Peace be unto you. . . .*

Yosef, a voice whispered as the trio melted into darkness. *Fear not. Yosef, son of Jacob, son of David. Greater is He that is with you than he who is in the world.*

—p. 238

ASK

Do you think suffering could be a part of God's plan? Why or why not?

____

____

____

Have you ever felt the presence of God? As if His wings of comfort and protection were covering you? As if angels were accompanying you during a difficult time? If so, tell the story. How did this experience impact your view of God, angels, and heaven?

____

____

____

READ

The host of four hundred men, women, and children who traveled south with the great Teacher believed His homecoming meant that soon Jerusalem would be rid of the Herodian dynasty and the tyranny of Rome.

At last the kingdom of David would rise, and Yeshua Messiah would ascend like a star to reign forever on David's shining throne. It was Judgment Day. Death to all enemies. The impending redemption of Israel!

—p. xi

"How small are all the things we wrestle with every day until this immense enemy comes to wrestle with us. We're busy in our gardens, and we look up and see the storm clouds gather. But always in the distance. We never believe it will reach the place we stand. Never believe it will sweep away everything. Everyone.

"Then suddenly here it is. The Curse, unbroken since Eden, finds us. It crouches on our doorstep. It knocks. *Death.* It calls on us to pay the debt of sin. The wind is always swirling. Gathering. Blowing. Changing everything . . . and leaving an empty place none can fill. It makes everything else we fuss about in life seem petty and insignificant, doesn't it?"

"Small. So small." Salome exhaled slowly.

Then Mary suggested, "Or maybe . . . instead, death makes the small things about our life *holy.* Details we think are insignificant are . . . truly sacred."

—Conversation between Mary and her sister Salome (pp. 196–197)

ASK

Do you believe in a Judgment Day? Why or why not? How does your belief affect how you will live today?

____

____

____

When was the last time you encountered death? Have any "insignificant" details become "truly sacred" to you as a result? If so, which ones—and why?

WONDER . . .

I would have despaired unless I had believed
That I would see the goodness of the Lord
In the land of the living.
Wait for the Lord;
Be strong and let your heart take courage;
Yes, wait for the Lord.
—Psalm 27:13-14

"Sometimes it all seems so big. I think about Aunt Elisheba. Uncle Zachariah. Herod searching for them. Herod so afraid of a baby that he would kill it. Afraid of the message of an angel because he is so evil. And I wonder about our safety too. The great events of the world and I am so small. I think about the angel, and it hardly seems it can be real. Then the baby moves and I know: Nothing is too hard for God."
—Mary (p. 154)

In the midst of great tumult, Elisheba tells Mary, "The birth of our son is proof that the angel's promise to you is true. Don't be afraid. Nothing is impossible with God."
—p. 16

In what area(s) of your life are you afraid? What do you need to believe is possible?

2 A BOLD STANCE

The Lord is my light and my salvation;
Whom shall I fear?
The Lord is the defense of my life;
Whom shall I dread?
—Psalm 27:1

Who is the boldest person you know? What made you think immediately of this person?

____

____

____

According to *Webster's*, *bold* means: "fearless before danger; showing or requiring a fearless daring spirit; assured, confident, standing out prominently." Do you consider boldness a positive quality, a negative quality, or somewhere in-between? Explain.

____

____

____

Three bold women can accomplish a lot—especially if their hearts are in the right place and their ears are tuned toward hearing the Truth.

The prophetess Hannah was eighty-four, but she certainly hadn't outlived her usefulness. With every breath she spoke the truth of Scripture from the steps of the Temple in Jerusalem. "A light seemed to shine from within her" and "every word Hannah uttered came true" (p. 10). And she didn't back down to anyone—not even King Herod or High Priest Boethus!

Rachel, the midwife of Beth-lehem, was determined to keep wee Obi, whom she declared had been "sent to us from heaven" (p. 98). She was not about to give up this precious orphan, in spite of the rules of the day.

Anna, Mary's mother, was fierce in her protectiveness of her family. To keep them safe, she "would have taken on a Roman legion without a second thought" (p. 35).

What made these women so bold?

READ

Hannah

The prophetess was, by virtue of her age, untouchable. Herod could have killed her for the things she said about him and his reign. In fact, he longed to kill her. But he did not dare lay a hand on her.

The old woman's life story was an artifact of Jerusalem before Herod and before Rome. She was a living tower dwelling within the Temple grounds. Her face, venerable as weathered stone, had witnessed too much turmoil to be affected by Herod's threats.

Had Herod tried to dismantle her, his kingdom would have been toppled by riot and revolt. . . .

Hannah had married a Pharisee, whose name was now forgotten by everyone but Hannah. Hannah loved her husband and loved the Lord. Her gentle spirit and infectious laugh made her a favorite with Queen Alexandra, the last righteous ruler descended from the brief line of Maccabee kings. . . .

She who had witnessed revolution, civil war, and the Roman general Pompey's desecration of the Holy of Holies had no fear of what Herod the Butcher King could do to her. Hannah was a tower. A cornerstone. A tree that cast shade on the humble. . . .

The people despised Herod as much as they adored Hannah. Young women looked for her when they brought babies in for redemption. Widows brought her flowers. Housewives brought her cakes of raisins when they paid their two-penny sacrifices or dropped a coin into the trumpet-shaped container for widows and orphans.

—pp. 9–11

ASK

What was Hannah's reputation? Do you think it was deserved? Why or why not?

Hannah not only stood her ground, but stood it with boldness. When the Temple officials asked her a question, trying to trip her up, she merely responded with Scripture (see pp. 215–218). When the high priest swept past with his vestments, "everyone else in Jerusalem bowed and stepped aside. . . . She did not budge" (pp. 111–112). Even further, she pointed an accusatory finger and lectured him with the words of Scripture!

Hannah had a lot to lose by being so bold (including her own head!), but that didn't stop her. Why do you think she continued to speak the Truth?

How could you be bold like Hannah? speak the truth even in a difficult situation?

READ

Rachel

"But the baby, Zadok! We must keep him. . . . A baby isn't property. . . . If there was any justice in Israel, the master of that poor murdered girl would be taken out and given a taste of the lash for what's been done to her. I myself would braid the whip and wield the scourge. . . ."

Zadok smoothed his mustache. "Eliyahu is right. We'll have t' think carefully on what we do."

"Do? Think? Do! Raise him as our own!"

"Be reasonable, Rachel girl! Look there! His skin is black as night, Rachel. Ebony black. Like his mother's. We can't claim he's an orphaned relative. Can't tell the neighbors that Rachel, the shepherd's wife, has thrown a black lamb in his flock of sons . . . ?"

"And the Almighty God of Israel has chosen to put this one fragile life in our care. . . . We'll redeem his life. Buy his freedom if we must! Zadok! Honestly. We tell the officials what happened. How she came to us. A few coins in the palm of Herod's steward to buy a newborn infant of no use to anyone. They'll take the money. Surely!"

—RACHEL (pp. 98–100)

All Rachel had—all her possessions—what were they when weighed in the balance with Zadok and her three sons? . . .

How grateful she was that Obi's mother had come to Beth-lehem so the child could live and be loved in a real family!

Rachel caressed his cheek and kissed his curly hair. Yes! Obi had become her son just as much as Enoch and Samu'el.

What would Rachel give to keep them safe? What price could she put on love? Compared to her boys and Zadok, nothing in all the world had any value.

—p. 155

ASK

If you got in an argument with Rachel, would you win or lose? Why?

____

____

____

What do you think made Rachel so bold in pursuing baby Obi's redemption?

When you look back on your life, what price have you put on love? How has your life reflected that value?

READ

Anna

Her physical strength was matched by her strength of character. When a legion of whisperers closed in on Mary, as well as Yosef, Anna's sound advice, fierce faith, and constant prayers of intercession kept the hounds of hell at bay.

Along with Yosef, Anna was Mary's greatest defender, her most ardent supporter. Yosef knew that Anna had been the first to hear of the appearance of the angel to Mary. She had been the first to believe with unwavering faith the heavenly message given to her daughter: *You will conceive in your womb and bear a son and you will name Him Yeshua. He will be great and will be called Son of the Most High; and the Lord will give Him the throne of His father David . . . and His Kingdom will have no end.*

Only yesterday Anna had instructed, "*Head high at the bar mitzvah. And keep your mind clear. . . . Smile at them if they fall silent as you pass. Remember, when they're talking about you, they're giving somebody else a rest. Pray for them, children. They violate the commandment not to murder with words as sharp as daggers. With speculation and lies passed on to others they bear false witness against the Lord's Anointed. Against the Son of David! An unkind word is a sword aimed at your heart, Mary. Meant to pierce you through with discouragement. The Lord, who is judge of all, will break the blade of the slanderer one day. Pray for those who speak badly of you. Pity them."*. . .

How easy it was for Yosef to understand "Why Mary?" as he observed Anna. Was it not written "the apple does not fall far from the tree"?

Anna of the steady heart! Anna of the easy laugh! Anna of the Lord's keen insight! Anna, believer in miracles. Anna of praise and prayer. Anna selected as grandmother to the promised King of Israel!

—pp. 35–36

ASK

Would you choose someone like Anna as a friend? Why or why not? If so, what qualities of hers would attract you?

____

____

____

Have you ever found yourself falling into the discouragement trap? If so, how could Anna's advice to Mary encourage you and give you perspective?

____

____

____

Insert your name at the beginning of each line:

_______________ of the steady heart!

_______________ of the Lord's keen insight!

_______________, believer in miracles.

_______________ of praise and prayer.

How can you begin to develop—or develop further—these qualities?

____

____

____

WONDER . . .

Do not be afraid; do not be discouraged. Be strong and courageous.
—Joshua 10:25

The righteous are as bold as a lion.
—Proverbs 28:1

In what one way can you—like Hannah, Rachel, and Anna—be bold this week?

____

____

____

3 AN ORDINARY DREAMER

When Yosef woke up, he did what the angel of the Lord had commanded him.

—Matthew 1:24

Imagine that you've been engaged ("betrothed") to a girl for several years but have only admired her from a distance. Right before your wedding she claims to be pregnant "by the Holy Spirit." What would you think? What emotions would you experience? What would your conclusion(s) be?

____

____

____

Then imagine that you fall asleep . . . and dream. In that dream you are visited by an angelic messenger, who tells you that the one you are "engaged to wed is the virgin of the prophecy of Isaiah: *Therefore the Lord Himself will give you a sign: The virgin will be with child and will give birth to a son*" (Isaiah 7:14). What, if anything, would change about your thoughts, emotions, and conclusion(s)?

____

____

____

Yosef is just an "ordinary guy"—a simple man, a carpenter. "I am plain Yosef," he says to the angel (p. 46). He calls his father "Jacob the ordinary" (see p. 47). It's no surprise he wonders, *Who am I, Lord, that you have chosen me? I am only Yosef, son of Jacob* (p. 36).

None outside Mary's immediate family knew the true circumstances of

Yosef's marriage to Mary. Yosef didn't even dare tell his closest friends about the angel's visit. They would have thought him crazy.

But in remaining loyal to Mary, this humble man had to suffer the condescension of his entire hometown. Worse, he couldn't defend the honor of the woman he loved against the gossip because he had to protect the fragile child in her womb.

READ

Yosef was certain Mary was blessed by Adonai and chosen from all the women of Israel to carry in her womb the Messiah, the only begotten Son of the Most High. . . .

To help her, the angelic messenger had appointed Yosef to be protector, friend, and brother to Mary.

As a carpenter, Yosef was a man of great physical strength. His prowess would be used to defend her life and the life of the child if required. He carried a short sword concealed beneath his tunic these days and was willing to fight and die shielding her if called upon to do so.

Yosef's standing as a righteous man would also shield her reputation and deflect emotional assaults when they came. His calm, quiet spirit would stand between her and the dark unseen force that must surely be seeking to destroy her respectability even now.

—pp. 19–20

The responsibility of providing for Mary and the baby she carried was a heavy one. Yosef shouldered the burden with the prayer that he would never let The Lord of All the Angel Armies down.

That meant never letting Mary down.

—p. 18

The carpenter crossed his arms. He felt the weight of his concealed sword. He could defend Mary against a half-dozen stout fellows with weapons. But how could he protect her heart against the sword of gossip from friends and neighbors?

—p. 91

ASK

Why do you think God chose Yosef—out of all the men in Israel—to become the baby Messiah's earthly father and Mary's protector?

____

____

____

Do you believe that God can speak to us through dreams? Why or why not?

____

____

____

READ

"I've been feeling very uncertain of myself, you see. So unworthy. I understand why he chose Mary . . . never was a heart more willing to serve the Lord than hers. But me? I am caught up in this great event with some reluctance. I wanted nothing more for myself than a humble life, you see. A house. A business. A wife and children."

And so humble lives are all a wonderful part of the Master's plan.

—Conversation between Yosef and Joseph, the Dreamer of dreams (p. 48)

Comprehension of the enormity of his task pressed Yosef onto the hard cold stone of earth. "Yeshua is the Son and Heir . . . the Word . . . the Creator. And I am to be his father? I? I will carry Bar Elohim—the Son and Heir of Eternal God—on *my* shoulders? Rock him to sleep? He who has never slept? Teach him his *alef-bet*, though his is the story of the Scriptures and the word that spoke worlds into existence? Teach him to pray who is Lord of the Sabbath, existing in equal power and glory with Elohim from the foundation? Yeshua bar Yosef, the son of a carpenter? It's too big for my mind to comprehend! This dream brings so many unanswered questions. . . .

"Wait! Don't go! Don't leave me feeling so . . . so . . . small!"

It is written. Soon! Soon! He is coming soon! You will behold him face-to-face. Immanu'el . . . God-with-us.

—CONVERSATION BETWEEN YOSEF AND JOSEPH, THE DREAMER OF DREAMS (p. 107)

"None of this is the way I imagined it. The virgin who will give birth to the Messiah. Who would think that old friends would gossip about her? or that she would suffer? If a person is chosen to serve God—I mean, out of all the women on earth—shouldn't everyone recognize how special she is? . . . And why has the Lord begun his work of salvation with the birth of a baby?". . .

All of Torah points to this hour in history and to the birth of the One by whose word all of creation came into existence. If the Lord created all things because of His love for His children, does it not stand to reason that He would come personally to save everyone who calls upon His name?

And the Savior must come first as a long-awaited baby to reign on earth on the throne of King David, just as the prophet Samu'el predicted. This baby will be born to Mary, who, slandered and reviled like Hannah, has said, "Lord, may your maid-servant find favor in your eyes."

Yosef was troubled by the reality that even righteous men and women did not go through life without sorrows. "Will it always be this hard? Will there always be gossip? slander? opposition?"

The angel replied, *Even in her joy at Samu'el's birth, Hannah sang these words about the Messiah: "The Lord brings death and gives life; He lowers to the grave and raises up." Life follows death! Eternal resurrection follows the grave! . . . There are stormy seas ahead. Yosef! Be strong and be a man! Be strong for Mary! Stand by her. Comfort her. You also were chosen from among all men from the dawn of creation! For this moment you were born.*

—CONVERSATION BETWEEN YOSEF AND GABRIEL, THE ANGEL (pp. 122–123)

"I'm already so aware how small and powerless I am and how important is the birth of this child."

Yosef the Tzadik, your great gifts are your humility and your faith. But you are not so powerless as you suppose. Did you not learn today how your steps are ordered by the Almighty?

—CONVERSATION BETWEEN YOSEF AND JOSEPH, THE DREAMER OF DREAMS (p. 246)

ASK

In what ways did Yosef's dreams help him cope with his doubts? his questions? the daily pressures of his life?

When have you felt powerless? What difference would it make if you remember that "your steps are ordered by the Almighty"?

READ

"He'll be a boy like other boys. With a father. You. The Lord chose you. And a mother. Me. He'll learn from his father. From me too, I guess. And we'll protect him while he's growing up."

"Who could imagine such a thing? How will it work, do you suppose? Do you think he'll pretend he's like any other child?"

"Maybe he will be. What do you think he'll look like? The angel didn't give details. Oh! There! He just moved. Here—give me your hand." She grasped Yosef's fingers and placed his hand on her stomach. The baby moved.

Yosef laughed. Tears brimmed. So this was a real person. Immanu'el. God-with-us. God come to live among man.

The Lord of All the Angel Armies tapped from within Mary's womb again.

"Feel that?" Mary exclaimed.

"Yes. Yes."

"He's saying 'Shalom, Yosef. Glad to meet you.' He's saying, 'I will be happy to be a carpenter like you until I can become king and build a kingdom.'"

—Conversation between Mary and Yosef (p. 31)

ASK

What is "ordinary" about this extraordinary baby?

Why do you think it was important for God to come "as a real person. Immanue'l. God-with-us"?

How does this peek at the life of Mary, Yosef, and baby Yeshua impact your view of the traditional Christmas story?

WONDER . . .

Blessed are you, O Eternal, who made the stars. Blessed are you because you love us so much you are coming to live with us. Like an ordinary man. I promise, Son of David, I will take care of you! Protect you! Oh, Lord. Messiah. Maker of stars! I'll do my best to be a good father to you while you're here.

—Yosef (pp. 31–32)

God gave the ordinary Yosef a pivotal role in history. What might He be preparing you for? Why not open your heart and the happenings of your day to the "Maker of stars" and see what He can do through you?

4 A CONTENTED HEART

"I've been trying to figure it out. Why you and I were chosen, I mean."

"I try not to think about it much." Mary seemed so content. "It is what it is. Too big for me to understand it all. So I don't try."

—CONVERSATION BETWEEN MARY AND YOSEF (p. 29)

If something good happened to you, would you accept it—no questions asked? Or would you want to know every last detail? Why?

____

____

____

____

Recall the last time you went through a difficult situation. Did you accept it and move on—no questions asked, assuming hardship is just a part of life? Or did you respond with questions, anger, bitterness, etc.? Explain.

____

____

____

____

If a friend asked you, "How content are you with your life *right now*?" what would you say? Explain.

____

____

____

____

In the little village of Nazareth "the weaving of tales was a form of entertainment exceeding sewing, cooking, singing, or dancing" (pp. 35–36). And young Mary—pretty in a "fine homespun fabric" kind of way—was often the key figure in the weaving of tales. Everyone watched as she became ill from the smell of fish—and her stomach grew far too soon. It was clear to all that Mary was too pregnant for the conception of the baby to have occurred after the wedding.

The gossipmongers were in full swing, slicing up the private lives of Mary and Yosef.

READ

"The shame!"

"The expense! Why put on a wedding when there's already been a honeymoon, eh?"

"Poor Anna!"

"What sort of example is she to her little sisters, I ask you?"

"Never mind Anna! Anna's blind to it! Mary's her daughter; what do you expect? Poor Yosef! What if it isn't his?" . . .

"So, Mary, perhaps there'll be a *Bris* to celebrate soon in your home? Eh? How soon?" A pause and a conspiratorial whisper. "Does Yosef know?"

There was nothing subtle about the questioning.

—pp. 33–34

"Well, if she's not played the harlot, then no one ever has!"

"Thin in the face . . ."

"But look at that! Six months' bloom, or I don't know anything!"

"It'll have Yosef's name."

"Illegitimate though it may be!"

"Brazen."

"Bold as brass!"
"She doesn't give a copper about poor Yosef!"
—p. 91

ASK

If you were Mary, how would you respond to such gossip?

- Lift your head high and ignore it.
- Go about your business and pretend you didn't hear it.
- Confront it head-on and tell them the truth.
- Get angry inside but not show your anger in front of others.
- Other ______________________________

Why would you respond that way?

____

____

____

How do you think someone's personality affects his/her response to betrayal or hardship? Does a person "make or break" a situation, or does a situation "make or break" a person? Explain your theory.

____

____

____

READ

Mary and Anna kissed the cheeks of the most vicious one of the women and asked about her health and her children and grandchildren.
—p. 34

To Yosef's amazement, Mary appeared immune to the remarks. If she heard the gossip, her perpetually sunny disposition seemed unaffected by it.

How was it possible, Yosef wondered, that beneath a hail of Satan's flaming arrows, she was not wounded? . . .

Was Mary's unruffled demeanor in part because she spent so much time with her mother and her sisters, talking, laughing, praying about every concern? . . . Dark brown, honest eyes held the gaze of others and conveyed an unspoken message of both sweet humor and kindness.

—p. 34

Perhaps, Yosef reasoned, it was this powerful bond between mother and daughter that gave Mary the deep emotional keel by which she sailed on fearlessly through high seas.

Each day the women of Mary's close family circle were together as they kneaded bread or tilled the garden or churned butter. It came to Yosef in a sudden revelation that the Eternal One had carefully selected this family—these women—from among all in the tribe of Judah to help raise the Lord's Anointed. They were a clan not easily rattled.

—p. 36

ASK

Mary could have snipped at the offending women, refused to talk to them, gossiped about *them* behind their backs, told them off, etc. But what was her response to these people, who should have been her friends and loyal supporters?

____

____

____

If a friend betrayed you by slandering you or gossiping about you, could you forgive as easily as Mary? Why or why not?

____

____

____

Are you easily rattled? Or do you sail "on fearlessly through high seas"? Explain.

READ

She sat opposite him and leaned her cheek upon her hand. "Tell me. Help me put the pieces together. What do you see when you look at me?"

He answered without wavering. "You are our second beginning. Our second chance. . . . Like Avraham you offer your miracle child to the Lord. And the salvation your son brings the world will forever free us from the curse of sin and death. The chains forged in Eden will be broken at last. You are the virgin, the second Eve, who is obedient to the voice of the Lord. Because you trust—completely trust the Lord's promise to you—because you have said you would obey.

"Obey! It's more than a word with you. Because you really meant what you said the night the angel spoke to you. You believe whatever God does in your life is all right with you! Even if you hurt. Even if people are cruel. You trust the Lord! Because of your faith—a faith like Avraham's yet found in a woman—the chains of sin and death that bind us all will somehow be broken forever."

—pp. 154–155

What connection is there between Eve and Mary?

Is *obey* more than a word for you? Even if you hurt, even if people are cruel, do you trust the Lord? Or is something holding you back? If so, what?

____

____

____

____

WONDER . . .

"I almost forgot who our guest is. I almost let it be about me. But it's not about me. See? I almost forgot the One who has come to our house to stay with us. . . . Think what blessing our dear friends are missing when sweet baby Messiah is so near, and they don't even know who he is."

—MARY (p. 161)

Is your life about "me"—or about the Messiah?

5 THE CHILD WHO TURNED THE WORLD UPSIDE DOWN

> "Not just any baby. Such a baby! He'll know all the mysteries from the beginning of time. . . . No! Before the beginning! All that explained! Messiah. First Light. . . . He who sang the stars into existence . . . will be born."
>
> —Yosef (p. 56)

To you, who is the baby in the manger at Christmas? Is that baby simply part of holiday tradition, or something more? Explain.

____

____

____

To you, who is the baby in the manger *after* Christmas? If someone asked you, "Do you believe the Messiah has come?" what would you say?

____

____

____

For centuries the Jewish nation has longed for the promised Messiah, the Son of God and heir of all creation, who would descend to earth to bring ultimate peace and right all wrongs. They are expecting a mighty warrior—someone who will destroy all their enemies with a vengeful flash of the sword. Someone who will establish a very showy, obvious earthly kingdom. Someone who will roust the cruel, heathen nations who have controlled them and bring a just, new government. Someone who will help the needy and the poor. Someone who will bring righteousness and truth to all dealings.

Instead God arrived gently and quietly . . . in the womb of a young woman in the backwoods of Nazareth. It's not what anyone in Israel—much less Mary or Yosef—expected. In fact, it was all so ordinary that it wasn't until Mary is nauseated by the smell of fish that Yosef really realizes she is pregnant. "This was the first hint, the first tangible sign, that every detail Yosef had been told by the angel about Mary and the child was indeed a fact! And yet, it seemed so ordinary!" (p. 22).

READ

"He's a baby, growing in my womb like babies grow in their mother's wombs. He'll want me to love him just like a mother loves her children. And I already do love him."

—Mary (p. 57)

Could it be that Mary, chosen by the Almighty to carry the Messiah of Israel in her womb, would experience pregnancy with the same discomfort as every woman since Eve? Was such a thing possible?

—Yosef (p. 22)

"I'll thank him one day for making the stars and writing his story in the heavens for everyone to see." Mary's voice was tender. "But first . . . my part is a small one. I'll be his mama. Rock my baby in my arms. No cold, distant stars to hold him. A mother's arms, warm and gentle. I'll sing him to sleep. Sit by his cradle and be there to love him and care for him when all the stars have vanished and he wakes in the morning."

—p. 57

What a world you have decided to enter, O Lord. El Shaddai. All-sufficient. Almighty. A baby? . . . What a terrible time you have chosen to be born as one so vulnerable. And how will I protect you?

—Yosef (p. 103)

ASK

In the above passages, what is "ordinary" about Mary's pregnancy and the baby?

Although the coming of the baby Messiah had been prophesied throughout Scripture (see pp. 144–145, 178, 215–218), there were only a few—Simeon, Hannah, and Onias, for example—who had studied the prophecies so carefully and could reveal the true import of the words.

And such a revelation! Four baby boys would precede Yeshua. All of these earthly sons would be instrumental in the redemption of Israel. And all would point to the arrival of Yeshua—the Fifth and final Seal of redemption.

READ

"The Lord has placed four sons as royal seals from his signet ring upon the covenant he made with Avraham. By Avraham's faith and through Avraham's seed all the nations of the world will be blessed. The first seal is the miracle of Avraham and Sarai's son Yitz'chak, who was father of Jacob and grandfather of the twelve tribes.

"The second seal, Mosheh, at whose birth the stars shone like they shine now. He survived the massacre of the Hebrew firstborn babies and grew to lead Israel out from the bondage of Egypt.

"The third seal is the miraculous birth of the prophet Samu'el, who anointed David as king over Israel. Through Samu'el, Hannah's son, the Lord announced the promise that David's son will sit on the throne of Israel forever. Now, in our day, here is the miracle of the birth of Yochanan. The angel promised me that Yochanan will grow up to be the prophet of the Most High and forerunner of our Messiah.

"Four miraculous baby sons, each born and swaddled as is the custom and laid in his happy mother's arms. Listen to the Word of the Lord! Oh, how the Lord delights in wordplay when he speaks to us of mighty things! The word for a 'swaddled' baby is *chathal.* The word for the 'seal' of a covenant is *chatham.* The word for 'bridegroom' is *chathan.*

"The miracle of each of the four swaddled babes is God's seal on his covenant of love and the coming of the heavenly Bridegroom to redeem his bride, Israel.

"The miracle of Yochanan's birth is the fourth seal, set by the Lord's own signet ring, upon the scroll of mankind's final redemption."

—Zachariah (pp. 16–17)

Yosef raised his gaze to the stars rising in the east. From childhood he had heard from the rabbis that Messiah would descend from heaven to earth to establish His Kingdom with a host of angel armies and a flaming sword of judgment against the nations. He thought of the babies of whom Zachariah had spoken: Yitz'chak, Mosheh, Samu'el, and finally little Yochanan.

Yitz'chak, the promise of God's provision for redemption through the chosen *family* of Abraham.

Mosheh, the visible expression of God's redemption of mankind through His chosen *nation*, Israel.

Samu'el, the prophet to anoint David as chosen king of Israel from whom the eternal *kingdom* of a redeemed world would one day be established.

Little Yochanan, the chosen forerunner to prepare the way of King Messiah who would unite *Family*, *Nation*, and *Kingdom* beneath One Righteous Banner and One Name.

The first three men had been mighty in the history of Israel. But the record of their eternal significance had begun with accounts of their births. God, family, nation, kingdom . . . could it be that the Almighty and Eternal God planned all along to begin His greatest miracle with something as small and insignificant as the birth of a baby?

—p. 22

ASK

List the names of each of the baby boys.

First seal: ______________________________

Second seal: ______________________________

Third seal: ______________________________

Fourth seal: ______________________________

Fifth Seal: ______________________________

What was similar about each of these children? Why is each of the seals important?

____

____

____

If you were planning your greatest accomplishment ever, would you choose to reveal it through babies? Why or why not?

____

____

____

READ

In the Beginning, Yahweh created man and woman with a loving relationship in mind.

Peniel had learned from Yeshua that mankind's first father and mother had not loved God in return. They had turned away. After that, they had feared Him. The kind of fear that made them run and stumble away from Him instead of running toward Him for mercy.

From that time on, what mankind could not touch they proclaimed did not exist. What they could not comprehend they mocked.

Like color and light to a man blind from birth, they could not imagine God's power and righteousness and love for them. Instead, they ran to the lakeshore, filled their little bottles with water, and declared that god was in their bottle and that this was all the god they needed. The bottle was big enough to contain *their* truth, which was very small indeed.

—p. x

Blessed be the name of the Eternal God, the God of Israel, who alone performs miracles! The name of the Eternal shall be blessed from now and until forevermore!

—Yosef (p. 209)

ASK

In what ways have you scooped God up "in a bottle, carried home, and placed on a window ledge with the declaration that He occupied the bottle" (p. ix)?

Do you find yourself believing easily in God's miracles? Or are you skeptical? Explain.

When you consider our human tendency to proclaim that what we cannot touch does not exist, why do you think Yahweh chose to send Messiah in the form of a baby? What did sending Messiah as a baby accomplish?

READ

"Don't make the same mistake as others," Simeon warned. "They read of what Messiah will do as king—defeating Israel's enemies and purifying the worship of the Lord—and fail to understand that he comes first as a child."

Simeon clapped one aged hand on Zadok's shoulder and the other on Eliyahu's. "And you, my friends, may be the first to greet him!"

"Beth-lehem's no fit place for a king t' be born," Zadok complained. "There's naught but shepherds' babies born there . . . *am ha aretz*, every one. There's no palace there, no grand houses. Shepherds and sacrificial lambs—that's Beth-lehem."

"And kings . . . David!" Stabbing a crooked finger down on the scroll of Micah, Simeon argued, "Yet it is clearly so: Beth-lehem, birthplace of King David, who received the promise that the future King Messiah would be of his descent."

"So a child born in Beth-lehem," Zadok mused. "Could it be he's already there?"

Simeon and Eliyahu shook their heads in unison.

"Possibly, but unlikely," Eliyahu intoned.

Simeon added, "Mystery upon mystery. The Son of God, whose origin is from forever past, coming to earth as a man . . . Son of God, but also Son of Man . . . a human infant. Perhaps he'll need human assistance too."

—p. 145

[Rabbi Yismah] raised a crooked forefinger and jabbed the air. "To Beth-lehem? The city of David. Eh? Eh? I am blessed to see with my own eyes the virgin predicted from of old: she who will give birth to the Redeemer of Israel."

"But you know so much about us," Yosef said. "Our destination."

"Every detail—who you are, Yosef son of Jacob—is recorded in the Law and the Prophets. Your steps on this journey are ordered by the Lord from the foundations of eternity."

—Conversation between Rabbi Yismah and Yosef (p. 243)

ASK

Why was it ironic that not only a king—but the greatest King of all time—would be born in Beth-lehem?

Do you believe that God has every detail of your life planned—as Rabbi Yismah declared Mary's and Yosef's was? Why or why not?

____

____

____

As you've read more about the Messiah and Scripture's prophecies, have your perceptions of the baby in the manger or the coming Messiah changed? If so, how?

____

____

____

WONDER . . .

"You were barely a whisper of promise to our fathers. Now here you are. . . . Real. Living."

—Rabbi Yismah (p. 243)

Is Messiah real—living—in your life?

6 EXPECTANT HOPE

Zadok, his shaggy head bowed, spoke in a hoarse voice to those who were still awake around the campfire. "Aye. Do y' remember, Eliyahu? Do y' remember what those days were like? How we all were lookin' at the signs in the stars? The hopes we cherished for Israel? for our wives? our sons? Remember the hope?"

Eliyahu prodded the embers with a stick. "And the fears. I remember."

Zadok gazed into the face of Onias. "Ah, Onias, my brother . . . and here you are with us tonight. You've come hopin' to see a better end of the story. You, who knew all along what was ahead. You knew he was comin'."

—pp. xiv–xv

When you think of the past, what top three hopes and fears do you remember?

____

____

____

Has there ever been a time when you hoped "to see a better end of the story"? Tell what happened—and the end of the story, if you already know it.

____

____

____

When you think of the future, what do you look forward to with hope?

It has been said that hope is what makes the soul live on even under the greatest of loads. If ever any people needed hope, it was the Jewish nation of the first century A.D. They had been waiting so long and under such cruel tyranny for the promised Messiah that many had forgotten how to hope. Although they did "what was right"—such as making the yearly pilgrimage to Jerusalem—they left each year, deflated, when the Messiah did not come. It's no wonder that hope had dulled to a dim memory, and they no longer expected anything to happen. The Messiah had become, for many, a figure of their "spiritual history" but had lost relevance in their daily lives.

Although the people heard the prophecies about the Messiah and could recite the events in their nation's history, most, like Yosef, "had never thought to examine the depth and significance of the Hebrew words beyond what he heard read aloud. Was Torah more than the single thread of Hebrew history? Was Scripture rather a tapestry of many threads woven together to create a unified and living picture of Adonai's plan for mankind? Never had he wondered what the stories meant to him personally" (p. 119).

And he is not alone. How long has it been since you have thought of Messiah's coming not only with hope, but *expectant* hope? *active* hope?

READ

There are hopes unspoken in the human heart that groan and sigh and rise to reach the ears of the Almighty as wordless prayers. This is one of those occasions. The Lord has heard your sighs, Yosef. The Lord loves your questions. . . . He longs to teach you the answers.

—Joseph, the Dreamer of dreams (p. 48)

Heaven has spoken. Plainly. The truth of Yahweh is like a pearl a man drops in the sand. The wise man sifts the sand and throws the grains away and finds the pearl. Torah is the pearl bearing Messiah's identity. That truth is often buried in the shallow sand of man's arrogance, hypocrisy, and ignorance. Every word in Holy

Scripture is Truth. Everything in Torah—from the first letters of the first word to the last words—points to Yeshua, our Redeemer. All else is shifting sand.

—Joseph, the Dreamer of dreams (pp. 169–170)

ASK

If you could ask God anything right now, what would you ask? If it is a wordless prayer, a sigh, or a groan, what is on your heart?

____

____

____

Do you agree that Scripture is the "pearl bearing Messiah's identity"? Why or why not? Does this pearl shine in your life? Or has it, over time, become buried in the sand? If so, how can you dig it out and let it shine?

____

____

____

READ

The heart of every man longs to hear Adonai's true voice. Philosophies and false religions will come and go, but only the Word of Adonai recorded in Torah is eternal, and the Spirit will draw them to the truth. The stars remain a steadfast witness of the glory of their Creator and clearly speak of the story of redemption.

—Joseph, the Dreamer of dreams (p. 169)

That was all. Onias was afraid to say more, for fear of endangering Zadok and his family. But Onias had not stopped cherishing the study of prophecy, the longing for Messiah's birth, even though it had led to his crippling at the hands of Herod.

—p. 144

As He left Caesarea Philippi to return to the shores of Galilee, the *am ha aretz* were listening and perhaps, at last, believing that Yeshua was the Messiah, the Redeemer of Israel.

Men who had never walked before ran after Him.

Sons who had never spoken a word sang praises to His name.

Women who had lived lonely lives, barren of hope, danced at their own weddings while others carried babies in their arms.

Beautiful daughters, once marred by leprosy, were healed and whole and reunited with families who had grieved as though their girls were dead.

It was true what the prophets had said about Messiah: Yeshua healed them of all their diseases.

So it had come to pass. "*Those who have long lived in darkness have seen a great light.*"

Yeshua was that Light.

—pp. x–xi

ASK

How do you know what is true and what is false regarding philosophies or religions?

____

____

____

____

What evidence could you find in the above passages to prove that Yeshua is who He claims to be—the long-awaited Messiah? Make a list.

____

____

____

____

READ

How miraculous it seemed to Yosef that *all* the hopes of *all* the patriarchs and prophets for two thousand years were contained within the womb of one young woman riding humbly on the back of a donkey.

Surely Herod sensed Messiah's coming and trembled. Why else would the Butcher King send soldiers out to scour the land in search of Zachariah and Elisheba and their baby? Indeed, the whole world seemed to be waiting—some with dread and palpable hatred, others with hope and breathless anticipation.

—p. 232

If the Lord really, truly lived among men, suddenly all the deferred hope would be resolved. All the centuries of sacrifice would be evidence of faithfulness—not just rote obedience.

—p. 276

ASK

On what or whom do you place all your hopes for the future? Why?

___

___

___

___

As you think about the Messiah, are you waiting with "dread" or "breathless anticipation"? "rote obedience" or "hope and faithfulness"? Explain.

___

___

___

___

READ

"Can you believe it?" Lem chattered as they ran, stumbling and laughing, across the fields. "Angels! Angels came to us shepherds! Why us, Zadok? Why poor shepherds like us?"

"And why not?" Zadok demanded exuberantly. "Avraham. Yitz'chak. Jacob. Joseph. David. All shepherds. Five heirs of the promise. Five seals of the covenant. Every one of 'em. All hopin' for this day. And here we are, their shepherd descendants, alive t' see it!"

—pp. 278–279

It was all so . . . so ordinary seeming. This was not a palace or a fortress; it was a cave. The air was warm and moist with the breath of sheep and lambs and smelled of wool and manure, not incense and costly perfume. The teenage mother was not dressed like royalty. Her protector was clearly *am ha aretz* . . . one of the people of the land.

And yet . . . and yet . . .

There was the baby, wrapped in cloths and lying in a manger, even as the angel had foretold.

The accuracy of that fulfillment could not be doubted, which meant . . .

Head bowed, tears streamed down Zadok's furrowed cheeks. "My Savior and my Lord."

—p. 285

But who in all His people Israel knew it? A handful at most were aware of the miracle. And the majority of those were Temple shepherds! Inhaling, Yosef sampled the air in proof of the fact that *Immanu'el*, "God-with-us," had actually been born in a stable. . . .

Who could take everything in? Yosef wondered. Apart from more proclamations by heavenly heralds, how would anyone else accept it?

Baby Yeshua, Eternal Word of Yahweh, the One True and Living God, pursed rosebud lips and made sucking noises. Inside the feed trough, wrapped in swaddling cloths and cocooned in a blanket that was tucked over His head and around His shoulders like a prayer shawl, the Son of God blinked unfocused eyes at the lamp's flame.

—p. 287

ASK

After all the years of longing, of waiting in expectant hope, who are the first people to see the baby Messiah? and to believe who the baby in the lambing cave really is?

Why do you think God chose to reveal His plan this way—rather than to the priests and rulers, or with great fanfare?

If you were one of the shepherds who saw the baby Yeshua face-to-face, what would your response be? Why?

Have you, like Zadok, declared, "My Savior and my Lord"? If so, when? If not, what hurdles are holding you back from making this declaration?

WONDER . . .

"I am coming, and I will live among you," declares the Lord.
—Zechariah 2:10

"Thus says the Lord to you who live here and now! You will see him, and very soon! You will behold him, and he is very near!"
—Hannah (p. 218)

How can you live, day by day, in expectant hope?

"Blessed are you, O Adonai, who delivers us from evil.
Deliver us, Lord, from every evil, and grant us peace in our day.
In your mercy keep us free from sin and protect us from all anxiety,
as we wait in joyful hope for the coming of our Messiah!"
—p. 70

Dear Reader,

You are so important to us. We have prayed for you as we wrote this book and also as we receive your letters and hear your soul cries. We hope that *Fifth Seal* has encouraged you to go deeper. To get to know Yeshua better. To fill your soul hunger by examining Scripture's truths for yourself.

We are convinced that if you do so, you will find this promise true: "*If you seek Him, He will be found by you.*" —1 CHRONICLES 28:9

Bodie & Brock Thoene

Scripture References

[1] Isa. 9:2
[2] Isa. 53:3-5
[3] Isa. 53:6
[4] Isa. 53:7
[5] Matt. 17:22; Luke 9:44
[6] Luke 18:31-33
[7] Jer. 31:15
[8] See Luke 1:67-79
[9] Luke 1:37
[10] Luke 1:76
[11] Isa. 7:14
[12] Zech. 9:14-16
[13] Matt. 1:21
[14] Luke 1:31-33
[15] Isa. 40:12, 15
[16] Ps. 19:1-3
[17] Ezra 6:2-3
[18] The book of Daniel
[19] Gen. 37
[20] Gen. 28:10-17
[21] Gen. 32:24-28
[22] Heb. 12:1
[23] Rom. 8:26
[24] Gen. 37:3-36
[25] Gen. 42–45
[26] Prov. 3:34
[27] Deut. 11:19
[28] Prov. 9:10
[29] Luke 23:46, quoted from Ps. 31:5
[30] Song of Songs 1:4-5
[31] Luke 2:1
[32] Luke 2:3
[33] Luke 2:25-26
[34] Zech. 14:9
[35] Ps. 2:6
[36] Jer. 1:6, 8
[37] Dan. 4:34
[38] Dan. 4:37
[39] Prov. 3:6
[40] Dan. 2:44
[41] Matt. 22:21; Mark 12:17; Luke 20:25
[42] Job 1:21
[43] John 1:1-5
[44] Gen. 1:1
[45] Jer. 20:8-9
[46] Jer. 23:5-6
[47] Josh. 24:15
[48] Ps. 29:1-2
[49] 1 Sam. 3:3-4
[50] Gen. 18:10-15
[51] Gen. 1:2
[52] Gen. 3
[53] Matt. 18:12-14; Luke 19:10
[54] 1 Sam. 1:18
[55] 1 Sam. 2:6
[56] 1 Sam. 2:9-10
[57] 1 Sam. 1:28
[58] Deut. 17:15
[59] Matt. 10:29-31; Luke 12:6-7
[60] Zech. 14:1-11, 16
[61] Rev. 6:9-10
[62] Ps. 27:1
[63] Ps. 27:1
[64] Ps. 27:2-3
[65] Ps. 27:3
[66] Ps. 27:4
[67] Ps. 27:7-8
[68] Ps. 27:13-14
[69] Matt. 1:17
[70] Micah 5:2
[71] Isa. 11:1
[72] Gen. 3:14-15
[73] Isa. 11:6-10
[74] Gen. 22:9-10
[75] Isa. 11:6
[76] Isa. 61:1-2
[77] Ps. 19:1-2
[78] Gen. 32:28
[79] Gen. 48:1-4
[80] Gen. 37–47
[81] Gen. 48:8-16
[82] Isa. 60:3
[83] Ps. 19:1-4
[84] Num. 24:17
[85] Isa. 9:5-6
[86] Isa. 9:6
[87] Isa. 9:7
[88] Ps. 91:4-5
[89] Gen. 3:14-15
[90] Num. 24:17
[91] 2 Kings 4:8-37
[92] Gen. 35:16-20
[93] Mal. 3:1
[94] Isa. 40:3-5
[95] Mal. 4:5
[96] Isa. 11:1
[97] Isa. 11:2-3

[98] Isa. 11:3-4
[99] Num. 24:15-17
[100] Deut. 6:4
[101] Micah 5:2-4
[102] Isa. 53:7
[103] Gen. 22:9-11
[104] John 3:16
[105] Gen. 15:18
[106] Neh. 2:1-8
[107] Gen. 12:6-7
[108] Gen. 35:1-7
[109] Gen. 37:12-17
[110] Gen. 41:50-51
[111] Gen. 50:24-26
[112] Exod. 12:40-42
[113] Exod. 13:19
[114] Josh. 1:1-5
[115] Josh. 24:32
[116] Josh. 8:30-33
[117] Josh. 24:25-27
[118] Lam. 1:15
[119] Luke 1:28
[120] Luke 1:46
[121] Matt. 1:20
[122] 1 John 4:4
[123] Matt. 2:23
[124] Ps. 30:5
[125] Amos 6:1-7
[126] Gen. 18
[127] Rev. 19:6-9
[128] Ps. 50:10
[129] Job 2:9
[130] Gen. 2:15-17
[131] Gen. 21:1-7
[132] Gen. 18:1-15
[133] Gen. 31:1-55
[134] Gen. 31:32
[135] Gen. 35:1-4
[136] Gen. 35:16-20
[137] John 6:51
[138] Lev. 19:18
[139] Zech. 2:10-13
[140] Isa. 30:26; Zech. 14:6-7; Isa. 60:19-20; traditional Jewish prayer book
[141] Isa. 9:2
[142] Isa. 60:1
[143] Num. 7:1-10
[144] Zech. 2:10
[145] Luke 2:10-12
[146] Luke 2:14
[147] Luke 2:15
[148] Gen. 41:50-52
[149] Num. 7:89–8:2
[150] Micah 5:2
[151] Isa. 1:3
[152] Matt. 1:21
[153] Luke 2:12

Authors' Note

The following sources have been helpful in our research for this book.

- *The Complete Jewish Bible.* Translated by David H. Stern. Baltimore, MD: Jewish New Testament Publications, Inc., 1998.

- *iLumina*, a digitally animated Bible and encyclopedia suite. Carol Stream, IL: Tyndale House Publishers, 2002.

- *The International Standard Bible Encyclopaedia.* George Bromiley, ed. 5 vols. Grand Rapids, MI: Eerdmans, 1979.

- *The Life and Times of Jesus the Messiah.* Alfred Edersheim. Peabody, MA: Hendrickson Publishers, Inc., 1995.

- Starry Night™ Enthusiast Version 5.0, published by Imaginova™ Corp.

Our grateful thanks to Dr. Albert E. Cramer for his keen theological eye, knowledge of the Scriptures, and fastidious checking of biblical references on the A.D. Chronicles series. His credits in academia are many: a BA in history and a BS in education; master's degrees in colonial U.S. history, Old Testament, New Testament, and theology; a ThD in Old Testament; a PhD studies in modern European history, and over 40 years of college and graduate-school teaching and administration. A World War II combat veteran, Dr. Cramer's avocation is rural sociology.

About the Authors

BODIE AND BROCK THOENE (pronounced *Tay-nee)* have written over 45 works of historical fiction. That these best sellers have sold more than 10 million copies and won eight ECPA Gold Medallion Awards affirms what millions of readers have already discovered—the Thoenes are not only master stylists but experts at capturing readers' minds and hearts.

In their timeless classic series about Israel (The Zion Chronicles, The Zion Covenant, and The Zion Legacy), the Thoenes' love for both story and research shines.

With The Shiloh Legacy series and *Shiloh Autumn*—poignant portrayals of the American depression—and The Galway Chronicles, which dramatically tell of the 1840s famine in Ireland, as well as the twelve Legends of the West, the Thoenes have made their mark in modern history.

In the A.D. Chronicles, their most recent series, they step seamlessly into the world of Yerushalayim and Rome, in the days when Yeshua walked the earth and transformed lives with His touch.

Bodie began her writing career as a teen journalist for her local newspaper. Eventually her byline appeared in prestigious periodicals such as *U.S. News and World Report*, *The American West*, and *The Saturday Evening Post.* She also worked for John Wayne's Batjac Productions (she's best known as author of *The Fall Guy)* and ABC Circle Films as a writer and researcher. John Wayne described her as "a writer with talent that captures the people and the times!" She has degrees in journalism and communications.

Brock has often been described by Bodie as "an essential half of this writing team." With degrees in both history and education, Brock has, in his role as researcher and story-line consultant, added the vital dimension of historical accuracy. Due to such careful research, The Zion Covenant and The Zion Chronicles series are recognized by the American Library Association, as well as Zionist libraries around the world, as classic historical novels and are used to teach history in college classrooms.

Bodie and Brock have four grown children—Rachel, Jake, Luke, and Ellie—and five grandchildren. Their sons, Jake and Luke, are carrying on the Thoene family talent as the next generation of writers, and Luke produces the Thoene audiobooks. Bodie and Brock divide their time between London and Nevada.

For more information visit:
www.thoenebooks.com
www.familyaudiolibrary.com

suspense with a mission

TITLES BY

Jake Thoene

"The Christian Tom Clancy"

Dale Hurd, *CBN Newswatch*

Shaiton's Fire

In this first book in the techno-thriller series by Jake Thoene, the bombing of a subway train is only the beginning of a master plan that Steve Alstead and Chapter 16 have to stop . . . before it's too late.

Firefly Blue

In this action-packed sequel to Shaiton's Fire, *Chapter 16 is called in when barrels of cyanide are stolen during a truckjacking. Experience heart-stopping action as you read this gripping story that could have been ripped from today's headlines.*

Fuel the Fire

In this third book in the series, Special Agent Steve Alstead and Chapter 16, the FBI's counterterrorism unit, must stop the scheme of an al Qaeda splinter cell . . . while America's future hangs in the balance.

for more information on other great Tyndale fiction,

visit www.tyndalefiction.com

THOENE FAMILY CLASSICS™

✪ ✪ ✪

THOENE FAMILY CLASSIC HISTORICALS
by Bodie and Brock Thoene

*Gold Medallion Winners**

THE ZION COVENANT
*Vienna Prelude**
Prague Counterpoint
Munich Signature
Jerusalem Interlude
Danzig Passage
*Warsaw Requiem**
London Refrain
Paris Encore
Dunkirk Crescendo

THE ZION CHRONICLES
*The Gates of Zion**
A Daughter of Zion
The Return to Zion
A Light in Zion
*The Key to Zion**

THE SHILOH LEGACY
*In My Father's House**
A Thousand Shall Fall
Say to This Mountain

SHILOH AUTUMN

THE GALWAY CHRONICLES
*Only the River Runs Free**
Of Men and of Angels
*Ashes of Remembrance**
All Rivers to the Sea

THE ZION LEGACY
Jerusalem Vigil
Thunder from Jerusalem
Jerusalem's Heart
Jerusalem Scrolls
Stones of Jerusalem
Jerusalem's Hope

A.D. CHRONICLES
First Light
Second Touch
Third Watch
Fourth Dawn
Fifth Seal
Sixth Covenant
and more to come!

THOENE FAMILY CLASSICS™

✪ ✪ ✪

THOENE FAMILY CLASSIC AMERICAN LEGENDS

LEGENDS OF THE WEST
by Bodie and Brock Thoene

The Man from Shadow Ridge
Riders of the Silver Rim
Gold Rush Prodigal
Sequoia Scout
Cannons of the Comstock
Year of the Grizzly
Shooting Star
Legend of Storey County
Hope Valley War
Delta Passage
Hangtown Lawman
Cumberland Crossing

LEGENDS OF VALOR
by Luke Thoene

Sons of Valor
Brothers of Valor
Fathers of Valor

✪ ✪ ✪

THOENE CLASSIC NONFICTION
by Bodie and Brock Thoene

Writer-to-Writer

THOENE FAMILY CLASSIC SUSPENSE
by Jake Thoene

CHAPTER 16 SERIES

Shaiton's Fire
Firefly Blue
Fuel the Fire

✪ ✪ ✪

THOENE FAMILY CLASSICS FOR KIDS
by Jake and Luke Thoene

BAKER STREET DETECTIVES

The Mystery of the Yellow Hands
The Giant Rat of Sumatra
The Jeweled Peacock of Persia
The Thundering Underground

LAST CHANCE DETECTIVES

Mystery Lights of Navajo Mesa
Legend of the Desert Bigfoot

✪ ✪ ✪

THOENE FAMILY CLASSIC AUDIOBOOKS

Available from
www.thoenebooks.com or
www.familyaudiolibrary.com

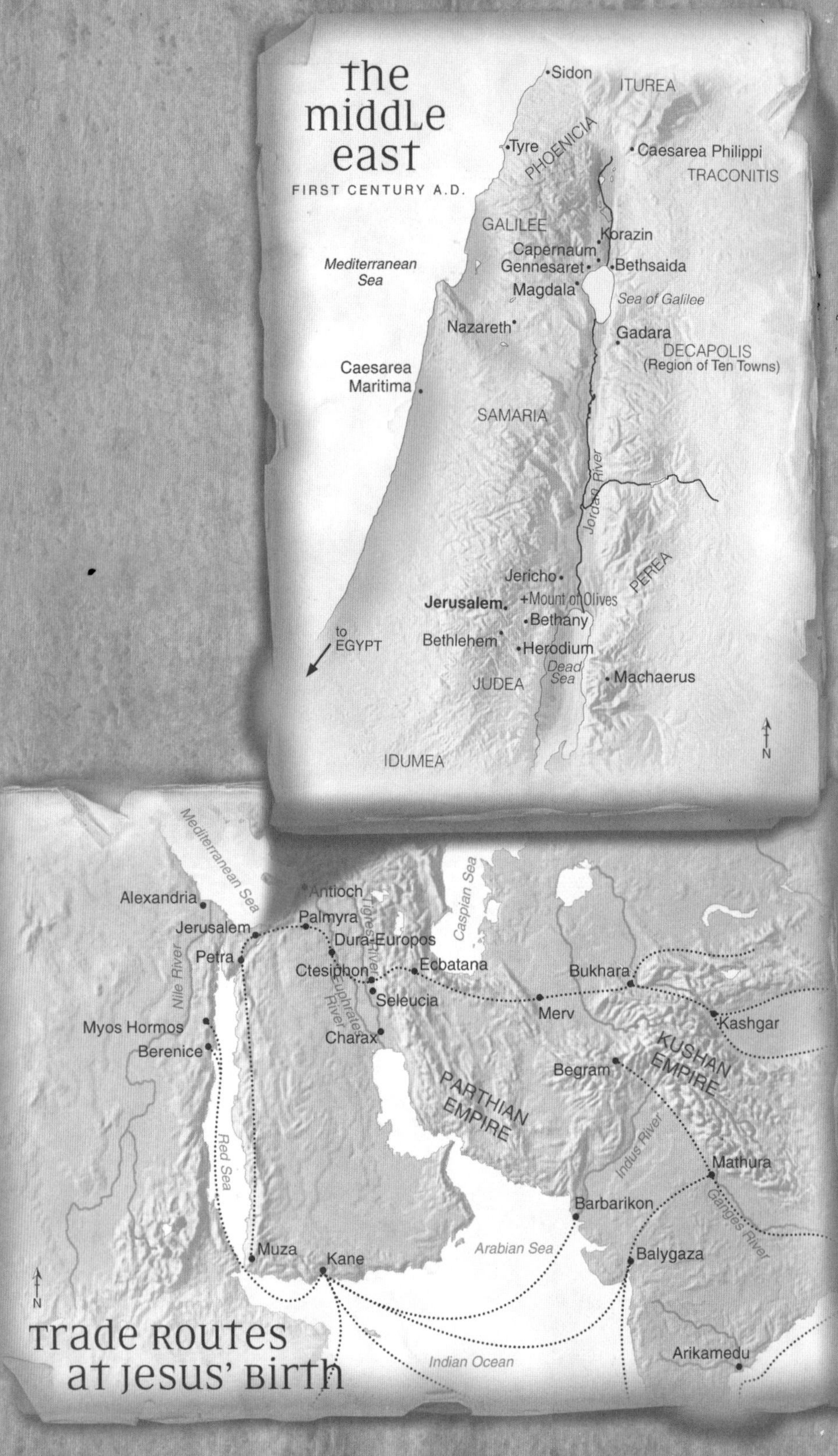
the middle east
FIRST CENTURY A.D.
Sidon
ITUREA
Tyre
PHOENICIA
Caesarea Philippi
TRACONITIS
GALILEE
Korazin
Capernaum
Gennesaret
Bethsaida
Mediterranean Sea
Magdala
Sea of Galilee
Nazareth
Gadara
DECAPOLIS
(Region of Ten Towns)
Caesarea Maritima
SAMARIA
Jordan River
Jericho
PEREA
Jerusalem
+Mount of Olives
Bethany
to EGYPT
Bethlehem
Herodium
Dead Sea
Machaerus
JUDEA
IDUMEA
N
Mediterranean Sea
Alexandria
Antioch
Caspian Sea
Palmyra
Jerusalem
Dura-Europos
Tigris River
Petra
Nile River
Ctesiphon
Ecbatana
Bukhara
Euphrates River
Seleucia
Merv
Kashgar
Myos Hormos
Charax
KUSHAN EMPIRE
Berenice
Begram
PARTHIAN EMPIRE
Red Sea
Indus River
Mathura
Barbarikon
Ganges River
Arabian Sea
Muza
Kane
Balygaza
N
Trade Routes at Jesus' Birth
Indian Ocean
Arikamedu